Praise for Cynthia Victor's novels

Consequences

"Dramatic. . . . A brisk and colorful tale, rich in its evocation of privileged lifestyles and well seasoned with a blend of sex and intrigue." —*Publishers Weekly*

"A good, strong story about the choices women sometimes have to make . . . wonderful twists . . . full of surprises."
New York Times bestselling author Eileen Goudge

"An expertly confected web of obsession and intrigue. Ms. Victor is a hypnotic tale-spinner."
—*New York Times* bestselling author Edward Stewart

"*Consequences* is a very special book, with characters that leap to life on every page, and a story that you squeeze every drop from to the final page."
—Elaine Bissell

The Sisters

"Enthralling . . . powerful . . . exceptional."
—*Rendezvous*

"A gripping suspense tale that keeps you on the edge. Fantastic." —*Bell, Book & Candle*

"Thrilling. . . . Should appeal to both mystery and romance novel fans. The sex is explosive and hot!"
—*Romance Reviews*

"A brilliant tale . . . clever . . . wonderful."
—*Midwest Book Review*

continued . . .

The Secret

"An entertaining, sly, and satisfying story of a woman's journey of discovery."
—#1 *New York Times* bestselling author Nora Roberts

"Victor evokes [her characters] with skill, a clear ear for their language, and a feel for family interaction. Readers will enjoy this tale." —*Publishers Weekly*

"Warmth and compassion. . . . A *First Wives Club* descendant." —*Kirkus Reviews*

"Great fun! Readers who enjoyed the humor of Olivia Goldsmith's *The First Wives Club* will find this novel much in the same vein." —*Library Journal*

What Matters Most

"Breezy dialogue, well-developed dramatic tension, and of course, the eventual triumph of love blend nicely. . . . Victor's characterization is deep and subtle. . . . Her prose is assured. . . . Readers will enjoy the excitement." —*Publishers Weekly*

"Delightfully engrossing." —*New Woman*

"Victor dishes some good stuff . . . left me wanting more." —*San Antonio Express-News*

"Excellent!" —*The Philadelphia Inquirer*

Only You

"Riveting. . . . *Only You* is a stay-up-late read with terrific characters, nonstop action, and an epic tale of love that will remain in my mind for a long time to come. Readers will savor it."
   —*New York Times* bestselling author Julie Garwood

"A complex story containing love, lust, blackmail, murder . . . Recommended."   —*Booklist*

"Steamy sex . . . delightfully and totally wicked."
                              —*Library Journal*

"Thrilling, absorbing, consoling . . . astonishing and enthralling. . . . I can't think of anyone who gets it all as right as Cynthia Victor."
   —*New York Times* bestselling author Edward Stewart

Relative Sins

"Two dynamic women, one involving tale. The gripping prologue of *Relative Sins* is only the beginning. . . . There's excitement and emotion on every page."
   —*New York Times* bestselling author Sandra Brown

"*Relative Sins* is a wonderful story packed with excitement and with all the longing and betrayals, misalliances and mistaken identities of great old fashioned drama. . . . Satisfying. . . . A book you won't want to miss. Hats off to Cynthia Victor!"
   —*New York Times* bestselling author Eileen Goudge

"A moving mother-daughter saga that completely engrosses."
   —*New York Times* bestselling author Olivia Goldsmith

"Compelling . . . entertaining."   —*Publishers Weekly*

ALSO BY CYNTHIA VICTOR

The Three of Us

Cynthia Victor

AN ONYX BOOK

ONYX
Published by New American Library, a division of
Penguin Putnam Inc., 375 Hudson Street,
New York, New York 10014, U.S.A.
Penguin Books Ltd, 80 Strand,
London WC2R 0RL, England
Penguin Books Australia Ltd, Ringwood,
Victoria, Australia
Penguin Books Canada Ltd, 10 Alcorn Avenue,
Toronto, Ontario, Canada M4V 3B2
Penguin Books (N.Z.) Ltd, 182–190 Wairau Road,
Auckland 10, New Zealand

Penguin Books Ltd, Registered Offices:
Harmondsworth, Middlesex, England

First published by Onyx, an imprint of New American Library,
a division of Penguin Putnam Inc.

First Printing, April 2002
10 9 8 7 6 5 4 3 2 1

For Amy Berkower

ACKNOWLEDGMENTS

Warmest thanks to the following people, all of whom were so generous with their time and expertise: Gregory Astor, Carole Baron, Richard Baron, Karen Bergreen, Betsy Carter, Amanda Clarke, Carolyn Clarke, Mackenzie Clarke, Jennifer Jahner, Audrey LaFehr, Linda Marrow, Susan Moldow, Marc Rosen, M.D., David Roth-Ey, Jennifer Skurnick, Carly Steckel, Jenna Steckel, Mark Steckel, M.D., and Emily Weiss.

1

Kip Hallman finished filling the ice bucket and shut the freezer door. Fitting the bucket's cover on tightly, she paused at the kitchen counter to consult her to-do list. All the items related to cooking and setting up had already been checked off. The turkeys, filled with pecan stuffing, and the sweet potato pies were in the kitchen's two ovens; the breads she had baked the day before were in baskets, covered with dish towels to keep them from getting hard; the cranberry sauce, her own special recipe, was in the refrigerator.

Thanksgiving was Kip's favorite holiday, and she made an elaborate feast for it every year. Relatives who lived nearby knew they could always count on an invitation. There was also a large, changing cast of characters in attendance: friends, friends of friends, and any long-distance relatives who could make it to the Hallmans' home in Rhinebeck that year. Today she was expecting twenty-one people, but only fifteen of them were adults, a moderate crowd compared to some of the get-togethers in the past.

"Oh, right," Kip muttered as she saw something she had forgotten on the list. She turned and grabbed two lemons that had been shoved nearly out of sight on the far end of the counter, taking them with her into the living room.

Kip's husband, Peter, was standing at the bar. It was actually just a section of the enormous bookcase that covered most of one wall. The bar was hidden behind a door that pulled down to reveal the crystal glasses and bottles of liquor within. Although Peter was supposedly setting up for drinks, he had only brought the bar glasses forward to be more accessible before getting distracted by a book. He was completely absorbed by what he was reading, his job forgotten.

"Hon, here's the ice and some lemons."

Kip didn't bother commenting on his abandoning the only task he had been assigned that day. Peter was just being Peter. She knew when she married him eighteen years before that nothing in the world could ever be more important to him than books. Back then, he was already a nationally known author, and he had only grown larger in stature as the years went on. His work continued to earn him literary praise and recognition, and was commercially successful, as well. In June, his latest book, a best-seller called *Norton's Ride,* had earned him the Middleton Award, one of the top honors an author could receive.

Peter struggled to tear himself away from what was on the page. He looked over at her. "Oh, sorry. Thanks." He snapped the book shut and put it on a shelf, reaching out to take the things his wife was holding.

"How do I look?" Kip asked him, twirling around so he could get a full view of her white satin blouse and long black velvet skirt. She had twisted her long, light brown hair into a French braid. She was generally more comfortable with her hair up, no doubt, she realized, from the many years she wore it pulled back when she was younger.

Peter tilted his head. "Proper. But sophisticated and very beautiful."

She made a face. "I'm not sure I like that. *Proper* sounds dreadful and old."

He came over, putting his arms around her. "No, I meant *proper* in a devastatingly sexy kind of way, of course."

She laughed and kissed him. "I see. Well, that's very different."

They stayed where they were for a minute, Kip enjoying the feeling of her husband's arms around her. For the first few years they were together, she couldn't get over the fact that this older, smarter, and incredibly handsome man wanted to be with her. As far as she was concerned, he had only gotten better looking with time, his thick black hair now full of gray.

She pulled back. "Thanks for the squeeze, babe, gotta run," she said.

"You make me feel so cheap." He feigned indignation.

She grinned back at him, but hurried into the kitchen. *Proper,* she thought, frowning as she crossed to the wooden island in the middle of the room. A euphemism for *matronly.* Ugh. But, hey, thirty-six wasn't so old. She sighed and made a mental note to buy something daring to wear for New Year's Eve.

Picking up a small knife, she began spreading pâté on small squares of black bread. Intent on her task, her back to the doorway, she didn't hear her daughter, Lisa, enter, a red one-piece bathing suit in her hand, an annoyed expression on her face.

"Mother, will you look at this?" the fifteen-year-old demanded. "There's a hole in my new suit."

She reached Kip, her arm outstretched with the offending garment, and waited for her mother to examine it.

Kip glanced over. "Sweetie, everybody will be here in about five minutes. Could we discuss this later?"

"But it's right in *front,*" Lisa exclaimed, underscoring the urgency of the discussion. "I mean, I really wanted to wear this tomorrow."

Kip put down the knife and began to neaten the concentric circles of bread on the large serving platter, straightening any errant hors d'oeuvre that deviated from the correct arrangement. "I guess you can't," she said mildly.

Lisa glared at her mother as if the whole business were her fault. "How the hell could this have happened?"

"Heck," Kip corrected automatically, knowing it was a futile gesture. "I can't imagine how it happened, dear. Swimming, perhaps?" she asked innocently.

Lisa dropped the hand holding the bathing suit to her side. "You *know* how much I hate it when you're sarcastic. Thanks a lot for your concern."

Kip paused in her task to look at Lisa. Her daughter was dressed in a tight velvet, long-sleeved top, an extremely short black skirt, and black shoes with heels that had to be at least three inches. The whole effect was sexier than Kip would have liked on her child, but she knew better than to complain; it could have been a lot worse. Funny, Kip thought, I now have to make an effort to look sexy, but these teenagers just *exude* it without trying.

Lisa's brown hair, cropped short so she wouldn't have to deal with swimming caps or hair dryers in her daily swimming practice, revealed the heart shape of her face, as well as the three diamond stud earrings she wore on her earlobes, one on the left, two on the right. The earrings had been a present from her parents on her fifteenth birthday, a response to two years of virtually nonstop begging; she never took them off.

Kip smiled at her, aware of how fresh and young and alive she was, but at the same time how grown up. "Boy, fifteen is really different from fourteen," she mused aloud, thinking of how Lisa had looked at last Thanksgiving's dinner.

"Don't change the subject, please. There'll be some important people watching practice, and I really want to wear this suit. Maybe you could call the store, or the manufacturer. You can do it now, before everybody gets here."

"On Thanksgiving? It's hardly likely they'll be at work. Is the suit lucky in some way?" Kip knew firsthand about athletes and their superstitions, and if the suit had a history associated with winning, she could sympathize.

"No, I've only worn it once. But I think the color is great for me."

"That's what this is all about?" Kip was getting exasperated. "Honey, please. I can't do anything about it right now. You'll have to handle this tragedy by yourself."

Lisa glared at her. "Fine, fine, never mind." She spun on her heel. "Now what am I going to wear tomorrow?" she demanded as she stormed out.

"Perhaps one of the nine million other suits you have might somehow suffice," Kip answered under her breath.

She couldn't help shaking her head at what was just the latest example of her daughter's unrelenting self-absorption. Then she grabbed an oven mitt and pulled open the top oven's door to baste the turkey. The bottom oven held the second turkey, which she attended to next. As she was finishing, she heard the doorbell ring.

"I got it," Peter called out.

The gravy was simmering on the stove. Kip stirred it with a wooden spoon as she listened. Her sister, Nicole, had come in with her husband, Larry, and their two boys. The grown-ups were greeting each other, as usual, her husband and her sister disguising their mutual dislike of one another. She heard the sounds of coats being collected, hats and scarves removed, boots pulled off.

"Where's J. P.?" It was the voice of Nicole's eight-year-old, Ethan.

"Yeah, where is he?" echoed seven-year-old Jordan.

"In his room, I guess," replied Peter.

There was a small stampede as the two boys raced up the stairs. Kip smiled. Her nephews adored her son—at age eleven, J. P. seemed practically adult to both of them—and followed him around every chance they got. Her son was good-natured about it. But, of course, her son was good-natured about practically everything.

Nicole came into the kitchen, holding a brown shopping bag, her cheeks reddened from the cold. She was shaking out her long blond hair, running a hand through it.

"Freezing out there," she said to Kip by way of greeting, coming over to give her a peck on the cheek. She set the bag down on the counter and started to pull out plastic containers. "I have the boys' veggie burgers and carrots, and a little surprise dessert for them," she explained.

Kip nodded noncommittally. Nicole believed that her sons were allergic to everything on earth as far as Kip could tell. She never let them eat food prepared outside their home because she couldn't be sure what was in it. They had to avoid wheat and dairy and nuts and a whole list of things Kip couldn't even recall. Otherwise, Nicole claimed, they developed rashes and runny noses, or became hyper, or sleepy, or came down with any one of twenty other symptoms Kip had never seen them display in connection with anything but normal childhood illnesses. Even coming here for the holiday, Kip reflected, amused but a little hurt as well, Nicole couldn't trust that something special could be prepared for them according to her directions. Kip believed it all to be nonsense, but she wouldn't dream of saying that to her sister. Things were strained enough between them.

"And here's some wine for you," Nicole went on, pulling out a bottle and handing it to Kip. "Not that it's in a class with what you usually drink, I'm sure."

Kip stopped herself from saying anything other than thank you, she was sure it would be perfect. By this point, it was clear that her sister was never going to stop making remarks about the disparity in their economic situations. Nothing Kip could do would remedy that, though she had tried her best. Apparently, it would always drive Nicole crazy that *she* was the one who was supposed to be the golden girl when they were growing up, but instead, it was Kip who won all the prizes. Nicole had been the one with the beautiful face and body, the one with all the boyfriends, the one who was going to land some fabulous husband and live happily ever after. But then Kip came along with her figure skating and the medals and the attention. As a teenager, Nicole had been insanely jealous. And she had always done a poor job of hiding it.

Even when Kip's skating days were over, the situation didn't improve from Nicole's viewpoint. Kip married a nationally known author and lived in a huge house in a beautiful town with two talented children. Nicole, on the other hand, married Larry Thurston, who she believed was going to accomplish great things. She met him on a train ride from New York to Philadelphia, and they were married a year later. Kip found him genuinely nice, but he had proved a bitter disappointment to Nicole. He certainly had never developed into the tycoon she imagined he would become. Now about twenty pounds overweight with a receding hairline, he worked at a cable network, selling time to advertisers. He was actually very successful, and made more than enough to support a family, but it was a far cry from the sort of income Nicole envisioned for the man she chose.

It remained a puzzle to Nicole how everything had gone so wrong. She didn't have the man she wanted, the money she wanted, the house she wanted. There wasn't enough in their budget to allow for a nanny for the children, and Nicole repeatedly informed Kip that she couldn't possibly imagine how exhausting it was to run after two young boys only a year apart.

Nicole never came right out and said it, but Kip felt that she might as well have. Life had owed Nicole something and then cheated her out of it. Her younger sister, Kip, on the other hand, had it all and didn't deserve it.

Kip watched Nicole busy herself finding space for the plastic containers in the refrigerator. As she rearranged the packed shelves, Nicole leaned over so she could see out into the dining room. Three folding tables extended out from the regular mahogany dining table, stretching well into the living room. It was a sea of white linen, ivory and gold china, sparkling crystal and silver.

"Wow," she admired, taking in the arrangements of

small pumpkins, colorful gourds and cranberries nestled here and there amidst the place settings. "How many are we?"

"Kip, darling, hello!" They were interrupted as Peter's mother swept into, rather than entered, the kitchen, followed by his father. Vivian Hallman gathered Kip into a hug, her numerous silver bracelets jangling.

"Welcome," said Kip with a warm smile.

"So wonderful to be treated to one of your dinners, especially this one," Vivian exclaimed, pushing her long, nearly white hair back from her face.

Vivian looked at least ten years younger than the seventy-eight she was, with her hair still thick enough to be worn loose, flowing partway down her back. Long earrings dangled almost to her shoulders. Beneath a colorful woven shawl, she wore a full-length, dark blue, heavy cotton dress with large patch pockets below the dropped waist. She was always warm to Kip, but sometimes Kip couldn't help suspecting that her mother-in-law didn't truly give a damn whether she ever saw Kip again or not. Kip didn't like the feeling, and she preferred not to examine it too closely.

Vivian held one hand daintily in the air over the plate as she considered the food before her. Deciding, she selected a piece of the bread and pâté and popped it into her mouth.

"Ummm, delicious," she pronounced, still chewing. "Peter's getting Grandma Bess settled in the living room."

Without realizing what she was doing, Kip rearranged the bread slices to close up the hole Vivian had left. "I'm so glad she was up to coming today."

Grandma Bess was Vivian Hallman's mother, now approaching ninety-eight. The older woman was tiny and frail, barely able to see or hear. She lived with Vivian and her husband, who tried to take her out with them whenever it was feasible. It wasn't as difficult as it might have been, because she usually stayed put in a chair, saying nothing. People shouted pleasantries to her until they got bored and then more or less ignored her until the end of the event, when they leaned down to say good-bye. Whenever she saw Grandma Bess, Kip liked to sit with her for a few minutes, holding her wrinkled hand, not saying anything. The elderly woman would smile, but she never seemed to be fully aware of Kip's presence. Still, for some reason she couldn't explain, Kip found her company very peaceful. Selfish of me, she reflected. As if I'm using this poor old woman like a string of worry beads.

Kip could hear more people arriving. Her parents were here, she noted as she listened to her mother exclaim over J. P., who must have just come downstairs from his room.

Vivian turned to Nicole.

"How are you, dear?" She extended a hand.

Nicole smiled, but she took the other woman's hand almost warily. Vivian Hallman was hardly that free-spirited or zany, but Nicole privately referred to her as the wild old hippie. A reasonably successful writer, Vivian continued to publish, although it had been many years since her big novel, *The Catalyst*. She was, in fact, down-to-earth and completely practical. Unfortunately, Peter hadn't inherited that gene from his mother, Kip thought with a small smile. Instead, he had his father's absentmindedness, along with a special bewilderment gene for household repairs and the like. It was starting to look as if their son had inherited it, as well; sweaters, backpacks, gloves, sneakers—everything in J. P.'s care eventually disappeared.

Peter's father came over to Kip, at six feet three towering over her as he gave her a hug. "How's my favorite and only daughter-in-law?"

"Hey, there, Art," Kip answered, hugging him back.

She could smell his pipe tobacco on his tweed jacket. She liked her father-in-law, although to this day she found his intellect intimidating. Art worked at a small publishing house as an editor of what inevitably turned out to be obscure literary novels. Occasionally he would write articles for literary journals, but they were so dense that Kip usually found it impossible to get past the first paragraph. He had the pipe and wire-rim glasses to go with the image, but, in his case, none of it was an affectation. He was the real deal, as Peter put it. Once Peter and his parents got started on a discussion about books or philosophy or politics, Kip didn't even bother trying to follow along, much less join in. When it came to that sort of thing, she thought, those three Hallmans breathed a rarefied air indeed.

The sudden appearance of Kip's brother, Dirk, in the doorway caused everyone to turn. His wife was behind him, and their two little girls, ages five and seven, were shyly hanging on to her legs. They had flown in from Seattle especially for the holiday, spending the night in a Manhattan hotel before driving up to Rhinebeck. Traveling was a significant expense for them, and this was the first time in three years that Kip and Nicole had seen their brother.

"Duck!" Nicole threw herself into his arms, using her childhood nickname for him. "I can't believe you're here."

"Baby sister number one. Gorgeous as always." He kissed her and gave her a bear hug. Then he turned his face to Kip. "And baby sister number two, also a vision of loveliness."

Kip laughed and came over for her hug, as Nicole reluctantly surrendered him and turned to greet his wife, Sue. Both girls had always adored their older brother, but Nicole had a special attachment to him. The sun rose and set on Dirk Pierson as far as she was concerned.

Kip kissed Sue hello, as well, and knelt down to hug the two little girls, who were still uncomfortable in the new and strange environment. After a minute or so of Kip's chatting with them, they began to warm up to her. They even allowed her to give them each a hug.

"Hey, old man," Kip said playfully to her brother, rising from the ground, her five-year-old niece Jocelyn in her arms. "You've aged horribly. Glad you could hobble back East for a bit."

Dirk grinned. His youthful appearance was a family joke by now, although it had annoyed him to no end when he was in high school and, later, in his twenties. Despite his height, he looked so young that he had trouble getting dates. Girls either didn't believe how old he was or weren't interested in his baby-faced appearance. That was the reason, he often said, he was able to devote so much time to basketball. The sport had earned him a scholarship to college and, eventually, a job as a high school basketball coach. The team he worked with in Seattle had enjoyed four consecutive winning seasons, he informed Kip when he called about coming for Thanksgiving A winning team, a great wife, two great daughters—he was a happy man, he had said.

Kip was delighted that things had worked out so well for her brother. He was just so easy to love, so much fun to be around. Nicole, on the other hand, was invariably difficult and unhappy. And Kip herself, as she knew all too well, was another story, always on the run, wanting everything to be just right, trying to take care of the whole world. It was as if they came from three different families.

Jocelyn was reaching out for her father. Kip handed the little girl over and gave Dirk an affectionate squeeze on the arm. "All right, everybody into the living room. It's too crowded in here, and, more important, the drinks and hors d'oeuvres are out there."

Ushering everyone out, Kip took a few minutes to recheck her list and attend to her turkey basting again. She figured she could sit for one drink with her company before she had to come back into the kitchen to stay.

The living room was already busy and noisy, with more guests still expected. Kip greeted her parents, who were talking to J. P. over near the piano. As she approached, Kip smiled at the pleasing sight of her son, lean and tall for his age, his brown hair thick and shiny, his large eyes fixed attentively on his grandfather. Despite J. P.'s efforts to dress up for the holiday in gray flannel pants and a white shirt, he still looked as if he were taking a break from a game of touch football; his shirttail hung out, and his freshly ironed pants were somehow already rumpled. Ruffling his hair, she pulled him to her and kissed the top of his head. J. P. rolled his eyes, but didn't pull away.

Peter's parents went over to Lisa and congratulated her. Two first prizes at swim meets, they marveled. Quite an accomplishment for her first year in competition outside her own school. Lisa smiled and then turned to see her Uncle Dirk and Aunt Sue coming closer to offer their congratulations, as well.

Kip stood, watching. Her daughter was the center of attention in the room. Everyone was praising her dedication to swimming, her talent, her awards. Lisa usually kept her more upbeat emotions to herself these days, but right now, Kip thought, she was glowing, actually glowing.

J. P. asked her a question. Turning back to ask him to repeat it, Kip's eye fell on a photograph on the mantelpiece, an eight-by-ten in a silver frame. It was a picture of her when she was sixteen. She had just stepped off the ice after winning first place in a district championship. Someone had handed her an enormous bouquet of flowers, which she was clutching tightly. Her hair was pulled up in a bun, the way she always wore it when she skated, and she had on a red skating outfit, the skirt sparkling with gold glitter. She felt a familiar pang of longing, one she had pushed away so often. She immediately did so again.

What struck Kip about the photograph was the expression on her face. It was identical to the one on her daughter's face at this very moment.

2

Nora Levin leaned back and immersed her head in the water. She might as well apply the shampoo in the tub before standing up and showering off, she figured. She had at least fifteen more minutes before she had to leave for her sister's house. Coming up for air, she saw that Duncan was entering the tub beside her. He lifted her body, slid in underneath her, and began to soap her breasts from behind with a large white washcloth.

"I was about to get out," she murmured, not moving a muscle as her skin responded to his continuous circular caresses.

"Feel free," he replied, propelling the soapy cloth down over her stomach and finally bringing it to a resting place between her legs.

Nora realized she was not about to go anywhere as his hand once again started moving, this time staying in the small area that sent waves of pleasure throughout the rest of her body. Her back arched while his fingers explored further, moving deeper inside her. It was another twenty minutes before they emerged from the tub. Nora hurried into her clothes and then reached for the small hair dryer she kept in her backpack.

As she dressed, Duncan kept up a steady stream of conversation.

"So, if I stay here in Ardsley, I have all this suburban crap to deal with. I mean, I hate using the car all the time. Nothing is convenient. Everything is a few miles away. If I have a gig in the city, I have to get on the train, or—worse yet—drive there and spend forty bucks on parking. It's impossible."

Nora had heard this diatribe many times before. In fact, she'd been listening to variations on it for as long as she'd known him. She and Duncan would get together for lunch or dinner, spend a few hours in bed; then she'd bear witness to the decisions that were the bane of her friend's existence. The interesting thing was, the issues never changed. As she stood in front of the mirror, applying lip gloss, she knew exactly what was to come. Duncan would reminisce about how great it was to have lived in downtown Manhattan for several years, and then he'd start to list all the disadvantages. At the end of the discussion, he would go back to the subject of his current life in the suburbs, and the endless debate would continue.

"I never had these problems when I lived on Seventeenth Street," he said, lying across his bed, still naked but dry now. "That was the thing about New York. No car, no hassles with garbage pickup. The restaurants stayed open till three in the morning. It was great." He scratched his head and then stretched out and covered himself with the sheet. "Of course, you also were attacked by the sound of car alarms going off in the middle of the night, not to mention enough filth in the air to stunt a person's growth."

Nora turned to him. "Gee," she said, unable to stifle a smile, "I didn't know that clean air kept people tall."

"Hold on, hold on," he said. "I'm not claiming that clean air makes you taller. I'm just suggesting that there has to be some correlation between the agents of filth that try to enter a person's body, and the body's response to them. I mean, it seems to me the cells have to react in some way to protect themselves. Maybe they don't shorten exactly, but I think they must constrict in some way. You know what I mean?" He couldn't have sounded more earnest.

Nora smiled. No, she wanted to say. I don't in any which way know what the hell you're talking about. But she wasn't about to hurt his feelings. She was fond of Duncan. For almost seven years, they'd been friends, for six of them occasional lovers. They were kind to each other and affectionate. And if Duncan was the most ambivalent person Nora had ever known, she still loved having him as a pal. After all, she was not about to settle down, and enjoying an attractive guy like Duncan every couple of months was not exactly a poke in the eye with a sharp stick.

"I sort of know what you mean," she answered him. "And at worst, it's a fascinating theory."

He smiled up at her as she came across the room and sat on the edge of his bed.

"You have some crazy ways of your own, you know," he said, reaching for her.

Fully dressed now, Nora resisted his attempt to pull her down alongside him on the bed.

He continued to speak as if she had all the time in the world, although it was obvious that she was trying to leave. "You're the one who started asking the crazy questions. What was that line you picked me up with at the studio? 'If you were going to die, and you could choose between one perfect month and two so-so years, which would you pick?' Wasn't that it?"

Nora laughed. She pulled away from him and stood up. "Maybe I did and maybe I didn't. Either way, aren't you glad?"

"You bet," he said cheerfully. He crossed his arms behind his head. "It certainly made the six weeks we spent on that job more fun. I could use some fun at work these days. You know, I had a conversation with Jim Percivale. We talked about my coming down to work with him in Orlando."

Nora looked at her watch. She knew this conversation by heart as well. Duncan was a sound engineer, and every few months he would talk to the guy he'd learned the business from right after college. Each and every time, it would impel him to debate the merits of leaving studio work in New York and moving to another area. Some months the decision would be between Florida and New York. Then the discussion would switch to the possible merits of Northern California. She usually got a kick out of Duncan's lifelong dilemmas, but it was time to leave for Wendy's house.

"I've got to get on the road," she said, picking up her leather jacket from the back of a chair.

She walked back toward the bed and bent down to kiss him on the lips. "The family awaits," she said, walking toward the door.

"Hey, happy Thanksgiving," he said, turning over and burying his head in the pillow.

"You, too," Nora answered, letting herself out the door. "Have fun at your grandmother's."

As she walked toward her car, a sudden breeze forced her to close her jacket. She breathed in the fresh, cold air and pondered her encounters with Duncan. They would never be more than casual, but they were never less than satisfying. Maybe there was a prince out there, she thought, whose pea only she could find. Frankly, she doubted it. Making love with Duncan was fun. For that matter, she laughed to herself, maybe he's right about the clean air. As she approached her Toyota, she felt energized and alive. So why not believe that in the clean Westchester air, she might even be taller. The thought made her laugh out loud.

"If you were a character in a novel, who would you pick to write it?" Nora asked, taking a sip of water.

Her sister closed her eyes, clearly trying to think up an accurate answer. Nora was certain that Wendy's good manners would keep her from expressing the impatience she undoubtedly felt. She also knew that Wendy was unlikely to come up with anyone who could really capture her. No writer Nora had ever read would fully appreciate the care and craft Wendy poured into everything in her world, from the origami animals she'd formed for the bookshelves in the kids' rooms to the hand-loomed placemats already set under the plates in the dining room.

"Louisa May Alcott," Wendy responded, opening her eyes.

Nora nodded. "And Mr. Berlinsky?" She smiled at Wendy's husband, Andy.

He responded right away. "Kafka."

"A cheerful little answer," Nora said. "Okay, now, it's your last meal before you go to a desert island for the next twenty years. You get three courses. What do you want?"

Wendy once again looked thoughtful, but Andy lay his face down in his hands, crying, "No more, please God, no more questions."

Nora laughed, but her fingers drummed impatiently on the end table beside her chair and her bright blue eyes traveled longingly toward the next room. Her sister's dining room was spotlessly clean, the wooden chairs newly polished, the fresh tea roses lodged artfully in three short white porcelain vases, their perfume embracing the whole room. But, on the sideboard against the wall sat the enormous platter of turkey her brother-in-law had so carefully carved three hours before. At four o'clock, the hour dinner was called for, the slices had been moist and inviting. Now, the white meat seemed to curl up at the ends, and the dark meat resembled small dead gerbils. Given the time and effort Wendy must have put into the preparation, Nora knew this must have been teeth-gnashingly painful, but her sister's ability not to be thrown—or, at the very least, not to *seem* thrown—was legendary.

In the center of the table was the large bowl of cranberry sauce, still encased in plastic wrap, and the basket of seven-grain rolls that had stayed promisingly full and delicious up to about an hour ago, but now lay on their backs like soggy brown paper balls.

In a wing chair next to Wendy's, Andy sighed and checked his watch, as he'd done every few minutes for the past couple of hours. Nora had left Duncan's house at noon, arriving at Wendy's around one. In retrospect, she wished she hadn't hurried.

The scene felt entirely familiar to Nora. From earliest childhood, Nora and Wendy Levin had spent an inordinate amount of time waiting for their father to get home so they could go to the beach as their mother had promised, or attend the wedding or bar mitzvah of a cousin or a friend. "You wouldn't believe . . . ," he would say when he'd finally walk through the door, perspiration running down his face, practically shaking from the tensions of running Levin's Corner, the coffee shop on Rhinebeck's Main Street that seemed to drain all the strength from his body on a daily basis.

Between tales of the counterman filching twenty-dollar bills from the cash register and waitresses leaving on a moment's notice, or worse yet, breaking down in tears in the middle of the breakfast rush, Nora's father was almost completely undone. And late. So very late all the time.

Nora got up from the couch and walked into the dining room, taking a seat at the large maple table. Unconsciously, she tapped a soup spoon against the tablecloth in time to the music that was coming out of the CD player. In addition to the cheeses she'd brought from Zabar's, Nora had stopped at Tower Records and picked up an old Nina Simone collection that had just been transferred to disc, knowing Wendy and Andy would enjoy listening to it. Of course, she'd also realized that her parents were unlikely to be there early enough to hear much of anything, but the waiting around drove her crazy anyway. She tried to calculate how many hours she'd spent not actually *doing* something but *waiting* to do something. Forget it, she thought. The number was infinite.

Wendy followed Nora to the dining room, bringing with her the mostly eaten bowl of pistachio nuts from the coffee table. Her husband followed a few seconds later. They each sat down, Andy at the head of the table,

Wendy across from Nora. Neither said anything, though Andy sighed one more time. Nora watched her sister take in the clenching and unclenching of her husband's fingers as he sat there. Internally, Andy was not the model of calm he liked to project on the outside.

Too exasperated to try another of her questions, Nora found herself sighing along with him. Here it was, Thanksgiving. Wendy had been cooking for two days straight, and by now her two children had been so hungry they'd already gone through an entire bag of Goldfish crackers, a container of grapes, almost the whole bowl of pistachio nuts, and the two large Swiss chocolate bars their aunt had brought them as a special dessert treat.

"I think we should start," Nora said. "This is crazy. The kids must be ready to eat the curtains."

Wendy smiled. "I doubt that they have room left for anything. Besides, you know how Daddy hates eating alone."

Nora shook her head. "Interestingly enough, *I* hate waiting around and I bet *you* hate having all your food turn to dust. Everyone hates something."

"Oh, Nora," Wendy answered beneficently as she stood up and walked across to a chest of drawers, taking out some kind of fabric with a needle tucked into it and bringing it back to her place at the table. "At least we're all here together. Mom and Dad must be just killing themselves to get here." She sat down once again, this time withdrawing the needle from what turned out to be a large square of tapestry fabric and beginning to make tiny, neat stitches in pale blue thread on the outline of a leaping deer.

Nora tried to imagine a scenario in which her father would "kill himself" for someone else's benefit. There was not even a glimmer of a possibility of coming up with one. But her irritation wasn't going to move dinner along.

"You're right," she said. "With Daddy finding the cure for cancer and all, it's no wonder he's a little late." She waited for her sister to object, but Wendy was smarter

than that. She just kept on with her sewing. Which only
made Nora continue. "The last thing Mom and Dad
would want is for everyone to have to wait for them.
They're probably climbing snowdrifts in their bare feet
to get here."

This time, Wendy did respond. "You know Mom's
dying to get out of there."

Nora nodded. In fact, her mother rarely even worked
at the coffee shop, let alone stayed there hours past closing. Belinda Levin had designed the flowered menus and
the watercolor paintings that lined the walls, but she
didn't usually work with her husband. In fairness, Nora
acknowledged to herself, she'd only gone there with him
today to hurry him out when the coffee shop closed,
special for Thanksgiving, at two-thirty. Nora sighed
loudly one more time, laughing as she saw her brother-
in-law check his watch yet again. It was almost seven
o'clock. Clearly the restaurant hadn't closed on time, and
just as clearly, her mother hadn't been able to move her
husband out the door at whatever time the shop actually
had closed its doors.

Nora sat back in her chair and gazed at her sister. As
usual, Wendy seemed a model of serenity. With her daughters playing—and screaming—in the living room, out of
sight if not out of earshot, and her husband a human time
bomb, Wendy just sat there, working on the tapestry and
gazing out the dining room windows to the late fall in
Rhinebeck, the leaves long gone from the trees, but their
branches graceful and imposing against the darkness.
Wendy was dressed beautifully, her compact frame encased in a navy blue wool skirt, with a matching navy
sweater set. Her hair, straighter and lighter than Nora's,
fell neatly behind a tortoiseshell hairband. Pretty, a per-
petual slight smile on her face, Wendy Berlinsky ema-
nated contentment.

Her sister never failed to amaze Nora. She never quite
understood how Wendy got that way. As for herself, she
possessed neither the look nor the personality for such
placidity. Dressed in her blue work shirt, an oversize

sweater she'd borrowed from Duncan earlier in the day, and a black watch plaid miniskirt she'd worn since high school, Nora was no exponent of the stylish match. Her shoulder-length dark, wavy hair fell, as it always did, at will around her face. She was tall where Wendy was shorter, impetuous where Wendy was thoughtful, sloppy where Wendy could turn any room into something resembling an antique dollhouse.

Her attention was caught by the sounds of her nieces' outraged screaming as they ran in from the living room. No real surprise, given the fact that they only scurried to their parents when they found themselves in the middle of a fight.

"Tamara hid my sneakers!" six-year-old Sarah exclaimed, standing in front of her mother, demanding attention.

Tamara, still round and cherubic at four, ran up behind her older sister, a look of perfect innocence on her face.

Nora took in the glances that passed between Wendy and her husband. Since the birth of their first child, Andy had hoped for an atmosphere of calm to prevail in his household. "The office is a sea of land mines," Nora had heard him say countless times, "home should be my island of tranquillity." It seemed to Andy that his wife should possess some magic trick that would make his little darlings into the perfect porcelain figurines that filled his imagination when he had envisioned life as a parent. Wendy, on the other hand, took all behavior in stride. Not even when the girls were making a cyclone out of her hard-wrought environment did Wendy lose her cool. When the kids were acting out, her theory was that the fighting was bound to end sooner or later. When they were behaving like angels, she knew that that, too, had a limited lifespan.

Nora watched as her sister weighed her options. Doing nothing would enrage Andy, but have little impact on the girls. Making a fuss would please her husband, and effect exactly as little change on the kids.

Nora spared her from having to decide.

"Sarah," she said, walking over to the child and taking her hand to lead her back to her place at the table. "I bet you can think of a song about the butter."

"Huh?" Sarah said, climbing into her aunt's lap and making corkscrews of Nora's dark curls, as she'd done since she was a few months old.

"Well . . . ," Nora said, looking up at the ceiling as if lost in thought, "how about something like this? 'There's one food that has little to say, and we all call it butter. There's one thing it's unlikely to do and that thing would be mutter.' " The melody she'd picked began a little like "Old MacDonald" and then turned into a vague patter. But the lack of perfect musicianship didn't stop both her nieces from giggling.

"I can make up a song about the stuffing," Tamara cried out, running over to Nora to claim equal attention.

"Let's hear it," Nora said, picking the child up and arranging each girl on one knee.

"Stuffing, wuffing, tuffing, fuffing!"

"That's not a song," Sarah cried indignantly, reaching out to tickle her younger sister, something Tamara couldn't bear.

"Okay," Nora said, extending her arms to keep them apart, "you're going to a desert island. You can bring one room of your house. Which one would it be?"

"The kitchen! The kitchen! The kitchen!" Tamara shrieked. "So I could eat and eat and eat and eat!"

"But how would you go to the bathroom?" Sarah asked. "Oh, I know," she added, sliding along her aunt's knee so she was a little closer to her sister, "you'd go in your pants, 'cause you're a baby!" With that, her tormenting fingers reached out to the smaller girl once more, causing Tamara to shriek.

Nora fixed an arm around each of her nieces and stood up, still holding both girls. "Time out," she said, meaning it.

The girls stopped screeching and looked at her.

"I have something you creatures will enjoy." Nora walked over to the CD player, next to which was a large black leather bag. She reached inside and pulled out a CD, replacing the one they'd been listening to. She skipped tracks until she found exactly what she was looking for.

Sure enough, as "Tomorrow" began to play, both girls began to dance around the room, singing along. *Annie* was a show Nora loathed, but she knew the girls would love it.

Wendy lay her fabric square in her lap and turned to her sister. "I thought in your profession musical taste was everything."

Nora smiled. "In my profession, it *is*. In my personal life, expediency rises to the top of the list."

"The next time someone requests 'Sunrise, Sunset' instead of Schubert or Miles Davis, I'll remind you of this," Wendy laughed, picking up her needlework and starting another series of stitches.

Nora sat back down at the table. At thirty-nine, she'd spent fifteen years building a career as a music producer, putting together reels for a variety of events. At first, she'd done weddings and small parties. She'd even had the slightly dubious distinction of creating collections of songs for elevators and stores, although she had put her all into making the pieces more interesting than the easy-listening stuff most malls featured. In the past couple of years, she'd worked steadily, moving her business out of her apartment on Manhattan's West End Avenue and into a small office downtown. Nowadays, she didn't have to scrounge for business, as she'd had to do in the beginning. People sought her out. Although she had yet to break into film work, which was her ultimate goal, her work had become both more interesting and much more profitable financially. But even back when the bulk of her jobs were birthday parties and discount clothing stores, she would never have chosen "Tomorrow" for a client. Not even an elevator client.

"How about if the five of us just have a bite of the stuffing," Nora said, sitting back down and reaching out for a tired-looking baby carrot. "We don't even have to

make a dent in the dish. We can even it all out with a
fork after we finish, and they'll never know anything's
missing."

Andy looked interested, but Wendy just smiled and
shook her head.

"So, how's the guy you were seeing the last time you
came up here?" Wendy asked.

Nora had to think. Wendy and Andy knew nothing
about Duncan, so her sister must have meant the lawyer
Nora had met at the vegetable counter in the supermarket. "You mean Sam?"

"I don't know," Wendy said. "He was an architect or
something. You said he was really nice."

Nora yawned. "Actually, I said I'd gone out with him
three or four times. You were the one who said how
nice he sounded."

"Okay," Wendy responded. "So, how's it going?"

"I guess you might say it's gone," Nora said, laughing.
"He left to do some trial in Austin a few weeks ago."

"You don't seem too shaken by it," Wendy observed.

"Actually, I started seeing someone else last week. An
advertising guy." And this morning I slept with someone
I've been seeing for years whom you don't know about
and never will, 'cause it's never going to matter, she said
to herself.

Nora was aware that her brother-in-law was shifting in
his chair. She knew the conversation was making him
uncomfortable. When subjected to the personal details
of his single sister-in-law's life, Andy veered between
fears for her personal safety and disgust at her presumably low morals. Wendy's attitude had always been more
benign. She hoped Nora would find the man of her
dreams and bring him along to family dinners, so yet
another person could sit there, hour after hour, waiting
for their parents to walk through the door.

"What's his name?" Wendy asked, the needle in her
hand held in midair as she searched her sister's face.

"His name is Rick, and, yes, he's very nice, too." We
slept together a couple of times and it was very pleasant,

but he's probably not going to matter much in the long run either, she thought, again careful not to say it out loud.

Wendy started to respond when they all heard the front door opening.

"So, where is everybody?" her father's booming voice rang out. He and his wife entered the dining room, Belinda Levin weighed down by dishes she'd undoubtedly been cooking for days. Her face was apologetic in the extreme.

Not so David Levin's. "You wouldn't believe how slow the new girl was today! Like everyone in the place is on a plane, and this one's on a bus." He peered at his daughters, obviously annoyed. "So, what are you waiting for? Your mother and I are starving!"

3

Eloise Bentley emerged from the bedroom before her husband and put her suitcase down in the front hallway. She frowned as she noticed that the bag was overstuffed, bulging on both sides. John and she would be away for only three days. By the time they got to her parents' house, the elaborate holiday dinner would be under way, so the suit she was wearing would take her through the whole evening. That left only Friday and Saturday afternoons to dress for. It was silly to pack so many outfits and break an expensive piece of luggage on top of it. Besides, she realized, all the outfits in the world couldn't disguise how overweight she was. She sighed as she picked up the valise and went back to the bedroom.

She expected to see John finishing up his packing. Instead, he was standing by the window, holding a blue cashmere sweater she'd given him for Christmas a few years before. It was odd to see him so still, his head down as if he were in deep contemplation. Usually, John's ebullience made him appear to be in almost constant motion. Eloise placed her suitcase beside his on the king-size bed he had purchased after winning his first case. She opened the valise and withdrew the chocolate brown suit she had thrown in at the last minute.

"I packed too much," she said as she carried the suit to her closet. "As usual."

She placed the skirt and the jacket on hangers. Then, for a few seconds, she stared at them, tempted to stuff them back into her bag. Forcing herself to leave them where they were, she closed the closet door and turned her attention to her husband. She was surprised to see him still at the window, holding the sweater, staring into space. In the course of their marriage, she was usually the one urging him to slow down, to take it easy. Not that he ever listened. In fact, in the past couple of years, each of their careers plus John's insistence on taking up each and every invitation he ever received made their quiet times together just about never. She often thought about how much she missed the way things used to be, when the two of them seemed the only people on earth. The memory made her look at him more closely. She suddenly realized that his shoulders had begun to shake.

"John," she said, coming to stand beside him, "is something wrong?"

When he turned around, she was shocked to see tears running down his cheeks. "Oh, Eloise." The words seemed to burst from him. "Oh, my darling Eloise."

He drew her into a tight hug.

"My God, what's the matter?" she gasped, sliding her arms around him with an answering closeness.

"It's all too much." He buried his head in her neck, the moisture of his tears leaving her jacket collar damp.

Fear crept up Eloise's spine. Until now, he had been perfectly fine, making small talk while they packed. He must have been hiding something behind his casual demeanor. He had to be ill, she thought. That was the only explanation. John was a buoyant man, someone whose limitless energy had helped to turn him into the success he had become. In their fifteen years of marriage, she'd learned almost everything about him. He wasn't a whiner and he wasn't a quitter. For him to behave this way could mean only one terrible thing.

Eloise held on to his hand as she turned him around and led him to the foot of the bed. She sat down, indicating that he should sit next to her. But rather than sitting beside her, he fell to his knees in front of her.

"It's cancer, isn't it?" she asked, steeling herself for his answer.

He looked at her, amazement on his face. "You're too good for me," he said, rising slightly to take her face in his hands and kissing her on the mouth. "You always were and you always will be."

Eloise's heart was breaking for him. "Listen, honey," she said, throwing her arms around him, "we're going to fight it, and you're going to be fine."

John pulled away from her, taking both her hands into his own and kneeling back down at her knee. "Ah, Eloise, I'm going to miss this so much."

No, Eloise thought, please, God, don't let this be happening. "You're wrong, darling," she said fiercely. "You're going to be fine. Everything's going to be fine."

John smiled up at her. "That's so *you*, El. And you're right, you *are* going to be fine. You're too great a girl not to be fine. We're all going to be fine."

We're all going to be fine? Eloise was confused. Who *all*?

"John," she started, "what—?"

"I'm healthy," he reassured her as he reached up to trace her mouth with his fingers. He moved the ends of her lips into a smile.

The smile vanished the second he pulled his hand away. "If you're healthy, what's this about?"

He emitted a heavy sigh before he answered. "I've been so lucky," he said, talking more to himself than to her. "For all these years, I've had you in my life, and now I have the rest of my life to look back on our marriage with the gratitude it deserves."

Eloise took her hands out of his. She realized they were trembling and clasped them in her lap. "John, please. What are you telling me?"

He got up off the carpet and stood in front of her, his entire six-foot frame suddenly pulsing with life. "I know it's a surprise to you, but I'm in love." He smiled at her as if she would share his joy.

"You're in love. . . ." Eloise's voice broke, and she waited a few moments before going on. "I take it this doesn't imply that you're in love with your wife. Namely, me." She was making an effort to keep from crying or screaming. Somehow, for reasons she couldn't possibly have articulated, it seemed very important to maintain her dignity.

"I've found something incredible, something I'm sure you'll find as well." He beamed at her. "That's my wish for you."

She stared at him. This is a dream, she thought, and I'm about to wake up. I will laugh about this in the morning. We'll be lying in bed, and John will be next to me. His mouth will be slightly open, and he'll be snoring, and then he'll awaken and ask me how I slept and whether I feel like having blueberry pancakes.

"I want you to be happy for me." His words were all too clear for a dream. "What we've had was so very special. I can't be happy unless you're happy, too."

She took in his eager expression, wanting to pummel him with her fists, to claw at him until he told her that he didn't mean what he was saying. That this was a scene from a play or a very bad joke. But she found herself saying nothing. Instead, she sat, silently, as he talked about the woman who had "made him feel eighteen again." She lived in the next building and walked her schnauzer every evening at ten-thirty. That was how they'd met. Walking the dogs. John would go out with Buster, their chocolate Lab, and he'd fall into conversation with her.

Now, he was in love with her and she with him. It wasn't anything he expected, but she made him feel a kind of passion he had thought was gone from his life forever. It was a gift. It had to be accepted, welcomed with open arms. He wanted Eloise to understand. That was so very important to him, he kept saying, that she understand and be glad for him. And he knew that she would. She had always wanted the best for him. That was one of the reasons he was so grateful to her.

Eloise watched him as he talked, one realization after another hitting her as hard as blows to the stomach. He had been having an affair, probably for quite a while.

He had deceived her so expertly that she'd never suspected it, not even for a second. This man she thought she knew so well had maintained a perfect facade right up until now, the moment when he decided he simply had to share his news. He wasn't going to give their marriage another try or make any effort to salvage the fifteen years they'd shared. And he genuinely seemed to believe that the wife whose heart he was breaking would congratulate him on his new romance.

Eventually, she stopped hearing his words altogether. She watched the light in his eyes, his obvious relief at getting everything out in the open. Now he would be free to go. The hard part for him was over.

"I'm going to leave, El, no reason to put it off," he said, patting her hand. "I've got my bag packed, so . . ."

She saw that he could hardly wait to get out the door. Nodding, she stayed where she was as he closed his suitcase, grabbed his jacket, and kissed her on the cheek. She heard the front door to the apartment open and then slam shut.

So, that's it, she thought. Simple. My husband's gone. My marriage, the life I've been living—over, erased as if they'd never happened.

It was odd how numb she felt. She clasped her hands in her lap again and stared at them. Now what? She stood, knowing the answer.

It was several hours later that Eloise sat back on the white silk couch and viewed the coffee table before her with disgust. The remains of an Entenmann's coffeecake rested near two empty cartons, one bearing the traces of beef lo mein, the other sauteed garlic shrimp. In the center of the table stood what had been a half gallon of Breyer's Vanilla, an empty jar of cashew nuts, and one lone eggroll, left over from a bag that had held five.

She felt her stomach clench in pain, yet even now, after all she'd eaten, she felt as if she could just go on gobbling everything in sight. She thought about what was in the refrigerator. Year-old Skippy Super Chunk, half a roast beef sandwich her husband had brought in from a nearby deli weeks before that neither of them had bothered to throw away. All of it was fair game.

She looked at the antique gold clock on the stone fireplace mantel. Thank God, she thought. Thanksgiving would be over in an hour and a half. Maybe tomorrow would be easier. Maybe sunlight would bring her back to some kind of control.

Then again, why the hell should she bother to be in control? Would it make John come back to her? No way. Would it make her beautiful? Sure, she thought, looking down at herself, her stomach distended in the royal blue wool knit she'd paid over a thousand dollars for, her feet swollen and pinched in their Manolo Blahnik pumps. Ironically, the sight of herself made her think of her childhood. She could hear her father's voice in her ear. *"My beauty,"* he would say, putting an arm around her as he'd introduce her to someone. Her brother, George, had been "the brain." She had been "the beauty." Her naturally blond thick hair fell to beneath her shoulders. Her blue eyes were almost turquoise in the light. Her skin was smooth and lightly tan, her nose elegantly narrow, just long enough to give her face some seriousness.

"My beauty!" Her father had repeated that phrase over and over until she'd reached sixteen, when five extra pounds turned mysteriously into twenty and then twenty into thirty. Only after she'd graduated from Chapin and started at Vassar, finally the perfect 118 pounds that had eluded her for so long, had she heard the words from him again.

Her weight had not been a problem all the time she'd been away at college. Or, for that matter, when she'd started her career. She'd been so busy, working her ass off to prove herself at Bentley Communications. Not just the boss's daughter, but someone who earned her success. A crack assistant to the editor of *USA Now.* A fifteen-hour-a-day, seven-days-a-week reporter for *Manhattan Daily.* Extra pounds? Please. Who had time to think about eating?

Now, in the top spot of the company's most widely

circulated women's glossy, she took, maybe, three vacation days a year. She had no free time at all. Not a minute. Yet she'd managed to work her way up to 178 pounds. She frowned. That was this morning's weight. Tomorrow's number would be even higher. For a second, she thought about making herself vomit, as she'd done for a year or so as a teenager. She remembered hiding the noises in the bathroom, worrying that one of the many guests her parents had invited to their house each summer weekend would hear her, would expose her. Oh, would Grey and Felicia Bentley have loved that! She could still imagine the scene, just as she used to fear it years before. She would be in their weekend house in New Hope, in the small bathroom on the main floor, the one right off the den, and someone—a president of some country or a cardinal from the Vatican or something— would stop by the door. "Your daughter is purging!" the person would scream. And then her father would get that dignified scowl he so rarely showed in public, and her mother would weep into a lace handkerchief. And the worst part was that they probably wouldn't even say anything. They'd just be mortified. Or, to use the words they might have chosen had they actually deigned to speak of it, "so disappointed."

It was small comfort, but at least she was in her own apartment, alone, right here on Fifth Avenue. Her parents and her brother and his wife were down in New Hope, eating turkey and goose, and beautifully made pumpkin soufflés. Not that they'd be there alone. She forgot who was on tap for this weekend. Was it the secretary of state or the guy from National Public Radio? No, she thought, that was last weekend. What was the difference? For once, Eloise didn't have to smile at a group of strangers, make small talk with the well-bred.

Jesus, you're ungrateful, she thought, reaching absently for the last eggroll. Her parents had been loving, supportive, family-minded. If her father's communications empire had taken much of his time and forced his family into a constant stream of public events, his affection had nonetheless been clear. Grey Bentley was there on every birthday, and, despite their affluence and the abundant help that always surrounded them, both her father and her mother had always been attentive to their children.

She took a bite of the cold eggroll. She was glad her parents hadn't been in her apartment earlier, when her husband announced he was leaving. At last, she'd had the presence of mind to call them. "We've decided to go to Bermuda," she'd lied. "A romantic weekend. Just the two of us."

She hadn't said what hotel they'd be staying at, had hurried off the phone when her mother started asking questions.

Eloise pictured John's inamorata in her mind, the woman's face the same as the one on her schnauzer. It almost made her smile. But, of course, whatever-her-name-was bore no resemblance to a schnauzer. Although Eloise had never seen her close up, she had noticed the woman with the dog a couple of times over the last year or so. She hadn't gotten a good look at her face, but the woman was well dressed and slender. No, she thought, not slender. Reed-thin. The way women were supposed to be. The way she herself would be if she weren't a fat disgusting pig.

Her head turned to a picture of John and herself, taken the day he'd opened his first office. That had been three years after they'd met at a dinner party, when John was in his third year of law school. She'd helped him hang his law degree up on the wall, rearranged the pieces of furniture he'd bought from the small store on Broadway. The teak desk, the round conference table with the four chairs gathered around it. She could recall the pride in his eyes when he'd introduced her to his first big client, the president of a supermarket chain who needed help with bankruptcy proceedings. She sighed. Those early days, before he joined Carter, Hamill, Brusker & Strong. Before she'd put on sixty pounds and turned into—

The sound of the telephone ringing shocked her. She didn't move from the couch, but found her hands were

shaking. What if it was John? She almost rose to answer
it; then she stayed where she was. It was more likely a
wrong number or a solicitation from PBS or the American Heart Association. So few people called her at home.
Her whole social life seemed to take place in her office.
At *Metropolitan Woman,* she got hundreds of calls a day,
every one requiring a response. Writers wanting assignments, agents and managers who longed for their clients'
faces to be on the cover, photographers begging for
work. Then there were the scores of people who believed
they wanted to be her friend.

But, of course, she thought, all those people didn't
know her at all. They knew the editor of a magazine,
the daughter of "a leader of men," as she'd once heard
her father described in a speech. They didn't know the
person who just ate Thanksgiving dinner alone out of a
mass of cardboard boxes. And they surely didn't know
the woman who was so unattractive and boring, her own
husband left her for a woman who might or might not
look like a schnauzer.

She listened as the phone stopped ringing and the machine clicked on. "Eloise and John aren't home right
now," she heard her own voice chirp. "Do leave a message and we'll get back to you as soon as we can."

"Darlings . . ."

Eloise recognized her mother's voice. "Seth and Co-
rinne couldn't believe you weren't coming." Her father's
chimed in next. "Fania and Guillaume and Susie and Bill
all send their love."

Her father's voice carried on. "Your mother and I
hope you're having a good time, but, please, never do
this to us again. It's terribly lonely without you two.
You're going to have to do double-time at Christmas."

Eloise heard her father hang up his phone, listened to
the noises of her machine shutting off. He'd made his
last remarks sound funny, but she was certain he wasn't
finding it humorous in the least. There were certain times
you had to do certain things. That was the price you paid
for affluence and influence. The Bentleys were a lucky

family, and lucky families owed certain things to those around them. Thanksgiving was a family holiday, so the family was expected to appear, in total, even if—no, especially if—there were a lot of nonfamily on the scene, as well.

I'm sorry, Dad, Eloise thought, taking another bite of the eggroll. She was a bad wife and a bad daughter. If there were anything she could do about it, really, honestly, she would do it. She felt tears gathering in her eyes, which made her even angrier at herself. She didn't deserve self-pity. She'd made this happen. She found herself repulsive—what was her husband supposed to feel?

Wiping the tears away, she popped the last piece of eggroll into her mouth and stood up. She walked over to the window, looking out at Central Park, eleven stories below. The city was quiet tonight. Everyone would be in their apartment, half-asleep after the stuffing and the pie. Safe with their husbands and their children. She felt like hurling herself out the window. That would end the pain. She'd never have to tell her parents about John's leaving. Hell, she'd never have to resist another piece of chocolate cake. It would be the perfect solution.

Buster trotted over to her. She reached to scratch behind the dog's ears. Of course, she'd never do it. She couldn't even pretend to mean it. She couldn't have stood hurting her mother's feelings like that, exposing her father to the public humiliation of a daughter's suicide.

But, oh, she thought, staring down at the streetlights on Fifth Avenue, oh, how I wish I could.

4

Todd Lyle lay on his bed, his eyes closed, his hands clasped behind his head. The music of The Doors, the volume turned way up, seemed to envelop the small bedroom. Todd didn't notice. He was trying to decide which idea he liked better: electrocuting Harold Volman or setting him on fire. Dousing him with gasoline and lighting a match would be more satisfying, he thought. But it would really be a trip to throw a plugged-in hair dryer into his lap when he was sitting in a bathtub full of water. Todd tried to imagine what that fat, old-man body would look like, with all those volts running through it. He smiled.

"Hey, Professor Volman, looks like I know a little bit more about science than you thought, huh?" Todd would say as he held the hair dryer up above his head. The guy's mouth would be taped shut, but Volman's baggy eyes would be begging for mercy. "These are scientific principles at work here—water conducts electricity."

Todd laughed out loud. The biology professor was the first one who had warned Todd that he would fail if he didn't, as the teacher put it, "buckle down." The rest of his college teachers had followed, but fair was fair, the first to screw him should be the first to die.

"Oh, crap." He got up and went to sit at his desk chair, a castoff he had found at the side of the road two years before, with a ripped green vinyl seat and chrome legs on wheels. Volman had no doubt forgotten all about him. So had everyone else—the other professors, those condescending administration shitheads, the entire student population of SUNY's Buffalo campus.

Not that anyone there had ever noticed him or given a damn to begin with. By the time he had turned eighteen, other kids weren't interested in him or his problems. Todd snorted aloud. They were all too busy figuring out how to get laid or drinking until they puked. They made him want to puke himself.

This past semester at SUNY—his first and last semester there, he corrected himself—only proved what he had always believed. People were just repulsive morons. He'd even had to give up his late-night walks after a few weeks of coming upon students staggering home drunk, making out on the sidewalk, standing around on a corner sharing a joint, urinating on the snowdrifts.

They were so pathetic. He couldn't believe he was even part of the same species. Watching them make fools of themselves helped him ignore the pain in his chest whenever he wondered how long he would be a virgin. Or if any girl would ever want him the way those girls wanted those boys they were holding and stroking as they sat around the bars, their tongues down each other's throats.

He reached out with his index fingers to trace the carvings in his wooden desk, dozens of aimless markings he had made over the years. As usual, the room was dark, even though it was after ten in the morning. Short, faded corduroy curtains covered the two windows. Todd didn't mind; in fact, he preferred it this way. His small, crowded room was the one place he felt comfortable. No one came in there to bother him. Ever. He spent most of his days and evenings there. Sometimes he thought people had forgotten he was alive.

Of course, he could recall plenty of years when kids were *very* aware that he was alive. He let out a hollow laugh. "Come see Todd Lyle," he announced to no one, as if he were a circus barker, "our main freak attraction."

He was the kid who peed in his pants. That's who he

had always been. All the way up through fifth grade, for some reason he never understood, he couldn't always control his bladder. He never knew when it was going to happen, but there it was, urine leaking out onto the front of his pants. Every so often, a total release, urine streaming down his legs, soaking him, wetting his chair. The other children in the class invariably went wild, groaning, making retching noises, holding their noses. It was like a party for them. They could hardly wait for the next incident to break up the boring school day.

Year in and year out, it was always the same. It didn't matter if some kid was stupid or ugly. What mattered was that the kid wasn't weird like Todd. So he was better. And he could make fun of Todd.

Todd got up to replace the Doors CD with Jimi Hendrix's *Are You Experienced?* The teasing had gone on for his entire prison term—which was how he regarded his time at school. He couldn't remember being called a name outright for the last few years, but he had no doubt that they all talked behind his back. There was so much for them to talk about, wasn't there?

He collected saliva in his mouth, leaned over the wastepaper basket, and slowly let it dribble down, a long white strand, until it broke off. Things never changed. Nobody *got* him, not in elementary school, junior high, high school, or college. And it wasn't like his parents ever had a clue about anything, either. His mother's only job in life was to suffocate him, to bother him and hound him about every little thing until he wanted to slam her head against a wall. His father barely even spoke to him, much less tried to understand him. Last night, like every night, Todd had heard him ranting to Todd's mother over dinner. The two of them were alone at the table in the kitchen, as usual. Todd refused to eat with them, a decision he had made when he was fifteen.

"The kid doesn't even feel bad about it," Mike Lyle said in disbelief. "He doesn't care that I have to kill myself just to keep us in this crappy little house, much less cough up the money for college. Does he do what he's supposed to do on his end? No, he can't be bothered." There was silence, and the clink of silverware on plates. "Don't get me started," he went on. "The biggest break that screwup ever had, and he blows it. He doesn't appreciate one GD thing we've done—not one."

The house was too small for Todd to avoid overhearing them. If he had tried to drown them out with music, his father would yell at him to shut it off. Mike Lyle was a lot bigger and stronger than Todd, and perfectly willing to hit him when he got angry enough. Todd had no choice but to do what he was told. He had just sat on the floor, his back against the side of the bed, staring up at the ceiling and mouthing the words to Pink Floyd's *The Wall*, as he tried to ignore their conversation.

"It's not his fault," Shirley Lyle responded to her husband in a soothing tone. "And I'm sure he does appreciate you, somewhere inside him." Todd gave a derisive laugh at her answer. He had figured out a long time ago that she got off on being the saint in the family. Just the sound of her calling his name in that anxious, squeaky voice of hers made him want to punch something.

Not that her words had any effect on Mike. "Face it, Shirley," Todd heard his father say in exasperation, "he's a loser. Does he have a friend in the world? No. What the hell kind of kid doesn't have a friend, even one? Christ, *I* can barely stand to look at him."

There was a large black book on the floor beside Todd's feet. He leaned over to pick it up, opening it to the page where a piece of Kleenex tissue marked his place, and began to read.

It was a medical textbook on infectious diseases. The subject had fascinated him since the day his eighth grade history teacher happened to mention the Black Death in a lesson on the Middle Ages. Uncharacteristically, Todd had waited to talk to him after class to ask how he could find out more about it. He couldn't stop thinking of the thousands of people dying in the streets, moaning for help as they spread their fatal illness to anyone kind enough—or, in Todd's opinion, dumb enough—to help them. After reading several books on the subject, he moved on to the influenza epidemic of 1918. He was intrigued by the process of viruses and bacteria moving from one person to another, and the astounding amount of damage they could do.

He had been stupid to think he would want to study other things in college. He could see that now. Left on his own in a dorm room, no one keeping tabs on him or bothering him, he could concentrate on the stuff he liked to his heart's content. After the first week, his roommate transferred to another dorm, so he even had a double room all to himself.

Enjoyable as it was, none of his reading had anything to do with his courses. Every so often, he had tried to go along with the system, sometimes going to classes for weeks in a row. It was so hard to pay attention, though. The professors droned on and on. Suddenly, the class would be over and he realized he hadn't heard a word anyone had said. He would sit there, observing the other students filing out, the boys like hulking gorillas in their athletic jackets, the girls dressed like Hooker Barbie, tugging on their tight sweaters and short skirts, tittering away about their little secrets. Eventually, he gave up going to class altogether. He really liked that month when he virtually never left his room, but stayed in surrounded by his medical books and music. His diet consisted primarily of Twinkies and Coke, which suited him fine.

His absence from all his classes and tests didn't go unnoticed. First came Volman's warning. Then the other teachers. The school administrators started out with concern but finally switched to tougher talk, and, with four F's on his finals, a suspension. His return was conditional on his taking some steps to show his desire to improve. He hadn't even bothered to find out what those steps were. College was over.

If he had had any money at all, he would never have come back to live with his parents. But, for now, there wasn't any option. No other choice but to listen to his parents nag him about getting a job. Each had a particular technique: His mother used her sappy sweet encouraging words, while his father called him a worthless slob. Neither technique did he find particularly motivating. He didn't think *they* would be so eager to bag groceries or pump gas, but they felt he should jump at the chance.

Distracted, he pushed the book away and got up. If it weren't for Arden, he didn't know what he would do. Thoughts of her were what kept him going while he was away. Most of the time, he felt as if the walls, floor, and ceiling were closing in on him. Conjuring up her face in his mind would make the feeling go away so he could breathe again. He went over to the night table next to his bed and pulled open its one small drawer, revealing a blue velvet box. He couldn't wait to give it to her.

They had met a few weeks before he'd left for college in a small grocery store about two miles from Todd's house. His mother had asked him to go out for a half-gallon of milk; there wasn't a drop in the house, and she couldn't stand drinking her coffee black. Todd was standing in front of the magazine rack, leafing through *Today's Computing.* He was in no rush to get the milk home. For all he cared, his mother could wait until she dropped dead for her beloved cup of caffeine.

He had replaced the magazine on the rack, and as he reached for a different one, he happened to glance at the girl standing to his left. She was engrossed in what she was reading. Apparently sensing his gaze, she looked up. Her complexion was a deep olive, and her eyes were so dark they were nearly black. Shining brown hair flowed down to her waist. She wasn't too tall, but she was wiry, wearing blue jeans and a faded brown T-shirt.

The girl continued to stare at him, saying nothing. He desperately wanted to look away, but he couldn't. His mouth dry, he spoke, barely aware of what he was saying.

"What're you reading?" Jerk, he berated himself silently.

She held up the magazine for him, a copy of *Time.* He didn't recognize the two men on the cover, but he could see that they were in front of an image of the White House.

Instinctively, he snorted loudly. "Politicians. Bull-shitters."

She rewarded him with a smile. "I agree," she said, so quietly he almost didn't hear her.

"You do?" Emboldened, he went on. "They don't care about anything but holding on to their little pockets of power."

"Jumping from one election to the next," she responded softly, putting the magazine on the rack. She turned to him, her intentions unreadable on her face. Silent again, it was as if she were waiting.

Quickly, not wanting to lose her attention, Todd began talking. Afterward, he couldn't remember a single word of what he said. All he knew was that they wound up buying two cans of Coke and taking them outside. They sat down on the grass behind the store.

She didn't say much, but Todd felt that she didn't have to. It was the first time he ever believed a girl understood what he was talking about, maybe even understood *him*. She didn't interrupt; she didn't correct him. Every so often she would nod or give him one of her mysterious little smiles. He was frightened by how beautiful she was. It turned out that the reason he had never seen her before was that she had moved to town the previous June. In September, she would be starting her senior year in high school.

When she got up to go, he asked for her name and telephone number, his heart hammering in his chest. In the same soft voice, she told him. He repeated the number frantically in his mind until she was gone, then raced inside the store to get a pen so he could write it down on the back of his hand. When he called her the next day, she agreed to meet him again for coffee, this time in a diner.

They spent two hours in a booth, slouched against the wall with their legs spread out on the red leather seats. Arden seemed even more beautiful to him than she had the day before. She had on a short, torn gray T-shirt, and he loved the way her baggy khaki pants hung down below her tiny waist, revealing a peek at the smooth skin just under her navel. She wore no makeup, but had on earrings and a matching bracelet, silver with turquoise stones. That Southwest, Indian sort of stuff.

Noticing her jewelry was what had led him to buy the sterling silver bracelet that lay in the blue velvet box. He had seen the bracelet in a store window in Buffalo, and knew instantly he had to get it for her. It was a twisting serpent that bit its own tail. Todd paid for it by cleaning out the checking account his parents had set up for him to buy books and supplies.

He opened the box to inspect his treasure once more. Arden didn't know he was back in town. He had written to her while he was away, long letters describing what he saw, what he felt. She hadn't answered, but he liked it that way; it was as if she were waiting at home for his news. She obviously didn't feel the need to write if she didn't have something important to say. That was part of what he liked about her. She wasn't like other girls, caught up in idiotic social conventions.

He hadn't told her he was coming back. It would be better as a surprise. He pictured the two of them, walking and talking, going everywhere together. Inseparable. At night, they would have incredible sex—he caught his breath just thinking about it. Then they would sleep wrapped up tightly in one another's arms. They had waited to find each other, waited so long.

But he didn't have to wait anymore. He snapped the box shut and looked at his watch—10:40. Her shift would be starting in twenty minutes. Arden worked at the drugstore in downtown Rhinebeck. He was planning to surprise her with the bracelet. He imagined her eyes lighting up when he walked in the door, her happy reaction when she opened the present. It was going to be perfect.

There was one more thing he wanted to show her. He went to his closet, reaching up to push aside a large carton packed with some junk that his mother kept stored in it. He pulled down a plaid blanket, which appeared to have been carelessly stuffed in the back on the shelf. Setting the blanket down on his bed, he unfolded it. He smiled at the sight of the contents.

They were still there, the .45 and the box of bullets. He picked up the gun, enjoying its black shine, its coldness. It had been an unexpected purchase one October night in Buffalo. He had been out walking in what he knew was a bad neighborhood, but he found it real and unpretentious. It was about one-thirty in the morning, and he had stumbled upon two men on a corner transacting a gun sale.

In that first moment when the men spotted him watching, he could tell from their expressions that they were going to shoot him. But he thought fast, telling them he wanted to buy a gun if they would sell him one. They had gotten quite a kick out of that. They had practically guffawed, asking what a cute little white college boy like him wanted with a gun. It may have started out as a stall, but he got progressively more excited about the idea. They opened the back of a black van, showing him a small arsenal. In the end, he bought the .45 and a box of bullets, and the men sent him on his way with more laughter and a hearty pat on the back.

He was extremely pleased with the way that evening worked out. He used to take the gun out in his dorm room nearly every night, admiring it, aiming, and pretending to fire. He wanted to show it to Arden. It was another thing they could share. They would find a field to practice firing it, really get good with it.

He reached down to retrieve his black winter coat from where it lay on the floor. Yanking it on, he stuck the velvet box in one of its deep pockets, the gun and bullets in the other. As he passed his desk, he grabbed a half-empty bag of popcorn to eat in the car.

A mirror hung by the front door, just big enough for his mother to check her appearance before she went out. Todd could never stand to watch her preening in front of it. As if she was ever going anyplace important, as if any person on earth was ever going to look at her. He caught a glimpse of his reflection as he paused to open the door and stopped. Not bad, he decided, trying to imagine what Arden saw when she looked at him. He was tall and had black hair that he kept cut short. He didn't like his thick lips or the acne that perpetually covered his forehead, but those things might not bother her. His eyes were small, too, he had to admit it. He turned away, not wanting to look any longer.

His mother must have heard his footsteps. She called out his name from the kitchen. He ignored her. His mind was racing as he got into his car, an old orange Datsun his father was grudgingly allowing him to use now that he realized Todd was stuck in the house for the foreseeable future. He turned the ignition key, relieved that it started. What a piece of garbage this car was, he thought as he pulled away from the house. Must have set his father back, oh, a good two hundred bucks.

He sped along the roads, past the seemingly endless acres where the local farmers grew corn, soy, apples, and pears. Everything looked bare and desolate in the gray December day. Todd didn't care, any more than he would have cared had the fields been bursting with crops. Farming held no interest for him. This whole place held no interest for him. New York City was where he should be. Maybe he and Arden could move there together, get an apartment downtown.

Rhinebeck was over twenty miles away, but he made it in a little under fifteen minutes. The drugstore was on Market Street. He turned left and pulled into a parking lot. Despite the cold weather and the car's heater being broken, he was sweating heavily as he got out. It was difficult for him to keep from running, but he forced himself to slow down.

The street was crowded with people from the area, plus the usual assortment of tourists, weaving in and out of the stores, doing their holiday shopping. He walked up the long block, past the gaudy electric lights and the tinsel that was draped on almost every doorway. He barely took in the Christmas decorations. He had his eye on the drugstore sign, sticking out at a ninety-degree angle from the building.

His breath was coming in short bursts as he drew closer. So many months since he'd seen her, he thought, so many months. He must have been crazy to go away.

He reached for the glass door, its rim sprayed all around with artificial frost. Taking a deep breath, he stepped inside. It was a small store, with high shelves dividing the aisles. The only customer was a man over to the left, browsing through the vitamins. Todd saw the store's owner, Ray Ford, counting some bills at the register. Arden was nowhere in sight.

Todd went over to the counter. "Is Arden here?"

The man glanced up from what he was doing. "She's busy," he answered curtly, looking back down.

Irritated, Todd reminded himself to stay calm. "Excuse me," he said slowly and deliberately. "I need to speak with her."

"I said she was working. See her on your own time," came the annoyed response.

"It's important."

Ray gave a small sigh of exasperation and put the money back in the register, shutting the drawer as he finally gave Todd his full attention. "Don't come in here to socialize with her. She's supposed to be taking care of customers, not visiting with her buddies."

Todd wanted to reach across the counter and shake the man. But all he said was, "Fine. I'm going."

He turned as if he were leaving, walking to the far end of the drugstore near the front door. Then he stopped beside the first aid supplies as if he had suddenly realized he needed something. He picked up a box of gauze, pretending to study it. The owner finished what he was doing then disappeared from view around a different aisle. Todd swiftly moved to the rear of the store again and ducked behind the counter. He guessed he would find Arden in the stockroom, which had to be back here somewhere.

Hastening through a small doorway, he saw long rows of metal shelves filled with cardboard boxes. This had to be the spot. He peered down the row. She wasn't there. But there was another row. His heart beat faster again as he hurried forward.

She was there, but she wasn't alone. Billy Tobias, the stock boy, was with her. He was leaning back against the shelves, and she was pressed up against him, kissing him. Even from here, he could tell they had their tongues in each other's mouths, and they were frantically running their hands up and down one another's bodies. Billy reached around to grab her behind, one buttock in each hand, and yanked her to him. She gave a squeal of pleasure.

"Oh, *you*!" she said in mock outrage before sliding her hand down to caress his crotch.

Todd was too stunned to move. Billy Tobias had been working at the store for years, all through high school, Todd knew. Arden had mentioned him once when she was talking about her job here.

But she sure hadn't mentioned any of this. She sure hadn't mentioned that she was interested in him. That she liked him enough to let him paw her, to let him touch her like that, so easy and familiar, as if he had done it a hundred times before. Which meant, of course, that he had. . . .

Todd took a step back, feeling as if his head were about to explode. The motion made the two look over as they released their hold on one another. Probably expecting to see their boss, they were surprised to find it was someone else. Neither one of them showed any recognition of him in that split second, the second before he turned and bolted, running back into the store's front area, past Ray Ford, who was shouting something at him. He shoved the door open with his shoulder and fled outside, still running. Little by little, he slowed down.

He couldn't get the image out of his head, the sight of Arden kissing Billy Tobias, her simpering voice, the disgusting way she thrust herself against him. When had it started? Recently? Or long ago? What if Arden had been with Billy back when she was with Todd?

The thought hit him so suddenly, he stopped dead. What if she were letting Billy put it to her back then, and was just stringing Todd along, having a little fun, toying with him? She thought he was a fool, a big, fat fool. He could imagine her laughing at him behind his back. Maybe even laughing about him with Billy. In fact, the two of them were probably laughing themselves silly right this minute. He thought he might vomit. Shoving his hands deep in his pockets, his head down, he resumed walking, faster this time.

His hand closed around the gun. Man, he'd like to blow her brains out, he really would. He had trusted her, and she had betrayed him. Like everybody always did. She hadn't wanted him; she was just amusing herself at his expense. The mysterious smiles, the soft skin. She had sucked him in and then punched him in the gut.

He had really believed that it was all going to happen. But, no, of course not, it was never going to happen for him. He was so stupid. What made him think that a girl like Arden would care whether he lived or died? He was nothing to her. Less than nothing.

Moving forward almost in a run, he put his hands over his ears as if he could block out the voice shouting in his head: She was laughing at you like everybody else. You're a useless piece of garbage who'll be living with your parents for the rest of your pathetic little life.

"No," he whispered. *"No."*

He wasn't going back to that house; he wasn't. He couldn't look at his parents for another day. For another second. Arden, his parents, everybody seemed to think they could crap all over him.

"Hey, young man, watch it!"

Todd hadn't noticed that he had bumped the shoulder of a thin, elderly man with such force that the man had lost his footing and nearly fallen. His wife helped steady him as she glanced over indignantly at Todd.

Todd stopped. "Hey, old man, *you* watch it!" he yelled,

liking how it felt. Energy surged through him. How he would love to haul off and slam this guy. He raised his voice even louder. *"You want to fight, come on, let's fight."*

The couple looked into his face and then drew back uncertainly, their courage failing. Murmuring to each other about his rudeness, they walked on.

But Todd was no longer watching them. He was staring at the name on the store right next to where he stood. In The Details, it said in an elegant black script on a golden sign. FINE CLOTHING AND GIFTS. RUTH JOHNSTON, PROPRIETOR.

Ruth Johnston. Mother of Leo Johnston.

Memories flooded his brain. Of all his tormentors throughout childhood, Leo had been the worst. From fourth grade, when he had moved here, through ninth grade, Leo had made Todd his personal whipping boy. But he wasn't satisfied to tease Todd about wetting his pants like all the other kids. He found more. Todd's unsuccessful attempts at baseball and basketball earned him a string of nicknames from Leo early on. Already known as *baby, stinky pants,* and *pisshead,* Todd had the pleasure of adding on Leo's creations of *lame-o, faggot,* and *mama's boy.* The other kids picked up those names as well, and they all stuck. But that wasn't where it ended. When Todd couldn't answer the teacher's question, or got singled out of misbehaving, Leo was always right there to ride him about it.

The worst day of Todd's entire life had come about because of Leo Johnston. It was that day in seventh grade when Todd had gotten an erection while he was sitting at his desk. Leo, sitting one row over, saw. He had whispered it to the kids in front of and behind him. By the end of the day, the story was all over school. Todd couldn't walk down the hall without everybody, girls and boys, pointing and whispering, laughing, or making jokes. Todd had been teased before, but never like this. It was the first time he knew what real hatred was.

Leo had moved away after ninth grade to live with his father somewhere upstate. But his mother was still there. Running her little store. Catering to all the rich bitches with nothing to do but buy sexy clothes so they could get men to spend even more money on them. Like I would have spent on Arden, Todd realized, revolted by his own weakness.

But I'm not weak, he thought.

Breathing hard, he clutched the gun in his pocket. In one stroke, he could get enough money to get away, and he could scare the crap out of Leo Johnston's mother. Those guys who sold him the gun wouldn't consider him so damned funny then. He could disappear and read about the whole thing in the newspaper. At last, he could *do* something instead of getting kicked around by the whole world. He grinned.

But first he had to think. He didn't want to make any mistakes. And he had to find someplace private to load the gun. Turning, he walked on. When he had it all worked out in his head, he would be back.

Arden, his parents, and all the rest of them could go to hell. He was getting out of there in a blaze of glory.

5

The wind was picking up. Kip Hallman clutched her jacket collar as she approached the front door to In The Details only a moment before a couple coming from the opposite direction. Smiling, she pulled the door open and held it for them. She was somewhat surprised as they sailed past her without a glance or a word of thanks. Absolutely right, I'm the doorman, she told them silently. When you're done shopping, I'll be glad to hail you a cab.

She followed them in. As she stood just inside the doorway pulling off her gloves and jacket, she watched them approach Ruth Johnston, the owner of the store, who was bending down, straightening the jewelry in a display counter. Ruth was a short, slight woman, around fifty, with faded red hair and a redhead's freckled complexion. Kip stopped in at the store periodically, and she and Ruth were on a first-name basis. The shop was large in comparison to many of the other ones along the street, but it managed to convey a cozy feeling that Kip liked, with its wooden armoires and shelves arranged in an apparently haphazard way, hats, jewelry, and scarves on hooks everywhere. The clothing was surprisingly sophisticated.

The couple she'd let in approached the counter. The man was tall, with thin, white hair. Kip judged him to be in his early sixties. He wore an expensive navy blue overcoat and black leather gloves. The woman appeared to be the same age, her wavy blond hair obviously colored and set at a beauty salon. She was still attractive, and Kip decided that she must have been beautiful when she was younger. She wore a brown mink coat, a white silk scarf tied around her neck.

Busy neatening rows of necklaces, Ruth didn't see the couple. The man was looking around as if he would rather be anywhere else on earth.

"This should have been taken care of before we left the city," he said to his wife in annoyance. "I'm hard-pressed to believe you couldn't find the time."

"Five minutes won't kill you," the woman snapped.

Kip watched in amazement as the woman made a fist and turned her hand over, using the large diamond ring she wore to rap sharply on the glass countertop. Startled by the noise, Ruth straightened up. Kip could see in Ruth's face that she was unsure whether this woman had actually summoned her in such a fashion, but decided to give her the benefit of the doubt.

"Good morning. What can I do for you today?" Ruth asked.

"We're going to my daughter-in-law's," the woman informed Ruth in an impatient tone. "I need a gift."

Boy, am I glad you're not *my* mother-in-law, Kip thought, pitying whatever poor woman had to minister to these two just because she'd married their son. Warm feelings toward Peter's mother welled up inside her as she walked in the opposite direction, not wanting to hear any more. Bless you, Vivian Hallman, she thought.

She focused her attention on the task at hand. Okay, dresses, dresses, she recited silently. Somewhere in here is the most fabulous dress in the world. And I'm going to find it.

She spotted a row of evening gowns hanging in a tall maple chest. They were probably a bit over the top for New Year's Eve in Rhinebeck, but it didn't hurt to look. Maybe a slinky number with spaghetti straps. Or think Marilyn Monroe singing "Happy Birthday, Mr. President." Too bad she didn't bid for that dress when it was up for auction, she thought wryly, but hindsight *is* twenty-twenty.

Kip had resolved to look for something sexy to wear for New Year's, but so far she had had no luck finding it. It made her nervous to be getting this close to the date and still not know what she was going to wear to the Wellses' annual bash. Worse, there were only a couple of weeks until Christmas; she was frantic with everything she had yet to take care of. This morning, she had gone onto a fourth page of her "Things I Gotta Do" pad. That didn't even include the usual stuff that took up her time, like driving Lisa to and from swim practice seven days a week, or picking up J. P. from piano lessons, karate or his Science Explorers Club. She was growing agitated just thinking about it.

"Remain calm, and please stay in your seat," she instructed herself in a soothing tone, as if she were a flight attendant on a turbulent plane. "There is no need to become alarmed." She realized she had spoken out loud, and it made her laugh. Peter always teased her about her habit of talking to herself.

She quickly went through the evening gowns, dismissing all the tulle and satin as beautiful but not appropriate. It was silly to waste time this way, she decided; she had barely an hour until she had to pick Lisa up from practice. She would ask Ruth to direct her to something.

Kip retraced her steps to see Ruth escorting the couple around the store, pointing out gift possibilities. The woman was holding a lavender silk pillow, turning it over in her hands, as Kip approached.

Ruth saw her and gave a small wave. "Hello, Katherine."

Ruth knew Kip's name from her charge card. She didn't realize that everyone always called her Kip, based on her full name before marriage, Katherine Irene Pierson. Kip had never bothered to correct her.

"Hello, Ruth. When you're done, I was hoping you could help—"

"Do you have one that's larger? Or brighter?" the woman interrupted, oblivious of Kip. "This color is a bit anemic, really."

"Miss, we have *got* to get out of here," the husband put in. "If you can direct us to something, please do so immediately."

Kip held up a hand to indicate to Ruth that she could wait. *Later,* she mouthed. Ruth nodded with a smile that thanked her for being understanding. Without realizing she was doing it, Kip made a face as she turned away. If rudeness ever became a medal event at the Olympics, she was voting for those two to represent the United States.

"Delightful, aren't they?"

The amused whisper came from just to the right of Kip. She turned her head to see a woman with dark, wavy hair, wearing jeans, a tucked-in white shirt, and a wide black leather belt. The woman smiled, obviously having witnessed the scene, as she shifted the jacket she was holding from one arm to the other. Kip returned the smile and nodded before resuming her shopping.

As she reached for a pink cashmere sweater, the door to the shop was yanked open by a young man in a long, dark coat. He took a few steps into the store and stopped. For a few moments, he looked around. Then he reached into his coat pocket and pulled out a gun.

"Okay, everybody is going to do what I say," he shouted loudly enough for all the customers to hear. "Get to the back. *Now!*"

For a few seconds, no one moved. Kip stood, frozen, one hand outstretched toward the sweater. She felt as if she didn't understand. This wasn't actually happening, was it? She looked at the man. He was a boy, really, maybe nineteen or so. His face was pale, and he was perspiring. She could see it even from this distance.

"Do I have to kill all of you?" His voice was growing louder and more agitated. *"Get to the back!"*

His words startled Kip into action. Jesus God, she thought, fear flooding her, what is he going to do? Shaking, she made her way toward the rear of the store. There was the woman with the wavy hair, her face ashen, and another woman, blond and somewhat overweight, wearing a black skirt and sweater, laden down with a long coat and two shopping bags. She was biting her lip. Ruth was on her way toward them, taking small, hurried steps.

The boy with the gun quickly approached, his weapon pointed straight at them. The blond woman dropped her coat and shopping bags on the floor and grabbed Kip's arm, though whether it was for her own support or to comfort Kip was unclear. They glanced at one another, reading the panic on each other's face.

"Come on, come on." Holding the gun in one hand, the boy was grabbing silk scarves off a hook with the other. "Get in there." He nodded toward the dressing room.

There was a noise over to the left. Kip realized that the older husband and wife were still in the store somewhere.

"Hey, who's there?" the boy shouted, backing up so he could keep an eye on the women. "Get your ass out here right now."

There was no response. He moved another step toward where the sound had come from, his voice enraged. *"Man, do you not hear me? Now. Out here. Or you die."*

The couple had been crouching behind a wooden trunk. They rose slowly, terror on the woman's face, anger on her husband's. He drew himself up and stared at the younger man. "How dare you, you little shit!"

The boy aimed at the ceiling and fired. Kip heard a scream, but she didn't know where it came from. The four women instinctively huddled together. Get a grip, Kip instructed herself severely, don't fall apart. Her stomach heaved in fear. It'll be okay, it'll be okay. She kept repeating the words silently, hoping she wouldn't lose control.

The boy flashed a quick grin, as if delighted with his performance. The brown-haired woman was shivering, her arms clutched across her chest. Ruth swayed slightly, as if she were about to faint. The blond woman noticed it, as well, because she put a trembling arm around the older woman to steady her.

"Get out here, old man," the boy shrieked. *"You're gonna listen to me or I'm gonna blow your head off!"*

The woman immediately came forward, trembling all over. Her husband followed, his mouth set in a tight line. Was he actually not afraid, Kip wondered, or did he simply refuse to let it show? They stopped near the group, standing stiffly apart.

"Everybody in," the boy ordered, gesturing toward the dressing room with his gun.

In silence, they filed into the well-lit room. The low wooden bench that ran around the perimeter was hand-painted with peonies and vines. Mirrors lined the walls above it.

"Get in the middle there."

Kip's heart was beating so hard, she was afraid she might actually have a heart attack. Terror was literally painful. She hadn't known that. The thought came to her with an odd sense of detachment.

"On the floor, facedown." He pointed to Ruth with the hand that clutched the scarves. "Except you. You're gonna get me money."

"But—," she started to say.

"Be quiet," he snapped in annoyance. "The rest of you, take off your shoes and get rid of anything you're holding. Hurry it up!"

They all kicked off their shoes and tossed down whatever they had in their hands; then they lay on the floor. One by one, he used the scarves he had collected to tie their hands behind their backs and bind their ankles together. He was mumbling to himself as he went from one person to the next, kicking coats, purses, and shoes out of reach. Kip couldn't understand anything he was saying, except when he paused to yell at the others for moving.

When he got to her, Kip struggled not to cry out as he gripped her wrists roughly and wrapped a scarf around them, knotting it painfully tight. She could smell the odor of his sweat, feel his breath on the side of her neck as he kneeled down beside her. Her face was buried in the rose-colored carpet, its harsh fibers hurting her cheeks. It was impossible to avoid inhaling the unpleasant odor left by the shoes of thousands of customers.

It's a dream, it'll be over soon, she said to herself as he gripped her ankles. Please, God, let it be a dream. Make it be over.

She heard, rather than saw, when he was finished tying them all up.

"Any of you assholes try to escape, you're gonna make me have to kill you."

No one said a word.

"Okay, *Mrs. Johnston*," he said with a sneer in voice, "you're gonna come with me. And on the way, you can tell me all about how little Leo is doing."

Kip heard Ruth's bewildered voice. "How did you—?"

His laugh was sharp. He spoke in a childlike teasing tone. "That's for me to know and you to find out." He laughed again.

Kip turned her head sideways to see them moving past her. She noted that Ruth was wearing beige pumps and the boy had on heavy black construction boots. For some reason, these details seemed critically important. She could hear their footsteps, the sound fading away as they moved to the register near the front of the store. Her blood pounded in her ears.

Todd aimed the gun at the small of Ruth Johnston's back as he followed her. "Faster," he urged, coming up behind her with a few long strides. Ruth was already hurrying, but, sensing him suddenly so close, she jerked in fright and tried to walk even more quickly.

He grinned. It was amazing to watch people jump when he gave orders. He had never realized how simple it was, that all he had to do was hold a gun and the world would obey him.

Her hands shaking, Ruth hit several buttons on the cash register and the drawer popped open. Todd came up behind her and peered over her shoulder. He saw a few one-dollar bills, two fives, and a ten.

"What the hell is this?" he snapped. "Where's all the money?"

"I tried to tell you," Ruth said, her voice unsteady. "There isn't any. Almost nobody pays cash anymore. It's all credit cards."

He stared at her. "What?" This was bad, this was really bad. "There's gotta be more somewhere," he said. "You're hiding it. From yesterday or something."

"There isn't any more here. We don't handle much cash, ever."

Todd looked back into the nearly empty drawer with a growing sense of horror. He couldn't leave here without money. He had assumed there would be hundreds, maybe a few thousand here. Credit cards. He cursed aloud. He had never considered that. What was he going to do? Don't panic, he told himself. *Think.*

His attention was diverted by a sudden noise near the dressing room. The older man who had tried to hide from him was coming through the doorway of the dressing room, practically dragging his wife with him. Todd saw that somehow they had gotten untied. Not this, too, he thought frantically. Everything was going wrong.

He shoved Ruth aside as he ran in their direction. They were heading for the front door as fast as they could manage.

"What're you doing?" he screamed, lunging to get between them and the door.

The older man stopped short. His wife let out a guttural moan and attempted to stand behind him, still grasping his arm.

"Step aside." The man spoke with authority, clearly expecting to be obeyed.

Todd exploded in rage. "Are you crazy, mister? I mean, are you fucking *insane*? I'm the one with the gun, see?" He brandished the weapon, planted his feet wide apart, and then aimed with two hands straight at the man's chest. "You want to tell me to step aside again?"

He was unprepared for what happened next. The man rushed at him, tackling him head-on. He wrapped both arms around Todd to pin his arms to his sides. Todd struggled wildly to get out of the man's surprisingly strong grip. He heard a woman screaming.

The man grunted as he and Todd toppled to the ground. Todd was choking, unable to see or think, trying desperately to get away. He wasn't even aware that he was still holding the gun. But he heard the blast when it went off, felt the jolt of the shot, and then the loosening of the older man's grip. The man slid off him, blood gushing from his chest, spreading all over his body, Todd, the floor.

He heard more screaming; then he looked up to see the man's wife bearing down on him, her face contorted. She was reaching out, either to attack him or to reach her husband, he didn't know. All he knew was that he had to stop her. He raised the gun, took aim and fired it again. She went down, her eyes opening in shock, blood spurting from her neck.

Why wouldn't the screaming stop? He rubbed his head with his free hand. He *had* to make it stop. Glancing up, he saw that it was the store owner—he couldn't even remember her name anymore. She was shaking violently and had her hands over her ears, but she was screaming, a terrible piercing wail.

He couldn't let things go this wrong. He had to fix them. Standing up, stumbling, he took a few steps in her direction, raised his right hand again, and fired. She sank out of sight behind the counter. There was silence. Thank God. The screaming had stopped. He almost smiled with relief.

A thin stream of blood trickled out from behind the counter, tracing a curved path along the wood floor. Todd went over to look. The woman was facedown, a puddle of blood around her. He bent over to grasp the sleeve of her flowered dress, lifting up her forearm. Her hand dangled uselessly. When he let go of the sleeve, her arm dropped with a thud. She was dead.

He stood up to see the other two bodies, lying close to one another, both of them drenched in blood.

Then Todd heard breathing, shallow and sharp. It was his own, he realized. He glanced down and saw that his hands and clothing were spattered with blood. Recoiling, he grabbed a garment from a nearby shelf to wipe off his hands. Then he rubbed it quickly up and down the front of his coat, but that only served to smear the blood further. He felt a wave of revulsion as he crumpled the material up and threw it on the floor.

He turned to the bodies, his anger rising.

"Why did you make me do that?" he exploded. *"You ruined everything!"*

Pacing, he began smacking his forehead repeatedly, trying to figure out what he was going to do now. Three dead people. Where the hell had that come from? He was as good as dead himself if he got caught.

But he couldn't get caught. That was all there was to it. Running over to the front door, he turned the brass knob to lock it. He had to do whatever it took. He couldn't go to jail, that was for sure.

"No fucking way," he muttered, kicking a large basket of beaded change purses so hard that it flew into a standing hat rack, knocking it over with a loud crash. Christ, he had the worst headache. He rubbed his temples. He had to figure out what he was going to do.

Kip found the sudden silence almost as terrifying as the gunshots and the screams. Maybe he was on his way back to the dressing room to kill them all. Maybe he would decide they had helped the couple get loose, that they were all acting in concert. Hardly. The husband had somehow managed to free his hands, and then paused only long enough to untie his wife and drag her, whimpering, out of the dressing room. The other two women had asked the couple to let them loose. But the man had ignored them, while his wife kept her head down as if she hadn't heard anything. Kip was struck by the thought that, even in crisis, people were what they were. That couple had shown their true colors when they first walked into the store. Having their lives threatened didn't suddenly improve them.

Still, that didn't mean she wanted to see them die. Lying on the dressing room floor, she and the two women with her had been able to hear footsteps and muffled voices, then scuffling and yelling. Why didn't they hear anything now? And Ruth Johnston, there was nothing more from her. Kip concentrated on taking a deep breath. She was trying with all her might not to think about Peter or the children. It would have been too much to bear. Kip exhaled slowly. Her chest hurt and her stomach was one big knot.

Minutes went by. Someone spoke, although Kip wasn't sure which of the two women's voice it was.

"What do you think—?"

Kip's body went rigid as the gunman suddenly burst into the dressing room. The blond woman shut her eyes, as if afraid to see what might be coming next.

The boy was covered in blood. It was evident to Kip that he was panicked, his eyes darting everywhere as if seeking some kind of answer. His hair was disheveled, his face slick with sweat. Accidentally, she caught his eye. She immediately looked away, but it was too late.

"What're you staring at?" he yelled. "You have something to say? Lemme hear it, come on."

Kip didn't answer. He came over to her, prodding her side roughly with the toe of his boot. She squeezed her eyes shut tight, willing herself not to make a sound.

"I might kill you, too," he shouted. "All of you. What's a few more?"

Peter. Lisa. J. P.

"What do you think of that, huh?" He was growing even more agitated. "Well? Answer me, damn you!"

Did he expect her to respond? Kip didn't know what to do. "It's not . . ." She faltered.

"*Shut up!*" He paced a few steps away in fury. "What the hell am I supposed to do with you fuckheads? If it wasn't for you—"

Abruptly, he swung back around and gave Kip a savage kick, the pain exploding in her chest so suddenly, the shock of it made her head jerk back. Instinctively, not even realizing she was doing it, she attempted to curl into a ball, drawing her knees up and trying to roll her body away from him. His second kick caught her in the side of her shin, and a scream escaped her as knifelike pain shot up and down her leg. She gasped, the agony forcing tears from her eyes.

Without another word, he turned and ran from the room.

"Oh, God, are you all right?" The blond woman's terror was evident in her voice. She struggled with renewed determination to free her hands, but her efforts were useless.

Kip felt as if she were suffocating, unable to get enough air. Every breath brought with it a stabbing in her chest so excruciating she was afraid she might pass out. Calm down, she told herself, you'll be okay, you'll be okay. She tried to take shallow breaths to minimize the pain, rounding her shoulders, which only increased the discomfort of the tightly knotted scarf binding her wrists. Her leg throbbed, sending waves of pain washing over the side of her lower body as well. She moaned.

"Take it easy there," the other woman said in a soothing tone. With difficulty, she rolled over to get closer to Kip, continuing to talk in a low, comforting voice. "You're doing great. You're brave, you know, really brave." She went on, murmuring reassuring words to Kip.

Her words helped Kip to steady herself. "Right, yes," she mumbled.

"Are you okay?" the other woman asked again. "Where are you hurt?"

"Broken," Kip got out. "Things are broken."

"We'll get you to a doctor. Hang in," the first woman said.

"Go back . . . where you were," Kip gasped. "If he sees you . . . moved . . . might kill us."

"He's not going to. He can't." It was the blond

woman, her voice barely audible. "If he's killed three people, he knows he's in trouble. He won't make it worse."

"I hope not," the dark-haired woman whispered back. "But, as he said, what's a few more? Three people or six people, it's the same conviction, the same sentence. If he kills us all, no witnesses."

"No. He's young. You saw how shook up he was. He didn't realize shooting people in real life is different from TV."

"He can't." Kip's words tumbled out. "I can't be killed. I have two children."

No one said anything.

Through her pain, Kip suddenly realized the implication of what she had said, as if being a mother made her life more valuable than the others'. "No, no, I mean—" She tried to take a breath, flinching at the pain that accompanied it. "—it's so unfair to . . . so terrible for children . . . be left without a parent. Imagine . . . your mother shot to death . . . Can't leave them this way." Her eyes filled with tears again.

"How old are your kids?" the dark-haired woman asked softly.

Kip fought to collect herself. Little by little, she got control of her breathing, finding the shallowness and pace that would enable her to speak. "My daughter's fifteen . . . my son's eleven." She paused, trying to ignore the pain by talking about something else. Concentrate, she directed herself. "You have children?"

"No. Not married."

"Oh."

After a moment, the blond woman spoke quietly. "I would have thought you'd be happily married with a big brood of children."

"What?" Startled, the woman craned her neck to look at her. "Why?"

The blond woman seemed to be considering something; then she sighed slightly and spoke. "I know you, Nora. From college."

The brunette stared, puzzled. "You do?" Suddenly, it came to her. "Eloise? Are you Eloise Bentley?"

"Yes, it's me."

"I don't believe this."

"Not quite the college reunion Vassar might have planned, is it?" Eloise said.

"Do you live here?" Nora was twisting around to bring her face closer to Eloise.

"We—I have a country house here. I live in the city."

Kip tried to straighten her leg slightly, but the movement was so excruciating, she screamed. Both women looked in her direction. "I'm so sorry we can't help you," Eloise said in an anguished tone.

"Soon," Nora added soothingly, "I'm sure we'll be out of here soon."

Stunned by the pain, Kip had reverted back to shallow breaths. She didn't want to focus on how much she hurt, but the only alternative was to wonder whether she would be leaving this room alive or not.

There was a crash just outside the dressing room. The women froze in terror. Holding onto the doorjamb, the gunman came careening around the corner into the dressing room. All three women flinched visibly.

"Hey," he shouted at Nora. "Get to where you were."

Quickly, she rolled back over.

"You know what happened to those people," he said. "If you move an inch again, you're next."

He looked around, inspecting for evidence of any efforts to escape. Shoes and packages were scattered about, still out of reach of the three.

"The door's locked, and nobody's coming in. So if you're planning on being rescued, forget it."

Nodding, he mumbled something Kip didn't understand and left. He seemed even less in control of himself than before, more frantic. That was a bad sign. Maybe he *would* kill them. These days, people got killed for no reason at all. Now that he had already shot three people, he might very well come back in and execute them, one by one.

"Are you all right?" Eloise directed her question to Kip.

Kip had been lying with her eyes closed. She opened them.

"Yes, thanks," she answered weakly. "You?"

"I'm afraid," was all Eloise said.

They lay there in silence for a long time. Kip concentrated on settling into the pain, which had now enveloped her like a blanket. Breathe through it. She remembered the Lamaze classes she and Peter had taken when she was pregnant with Lisa. Breathing was the key. She made a few short whooshing sounds. Labor pains weren't continuous. They gave you a break now and then. This pain did not.

"Do you want to talk?" Eloise whispered.

Kip nodded, her lips pressed in a tight line, appreciating that the woman sensed she needed distracting.

"Okay. What's your name?"

"Kip Hallman." She paused to gather her strength. "I live here in town."

"As I said, I'm from Manhattan. My husband and I have a house here. We . . ." Her voice trailed off.

"Yes?" Kip asked.

"My husband left me. Recently. I've been walking around wishing I were dead. I guess I may have my opportunity." She gave a short, bitter laugh. "Only now I see how stupid I've been. I don't want to die. Not at all."

"We're not going to die!" Kip insisted in a fierce whisper, paying for it with daggers of pain in her chest.

Nora shifted her ankles uncomfortably. "What's he doing out there? If he's going to try to get away, what's he waiting for?"

"Let's not think about it," Eloise said. "Let's talk about something else. Nora, do you live here, too?"

"No, in Manhattan. Ever since Vassar. I'm visiting my sister here."

All at once, they heard noises, crashes they couldn't identify, followed almost immediately by gunfire. The three women lay shaking, eyes shut, cringing as the sharp crack of guns continued. There was screaming far away.

Then, it was ominously silent.

"Dear God," Eloise breathed.

They heard footsteps moving slowly through the store. There was more than one person, but whoever was out there was being very quiet. It was only because the wooden floorboards were so old and creaky that the vibrations carried to the dressing room.

Nora let out a loud gasp as the policeman whipped into the dressing room. His gun was already drawn, aimed with both hands in front of him. When he saw the women on the floor, he lowered the gun and stuck it in his holster.

"You okay?" He spoke to all three of them as he knelt down to untie Kip.

Kip slowly brought her wrists around to rub them, the motion bringing on a fresh wave of pain in her chest. She clutched her left side and grabbed on to the policeman's arm as he started to help her sit up. In spite of her efforts not to, she cried out at the movement.

"She needs to get to a hospital," Nora said. "She's injured."

"Shot?"

Eloise answered. "No. But he kicked her, hard. She's in agony."

"Right. Lie down again." The policeman whipped a walkie-talkie from his pocket. He gave instructions for an ambulance to be summoned. "Anybody else here that you know about?" Quickly, he turned to untie Nora's hands and then went back to ministering to Kip.

"No, it was just us." Eloise answered. "Well, after he killed the other three people. At least, that's what we think happened."

The man looked grim as he pulled the scarf away from Kip's ankles. "It's bad. But we got him."

Nora was crawling over to help Eloise. She turned her face to his. "What do you mean, got him?"

"He panicked. Stayed in the store all this time, then

suddenly decided to make a break for it. I don't know why, he must have seen there were cops everywhere outside."

"Oh, Lord," Eloise said as Nora freed her hands, "he's been shot?"

"Yes, ma'am. He's dead."

Eloise's eyes welled up with tears. "He was young."

"You feel *sorry* for him?" Nora asked.

"No, it's not that," Eloise said. "But he was a boy. Oh, I don't know. I just want to go home."

"We'll be taking you to see a doctor, ma'am, but we'll call your family right away," the officer told Kip. "You can give us your statement later." He nodded toward Nora and Eloise. "The police need to speak with you ladies now. There are some people here who can take your statements. Why don't you gather your belongings and come with me?"

"We'd like to wait with our friend here until the ambulance comes, if that's okay," Nora said, her tone indicating they were going to wait even if he said it wasn't okay.

They heard the siren outside, louder and louder, until it was suddenly cut off. There was some yelling in the front of the store, and, almost immediately, two men came running into the dressing room, carrying a stretcher.

"What do we have?" one asked, as they deposited the stretcher alongside Kip.

"No gunshots," answered the policeman. "Kicked in a couple of places, some broken bones looks like. Maybe internal bleeding. Don't know what else."

Both men nodded. They positioned themselves at Kip's head and feet, one barking questions about where she hurt while the other busied himself cutting off her coat with some kind of shears. She responded as best she could, but she was feeling faint. Suddenly, in the midst of everything, all she wanted to do was sleep, to close her eyes and disappear. They were doing things to her, checking things, but she couldn't concentrate anymore. Dimly, she heard one of the men count to three, and, in tandem, they lifted her onto the stretcher. Kip screamed.

The men hurriedly maneuvered her out of the dressing room, Nora and Eloise rushing along behind them. Kip fought back tears against the jolts of pain, one after another, despite the men's efforts to keep their movements smooth.

As they entered into the main store area, Kip saw that there were at least half a dozen officers in the store. A tarp had been placed over what were evidently the bodies of the couple who had been tied up with them. Kip felt sick as they passed by, seeing the woman's black silk shoe lying just beyond the covering. A cluster of people stood behind the counter, conferring over what Kip guessed was Ruth Johnston's body. She had no desire to know for certain.

She saw Eloise turn her head in the same direction. It appeared as if all the blood had drained from her face.

"We're fine," Kip managed to get out. "See, like you said, we were perfectly safe all the time."

Eloise's haunted eyes met Kip's briefly before she turned away. A loud noise outside caused all three to look in the direction of the door. There was a crowd on the sidewalk across the street from the store. Several feet to the left of the store entrance were police barricades, and an officer was securing yellow tape indicating a crime scene. The store window was large, so the three of them had a clear view of what everyone was watching. A policeman was spreading a black tarp over the gunman's body, which lay in a fetal position. Then it was gone from view.

"Would you two ladies come with me?" A man in a black parka came over to them, his question aimed at Nora and Eloise. He gestured to one side of the store, as far from the bodies as it was possible to get. "We have some talking to do."

Eloise and Nora turned to Kip. Eloise leaned in close and took her hand. "Will you be all right?"

"She'll be fine," the man said. "Please come with me now."

"Maybe we should ride in the ambulance," Nora said, ignoring him.

Kip smiled weakly. "Thank you. No, please—just have them call my husband. Peter Hallman. The number's in my purse."

They nodded. "You're a lot tougher than you look," Nora said to Kip with a smile. "You're brave. And you'll be fine now, really."

"Fine—oh, yes, I'm fine," she murmured. Then she closed her eyes and let the world fall away.

6

"Hey, there." Peter stuck his head in the bedroom doorway and spoke softly. "How're you doing?"

Kip was in bed, her eyes closed, the fingers of one hand massaging her temples. At the sound of Peter's voice, her eyes flew open. "I'm okay. Thanks." She hoped her voice sounded reasonably pleasant.

"It's time for your pain medication." He went into the bathroom, where she could hear him rattling pills and filling a glass with water.

Kip sighed. She hated taking the painkillers, which made her groggy and nauseated. But, Lord, she thought, did she need them. Her leg ached inside its cast. Far worse, though, were the stabbing pains every time she breathed or moved her torso, and the enormous purple and black bruises on all the areas where she'd been hurt that made her cringe at the mere thought of moving.

Peter came over to the side of her bed. "Here you go." He set down the pill and the glass as he helped her sit up just enough to be able to drink. She bit her lip to keep from crying out.

"You're doing better, really," he said. "You seem less stiff than yesterday."

"Thanks." She dutifully swallowed the pill and drank.

"You need anything?" he asked as he took back the glass. "Can I make you some lunch?"

She shook her head. "No, thanks. Maybe later. The kids set for the afternoon?"

"Yes. J. P. wanted to go to somebody's house, someone from his class, but I told him no. I asked him, and he said you didn't know this kid or the parents, and I certainly don't know them. So he'll come home on the bus."

That was a shame, Kip thought. It would have been better for him to be out, not having to hang around his injured mother. Normally, she would have called up the other boy's mother, made sure a get-together was okay, and let J. P. go. She had met, or at least seen, all the boys in her son's class at one time or another, and none of them appeared particularly dangerous. But she was well aware of Peter's streak of overprotectiveness when it came to things like this, so she merely nodded.

"Lisa's getting a lift home later."

Kip summoned up a small smile. "So everyone's accounted for. You working?"

"Yup."

"Go ahead on back to it."

He nodded. "Shout if you need anything."

She listened to his footsteps going down the stairs. It was a relief to drop her strained cheerfulness. Not that I'm being so cheerful, she amended. Perhaps *normal* was the word she needed. Trying to appear as if everything was normal had started feeling like a monumental task.

Slowly, she settled back against two pillows, her head propped up just enough so she could see the television across the room. She retrieved the remote control from her night table, and aimed it at the screen, keeping her finger pressed on the "up" arrow, changing channels in rapid succession. Images came in a flood: talk shows, soap operas, music videos, cartoons, home shopping. All the smiling faces and incessant talking were making her want to throw something at the set. But she kept going anyway.

She saw something, so fleetingly that she wasn't even sure why it jogged her memory as it zipped past. Finding the channel again, she realized it was *Two for the Road,* her favorite Audrey Hepburn movie. She dropped her arm down onto the bed. The film's depiction of a marriage, cutting back and forth between the happy early days and the troubled later ones, never failed to entrance Kip.

"Look at her, just look at her," Kip whispered, as Audrey Hepburn grinned playfully at Albert Finney. So beautiful, so joyful—in these early scenes—so alive and vital, she thought. She watched for a few minutes, knowing what was to come—the hurtful words, the betrayals. Every time she watched the movie, Kip loved it more. Yet, now, it seemed unbearably sad. She lifted the remote and pressed the POWER button. The screen went black.

Now what? She pushed her hair back from her face, hating the way it felt. Her condition made taking a shower an enormous production, so she hadn't washed her hair since the day before yesterday. It's too bad, she thought, that when you're sick, you feel like a dirty slob, which, of course, makes everything worse. At the moment, she wished she could crawl out of her skin and have a total cleanup—shower, shampoo, and every beauty treatment she could think of. Hell, she thought, I'd like to be sandpapered from head to toe. Being a helpless patient had to be one of the worst feelings in the world.

She put the remote control on the folding bridge table Peter had set up beside the bed. The additional space gave her more room for newspapers, magazines, the telephone, and tissues, along with everything her well-meaning husband brought in his attempts to cheer her up. Not that he was having much luck, she reflected.

She felt sorry for him. For some reason she couldn't understand, she was practically indifferent to the shock and emotional upheaval he had gone through when she was in the hospital. Intellectually, she understood that his wife's narrow escape from a brutal robbery was harrowing for him. But, somehow, she was unable to summon up concern for him.

I *should* be concerned for him, I *should* be comforting

him and telling him everything will be fine, she thought. That's what I do—for him, for the children. It's what I do best.

And that's the problem.

She turned her head to look out the window at the steel gray December sky. For most of this horrible week, while she had struggled with her pain, she had been fighting just as hard to get away from her thoughts. But it was futile, and she knew it. The truth was right there in front of her. There was no way to pretend she didn't see it.

All her life, she had considered herself an athlete. That's who she *was*. Without realizing it, she had viewed herself as an athlete who didn't happen to be doing anything athletic. As if sixteen years away from her sport didn't mean anything. As if retiring from skating at twenty and never getting on the ice again was the same as taking a two-week vacation. She was still an athlete.

This was, of course, utterly ridiculous. She had stopped being an athlete long ago. The image was only a grandiose delusion. In fact, her body was weak and would only grow weaker with time. Her injuries made that brutally clear, but actually it had been true all along.

And the way she had acted for so long as if skating didn't even exist—it made perfect sense to her now. That was what was truly ridiculous, she mused. Sixteen years of viewing herself as an athlete for a sport she refused even to watch, let alone perform. Since getting married, she hadn't once gone skating herself or even taken the children. She skipped over ads for televised events, ignored articles about it, and never seemed to be around a television set during the Winter Olympics. She didn't think about why she did these things, she just did them.

It was so pathetically obvious, she thought. By staying far away from the sport, she could avoid facing that she wasn't part of it anymore. But she wasn't. With a bit of help from a deranged teenager in a clothing store, that had suddenly become crystal clear.

Which left her with her only other identity: the perfect

wife and mom. But that was only a role she had chosen
to take on, a job that kept her too busy to even consider
what she'd given up. It wasn't *her*. *She* was the person
underneath.

And the person underneath was . . . nothing. No one.

She had spent her entire life in service to either skating
or her wife-and-mother role. She drove herself at both,
as if working so hard, at first on one, then the other,
would kick up enough dust to make it seem as if there
were someone there. Yet, when she left skating, it had
been as over as over could be. Gone without a trace.
And now, she was engaged in delivering forgotten homework to school and vacuuming under the kitchen table.
A robot could do that just as well.

Hell, she thought, it's pretty pointless stuff, most of it.
The rest of the family didn't even need her, really. While
she had been in the hospital, somebody—she wasn't sure
who, but she suspected Peter's mother—had arranged for
a housekeeping service to come in three times a week.
Peter and the kids were doing fine, scheduling rides so
that Lisa and J. P. got where they had to go, arranging
pickups and deliveries to deal with the errands, eating
gourmet takeout and home-cooked dinners dropped off
by friends and neighbors. "Yes, everyone is just ducky,
thank you very much," she muttered to an imaginary
inquiry about her family.

Certainly, the children had been frightened when they
came to see her in the hospital, their eyes wide at the
sight of their usually competent mother lying flat and
helpless. Lisa appeared skeptical during both her visits,
as if she believed they were holding back information
about how bad Kip's condition really was. J. P. cried.
But they had bounced back with disturbing speed when
she got home and they understood that she would make
a full recovery. Her son sat at the foot of her bed before
and after school, telling her what was going on, but then
he was off to his activities and homework. Lisa's dis-
missal of her mother's brush with death appeared total;
just that morning she had come into Kip's room to ask

where some of her things were and to reel off a litany of complaints about Peter's ignorance of her daily needs and wants. It wasn't that she wanted Kip, though; it was more that dealing with her father was annoying. In fact, not *once,* Kip reflected, had Lisa offered to do or get anything for her mother. Clearly, her daughter was recovering nicely from the shock.

It was as if Kip were the Jimmy Stewart character in *It's a Wonderful Life,* except that in this version, it turns out that her not being born wouldn't have made one bit of difference.

Tears filled her eyes. She wiped them away with the back of one hand, detesting the way she was wallowing in self-pity. But she had spent her whole life running around without considering what she was doing, or, more important, why.

No, she couldn't do this; she couldn't let herself fall apart. Mentally squaring her shoulders, she looked around the room for distraction. Her glance fell on the flowers over on the dresser, colorful arrangements from Dirk and from Peter's parents, and other friends, so many that they filled half a dozen or so vases, which Peter had placed around the room. She hadn't written thank-you notes for any of them, she realized, feeling a twinge of guilt. Oh, for God's sake, stop it, she immediately wanted to shout at herself. You and your stupid thank-you notes.

The roses from Nicole were drooping, she observed absently, their edges turning brown. She knew those particular flowers were from her sister, since Nicole had handed them right to her during a brief visit the night before she left for Oregon. That had been the only time Nicole came to the house. Other than that, Kip had seen her once since the robbery, when Kip was still in the hospital. She had only a dim memory of the visit because it was just several hours after the operation to repair the shattered bone in her leg. Kip closed her eyes, recalling that day. There was nothing the doctors could do for her three broken ribs; they had to heal on their own.

But her leg needed more. The kick that had caused such agony had, in fact, fractured her fibula, the small bone on the outside of her lower leg. It had required surgical repair. Between the pain in her chest and leg, the massive bruising on both those areas, and the haziness induced by pain medication, Kip had been supremely uncomfortable when Nicole appeared at her bedside.

Her sister had gushed on and on about Kip's narrow escape from death, but even in her medicated fog, Kip had the sense that Nicole was almost enjoying the role of shocked and distressed sister. When the bedside telephone rang, Nicole seemed practically delighted to relay the gruesome news of Kip's experience to the shocked listener on the other end. Hearing her animated tone as she discussed how terrible it all was, Kip realized that it made Nicole feel important to be the one delivering the inside details.

The rest of what Kip remembered from that visit involved Nicole sitting by the bed, complaining about the trip to Oregon that her family was about to make, a trip scheduled long before. What was upsetting her was having to take the boys out of school, which she felt would throw them off their schedules for weeks after. Still, she kept repeating, she *couldn't* get out of attending her in-laws' fiftieth wedding anniversary party, now could she? When Kip, making a supreme effort to appear interested, suggested making arrangements to go without the boys, Nicole had snapped at her not to be ridiculous. She wasn't leaving her children with some stranger.

Kip recalled not being particularly sorry when Nicole finally said she had to get home. She felt the same way now, thinking that her sister's trip meant she didn't have to deal with any further visits for another few days.

Disloyal, ugly thoughts, she reprimanded herself. But she felt ugly inside. Furious and mean and ugly. Maybe as ugly inside as *him,* that Todd Lyle—she could barely stand to think about him by name, to think that he even *had* a name. There were moments when she thought she might choke on her anger at him. She kept reminding herself that he was just a boy, somebody's son, and maybe he had started out like *her* son, until something went wrong along the way. But in the darkest part of her heart, she had to admit that she was glad he was dead. Worse, she was also sorry he wasn't alive so that she could see him get punished for what he did to poor Ruth Johnston and those other two people. And what about what he had done to her, she thought, what about the consequences of those kicks? Effortlessly, he had stripped her life bare to reveal the raw nothingness beneath it. She might have fooled herself forever, if not for him. He forced her to understand that she was basically invisible, a windup doll keeping everyone happy, everything running. Because what else could she do? She had never managed to become an actual person.

"Okay, Peter," she whispered to her husband, in answer to his earlier question, "I do need something at that. Not a sandwich, thanks. I need a purpose. And I need an identity. I need to be someone. Could you do that for me, please? I'd really appreciate it."

Eventually, her bones would heal. What, she wondered, would happen then to the rest of her?

7

"How did I let them railroad me into this party?" Eloise said the words out loud, though she was alone in the bathroom. Dressed only in a slip, she'd emerged from the shower ten minutes before and was struggling with an array of cosmetics a model would have been proud to own. That was the perk of being editor of a women's magazine: makeup, stockings, combs, and brushes were donated to her by the pound. But she didn't feel the least bit like utilizing any of it. What she felt like was getting into bed with a good book and a pizza. Besides, there wasn't much she could do, she thought, with eyes that had been awash in tears at least ten out of every twenty-four hours since the robbery. It had almost been easier before that, right after John walked out, when she'd simply been too stunned to feel much of anything. Now, on top of feeling so sad, it was all she could do to get dressed in the morning; she felt terrified when a bulb blew out or a car drove by a little too fast. What she needed, she decided was . . . well, she had no idea what she needed, but she knew damned well what she didn't need. Namely, she had no desire to host the annual Christmas bash.

"Of course you're giving the party, darling," her mother had said when Eloise had suggested skipping it this year. "It's what you do! And we all love it so. Think how disappointed everyone will be if you don't."

Her father had put his hand under her chin. "You've never been a girl to bend to bad fortune," he'd said, grinning like a quarterback who'd just crossed into the end zone, "and that's how you have to look at it all—a bout of bad fortune."

I haven't been a girl in over twenty years, Eloise had longed to say, nor do I consider surviving a robbery that left four people dead a bout of anything. But she couldn't really argue with her parents' sentiments. Putting one foot in front of the other was never a bad thing.

If only it didn't *feel* so bad, she acknowledged, taking another glance in the mirror.

"I've been giving the Christmas party every year for over a decade. Why should the end of my marriage and a near-death experience alter that?" Even girls who experienced bad fortune must be entitled to a cynical expression in the privacy of their own homes, she decided.

She picked up the mascara wand and began feathering her eyelashes as a beauty editor had taught her to do years before. It wouldn't do anything for the red-rimmed area under her lashes, but at least it might make it less noticeable. Then she dabbed a brush in a small turquoise jar filled with powder blush, and accentuated the area of her cheekbones. No, she thought, disgusted. Where her cheekbones had once been. It was no use. She looked like a fat clown, makeup or no makeup.

As she lifted a tube of lip gloss to her mouth, she heard the front door bell ring once, briefly. Surprised, she glanced at her watch. It was only a quarter of six. Much too early for any of her guests to arrive. And how strange that the doorman hadn't announced that anyone was there to see her. She pulled her navy blue terry-cloth robe down from the hook on the back of the door and slipped into it before leaving the bathroom. She was astonished to hear a key scratching in the lock. She watched as the door opened a few inches, until it was stopped by the chain she had put in place earlier that afternoon.

"Oh, I didn't think you'd be home," John Kaline said as Eloise stood in front of the narrow opening. His key was still attached to the lock.

Eloise stared at her husband as if he were a ghost.

"If you thought I wasn't home, why did you come?" she managed to ask, clutching her robe tightly around her as if for safety. *Were you worried about me? Have you realized you still love me? Are you coming home?* These were the questions she managed not to ask.

John had the grace to look embarrassed. "Well, I thought you'd set up in the country. The firm's off-site at Killington starts on Sunday, so I need my skis."

Eloise felt like smacking him. She wanted to scream: *I've just been through an experience that almost took my life and you want your skis!* She imagined how the words would taste in her mouth, but instead of saying them she pulled the chain back and let him in.

John entered, visibly relieved to be allowed inside. "Honestly," he said, "if I'd known you were home, I would have called. I feel like a jerk."

You are a jerk, she almost snapped. But again, she held her tongue. John looked around the apartment as he entered, taking in the bottles of liquor displayed on the bar and the vases of overflowing roses and orchids.

"Oh, my," he said, "tonight's the party, isn't it?"

"Yes," Eloise answered, walking away from him and leaning against the arm of the couch. She felt like sinking down on to the floor, but she wasn't about to give him the satisfaction of seeing her dissolve right in front of him. "Everyone will be here soon."

John smiled. "How are your parents? And George and Bettina? Remember me to them, okay?" He looked around the room, pleasantness virtually radiating from his pores. "It's always a great party."

Does he even hear himself, Eloise wondered. The forced gaiety made it painful for her to look at him. There he was in a brown tweed jacket and one of his crisp, clean, casual blue shirts underneath, covering a beige turtleneck. Like a portrait out of the après-ski spread in *GQ*. He couldn't possibly feel at ease, as he was trying so hard to do, but that he even deigned to attempt it amazed her. "I don't know that sending my family your regards is especially appropriate," she responded.

"You know," he said, ignoring her comment, "I got Gil Coleman to speak to the partners Monday night."

How nice of my father to introduce you to him, she thought.

"Well," he said, a bit of the ease slipping, "I guess I'll go get my skis."

Eloise stayed where she was. She felt herself trembling. But it wasn't just the overwhelming sense of loss she'd become so familiar with, nor was it the fear that had joined it. For the first time, she felt angry at the man who'd behaved so badly. Not that it made her feel any better. But it was—however marginally—one step better than depression.

She could hardly believe that this was the man she'd married, the eager young law student who'd been so independent and energetic when they'd met. She'd been introduced to John by her college roommate, Lindsay Phillips, who was at Columbia with him. "You're gonna love this guy," Lindsay had said. "He's a house afire."

John had organized the study group, headed up Law Review, had even campaigned door to door for the Democratic senatorial candidate, who'd been a childhood friend of his father's in Pittsburgh. He's been so in charge, so different from Eloise herself. And so fiercely independent. She'd loved that. All her life, a piece of her had been aching to go out on her own. After graduation, she'd accepted a job at *Mademoiselle,* eager to learn from people outside her family. But that was the year her mother had had pneumonia. "Go and work with your father instead, dear," Felicia Bentley had said from her bed at Columbia Presbyterian Hospital. "Dad needs you around for now, and there's nothing he can't teach you about the magazine business."

Of course, that had been perfectly true. Her father was

an icon in the communications industry. But she'd so
wanted to test herself, to venture out of her familiar
circle. And when she'd met John, she'd felt as if that was
what she was doing. They'd fallen in love quickly. She'd
cared even more about his success than about her own
when he'd opened the law firm. But all that didn't matter. None of it counted. *Remember me to your parents*—
she didn't even matter enough for him to think twice
about what he was saying.

No, Eloise thought, sinking off the arm of the couch
onto the cushion. Now, she was just the unattractive
woman who'd happened to have temporary possession
of his skis.

"You certainly have your game face on," George
Bentley said, taking in Eloise's wide smile as she finished
greeting her latest guests.

"Leave it alone, George," Eloise answered, the smile
diminishing. After John had left two hours before, it had
been so much harder to continue getting dressed for the
party, let alone stand here trying to seem as if everything
was simply peachy without having her brother snip away
the thread of poise that was keeping her going.

George shrugged his shoulders in slight apology. "I
guess it's good that you're giving the party again. God
knows Mom and Dad seem to be enjoying it."

Both brother and sister looked across the large living
room to where Grey and Felicia Bentley were holding
court in the far corner. Their father, dressed in a bright
red sweater with a reindeer stitched across the chest, had
one arm around his wife, also in red, but in her case a
brilliant magenta Chanel suit with gold piping down the
front. With his other arm, Grey Bentley was greeting a
group of well-wishers who gathered around him. Every
minute or two, his hearty voice would ring out another
name, another introduction. "Jim, you remember Maggie
from *Vanity Fair*." "Horace, didn't you study with Ali-
cia's father when you were at Princeton?"

George turned to whisper into his sister's ear. "In another few years, that will be me. Promise to have me committed, okay?"

Eloise looked up at him. Well over six feet tall, George wore a blue, narrow pin-striped suit that emphasized his height. Underneath, he sported a yellow sweater, which hinted at an informality his patrician features and strong chin showed no hint of whatever.

She shook her head. "You'll love it, just as he loves it."

Her brother raised one eyebrow. "Maybe I'll be doing it, but please don't think I'll actually be enjoying it."

Eloise usually liked teasing her brother about how much he wanted to emulate Grey Bentley, but tonight she couldn't summon up the energy. It was all she could do to stand here trying to maintain the fatuous smile on her face. That she hadn't begun to scream in the preceding two hours was a small triumph in and of itself.

"Speaking of love," Eloise said, looking around the room, "where's Bettina? I said hello when she came in, and then she disappeared."

George lifted a hand to his brow, as if looking leeward from a ship. "Where is my wife? Oh, where oh where is my wife?" He lowered his hand and raised his glass of wine to his lips, sipping a few drops as if punctuating a thought.

Eloise found herself laughing. "Well, that was dramatic. Is there something here you're trying to tell me?"

George shook his head. "You're creating quite enough story for one family, dear sister."

Eloise expelled a long breath. "Yes, I suppose I am."

George put a hand on her shoulder. "I'm surprised you actually decided to throw the annual shindig. You know, one Christmas could have gone by without the public performance."

Eloise nodded. "Thanks, but I think it helped me. You know, it's what we do."

"Not for us to whine or cry, or feel any pain, right, El?

Not even when we're almost killed." He took another sip of wine. "Bentleys soldier on. We're so damn stoic, we're practically British."

"Oh, George, let's not get carried away." Eloise felt a dull pain begin behind her right eye. She pictured John standing in the hallway, and wished she could escape to her bedroom and settle in with a milkshake and the TV. She forced her voice to brighten, praying her spirit would choose to go along with it. "Actually, it was good to have to put the party together. It kept my mind on something, and that's not so bad."

George patted her shoulder. "I know, sweetie. But it can't be easy."

Eloise looked around the room, not even seeing the mass of people. All she really took in were the places John was not. He wasn't pouring drinks at the bar. He wasn't off in the dining room, with that eager, curious look on his face, chatting up someone he'd never met before, but whose work or whose life he was dying to hear about. Had he magically appeared in any of those places, she would have felt like planting a bomb under his feet.

"I guess nothing's easy, is it?" she finally answered, any hint of brightness gone.

"You don't know how right you are," George responded. "I guess I'd better find which hole my wife has fallen into. You never know what can happen after eighteen or twenty glasses of champagne."

Eloise didn't answer, but watched him as he walked toward the bedrooms at the rear of the apartment. She considered what George had said. It seemed as if Bettina had gone from being a cheerful if not overly complex young woman to an almost bedraggled, middle-aged matron overnight. She pictured Bettina after the Christmas party last year, seated along with her in-laws, talking about the evening's high spots as they always did after everyone had left. Eloise and John had been tired, Eloise's parents still filled with adrenaline, George companionably silent. But Bettina had been sprawled across the small divan in the corner of the room. Her speech had become a drawl, and both her lipstick and mascara had traveled from where they were supposed to be. In fact, she looked more like a woman who'd just gotten out of bed after a wild night than the wife of an executive, attending her husband's family holiday party.

Eloise felt guilty thinking these things. Guilty, but also worried. After all, she realized as she saw her brother reenter the living room apparently still searching for his wife, Bettina was not a middle-aged matron. She wasn't even thirty-five years old, for goodness' sake. Way too young to be described that way. Yet her lassitude, her drinking . . .

Oh, stop it, Eloise said to herself. Who was she to criticize Bettina's behavior? When she'd decided to give the party this year—or, more precisely, when her mother and her father had talked her out of *not* giving the party—she'd sworn to lose fifteen pounds before December 23. Well, here it was, and she wasn't a pound thinner, let alone fifteen pounds. She didn't dare look in any of the mirrors that lay in wait for her around the apartment. She'd compensated as best she could with a gray silk suit, the large jacket covering her most obvious flaws. But she certainly wasn't fooling anyone. No matter how much she paid a designer, an extra sixty pounds looked like an extra sixty pounds.

Great, she thought, now she was furious with herself, passive-aggressive about her parents, judgmental about her sister-in-law, and downright murderous about John. And it wasn't even about them, not even John, at least not all of it. Whatever pain she was in when he'd walked out had multiplied by one hundred since that horrible day in Rhinebeck. She'd hardly slept, hardly felt like talking to anyone. The magazine had pretty much run itself for the past few weeks. And as for this party, well, if anyone were having a good time—and, truth to tell, she didn't much care if anyone did or not—it surely wasn't because of anything she was doing as a hostess.

Damn it, just get on with it, she thought, forcing herself to walk into the next room. Standing right near her was the group from New Hope. Shelley and Michael Conrad were in earnest conversation with Absala Child, whose paintings of horses sold like wildfire to summer tourists. Eloise liked all three of them. The Conrads had been like second parents when she was a little girl. Whenever the Bentleys would go out of town during the summer months, as they often had to, it was Shelley and Michael who took care of Eloise and George. It was in their pool that she'd first learned to swim. And, of course—she smiled to herself—it was on the couch in their den that she'd lost her virginity on a hot August night the summer after her freshman year of college.

At the time, that experience had bordered on traumatic. Eloise was staying with the Conrads while her parents were in China. She and Doug Conrad had gone to some party together where they'd both drunk too much beer. And there they were, suddenly, having intercourse on his mother's couch, unsure of how they'd even started making out. She'd known Doug from the time she was four or five. What they were doing felt wrong. Incestuous, even. And she was sure it had been as awkward for Doug as it had been for her. They'd never dated afterward. In fact, it was only during the past couple of years that they'd even spoken comfortably to one another again.

She'd felt horrible the next morning. Had rushed out of their house with some excuse about having to go back to New York City for some nonexistent event. But now, twenty-odd years later, all she could really think about was how thin she'd been. Nowadays, she would never spontaneously, drunkenly, go to bed with someone. The notion of some man seeing her naked was enough to keep her from drinking for the rest of her life.

Shelley Conrad saw Eloise and motioned her to come over, but Eloise simply waved and walked on toward the den. She loved the New Hope crowd, but she was too rattled to settle into a group. As she approached the den, she heard the familiar voices of Ben Schimmel and Pat DeVries.

"Eloise, come here and tell him what an idiot he is!" Pat demanded.

Eloise smiled at the pair, but, rather than entering the fray, walked away from the room, striding toward the kitchen as if she had been called there. When she entered, the caterer looked at her.

"Was there something you wanted, Mrs. Kaline?"

Eloise frowned at the question. She'd arranged for the caterers before John had left, using his last name, as she did for most things outside her professional realm. Now, the sound of the words "Mrs. Kaline" filled her with fury.

"No," she answered. "I needed to check on something." She walked away, opening the door that led to a breakfast room. Closing it behind her, she sank down onto one of the white cane chairs. She'd left the light off and was glad she had as she gazed at the rooftops that formed the view out the window.

Laying her arms on the tabletop, she lowered her chin onto them. She was barely even aware of the party sounds behind her as she observed the stillness of the dark December night.

Nora Levin was surprised to find herself engulfed by the hearty gray-haired man in the reindeer sweater.

"So, you're Nora. Eloise has told us all about you." The man's voice boomed as if he wanted everyone in the room to acknowledge his bonhomie.

"Thank goodness you girls are all right," the carefully coiffed woman beside him said, clutching Nora's hand.

Nora backed out of the man's embrace, gratefully taking the glass of champagne the woman was holding out to her. "Are you Eloise's parents?" she asked after taking a sip.

"We certainly are," the man said, grabbing Nora once more and walking her toward a clutch of beautifully dressed older people standing a few feet away. "That was my wife, Felicia, and I'm Grey Bentley."

And I'm Red Toyota, Nora thought, concealing a smile.

"Now," he said, planting Nora squarely in front of an aged white-haired gent who, much to her surprise, was wearing actual spats. "Emil Gaspare, this is Nora Levin." Grey Bentley turned to Nora. "Emil was the ambassador to China during the Tiananman Square episode. He's a man who understands violence."

Nora couldn't imagine what she had to say that would interest a former embassy official, but Eloise's father didn't leave her there long enough to find out. She felt as if she had suddenly become a ventriloquist's dummy, whose strings were pulled exclusively by the august Grey Bentley. She half expected to feel his hand inside her back.

Almost immediately, he turned her around to face a young girl with straight brown hair. She was dressed in navy blue slacks and a white blouse. "And this is Virginia del Batterly."

Nora recognized the name. The girl had written a novel about miscegenation in the border states while still a junior high school student, which had led best-seller lists throughout the Christmas buying season. Unfortunately, Nora hadn't read it.

The girl peered at her. "Do you think that women can attain real equality in the new millennium, given everything that came before? I mean, don't you think it would be like Martin Luther King deciding to become a landscape architect or a playboy? You know, capturing the spirit of inherent choice while ignoring the centuries of *idée fixe* that preceded it."

Nora had no idea what the girl was talking about. Absolutely no answer came into her mind. That's two for two, she thought. I wonder how many other people I can bore to death before I get out of here.

But Grey Bentley wasn't about to leave her speechless. "So tell us, Nora, what is it you do?"

"Well," Nora said, feeling not even the least bit like going into the long explanation of her profession that always seemed necessary when meeting new people, "I'm a music producer."

The novelist looked at her curiously. "What is that?"

"Yes, dear," Grey Bentley said, "what does a music producer do?"

Nora felt too exhausted to answer. What in hell was she doing at this party tonight anyway? She'd been up since three that morning, having awakened from a nightmare she could hardly stand to recall. At the best of times, she couldn't imagine what she would be doing in this sumptuous apartment, talking to complete strangers who couldn't possibly give a damn about anything she had to say.

"You know, Mr. Bentley," she said, "I'll be happy to tell you all about it, but could you excuse me for just a minute?"

Without waiting for him to answer, she walked away, heading for the bathroom. She'd take a five-minute break, find Eloise to say hello, and then head on home. She knew there were probably many people in the room she'd have found interesting if she'd gotten to know them, but since that day in the store, she hadn't felt at all sociable.

"Nora!"

Nora turned around at the sound of her name. She felt unexpectedly overjoyed to see Kip Hallman behind her, leaning slightly on a cane. She threw her arms around the other woman, surprising both of them.

"I'm so happy to see you here," Nora said.

"Me, too," Kip responded, grabbing Nora's hand with her free one.

"How are you feeling?" Nora asked, glancing down at Kip's leg, hidden beneath loose black silk pants.

"Cast's off. I'm getting there," Kip answered. She looked around. "I haven't even laid eyes on Eloise, but her mother just introduced my husband and me to two Booker Prize winners and a fifteen-year-old whiz kid."

Nora grinned. "I met the whiz kid."

Kip grinned back at her. "She made me feel stupid."

Nora laughed. "She made me *happy* to feel stupid." She looked around at the lush carpets and obviously expensive furniture. "It's a fabulous apartment, isn't it?"

"Sure is," Kip agreed. "Do you think we can walk around and see the rest of it?"

Nora raised her shoulders an inch. "Why not?"

The two left the room, Nora slowing her pace to match Kip's slower gait with the cane. Aiming for the bedrooms, they found themselves in the kitchen instead. Plain wooden cupboards lined two walls, the floor was the same wood, highly polished and urethaned, and a very large white refrigerator sat next to a double oven. There were trays of hors d'oeuvres on top of the counter and the pleasant smell of apple cider coming from a huge pot that was bubbling on the stove.

"I could live here," Nora said, inhaling the scent. "Just so long as everyone else promised to go away."

"That's mighty nice of you, Nora," Kip answered. "Shall I leave you alone?"

"God, no." Nora smiled at her. "Actually, you're the first person I've been glad to see in a month."

Both women were surprised by the creak of a door opening across the room. They could see Eloise's face peeking through the space. She looked around as if to make sure they were alone.

"Come and join me in the cave," she said in a stage whisper.

The two women hurried to the small room behind the kitchen. Eloise shut the door behind them and once again took her seat at the table. "It's all unreal, isn't it?" she said.

"Boy, is it ever," Nora agreed, sitting down across from her. She couldn't have said why, but she knew just what Eloise meant. In fact, since the robbery and Ruth Johnston's funeral, nothing had seemed real. People she'd known all her life looked unfamiliar. Even the CDs she most loved sounded tinny and odd.

Kip stood by the window for a while, taking in the view, and then sat down next to Eloise.

Nora looked at both women. It was somehow as if

she'd been drowning and these two had swum out with a life raft. She'd felt the same way when she'd seen Eloise at Ruth Johnston's funeral. The past weeks had been so confusing for her, and here were people who maybe, just maybe, would understand what she'd been going through.

"Listen, guys . . ." She hesitated and then took the plunge. "Maybe you'll think I'm crazy . . . actually, *I'm* starting to think I'm crazy . . . anyway, I've hardly slept since, well, you know since when. I lie in bed and all I can think about is killing that stupid kid. Which is crazy, since he's already dead. But it's making me nuts." She looked at Eloise then at Kip. "You know, I intended to get on the subway tonight. I was downtown and it would have been the easiest way to get up here. But I've hardly had the nerve to walk down the stairway, let alone to board a train with a ton of strangers on it since that kid got ahold of us. When I'm at home, I find myself going to the front door ten or fifteen times, to make sure I locked it."

She was surprised to see tears appear in Kip's eyes, ones she brushed away quickly. "I know exactly what you're talking about. I have temper tantrums about a hundred times a day. At my husband, at the kids. And it's so unfair, 'cause the person I'm furious at is Todd Lyle."

Like Kip, Eloise had tears in her eyes, but, unlike Kip, they began to spill over, running down her cheeks. "I'm crazier than both of you. I'm filled with rage, but it all seems to be against my horrible, disappeared husband. Like, maybe if he hadn't walked out, I wouldn't have been shopping in that store, wouldn't have been tied up on the floor for all that time thinking I was about to die." She swiped at her eyes with a tissue. "I know it's ludicrous. John had nothing to do with it, but somehow, during my sleepless nights, he's the one I want to mangle." She smiled at Nora. "I guess the good news is there's someone you can call at three or four in the morning if you get bored."

Kip smiled as well. "That would make three of us. I've been feeling as if no one on earth could understand what's going on inside me."

"What the hell *is* going on with us, anyway?" Nora responded. "Whatever it is, it doesn't seem to be abating in any hurry." She shuddered suddenly. "What if it never goes away? Maybe, when something like this happens to you, it stays with you for the rest of your life."

"I don't know about the rest of our lives," Eloise said, "but if the three of us could stay in this room for the rest of the evening, I'd be perfectly content."

"Eloise, dear, where are you hiding?"

All three women looked toward the closed door. Grey Bentley's voice started up again, this time from slightly farther away.

"I checked the kitchen, Felicia, and she's not here. Maybe she ran out for some ice or something."

They listened to his retreating footsteps, none of them moving an inch. Finally, Eloise sat back against the chair and smiled toward Kip.

"Have you seen Eloise?" she chirped.

The corners of Kip's mouth turned up. "Me? No." She turned to Nora. "How about you?"

"Eloise who?" Nora asked, straight-faced.

8

Sitting in the passenger seat of the Lexus, Lisa Hallman groaned. "I can't believe you stopped. You had plenty of time to make the light."

Kip glanced over at her daughter. "So sorry," she said. "Stupid of me not to run it."

Lisa fumed. "I *have* to be home by eight."

"You made that quite clear." Kip gripped the steering wheel. "You've told me at least a thousand times."

"Then why did you have to stop to talk to Melanie's mother? You're not even friends."

Kip wasn't sure she could keep her temper in check for much longer. Lisa had been complaining about one thing or another from the minute Kip had picked her up from swim practice. The traffic light turned to green, and Kip pressed down hard on the gas, going faster than she normally would.

She enunciated her words precisely. "Melanie's mother is a perfectly nice woman with whom I have come in contact many times over the years. It would be rude to ignore her when she was standing right there by the pool. Not that I wished to, anyway."

Lisa scrutinized her fingernails, apparently sensing that she should go no further, but unable to stop herself. "Talking for fifteen minutes about some stupid house that's going to be torn down is a lot more than not ignoring her," she muttered.

"That stupid house is a landmark of historic significance," Kip snapped. "We're trying to preserve it for future generations. Not that you would care. Perhaps your children will appreciate it."

With a sharp jerk of the wheel, she turned the car into their driveway.

"Here we are. And not a moment too soon for me either," she said, pressing the garage door remote.

Within seconds of Kip's stopping the car, Lisa had grabbed her gym bag and backpack and was dashing into the house. Kip could hear her yelling as she ran up to her room. "If anybody's on the phone, get off! I'm expecting an important call!"

Kip turned off the engine. She put both hands back on the steering wheel and shut her eyes. Grateful for the quiet, she remained there, motionless. No one needed her inside just yet. Before she left to pick up Lisa, she had made dinner for J. P. and Peter. J. P. would be doing homework up in his room, while Peter was probably reading in his favorite wing chair, feet up on the ottoman, a glass of wine on the small table beside him. Still, she shouldn't be sitting here, doing nothing. There were those phone calls to make about the PTA fund-raiser, and she had to write that letter to the kids in J. P.'s class about making a Teacher Appreciation Day gift.

Kip rubbed her eyes. She didn't want to do any of it. She wanted to be left alone. Forever. It was all too much. Right now, though, she decided, Lisa's swimming was annoying her most of all.

But it wasn't as if she could blame anyone but herself. No one had forced her to let her daughter become a swimmer. She could have refused to take on this monster of a commitment; there was no law stating that parents had to go along with any sport their children selected, regardless of how consuming it was. Lisa might have been unhappy at first, but she would have gotten over it. Once her daughter became serious about the sport, Kip had known that it was going to be an endless round of morning and evening practices, sometimes six hours a day, more on the weekends, not to mention the meets and competitions themselves. So it was tough to blame Lisa for the fact that all this chauffeuring and ministering to her needs was driving Kip crazy.

Part of the problem, though, was that Kip believed it would all be for nothing in the end. Eventually, Lisa would tire of the sport. She would drop it and move on to something else. Kip would have expended all this time and energy for absolutely no reason.

Beyond that, she knew better than to actually expect an adolescent girl to be sweet and polite. They were horrors, with few exceptions. Other mothers who had been through it swore that time could indeed be counted on to restore the daughters to their former selves, if everybody just hung on long enough.

Still, still . . . she was continually confounded by the depth of Lisa's selfishness. Kip was often reminded of one of the expressions her mother used to use: "She doesn't know anyone else is alive." That was Lisa. She was sullen and uncooperative—and that was putting a good face on it. Apparently, to Lisa, the members of her family were servants to be ordered around, and not very bright ones at that. Was I that bad as a kid? Kip wondered.

None of this was helped by the extra attention Lisa was receiving from everyone around her for her athletic achievements. Of course, Kip knew full well what it was like to be kowtowed to when you were a winner. Along with the perk of instant popularity, coaches, other athletes, total strangers fussed over you. You were lifted above the world of the ordinary.

But was it necessary to become a diva? Despite Kip's very real successes when she had skated, she had always been more focused on her failures, concentrating on how she could improve. That attitude probably kept her from being too full of herself. Lisa seemed to suffer from a surfeit of confidence. She reveled in her victories and ignored her defeats as temporary, meaningless setbacks. Maybe that makes her a better athlete, Kip mused.

She maneuvered herself out of the car. She was grate-

ful the broken bone was in her left leg, so she could still
drive with her right. It had been a thrill to get rid of the
cane, and walk on her own again, but the strain of keeping up with her usual activities was taking a toll. She
moved more slowly, afraid of making sudden movements.
One step at a time, she reminded herself. The pain she
felt with every inhalation was easing, although it was still
enough to keep her ever aware of her broken ribs. Plus,
as a result of compensating for her bad left leg, her lower
back and right hip hurt. Still, it wasn't the pain that bothered her the most. After the initial discomfort of the first
couple of weeks had subsided, it turned out exactly as
she had feared: her mental devastation over the injury
was actually worse than the injury itself.

She went inside the house, pausing to drop her shoulder bag on a chair, and going around to the front hall
closet to hang up her coat, a process that now took far
longer than usual. When she turned to go into the
kitchen, she nearly tripped on a pair of J. P.'s sneakers,
haphazardly thrown on the floor. Anger exploded inside her.

"J. P.," she yelled, "get down here and pick up these
sneakers."

There was no answer.

"Do you hear me?" she screamed.

His voice drifted down. "I hear you, I hear you. I'm
coming."

Her son appeared before her on the steps, hurrying,
with a puzzled look on his face. "What's so terrible?"

"I nearly killed myself." Kip pointed to the shoes.
"How many times do I have to tell you—?"

He put up a hand. "Hey, all right, don't go ballistic."

Grabbing the sneakers, he scooted back upstairs, eager
to get away from her. "Sorry. Jeez."

Kip went into the kitchen and sank down onto a chair.
What was wrong with her? she thought. She was losing
her mind. Since when did she scream at J. P., who was
about as obedient a kid as ever lived. Besides, if it had
been Peter who happened to be in her path, she would

probably have yelled at him about something or other instead.

She wasn't the same person she had been; there was no question about it. Ever since that day, the day she thought she was going to die, she had been inexplicably irritable, quick to anger. No, she amended, more like fury. Peter, the kids, her friends—no one was exempt from her new nasty temper. She was out of control and had no idea what to do about it. You would think she'd be happier, more appreciative of her life after having almost lost it, she reflected. Instead, she felt as if she hated everyone.

The ringing of the telephone startled her. After one ring, it stopped. Lisa, of course, would have leaped on it. Apparently, some supposedly perfect boy had said he would call at eight o'clock, which was what led to Lisa's urgent need to get home. Kip was surprised to hear Lisa come bounding down the stairs.

"Mom," she yelled out, panic in her voice at this unplanned hitch, "it's for you. Please make it fast."

Kip didn't reply. She picked up the portable phone on the table just beyond her elbow.

"Hello?"

"Kip, hi. It's Nora Levin."

Kip smiled, for what felt to her like the first time all day. "Oh, Nora." There was such relief at the sound of her voice on the other end of the line. "You have no idea how good it is to hear from you."

"The same goes for me. How's your leg?"

Kip didn't want to complain. "I'm pleased to report that I tossed the cane."

"That's encouraging. How are you doing otherwise?"

Kip hesitated. "The truth?"

"No," Nora said, "lie to me."

Kip laughed. "I'm doing horribly. How about you?"

"Also not so good. Lots of stuff still bothering me."

"Ditto. But it appears the new mean and rotten me is here to stay. I can't seem to shake it."

"Well, that's not as festive as one would like, I imagine."

"No, it certainly isn't."

Nora paused. "That's sort of why I'm calling."

Kip smiled. "You heard I had become mean and rotten? Boy, news travels fast."

Nora chuckled. "No, I mean I have this feeling, like we three should see each other again. I really want to. I was hoping you and Eloise would meet me for dinner one night."

Kip brightened further. "That's a wonderful idea."

"Since we're both here in New York, would it be possible for you to come to the city one night?"

Kip envisioned the juggling of schedules that would have to be managed in order for her to drive into Manhattan and spend an evening. No, driving locally was one thing, but she wasn't up to a drive to the city. She would have to take a train, which made it even more involved. Easier to schedule a rocket launch, she thought. "Absolutely. Name the night."

"Thursday? Or, if Eloise can't make that, the following Monday?"

"Either one."

"Great," Nora said, "I'll call Eloise and get back to you."

They said their good-byes, and Kip put the telephone down. She was feeling better already. She went to the living room, where she found Peter, reading, exactly as she had envisioned him. She crossed over to stand behind his chair, leaning down to hug him from above. Whatever was wrong with her, she thought as Peter looked up at her with a smile, she just knew that seeing Nora and Eloise was going to be the medicine for it.

"I don't know what I'm doing anymore. Or rather, I don't know *why* I'm doing anything anymore." Nora slowly wound several strands of pasta around her fork. "It's as if I've been given a second chance, but I'm not doing anything with it."

Eloise nodded as she broke off a piece of a roll. "I feel like such an idiot when I think of how I was going around wishing I were dead. My life may be bad, but I sure snapped out of it when the alternative was staring me in the face."

"I agree—we were lucky. So why are we all of a sudden going crazy?" Kip sipped at her glass of red wine. "I was happy before it happened. Now I'm *un*happy. What the hell is going on?"

The waiter appeared next to their table. "Is everything satisfactory?"

Eloise smiled at him. "Yes, fine, thank you."

They were seated at a table near the front of Lattanzi's, an Italian restaurant on West Forty-sixth Street. Eloise had selected it, and they had all arrived several minutes early for their seven-thirty dinner reservation. They hugged and kissed, overwhelmingly glad to see each other, exclaiming over Kip's recuperation. Halfway through the meal, they all had acknowledged that they were talking more comfortably together than they had with anyone else, not just since the robbery, but in months. Perhaps, Kip thought, even years.

"What a nice restaurant. I've never been here before," she commented as the waiter walked off. "Thanks for introducing me to it."

Eloise took a bite of her lasagna. "I eat lunch out practically every day of the week for business. Knowing restaurants is one of the critical parts of a publishing job."

Kip raised an eyebrow. "This is the essence of great journalism?"

Eloise laughed. "Sort of. But you have to know the restaurants that impress, the restaurants that indicate displeasure, the restaurants that say 'You haven't got a chance, but make your pitch anyway.' "

Nora grinned. "Such devotion to high art."

Eloise paused, a forkful of food halfway to her mouth. "Which brings us back to what we were talking about before. Now that I'm glad I have my terrible life back, what am I supposed to do with it?"

"When I was lying on that floor, all I could think about

was my family, how much I love my kids," Kip said.
"But after the first days when we were all grateful I made
it out of there safely, well—then they started ticking me
off right and left. I'm so—" She searched for the word.
"—*resentful* of them now, of what I have to do for them.
It's a new feeling. And not a very nice one."

Nora leaned forward. "Can you say exactly what's
making you feel that way? Try to nail it down."

Kip considered the question. "My *life* is making me
feel this way. It's like I'm suddenly sick of doing everything for everybody. I never do anything for myself."

"The lament of the American woman," Eloise put in.

"Well, yes and no," Kip said thoughtfully. "It's more
as if I had been perfectly fine with my life, and suddenly
I'm not. I want something, but I don't know what it is.
It's as if I *missed* something. I feel loss."

"Loss?" echoed Nora.

"Like I let something slip through my fingers." Kip
shook her head. "Oh, I don't know what the hell I'm
talking about."

"No, wait," said Nora, "this is important. What did
you lose? There's something you miss. Something you
regret, maybe?"

Kip started to say something; then she stopped. She
stared at Nora.

"What is it?" Eloise asked.

"Yes, that's exactly what it is," Kip said. "I regret
something. And until this minute, I had no idea what
it was."

"And? Tell us," Nora urged.

Kip didn't answer right away. She began tracing patterns on the tablecloth with her finger, apparently having
a difficult time bringing herself to say what was on her
mind. At last, she sighed and spoke.

"Skating. I regret having given up skating. I didn't
realize it, but I do now."

Nora pulled back slightly in surprise. "What do you
mean, skating? Roller skating, ice skating, what?"

"Ice skating." Kip smiled at them. "I used to be a competitive figure skater. Serious. Before I got married."

"Whoa, hold on here," Eloise said in amazement. "You're kidding."

Kip shook her head. "Nope."

Nora's eyes were opened wide. "Well, I'll be damned. I've never met a professional ice skater before."

"Not professional," corrected Kip. "I was working toward the Olympics."

"You actually skated around to music in those little sparkly costumes?" Nora was intrigued.

"Nora," Eloise interjected as if she were talking to a child, "what are you doing?"

"Sorry," Nora said. "I got carried away. No offense."

Kip laughed at the two of them. "It's okay. I know it's not the most usual job in the world. But, yes, I did the whole thing. Practiced every day from the time I was six. Competed. Won lots of championships, actually. Then I met Peter and fell in love. He was already a successful writer at the time. He was so handsome, and so smart—oh, God, was he smart."

"Who wouldn't love that?" Eloise asked rhetorically.

"Anyway, he was going away to France to research a book. I knew if I let him go, that would be it for us. I left skating to travel with him, and I never went back."

"Like a storybook," said Nora, not unkindly.

Kip nodded. "Exactly. But, truthfully, I never minded. Or I *thought* I never minded." She shrugged. "Apparently, I did. Or, rather, I do."

"That's a big deal," Eloise said.

Kip spoke reflectively. "There was a moment when I was crossing over from childhood to adulthood. I was just starting to be on my own. But I never went down that road to become an adult. I took a different road with Peter. It's like I want to go back there and get at that moment again. Does that make any sense at all?"

The other two nodded.

"All this is forcing me to look at how little I've done

to steer the course of my own life." Kip sipped at her water. "It's not as if I could go back to skating. It would be silly to think I could compete again in the same way. But I was an athlete, that's always been a big part of my identity. I need to go back to that girl I used to be and sort out what the hell I did with her."

"That's quite a regret," said Nora. "Hmmm. It's a good question for my game."

"What game?" the two women asked simultaneously.

"It's just something I like to do. What book would you take with you if you were going to a desert island? If you were being executed and had only one meal, what would it be? Like that. But this question is more serious." She turned to face Eloise. "What's your biggest regret in life?"

Eloise, startled, stopped chewing her lasagna. She swallowed. "What a question."

"Kip told us. Now you tell," Nora said.

Eloise reached for her glass of water. "That's easy, but I'm not sure I want to say it."

"Why not?" asked Kip.

"Too mortifying. You can probably guess it anyway."

"Come on," prodded Nora. "Out with it."

"Okay, okay." Eloise sighed. "My biggest regret is that I let myself get fat. It might not seem like such a big deal to you two, but you've obviously never been fat." She grinned at Kip. "A professional figure skater, no less. I wonder if you even saw triple digits on the scale when you were doing that." She turned to Nora. "I don't have to ask you. I saw you at college, and I just know you were never fat as a child."

Nora made an apologetic face.

"But it's a truly big deal to me. It has informed every minute of my life since it happened. All the articles we publish about women's self-esteem? I could be the queen of the universe, it wouldn't make any difference. I have loathed myself without letup." She paused. "Oh, and did I mention the tiny fact that it cost me my marriage, too?

My husband left me because I became a whale. He didn't want to be married to the largest mammal of them all."

Kip reached over to put a hand over Eloise's. "Stop being so cruel to yourself."

Eloise looked at her, pain in her eyes. "You wanted to know my biggest regret. That's it."

Nora spoke. "You were the same weight as everybody else at Vassar, as I remember it. So when did this start for you?"

Eloise thought back. "I went up and down as a teenager. I guess I was reasonably thin at college and for a while after. But then I married John, and, I don't know why, but the weight came back on. And here it still is." She gave a rueful laugh, then sat up a little straighter in her chair, exhaling as if done with a difficult task. "Okay, Nora, your turn."

Nora opened her eyes wide. "Why would you ever dream I had anything to regret?"

Kip laughed. "Silly of us."

Nora waved a dismissive hand. "*Je ne regrette rien.* I have a perfect life."

"Ms. Piaf, you're *une grande* liar," Kip said amiably as she took a bite of her veal. "Nobody has a perfect life."

"I'm going to get very upset if I find out your life really is as wonderful as it appeared to be in college," Eloise said.

Nora smiled. "Well, you don't need to get upset. I mean, college was a terrific time for me in a lot of ways." She stopped.

"What?" Kip asked.

"Things sort of went awry back then. Do I really have to talk about this?"

Eloise and Kip nodded.

Nora put down her fork. "I had this boyfriend. It was the greatest thing in the world. He was adorable and smart, and we had that incredible sex you have in college. But what I loved the most was that we were independent, free as the wind. Everyone was always wanting me to be somebody else or do what they wanted me to do. But he loved me exactly as I was. He encouraged me not to change for anyone. What a feeling that was. I loved him to pieces."

She smiled briefly at the memory. Then she said matter-of-factly, "He married my roommate who also happened to be my best friend, the summer between junior and senior year. They quit school to go hiking in Nepal. I never even knew they were remotely interested in each other."

"Oh, my God," Kip breathed.

"Ouch," Eloise said.

"Yeah," Nora laughed. "Anyway, life went on as it tends to do. There was a guy after that, though. I was so lucky to find a man who was great and smart and kind and all of that. But after Roger in college, I couldn't open up with anybody the same way. I just couldn't. We went out for over a year and this guy, Alex, proposed. I freaked out. I ended the whole thing."

She sighed. "I thought about him after that day in the store. I've managed to keep everybody at a distance for all these years. I've kept myself alone in the world. I don't connect. On the surface, sure. But not underneath it."

"To meet you, no one would believe this," Kip said, shaking her head. "You're so—warm."

Nora straightened up in her seat. "So," she said as if summing up, "if I'm really going to pinpoint what I regret, it would have to be that I didn't marry Alex. We loved each other, and we would have had a good life together. He was the one, absolutely, but I ran like a bunny. That was the worst mistake I ever made."

Eloise tilted her head. "Where is he today?"

Nora shrugged. "No idea."

"Do you think you'd want to find him?" Eloise asked.

"Good Lord, it's got to be fifteen years since I saw him," Nora responded. "He must be married with nine children. What would be the point?"

"Maybe he isn't," Kip said. "You never know. Not to

be cynical, but he could be divorced by now. Enough
time has gone by so he could have gone through a whole
first marriage.''

Nora stared at Kip. "Not to be cynical, huh? You surprise me.''

Kip looked abashed. "Well, you know . . . he *could*
be divorced. Or never married.''

The waiter came to clear away their plates. They sat
in silence until he finished, each of them lost in thought.
He took their order for three coffees and one piece of
cheesecake with three forks. Then he left.

"So," Kip said, "what are you going to do about
this, Nora?''

She looked startled. "What do you mean? I'm not
going to do anything.''

"Why not?" Eloise asked. "You could track this Alex
down and see what the story is.''

Nora looked from one woman to the other. "Are you
crazy? We were just *telling* each other our regrets. We
weren't going on a crusade about them.''

Kip picked up a spoon and tapped it on the table.
"Maybe we should," she said. "You know, I imagine
everybody walks around with a big regret. But after almost getting killed, we three should certainly get the fact
that life is short. So why *don't* we actually do something
about all this?''

"Like what?" asked Eloise.

"Nora should find Alex. You should lose whatever
amount of weight you want to lose. I—and I can't believe
I'm actually saying this—should skate again. I could go
back to it on a different level. The oldies circuit.'' She
grinned. "In a skater's life, I'm ancient. But there are
competitions for people my age.''

"That sounds fine for you." Eloise shifted in her chair.
"But if I could have lost the weight, don't you think I
would have?''

"This would be different," said Kip, "because now you
would have us. We'd help you. Because you're going to
help us, too.''

"So, Kip, this means if Alex proposes again, I could get *you* to marry him for me?" Nora said with a grin.

"Very funny," Kip retorted. "Come on, I'm serious."

Eloise was nodding her head. "It's a good idea. I don't know where my life is going, now that it's been saved. This would be a chance to really do something."

"Oh, wait a minute," Nora said. "I can't imagine . . ."

"We'll help you," Eloise reassured her. "We will."

Nora turned to Kip. "And you're going to be a figure skater again?"

"No, not a big-time figure skater again. That's out of the question." She thought. "But I could do the Adult Nationals. They have them every year. I could compete in the twenty-five and up category, the Intermediate Ladies. Maybe the Adult Masters level. I don't have to win a gold medal. A third place bronze would be a big accomplishment. That would satisfy me." She smiled. "You want to hear something weird? Just thinking about doing it, just having said the words, it's as if a knot in my stomach has been untied. I'm not even feeling the urge to send my daughter to boarding school in the Ukraine anymore."

The three of them looked at each other.

"Well, okay," said Nora slowly. "Now we all have our homework assignments. Let's see what everybody brings in to class."

9

"Well, at least Ella Fitzgerald is dead, so we won't have to bother paying for any damned license." Charlie Hardwick's smug assertion was completely wrong, but nonetheless put forth with utter self-confidence.

It was a good thing he was on the other end of a telephone, Nora thought. Had he been in front of her, she might have given in to one of the hundreds of destructive fantasies he inspired in her every time they had a conversation. She kept her tone reasonable as she tried to answer.

"Charlie, we have to pay for 'One for My Baby.' We need a synchronization license for any existing recording of a song. Whether it's Ella Fitzgerald or Frank Sinatra or Bette Midler or my cat Blanche for that matter . . ." She realized her voice had risen. She stopped talking, knowing she couldn't afford to do any damage.

She looked across the room at her assistant, Kelly Fox. Petite and red-haired, Kelly was seated at her desk cataloguing scores of CDs scattered in front of her. Hearing Nora's end of the conversation, the young woman crossed her eyes, which might have made Nora laugh, had she been capable of finding anything funny at that moment. But she merely swiveled in her chair and faced the other way.

At the sound of the other line ringing, she looked back toward Kelly, who picked it up. Her assistant mouthed the word *Frank,* and pointed at the receiver. Nora shook her head, indicating that she couldn't take the call right now.

"But the song is a thousand years old. It must be PD." Hardwick was nowhere near the end of his complaints.

"The license covers specific recordings of any song," Nora responded with forced patience, "even those in public domain. Which, by the way, 'One for My Baby' is not. PD only applies when a song is seventy-five years or older. And even then, we'd have to get the mechanical license."

She listened to her client expostulate further on the unfairness, the outrageousness of paying people for their work; then she turned back toward Kelly, raising her right hand and forming her fingers into an imaginary gun. Raising her hand to her head, she pulled the virtual trigger and slumped down in her seat.

Charlie Hardwick could not have guessed at her actions by her professional tone.

"No, the synchronization license applies to the performer and the recording; the mechanical license covers Harold Arlen, the man who wrote it."

She listened for ten more minutes as the promotion director of Quad Industries held forth on how "demoralized" he felt, how "ripped off" and "demeaned." By conversation's end, she began to be sorry that she had ever taken on this particular client. Getting hired by such a large corporation would have seemed like a coup five or six years before, when her clients had been tiny operations, paying an independent the least possible money. But Nora's business had become a going concern. Which, she realized in fairness, didn't make the money she was making from Quad Industries any less attractive. It just made her more impatient.

"What does he want this time," Kelly asked as Nora hung up the phone. "Pat Boone instead of Little Richard?"

Nora shook her head. It was so like her assistant to turn the small matter of a jerk into the large matter of political correctness and racism. Kelly was drawn to the darkest possible scenario the way a moth was attracted to a hundred-watt bulb. Besides, Nora had little time for feeding Kelly's political paranoia. "Actually, he doesn't usually question my taste."

She had too much work to do to elaborate, but her answer to Kelly's question was mostly true. Hardwick's mission wasn't to dilute Nora's choices. It was more an effort to bring everything down to its cheapest level. Why go for the best rendition of a melody when you could get one for less cash? It drove her crazy. She'd started her business out of her deep love of all kinds of music. Even as a child, she'd been apt to sit by the record player, listening to favorite cuts twenty, thirty, fifty times in a row. She'd collected every Beatles album, all of The Rolling Stones, not to mention every Broadway show that opened and all the jazz she could find.

When her father was home, he would play classical music for hours. Symphonies, operas, choral music. For a largely uneducated man, David Levin knew a lot about music. Just as he worked hard to earn the money to buy record after record, Nora went through high school babysitting, selling magazine subscriptions, doing all she could to buy the albums she wanted. Her graduation present had been a stereo, and most of her summer's earnings before she started college went for albums.

It hadn't occurred to her to make her passion into a career. In fact, after college, she'd spent ten years working at different jobs. She'd tried publishing, which was interesting, but a hard business in which to make any real headway. After being an editorial assistant for two years, she'd finally become an assistant editor, a job that paid slightly less than her rent. Finally, she'd switched to an advertising agency, writing copy and trying to satisfy the demands of people who hadn't been satisfied ever in their lives. The stress level at the company was always at a fever pitch, and the work itself was without the redeeming quality of producing literature, which, if financially unrewarding, was at least something that allowed her to face herself in the mirror every morning. The one thing she did get to do for the advertising agency was to suggest possible music for a couple of the campaigns. It was this that gave her the idea for Levin Music. She figured that no matter how badly she might do for the first few years, it had to pay as well as book publishing. Plus, it was thrilling to think about making a business out of something she actually loved.

And the whole point of that business was taste. Her taste. That a client like Charlie Hardwick preferred saving twenty or a hundred bucks to using the best version of a song drove her wild. Hardwick only cared that old music tended to be less expensive to use than new music, and bad singers cost less than good ones. To him, as he'd said about fifty times, one thing didn't sound much different from another. Despite the fact that she'd made her corporate reputation, she couldn't wait until she'd conquered a field that was more creative, where people cared about what they listened to. Where one thing didn't sound at all like another.

Which was why her afternoon appointment was so important to her. Nora had been trying to break into supervising music for films for the past three years. Up to now, it had proved impossible. It was like breaking into jingle-singing—producers tended to use the same music houses over and over again. A closed system, with doors that never opened. But, finally, she was getting to talk to a film director. True, Will Stanley was only seeing her because she had designed the music for his cousin's wedding—not exactly the most auspicious professional credit, but at least he had agreed to see her. Stanley was doing some kind of documentary for PBS, and that would be a credit worth bragging about. She was certain she'd never have to have a conversation with a filmmaker that was anything like the one she'd just had with Charlie Hardwick. Then again, she acknowledged to herself, at least Hardwick paid his bills on time.

"Charlie Hardwick isn't the worst client I'll ever have," Nora said, as much to herself as to Kelly. She looked down and began to shuffle the papers in front of her into a neat pile.

"Oh, sure," Kelly offered, fresh outrage in her eyes. "Remember the man who offered me money to sleep with him?"

"You mean Morton DeLeon?" Nora replied, not looking up. "As I remember, he asked if you knew of any reasonably priced student hostels in Manhattan for his niece from Tampa. I think the sexual inference was your own."

Had Nora been looking, she would have seen the disbelief on the young woman's face.

"Oh, please," Kelly said. "I know what a man means when he asks you about a hotel."

Nora wanted to laugh, but insulting Kelly would have been stupid. Despite the daily drama, she really was efficient. Nora was grateful to have someone in the office who cared about the work as much as Kelly did.

"Listen, kiddo," Nora said, "I have that appointment with Will Stanley. I'll be gone for a couple of hours at least. By the way, what did Frank have to say?"

"You're not gonna like it." Kelly's voice had the grim satisfaction that always accompanied what she considered really bad news. "He can't make it tonight. Has some gig that's gonna run late at the studio."

Nora shrugged. "That's okay. I have so much work to do, I can use the time." She stood up, walked over to the closet, and removed her peacoat. "I'll check in when I leave this guy's office, but don't wait for me if it gets too late. Just leave any messages on voice mail, okay?"

Kelly looked at her, bewildered. "Don't you mind about tonight? These guys, canceling right and left. It's like they all signed a pact to torture us and make us feel like crap!"

"You mean, kind of a Million Man misogyny convention?" Nora replied.

"You can joke about it if you want, but ninety-nine women out of a hundred would be really pissed."

Nora laughed, but she was surprised to find that Kel-

ly's remark stayed with her as she left the building. Not
that she was looking to be angry. You either were angry
or you weren't. It was stupid to get all worked up about
something you didn't really care about. But that was just
the thing. Why *didn't* she care? Her evening with Kip
and Eloise flashed through her mind. How could she
complain about not having a man in her life when a
broken date with the guy she was sleeping with left her
grateful to stay home and wash her hair? What kind of
woman was she anyway?

Or maybe the problem was the guy. Frank was fine,
but he wasn't Alex. Alex was the real guy, the guy she
should have taken seriously. Alex was the one she was
supposed to be tracking down and getting in touch with.
So why wasn't she? Hell, she couldn't think about that
right now. There was so much to do, so much to contend
with. She wrapped her scarf more tightly around her
neck. The whole question was pointless. She was relieved
to have the night to herself because there just weren't
enough hours in the day. Who could cope with love? She
could barely cope without it.

As she walked up the subway stairs at Seventy-second
and Broadway, Nora looked behind her. The men and
women in her wake seemed perfectly normal, she was
relieved to see. As if she could tell anything about anyone from observing their outfits, she thought, once again
caught by a clutch of fear. She hated being so afraid. In
all her years of living in New York City, she'd never felt
scared at all. Sure, she was careful about walking down
dark streets late at night. But she'd never looked at other
people with the idea that they might be out to harm her.
Well, she thought, one afternoon in Rhinebeck with
Todd Lyle and her nonchalance was gone forever.

She forced herself to focus on what it was she was
supposed to be doing, pulling the piece of paper on
which she'd written Will Stanley's address out of her
pocket. Figuring out where it would be, she headed east
to Columbus Avenue and walked three blocks north to

Seventy-fifth Street. His office turned out to be a brownstone, with a broad stairway leading up to an inlaid wooden door. Although the building was old, the steps scuffed, the wood in the door faded and scratched, she could tell it had been quite elegant in its day.

She rang the bell marked STANLEY PRODUCTIONS, 3B, pushing open the heavy door when the answering bell released the lock. As she climbed up the two flights to the third floor, she noticed a number of black-and-white photographs lining the brick walls, an unusually homey touch in a city building. There was even a chair outside one of the apartments on the second floor, on its seat a copy of *Elle* magazine from two weeks before. Amazing, she thought. In her building the magazine would have been stolen in two minutes, the chair in five.

She had no idea what to expect from Will Stanley. He was the cousin of a client for whom she'd done some of her earliest work seven years before. Although Edith Marcus had only needed a group of sentimental songs amassed for her second wedding, she had been impressed with Nora's work and had recommended her a number of times. She wasn't sure exactly what kind of film Will Stanley was making, but at least it was a film. Then again, she thought, keeping her excitement within bounds, if he was taking recommendations from his cousin, it might not be much of a film after all.

She rang the bell and was greeted by a tall man wearing blue jeans, the color of which had been washed away long before. His hair was light brown, mixed with strands of gray, and in serious need of cutting. The black T-shirt he wore looked clean but had obviously never met an iron. There was a boyishness in his even features, a restlessness that made him seem very young. He has to be older than he looks, Nora thought, considering the fact that his cousin Edith had surely hit fifty.

"Nora Levin?" he asked, looking at her almost suspiciously.

"That would be me," Nora replied. She put out her hand.

He took it briefly before moving inside, indicating that she should follow.

She entered a large room, whose original oak paneling covered all but one wall of exposed brick, the burnished red giving the whole apartment a warm glow. The brick wall housed a fireplace with logs set in it but not lit. At one end of the room was a bay window with a cushioned window seat facing onto the street. Nora was drawn to it immediately.

"This is really beautiful," she said, looking out onto Seventy-fifth Street and then turning back toward the fireplace. She took in with pleasure the wooden mantel, paneled in the same rich oak as the walls.

Will nodded. "They've never renovated anything in this building." He sounded more annoyed than appreciative.

Nora expected him to say more, but he didn't. She continued to look around the room. There were at least forty stacks of photographs in piles everywhere. "So, you're a photographer."

He nodded.

"Is that related to what you need me to do for you?"

He walked across to a large work table and sat down on a stool. "I'm doing a documentary. It needs music."

"What's it about?" She made herself comfortable in the window seat.

"It has to do with a town in Mississippi. But you don't have to worry about content. You just have to find ten or twelve gospel numbers."

Nora felt a prickle of anger. "You can't really produce the music for a documentary without knowing something about the content. It's not like picking numbers out of a hat."

He looked at her, one eyebrow raised. "I know that mixing Billy Joel with Elton John is complicated work, and I'm sure you're very good at it, but I've been working on this project for over two years, scouting out the town, raising grant money, researching the politics. I know what I want my movie to sound like."

Nora stood up. "Well, then, what do you want me for?" She started walking toward the door.

"You're what I can afford. The big music houses cost three times as much." His response was factual. He didn't even try to sound apologetic.

"Maybe when they find out you've done all their work for them, they'll give you a big discount." She put her hand on the doorknob.

"Oh, come on," he said, getting up and walking toward her. "I didn't mean to be rude. I *do* need help. Otherwise I wouldn't have bothered you." He ushered her back toward a black leather couch. "Here, let me give you some idea of what the documentary is." He pointed to a pile of photographs on the coffee table in front of them and started to pick them up, one by one.

"See this," he said, pointing to two middle-aged women, one black and one white. "These are Mattie Dalloway and Elise Jackson. They started at Hallport High School just before 1966, one year after it had been integrated. They once almost killed each other in a fight in the cafeteria. Now they're running a mail-order business together. Handmade baby mittens."

He picked up another, this time a gas station with three angry-looking black men, their arms folded in front of them, standing in a line behind one of the pumps. "A black teenager named Barry Dalmain was shot right where these guys are standing over twenty-five years ago. That was when the white owners refused to fill up the kid's father's gas tank on Christmas Eve. From what I observed, not much has changed. It could happen again right now."

Nora was impressed with the photographs. Unstaged, they had captured the emotions of the subjects perfectly. The people seemed to radiate from the page. "So, the documentary is about these people?"

He leaned back. "Actually, it's about the town. Before and after Brown versus Board of Education. How it's changed, how it's stayed the same."

Nora thought about how interesting that could be.

What a nice change from parties and weddings! But Will Stanley was not going to be any picnic to work for.

"How much of it is done?" she asked, leafing through the rest of the photos.

"Oh, I've shot a bunch of stuff. There's a lot more to go. I expect to be finished in about two or three months."

The pictures Nora was leafing through had been in color. But underneath them was a stack of black-and-whites. They seemed to be from someplace else, a foreign country. She stopped at a familiar face in the next photo. Who is that, she thought, trying to place the person. She snapped her fingers.

"This is that reporter from CNN, isn't it? The one who was killed in the Balkans?"

"Yes," he answered abruptly, standing up and walking over to the window.

Oh, Jesus. Of course it was the woman from CNN, she realized suddenly. Her name was Theresa Stanley. She must have been a relative. "I'm sorry," she stammered. "I didn't mean . . ." She had no idea what to say.

"I don't think we need to discuss my wife."

Nora was mortified. All she could think to do was change the subject. "Can I see what you've done so far? It would help me in selecting the songs."

He turned to her, his lips still tight. "Can't you just come back to me with some of the great gospel music? You know, the standards. Mahalia Jackson. Cissy Houston."

"Really, Mr. Stanley, I'll do a much better job if I know what the music is going with. In fact, I'd like to go down to Hallport with you for a few days. The music shouldn't be arbitrary. Honestly, you'd be doing your own film a disservice."

"You'd have to pay your own way," he answered. "The Ford Foundation money is just about gone and PBS isn't exactly footing extra hotel bills."

"I may charge less than the music houses, but I think I can raise the cash for a Motel Six in rural Mississippi."

He shrugged. "Feel free. I'm going down in the next

few weeks. Tag along if you like. But, I'm telling you, I know the sound I want."

"Are you certain you want only gospel music?" she asked. "There may be a mix that would add more texture."

"It's a documentary about the South," he answered.

Nora couldn't help going on. "But what if there's a better sound, one you haven't thought of?"

"And what if an angel flies into my window tonight and leaves half a million dollars on the rug?" He smiled briefly. "Just about as likely, I'd say."

Nora had the urge to smack him, but she kept her hands in her lap. "Why don't I call you toward the end of the week. I'll have done some research by then, and I'll have some stuff for you to listen to. Then, we can talk about travel arrangements, okay?"

She stood up and pulled her coat around her, keeping her hands tucked inside. She didn't feel like shaking his hand again.

"Sounds all right to me." He walked her to the door, opening it for her and standing to one side as she passed through. "By the way, Edith sends her best."

Nora turned around and smiled. She'd enjoyed Edith Marcus as a client. A nice woman, and a smart one as well.

He attempted a smile of his own. "She said you got her to use Louis Armstrong instead of Julio Iglesias. I salute your taste."

"Well," she answered, flattered despite herself, "let's hope you're pleased with what I come up with for Hallport."

She walked down the stairs, once again taking in the photos along the way. She heard the door close behind her. At the landing between floors, she saw a picture she hadn't noticed on her way up. It showed a group of grim-looking empty shops, their doors half-open, surrounding what might once have been a beautiful town square. She wondered if it was the town where his wife had been killed. She remembered the story well. The beautiful reporter had been working on a story when she'd been hit by a sniper's bullet. She'd been maybe thirty or thirty-five. Young. And really talented, according to the news accounts. A woman on her way up.

Nora continued down to the building's lobby. Just like that, you could lose the people closest to you. Without a moment's warning. The image of Alex flashed in her mind. What the hell was she doing, wasting time? There might not *be* any time. Life had its own bag of tricks for everybody, and there was no reason to believe she was exempt.

She pulled open the front door and walked out onto the graceful stairway leading to the sidewalk, pulling her cell phone out of her pocket. Dialing her own number, she waited impatiently for Kelly to pick up.

"Levin Music." Kelly always sounded guarded when she answered.

"Listen, it's me," Nora said. "Can you do me a favor? Go on the Internet and see if you can come up with an address for an Alexander Fenichel. He used to live on West Tenth Street; then he moved to Cincinnati, Ohio, or Madison, Wisconsin, or something. Do you have time to do that?"

"Sure. What did he do to you?" Kelly asked, more guarded still.

Nora laughed. "The worst thing possible . . . he asked me to marry him."

10

Kip frowned as she unstrapped the five-pound weight from her ankle. Having completed the stretches and twists to increase range of motion, she moved on to the quadricep sets for her knee. Each motion seemed to require a monumental effort. It occurred to her that if anyone had said she would one day have to work so hard at a little physical therapy, she would have run shrieking into the night. Yet, here she was, struggling to get through a thirty-minute program.

Another fifteen minutes to go, she noted, as she checked her watch. She supposed she should be thankful to be up and around without the cane. Her ribs no longer hurt when she breathed—another big plus. Still, her leg, its bruises faded to a ghastly shade of green, wasn't completely healed, and all the weeks of inactivity had left her out of shape and easily winded. The idea of being so weakened, her leg muscles atrophied, made her want to scream with frustration.

"Don't think about it," she reprimanded herself. Surges of anger still overcame her, not quite as often, but enough to let her know she had other kinds of healing to do, as well. The image of *him*, of Todd Lyle, was triggered in her mind's eye by any one of a thousand little things. With each stretch, she thought of him. With the fatigue that gripped her suddenly at different points in the day, she thought of him. When she held back from bending or hurrying, he was there, right in front of her, his eyes staring into her, his gun pointed at her heart. She had never experienced the red fury that threatened to overwhelm her when she envisioned him, never known she was capable of real hatred.

"Turns out I am," she muttered, pushing herself to continue.

Normally—before—she would do the treadmill as soon as she got up at a quarter to six on weekdays. She would grab her workout clothes, careful not to wake Peter, and slip into the extra bedroom down the hall. That was where they had set up a small gym several years before, with free weights, a StairMaster, the treadmill, and a mat. Peter used the machines only rarely; every so often he would lift weights for ten minutes or so, or perhaps do a short stint on the StairMaster. This was really Kip's room, where she worked to maintain the strength and flexibility that she had come to expect from herself early on. She had always enjoyed coming in here, until the first day she attempted exercising after getting her cast off. That morning had left her awash in both pain and tears.

The series of stretching and strengthening exercises she was doing today was based on the physical therapy routine she performed three times a week at a local rehabilitation facility. Trying not to acknowledge how much she wanted to stop, she thought about what she still had to do that day. It was half past one, but this workout, such as it was, had been delayed. J. P. had come wandering into her room at around five-thirty that morning, complaining of a stomachache. Kip led him back to bed, sitting up with him until he dozed off again after six. There was no point in her going back to bed, so she went downstairs to fix his lunch. When he got up again at seven, he was fine. After two bowls of cereal, he went off to school.

Kip might be walking a bit more slowly, but she had resumed all her old routines, deciding she was better off keeping busy. The other members of her family were only too glad to see her push the whole terrible mess aside and return to being her regular self. That would be her regular self on the *outside,* she amended. They had no idea that she spent most of the day feeling as if she could jump out of her skin.

She went over the errands awaiting her after she showered. To start with, the shirts had to be picked up at the laundry, and she had to buy cork and glycerin for some project J. P. was doing for his Science Club meeting tomorrow. She had to stop at the drugstore and get three videotapes back to Blockbuster before midnight.

She had also promised to make chocolate swirl pound cake for the bake sale at J. P.'s school tomorrow. Then there were the phone calls, the endless phone calls. Today she would try to call the orthodontist for an appointment for J. P., two different places to schedule haircuts for both children, and the plumber about a leak under Lisa's bathroom sink. She had to draw up a schedule and start signing parents up for shifts at J. P.'s school book fair, an event she organized every year.

None of this had anything to do with the preparations for Peter's birthday party in two days. On Sunday afternoon, a crowd would appear at her doorstep, bearing gifts and expecting to be fed. Today was the day to plan the menu, make out shopping lists, order flowers and decorations.

"After that, I just *know* I'll find time to practice that new brain surgery technique," she muttered.

So much flurry and motion, she thought. And it would take hours, particularly since she was slower in getting around. Despite all she had agonized about when she was convalescing, she found she didn't know how to change things. When she got out of bed, the errands were still waiting for her. The busywork was as demanding as ever. She found herself back in her old routine, unable to see any way out of it. She had said she was going to skate again. Saying it was one thing. Taking steps to make it happen, she had discovered, was another thing entirely. One minute she was determined to buy some new equipment and get started. But the next, she was certain it was going to cause havoc in her life. Besides, she couldn't just shove aside her family and responsibilities to the extent she would have to if she were going to do this right.

At last, she was finished. With a sigh of relief, she went back to her bedroom and turned on the television, hoping to distract herself from her thoughts as she got ready to shower. There was a slight popping sound as the picture appeared. Yanking off her T-shirt, Kip glanced at the screen and then stopped, frozen in place. The young woman before her was wearing a pink, lacy leotard and wrap skirt, her brown hair pulled up into a high ponytail. She leaned forward, lifting one leg straight out behind her, and extended her arms to either side as she glided across the ice.

In the past, Kip would have changed the channel. But now, things were different.

Mesmerized, she watched the performance before her. Without meaning to, she began checking off what was right and wrong. The girl didn't have it, Kip decided, at least not yet. She was technically proficient, but she was trying too hard, and it showed. The confidence she needed to communicate was missing, at least to the eye of someone who knew the sport. Being a good skater and getting the jumps right weren't enough. There was so much more to it, and this girl was years away from mastering the grace and power of good skating. Even the music was a poor choice for her, Kip noted with a frown, the heavy chords of the Wagner piece overpowering for this slight, uncertain girl.

Kip couldn't watch anymore. She shut off the television and sat down on the bed. She couldn't do this again, she thought, she couldn't go back to skating. It was ridiculous. She was going to make a fool of herself. Skating was done, it was behind her. She had walked away when everything was perfect. Now she was about to destroy it all by going back when she was too old. Besides, the injury to her leg might mean she couldn't even get around on skates well, much less train for anything, however minor it was.

She unlaced her running shoes as she continued arguing with herself. The fact was, she wanted so much to skate again. That feeling of flying, the dazzling exhilaration—she remembered it perfectly. The joy of a well-executed jump. There was nothing in the world like it.

Her sneakers off, she flopped back on the bed. It was such a big goal, such a stupidly big goal, she thought. Like running for president or deciding to become a rock star. You can't just *pick up* skating again.

She remembered practicing as a teenager in Utica, recalling the early morning drives in the dark to the rink, the hours on the ice, doing her figures over and over, practicing jumps. And the falling—on her hips, her behind, her back, onto an arm or a knee. Stumbling, tripping, somersaulting out of control. So many bruises and sprains and pulled muscles, hours with ice packs and heat. Then there were the ballet lessons and gymnastics for coordination and balance. Studying music and choreography for her routines. Worrying about costumes, what was right for the mood, what would hamper her movements. The list went on and on.

She didn't have the energy for it anymore. And her body, it was damaged now.

She stared at the ceiling. If she didn't have the energy, how come she could run around all day doing stupid chores and errands? Where did that energy come from? Unfortunately, when all was said and done, no one would even care about the minutiae of bake sales and clean shirts that was her life.

On the other hand, she answered herself, a family was supposed to be a team, and her job was to make daily life run smoothly. She had accepted that when she chose not to work. Of course, *"chose not to work"* wasn't really an accurate way of putting it. It wasn't as if she had been a lawyer or an accountant who quit her office job. She was an athlete who had given up her sport. Besides, Peter's books earned so much money, there was no need for her to work. It would have been like a hobby, and she had always been glad she was lucky enough to be able to stay home with the children.

But even before Lisa and J. P. were born, she and Peter had fallen into the arrangement of her staying home with him, fixing his lunch, being around for him. It was what she had wanted as well. Ever since she had gone with him to France, she had had no desire to leave his side.

She remembered the four months they spent in Saint-Malo. They had met only two months before that, when she'd been performing in a skating exhibition in Manhattan. She was only twenty, but a well-known name in skating. Peter had come there with a sportswriter friend. Afterward, the two men attended the informal party in a nearby bar, table-hopping and talking with the performers and various friends and hangers-on who were crowded into the noisy, dark back room.

Kip knew Peter's name—everyone there did—but she had never read any of his books. She'd had no idea he was so handsome. Tall and lean, that thick black hair, and blue eyes that sparkled with interest. She was glad when Peter followed the sportswriter, a man Kip didn't recognize, to the table where she sat wedged in between another skater and his coach. Introductions were made all around.

When he took her hand to shake it, she experienced a sensation unlike any she had ever felt before. It was an effort to keep herself from leaning forward to get closer and closer until she could touch his face with her own. She wanted to feel his slender but strong hand run down the length of her body.

Embarrassed by her own reaction, she looked away. She wasn't a virgin, but she had slept with only two men. Neither experience had had much of an impact on her. She had never felt anything close to what she was feeling just by looking at this stranger and shaking his hand.

Apparently, Peter had felt something, too, because he

came back to sit with her later when the crowd had thinned out. They made small talk at first, but quickly moved on. It was nearly three in the morning when they got up to leave. She had the next day off, so she stayed to meet him in the late afternoon when he was finished with his work. They spent the night in his hotel room. After that, she had no desire to be away from him ever again. What she couldn't understand was that he seemed to feel the same way.

They traveled to Saint-Malo so he could research the wealthy families who flocked to the resort town in northern France during the early 1900s. He was about to start a novel about two families who had lived at that time, and he had allocated several months to find what he needed before he began the actual writing. There was no question of his putting it off, because he had a deadline for the book. When he told Kip he had no choice but to go, she shocked herself by asking if she could come with him. Peter had said he was thrilled, although surprised that she was willing to walk away from her ice skating. Still, she insisted it was what she wanted. After all, she could always go back to the sport.

Walking the streets of Saint-Malo, discovering its restaurants and shops, making love every day in their hotel room—she was inexpressibly happy and never regretted her choice for a minute. While he worked, she studied French and read book after book that Peter recommended at her request. She didn't want him to think of her as some ignorant ice skater, a mere high school graduate who could never keep up with him. It was critical to her that she become more knowledgeable. She knew she would never be his intellectual equal, but she wanted to do her best.

God bless him, she thought, Peter had never made a disparaging remark about her education or inability to keep up with him. But she still believed, deep down, that he had to have a little corner of contempt for her in his heart. He had to look down, if only slightly, on a girl who spent all her time twirling around on the ice.

The bottom line, she reflected, was that she had made all these decisions by herself. Her husband had never tried to force her to do anything one way or the other. He just accepted whatever she chose. But she wondered how he would accept her wanting to be an ice skater again after nearly twenty years. She tried to picture herself announcing to her family that she was pursuing her lost youth, and the changes it would mean for all of them. The image made her wince. She closed her eyes, exhausted from the push and pull of her own emotions, her inability to settle this once and for all.

After a minute or so she became aware of noises downstairs, the sound of Peter moving around the kitchen. That's odd, she thought. He had already had lunch, and once he'd taken that half-hour break, he almost never emerged from his study until five o'clock.

She got up and went into the bathroom, turning on the shower before peeling off the rest of her clothes. The noise of the running water prevented her from hearing anything outside the room, so she was startled to look up and see Peter standing there.

"You scared me," she said, putting one hand over her heart.

His eyes traveled up and down her naked body. "But it appears I came at a most opportune moment."

Grinning, he came forward to slip his arms around her waist. Kip backed away.

"Please, Peter, I'm all sweaty and I have a million things to do. Not now."

He dropped his arms to his sides, the smile disappearing from his face.

"Hey, forgive me. It's wrong of me to want to make love to my wife."

"I'm sorry, I didn't mean anything." Instantly, she was contrite about her curt rejection. At the same time, she couldn't help wishing he would leave so she could just take her shower and get on with things. Irritable again, she thought. Was she never going to get over it?

"It's okay." He turned to leave.

"Actually," she said, not wanting him to go on such a sour note, "I'm surprised to see you. How come you left your office?"

He shrugged. "No reason." He made a silly face. "I'm just an unpredictable guy."

Kip laughed. Her husband's writing habits might as well have been written in stone. They were inviolate. Or, at least they had been up until now.

"Whatever you say." She smiled at him.

She stepped into the shower as he shut the door behind him. The water was too hot, but she stood there, enjoying the penetrating warmth. It had been horrible of her to push Peter away like that, she thought with a frown. Nor was it even like her. In the past, she had adored their sex life, and only wished she were less tired at night so they could make love more often than a couple of times a week. They had held off while her ribs were healing, and then had made love late one night. But that was pretty much it, she realized. They hadn't made love at all the last two weeks.

Although they almost always went to sleep together, Peter had gone to bed earlier than usual several nights in a row, falling asleep an hour or so before she came upstairs for the night. He was particularly tired because the nightmares that had always plagued him were occurring more often lately. Once every few months, Kip would be awakened by his moans, growing louder and louder, until he practically shot up in bed, sweating and gasping for air. But the only thing he could ever remember was that he was a child, running, running for his life. The same dream over and over again. For some reason, he had had the dream three or four times in the past few weeks. It had left him tense and apprehensive about going to sleep at all, not to mention exhausted. Whatever had brought on this bout of nightmares—and she hoped it didn't have anything to do with her injury—she could only pray it would pass soon.

She hadn't pursued the matter of their lovemaking. Her sexual desire seemed to have deserted her for the moment. In general, she thought, it was as if she wanted everybody to back off and leave her alone. Even J. P. had commented on it just before he dozed off after his stomachache. As she stroked his forehead, he murmured that it was nice of her to sit with him because he had hardly seen her lately.

Go ahead, stick that knife right through my heart, she told him silently now as she reached for her washcloth. Kids knew how to get to you like nobody else. They press that guilt button and stand back to watch you self-destruct. Just the suggestion of *bad mother,* and you would do anything to gain their forgiveness.

But she was tired of being a mother. The thought shocked her. She would never have dreamed she could feel such a thing. Or maybe she was just tired of not having anything for herself. I really *want* to skate, she thought.

"I wanna, I wanna, I wanna," she said rapidly, imitating Lisa's way of insisting on doing something when she was little. "So there," she proclaimed like a petulant child. She smiled to herself.

As she stepped out of the shower, she heard the telephone ringing. Peter wouldn't get it; he never picked up the phone during his working hours. She grabbed a towel and hurried into the bedroom, leaving wet footprints on the carpet.

"Hello?"

"You there? I almost hung up." It was her sister, Nicole.

"I'm here. What's doing?" Kip asked.

"You sound like you're in a rush." Nicole's tone indicated that she wanted to know where Kip was rushing to.

Kip felt water trailing in wide rivulets from her hair down her back. She bent over and quickly wrapped the bath towel into a turban around her head before she straightened up and answered. "No, only sort of. I have stuff to do, that's all."

"Oh," her sister said, disappointed. "I wanted to know if you and Peter could have dinner on Saturday night with us. Larry's parents are sleeping over, and they agreed to baby-sit."

"This Saturday?" Kip tried to remember if they had anything planned. "Um, wait, we're having dinner with the Deans."

"That bitchy Carol Dean and her midget husband?" Nicole asked.

Standing there without a towel around her body, Kip was wet and freezing. But she couldn't help responding. "I don't know why you think she's bitchy. She's really very nice."

"Oh, please," Nicole retorted. "She's so full of herself, with her house on Nantucket."

"It's not actually a crime to have a house on Nantucket," Kip said. "She doesn't discuss it unless the subject comes up."

"Maybe, but somehow she always manages to bring it up with me."

Kip sighed. "If you'd like, you and Larry are welcome to join us for dinner. We're going to Andolie's at eight."

"Andolie's?" Nicole gave a small laugh. "That place is way too expensive for us, you know that."

"Then we'll change the restaurant," Kip suggested patiently. "That's no big deal."

"And let the Deans know we can't afford to run with your crowd?" Nicole retorted. "I don't think so."

"I wish you didn't feel that way," Kip said, both saddened and annoyed by her sister's analysis of the situation. "They won't be thinking that."

Nicole's tone was sarcastic. "Not much. Nothing gets by those two." There was a pause. "Well, don't let me keep you."

Normally, Kip would have tried to salvage the conversation. But she was wet and cold, as well as disgusted with her sister's attitude. "I'll call you later if I can. If not, tomorrow."

"Whatever," Nicole responded airily.

"Bye." Kip hung up the phone, disgust escalating into anger at the way Nicole had managed to make it seem she had been slighted somehow. What the hell did Nicole want her to do? Renounce her earthly goods and join a nunnery? It probably wouldn't even help. Her sister would just resent the fine quality of Kip's wimple and the tailoring of her habit.

She laughed at the thought as she went back into the bathroom to finish drying off.

Kip folded the dish towel and placed it on the counter. Glancing at the clock, she saw it was almost ten-thirty. Just two hours after the birthday party, and everything was washed and put away. It had been a long day, the guests arriving around two o'clock and staying until after eight. But it was worth it. Everyone seemed to have a good time. Most important, Peter had looked happy, and more relaxed than she had seen him appear in a while. He moved among their friends with a wide smile, chatting, drinking a little too much, talking to everybody. He and J. P. had blown out the candles on the cake together, and then Peter had turned to hug Kip with a delighted smile. She was glad. In the past few days, something had definitely seemed off about him. He was distant, more preoccupied than usual. He just didn't look happy. Today, he had brightened up, at least for a few hours. Maybe his down mood was about turning forty-nine. He hadn't said much about it, but perhaps it was bothering him more than he let on. They used to laugh about the thirteen years' difference between them, but the subject rarely came up anymore. She wondered if he didn't feel he could discuss it with her because, at thirty-six, she was so far away from it.

Whatever was bothering him, at least he had a few hours' respite from it today. But even that had been ruined for him when he realized that his daughter wasn't going to be there to wish him a happy birthday.

Kip rubbed her back, aching from the long day. Her leg was throbbing, but she had accomplished her goal, which was to appear to be completely recovered. Everyone there had heaped praise on her, marveling at how well she looked, and that she had hosted a party so soon after something so terrible. She left the kitchen and went upstairs, anxious to take some aspirin for the pain. Still, it wasn't her leg that concerned her. Maybe she'd just have a stroke from being so angry, she thought, and then she wouldn't have to deal with this.

Lisa had done a lot of selfish things in the past year. But not showing up for her father's birthday party was something Kip would never have believed the girl capable of. At first, Kip figured she was simply late in getting home from her friend Olivia's house, where she had spent the night. She was already in trouble about that. Lisa had claimed they were going to hang out for the evening, maybe rent a video. At around nine, some girl whose name Kip didn't recognize called the house, asking for Lisa. Kip said she wasn't there, and the girl apologized, saying she had just talked to Lisa on the phone, and assumed she was calling from home. She had forgotten to ask Lisa what time they were meeting. When Kip began to question her, the girl realized her mistake and clammed up. Kip called Olivia's mother, who was aware the girls had just gone out to a party, but had no idea where and didn't seem the least concerned.

Lisa knew perfectly well she wasn't allowed to go to a party without clearing it with her parents and letting them know the whats and wheres. But Kip couldn't exactly cruise around in her car looking for a party so she could go in and drag her fifteen-year-old screaming out the door.

It didn't end there, though. This morning she had telephoned Olivia's, only to be told the girls had left already. Maybe Lisa had gotten a lift to swim practice, Kip thought. But she should have come home first. When it got close to noon, Kip began to get nervous. What if something had happened to her daughter? She called Olivia's mother once more, who reported that the girls had been back briefly, but left again. Yes, she had given Lisa the message to call her mother immediately.

Kip was furious. When two o'clock arrived and the party began, she kept one eye on the front door, expecting to see Lisa walk in at any second. As the hours passed, she was almost numb with anger and disbelief. Peter asked where she was a few times, and Kip indicated that she was delayed but would no doubt be there soon. By the end of the party, she could see the hurt in his eyes as he glanced over at the door. He never said a word about it, going upstairs after helping to clear the dishes and thanking her for making him such a nice party.

Kip looked in on J. P., who was snoring lightly in his sleep. She went over to his bed, straightening the covers. She bent down to push his hair off his face and give him a kiss on the cheek, not wanting to disturb him, but unable to resist. Then she went into her bedroom. Peter was in bed reading a book, his head propped up by several pillows. She went to sit near him. He looked up, and they smiled at each other. He closed the book, setting it on the night table.

"How're you doing, birthday boy?" she asked.

He reached out to take her hand. "I've been waiting for you."

She leaned over to him. They kissed gently at first. She put her hand on his cheek, feeling the stubble of his beard after the day. His arms came around her and his mouth pressed more forcefully against hers. Their lips opened, their tongues exploring. Kip loved the familiar feeling of kissing him, his wonderful smell, the excitement she felt in her stomach as he moved to pull her to him on the bed and then rolled them both over so he was above her.

Slowly, he unbuttoned her sweater, then slid it off her and dropped it over the side of the bed. He moved his mouth along her bare shoulder, his hands caressing her arms, her breasts, her stomach. Reaching underneath her, he unhooked her bra with a quick motion and slipped it off. His mouth moved to her breasts. She buried her hands in his hair, pulling him to her, her aches and pains forgotten. Desire, absent for weeks, suddenly flooded through her.

Peter was wearing only a pair of flannel boxer shorts, and she ran her hands along his bare back, loving the smooth firmness. As he brought his face back up to hers, he kicked his shorts off. They both quickly took off the rest of her clothes and pressed their naked bodies together, relishing the familiar excitement. Her hands roamed everywhere, along his tightly muscled thighs, his stomach, the curve of his buttocks. He was the only man she could ever want this way, she thought as his fingers found her center and he stroked her, causing her to groan with pleasure. When she reached to take his penis in her hand, he rolled over, still clutching her to him. From above, she guided him inside her. He pulled her down to him, their movements urgent. Deeper and deeper he thrust until she felt herself being carried away as if in a giant wave, and she cried out.

Her body still shuddering, she heard him call her name and felt him climaxing beneath her. She lay down, clutching him to her as he spasmed. When it was over, they lay there catching their breath. She snuggled up against him and he put an arm around her.

"Oh, Kip, I love you so," he said fervently as he reached to stroke her cheek.

She was slightly taken aback. There was something odd beneath the declaration, a sort of need she wasn't used to hearing from him.

"I love you, too," she whispered, kissing his shoulder.

They lay there, and in a few minutes she heard the slow, even breathing of his sleep. She was growing uncomfortable, so she gently eased herself away from him and moved onto her stomach, closing her eyes and waiting to fall asleep.

Then she heard it, the front door opening and the sound of someone entering the house. The footsteps on the stairs, especially quiet so as not to wake anyone, unmistakably Lisa's. Kip looked over at the clock radio—

11:30. And tomorrow was a school day. The door to Lisa's room was shut quietly and only the desk lamp turned on, sending a weak shaft of light into the hallway from beneath the door.

Kip was about to get up, but something stopped her. The two of them might get into a screaming match, which could wake Peter and J. P., and keep everyone up even later. And, frankly, she was sick of being angry at Lisa. She didn't think she was up to another face-off. Besides, she was lying peacefully next to her sleeping husband, which was a feeling she didn't particularly want to destroy. She wasn't going to let Lisa ruin absolutely everything about the day. Kip told herself she would go to sleep now and kill her daughter in the morning.

Having resolved to do nothing until dawn, Kip rearranged her pillow and settled her head back onto it. The only problem, she realized, was that now she was wide awake. She could hear Lisa moving around, getting ready for bed. The water was running in her bathroom; then the toilet flushed. The light clicked off. Kip lay there, envisioning a beach with palm trees swaying in the breeze, counting backward from one hundred, trying every trick she could think of. Nothing.

After what felt like several years, she got up, threw on a robe, and went downstairs. Her eyes hurt momentarily at the brightness as she switched on the kitchen light. Her feet were cold; she wished she'd remembered her slippers. She pulled open the refrigerator door then shut it. Now that she was down here, she didn't know what to do with herself. Moving over to one of the windows, she stared outside. The moon lit up the backyard. She leaned against the wall, looking out at the swimming pool, covered for the winter, and the lawn and trees beyond it.

Abruptly, she turned and went over to the cabinet where she kept the telephone books. There was a stack of them for towns and cities around the state. She pulled them all out. She still remembered the names, but not the phone numbers. There was one place to order the blades, another to get them sharpened, and a place to go for the custom-made boots. She put the heavy books on the kitchen table, grabbed a pad and pen from a drawer, and sat down. Picking up the Manhattan yellow pages first, she flipped through until she found what she wanted: SKATING EQUIPMENT AND SUPPLIES. Taking a deep breath, she began to read.

11

"How about a Summer Spiritual Makeover?" Missy Caulding, the executive editor of *Metropolitan Woman*, wore an enormous gold tiger pin on the shoulder of her navy blue suit jacket, which, along with her authoritative tone of voice, threatened to gobble up anyone in the conference room who dared to disagree with her. "You know, like *you are us, we are you*. Or, *everywhere you go, there you are*."

For over an hour, Eloise's editorial staff had been trying to come up with a theme for the June issue, but none of the ideas had raised much enthusiasm. Nor, it seemed, did Missy's.

"How about *everywhere you sit, there's your ass*?" offered Priscilla Seidner, the fashion editor.

Several of the women laughed, but Missy shot her a look of disdain. "I don't see you coming up with anything."

Eloise usually chose to let her editors fight things out themselves, and this time was no exception. In fact, she had little affinity for New Age themes, but contemptuous remarks didn't move a creative meeting forward. Nor had she herself come up with anything especially original. After so many years of running the magazine, it was hard to find new concepts.

Every year had a summer, a winter, a spring, and a fall—how many ways were there to highlight that fact in one glossy magazine? She felt as if she'd done everything there was to do. Summer fashion, summer fun, summer blues, summer reading, summer sports, summer concerts, summer colors. Besides, for God's sake, it was still January. Dirty, slushy snow covered the New York sidewalks. In fact, even the concept of summer seemed unimaginable.

Frustrated, she reached for a handful of M&M's from the large bowl that her assistant had left in the middle of the conference table.

"How about Summer Weight Loss?" Anne Latham's southern drawl came from the far end of the table.

Eloise withdrew her hand from the bowl of candy. "Thanks, Anne."

Anne's face reddened. "Oh, I didn't mean—" She colored even more darkly. "I would never—"

Eloise started to laugh. "I'm not insulted. In fact, I'm glad you said it." She turned her head toward the door. "Kara," she yelled.

Her assistant hurried into the room. "Yes?"

"Thank you for the candy. Now, please, take it away and never let it into my sight again." Eloise looked around the table. "If I say this to everyone at once, maybe it will help. I'm going on a diet. Don't feed me, don't encourage me to cheat, don't offer me cookies or doughnuts, okay?"

Most of the women in the room nodded, but Eloise noticed the doubt in Dee Johnson's eyes. Eloise knew what she was thinking. "That's right, Dee. I won't be buying Girl Scout cookies from Morgan and Courtney, nor will I be ordering any of the chocolates from their school drive. I'm happy to contribute as much money as your daughters want to raise, but, please, please, please keep the fattening stuff out of my office."

"Sure, Eloise," the art director answered. "You can go wild on the gift wrapping they're selling. Besides, the cookies won't be on sale again until next November."

"No," Eloise said. "I don't mean this only for now. No more sweets. Not ever. Now, can we get back to summer?"

Missy Caulding spoke once again. "How about this? . . . We go to eight or ten celebrities and they tell us the hottest summer night they ever experienced. Hottest, sexiest stories. Hottest summer fashion. What's hot and sexy and what's not in people and vacation spots and books and movies."

Eloise pictured Missy's suggestion in her mind. She liked the idea, she decided. Slightly edgy, maybe a little mean, but interesting. The kind of issue that people read all the way through and then talked about afterward. "What do the rest of you think?" she asked.

The response ranged from mildly receptive to genuinely enthusiastic, the only exception being Priscilla Seidner, who wouldn't have greenlighted an idea from Missy if it had included the discovery of electricity.

"Let's come up with some specifics and talk again around four." Eloise stood, a signal to her staff to leave her alone.

Dee was the last one to gather up her papers. "You want to grab some lunch?" she asked.

Eloise smiled at her. Of all the people she worked with, Dee was the only one who qualified as a real friend. The two had worked together for almost ten years. In fact, Eloise had brought Dee along with her when she'd been put in charge of *Metropolitan Woman*. Eloise couldn't imagine doing the magazine without her. It had been Dee who'd given it the look that had helped to raise circulation by almost 40 percent since they'd started together. And Eloise had always supported Dee with her complicated home life. Dee had gotten six months' leave when each of her daughters had been born, and she worked at home one or two days a week since, no questions asked.

"Thanks, I'd love to, but I think I've inspired myself. I'm going to the gym."

"Want company?" Dee offered.

Since Bentley Enterprises paid for half of any employee's gym membership if they went at least one hundred times in a year, almost everyone who worked with Eloise

belonged to the overpriced but luxurious Western Fitness
Club, located in the basement of the Bentley building.
Bentley employees who didn't take adavantage of the
gym membership sometimes complained that as much
policy was decided in the basement as in the boardrooms
upstairs. That had never been a problem for the *Metropolitan Woman* staff, since Eloise had visited the gym
exactly once since she'd become editor-in-chief, but it
was occasionally true for some of the other divisions.
Her brother, George, who worked in Corporate with her
father, was known to schedule business meetings in the
steam room from time to time.

Whatever the downside, most of the people in the
Bentley Building looked great as a result of the propin-
quity to the gym. Eloise took in Dee's trim figure. At
forty-five, with two children and a stressful job, Dee had
the body of a teenager. As close as they were, Eloise
could occasionally see signs of strain in Dee's eyes, or
notice the smile lines at the corners of her mouth harden-
ing into permanence. But, from the neck down, Dee
looked like a ninth-grader. That's all I need, Eloise
thought, evisioning her entry into a space filled with peo
ple who looked like Linda Evangelista on their worst
day.

"I think I'm better off on my own," Eloise responded,
"but thanks. Next time, maybe."

"Go slowly at first, okay?" Dee said. "You don't want
to hurt yourself."

"Oh, I have a scientific plan."

Dee gave her a patient smile.

"No, really," Eloise said. "Twenty minutes on the
treadmill at a moderate speed. Then sit-ups. That'll be
it for day one."

"It's a good plan." Dee squeezed her hand.

Buoyed by her friend's encouragement, Eloise collected her hairbrush and makeup bag from her purse,
locked the purse in the top drawer of her desk, taking
only a few dollars and stuffing them into the makeup
bag, and made her way to the elevator. God knows, this

is easy enough to do, she thought as she pushed the button marked B and traveled twenty-two stories down.

The entrance to the gym was subtly marked. As Eloise observed two young women coming from inside, she felt a stab of fear. That's absurd, she thought, squaring her shoulders and walking briskly through the entrance to the women's changing area.

Part of what made the Western Fitness Club so desirable was that they gave members fresh workout clothing. Eloise only had to have her running shoes with her. Everything else, from a T-shirt and shorts to shampoo and a hair dryer, was available from the gym. She went toward the pass-through window in the rear of the locker room, where an attendant distributed the gym clothes. The woman working that day was well into her sixties, neither stylish nor slim, which somehow made Eloise feel better about being there.

That emotion faded as she got undressed. There were several women changing near her. One was a teenager, the rest in their thirties or forties. But each of them was lean and fit. Eloise forced her eyes downward as she exchanged her regular bra for a running bra, and put on the tight-fitting gray cotton shorts and extra large gray cotton T-shirt. She tried to hold her stomach in as she walked across the floor toward the large workout area where the treadmills were located, but no matter how erect her posture, or how much breath control she was exerting, she knew she looked like an elephant compared to the other people who were working on the various machines.

A blond, muscular young man wearing a badge pinned to his T-shirt identifying him as a WESTERN PROFESSIONAL TRAINER stopped her as she approached an empty treadmill.

"Do you have your schedule?" he asked.

She hesitated. She knew that Western offered members several sessions of personal training as part of their package, but the notion of working with another person made her feel even less secure. "I'd rather be on my own for a while, if that's all right," she answered.

"I'll be here if you need me," the young man responded, his politeness making her feel even more ungainly.

Eloise stepped onto the treadmill. It was one in a line of at least fifteen of them, directly in front of a mirrored wall. All but two or three were in use. A number of people were walking very quickly. Most were running, sweat pouring down their faces. All she needed to do was turn the thing on and do her best, she told herself, turning her eyes from the athletes all around her. She looked at the instructions on the panel in front of her. It might as well have been written in Rumanian. She couldn't figure out which button to push without getting into some preset program that might be akin to climbing Everest. Her consternation must have shown, since the trainer who'd approached her earlier suddenly appeared at the side of the machine.

"How about if I get this guy turned on for you?" he said, reaching across to the button marked START and then moving his fingers to the speed buttons.

"I appreciate it," Eloise said, though, in fact, she felt humiliated. She was certain everyone in the room was watching her, laughing at her, or, worse yet, feeling sorry for her. Why did she have to do this at the office? She should have started by walking on the city streets, preferably with sunglasses and a woolen hat pulled over her face. No one would have known who she was.

As the machine started up and the rubber tread began to move beneath her feet, Eloise tried to get into the rhythm, but her eyes kept returning to the reflection in the mirror of the soft flesh of her stomach and her upper arms. She could swear that everyone at the gym must be laughing as her Santa Claus belly ho-ho-hoed itself in time to the treadmill. You're being narcissistic and crazy, she thought. People have more to think about than you. Even *you* have more to think about than you. Twenty

minutes and that will be the start of . . . Of what? she
thought. Of love? Sure. Of happiness? Give me a break.
Her legs were beginning to ache. Wondering if it was
nearly time to get off the machine, she checked the time
elapsed. She was shocked to see that she had been on
the treadmill for only four minutes. Oh, shit, she thought,
another sixteen minutes.

Willing herself to stop the internal monologue, she
looked around. She could see the people in the weight
room next door, separated only by a glass wall. Maybe
if she looked at others instead of focusing on herself, she
could get the damn twenty minutes over with and get
back upstairs, where at least she knew what she was
doing.

She noticed something interesting. There was her brother,
George, lifting what looked to be about a million-pound
dumbbell. She'd known her brother kept in shape, but
she'd had no idea how fit he evidently was.

She watched him more closely, taking in the smile on
his face as he put down the weight in front of him. He
was laughing and talking with the trainer who was guid-
ing him. It was the same young man who'd helped her
turn on the treadmill. The two of them were engaged in
what must have been a fascinating conversation. Even at
his most relaxed, George's expression was generally
more sardonic than openly friendly, but watching him
this way revealed a side of him she rarely saw. There
was an easiness to him as he talked to the boy, a friendly,
bantering posture that was so different from the responsible, almost uptight businessman she'd gotten used to
dealing with in the last few years.

Suddenly, she became uncomfortable. Then the truth
struck her with a force that almost rocked her off the
treadmill. George wasn't just talking to the trainer or
taking instruction from him. He was *flirting*. In fact,
she thought, as she looked once again, they were flirting
with each other.

It wasn't that she was completely shocked. She'd always suspected that her brother would have preferred

men. In fact, she'd heard stories about George when he'd been an undergraduate at Harvard. Tales of sexual escapades that never included women. She hadn't cared especially, outside of hoping he made a practice of safe sex. When he'd married Bettina, she'd been honestly surprised. But, she had to admit, also relieved. Maybe the rumors hadn't been true. But even then, she'd worried that he'd married only to please their father. She knew neither of her parents could accept having a homosexual son.

She thought about how unhappy Bettina had seemed for the past couple of years. If her brother really was gay, that could certainly go far in explaining it. Oh, George, she thought, please let me be wrong. Please be happy and uncomplicated.

Her eyes fell again on the mirror in front of the treadmill, reflecting the huge mass of moving flesh that was herself. Oh, yeah, she thought, like the rest of the world is so uncomplicated. Disgusted, she located the STOP button and turned off the machine, doing her best not to see the elapsed time. It would be nice to pretend it had been twenty minutes, but she knew it must have been closer to eight or nine.

Without looking back toward the weight room, and avoiding the eyes of the people on the other machines, she scurried to the locker room. As she gathered up her clothing from the attendant, she checked her watch. It was only one-thirty. She didn't have a meeting until two-fifteen. Plenty of time for a burger and a milkshake if she hurried through her shower.

12

Eloise wiped at her mouth with the white linen napkin. Although she'd finished the bread pudding ten minutes before and checked for crumbs several times since, she didn't quite believe that Nora and Kip wouldn't know what she'd done. When she'd made the conference call from her office to ask them to lunch, she'd suggested going to Sarabeth's; the restaurant was just blocks from Nora's apartment, where she had been working that morning. Nora had been grateful. *"So considerate of you, so thoughtful about how little time I have before I have to show the stuff to Will Stanley,"* et cetera.

It was miles from Eloise's office and not especially convenient for Kip either. Eloise had felt almost noble—until she actually arrived at the restaurant. She'd rushed out of a meeting and gotten there fifteen minutes early, which was very unusual for her. When she took a seat on the banquette at the front of the restaurant, facing the windowed displays of Sarabeth's homemade desserts, she suddenly understood the real reason she'd selected it. The fact was, Sarabeth's had the most incredible desserts on the Upper West Side of Manhattan, and Eloise was hungering for the berry bread pudding. There was no way she was going to eat it in front of her friends, and she'd gotten there so very early. . . .

Oh, damn, she suddenly thought. What if the waitress says something about my having dessert before the meal? Should she call the young woman over and beg her not to open her mouth? Miserable, she sighed. It was so undignified. In fact, everything about her weight problem was undignified. But this was a new low. She felt humiliated, as if she'd shoplifted from a department store or cheated off another kid's paper in the seventh grade.

But that was the whole point of this lunch. If she was going to fail at this weight loss thing, she might as well do it with some kind of honor. She was going to come clean about her defeat. She wasn't going to pretend.

Oh, yes, the little voice in her mocked her. That's why you came early to sneak in the pudding.

The waitress approached her with a pot of coffee in her hand, offering a refill. Eloise debated saying something to her, but didn't have a chance as Kip and Nora were right behind her.

"Thank goodness Nora rescued me," Kip exclaimed, kissing Eloise on the cheek before sitting down beside her on the banquette. "I'd been driving around looking for a parking place for almost half an hour. Then, I saw her in front of Zabar's, and, like magic, a spot materialized down the block."

Nora sat across from them. "And Kip rescued me from being the only one to be half an hour late. I'm really sorry. I've been so caught up trying to put the DAT together."

"What's a DAT?" Kip asked.

"It's the kind of tape you use when you put music together. It means digital audiotape. Nothing fancy, and not very interesting."

"Of course it's interesting," Eloise said enthusiastically. "Tell us what music you've found so far."

"Well, I've spent a zillion hours in the Lincoln Center Library, listening to all this wonderful gospel stuff, and I have other things I'd like to add—that is, if this Stanley guy lets me. I think the mix would make it stronger."

"Tell us about the gospel groups. I know so little about that." Eloise was sitting forward, her fullest attention displayed.

Nora gave her a long look. "Why is it you sound a little too interested?"

"Don't be a brat, Nora," Kip said, tucking her napkin into her lap.

Eloise didn't share her opinion. She knew that Nora was on to her. Nora couldn't possibly know what it was she had to say, but she had obviously picked up on the fact that she wasn't quite ready to say it.

"So, do you ladies know what else you'd like today?" The waitress had returned.

Eloise's heart sank at the word *else,* but the other two didn't seem to notice. "I'll have the soup and the smoked trout, please," she said, praying the young woman would keep silent.

"Shall I give you the soup for dessert?" the waitress asked, smirking.

Nora and Kip looked mystified, but Eloise wasn't about to explain. After twin orders for a small green salad and chicken breast, the waitress left the table. Then, Nora leaned across to Eloise.

"Okay, what's going on?"

Eloise wanted to just come out with it, but she found she couldn't. There they were, Kip and Nora. Both of them smart and beautiful and undoubtedly doing exactly as they'd promised. Eloise couldn't stand looking like such a fool.

She sat there quietly, hoping a wave would come up from Amsterdam Avenue and swallow up the restaurant.

"Well, *I* have something to say," Kip declared unexpectedly.

Both women turned to her.

"I can't do it." Kip's shoulders sagged. "I can't skate. I can't perform. I'm an abject failure."

Nora bit her lip, then she, too, spoke up. "And there seems to be no way in hell I'm going to get in touch with Alex Fenichel. My assistant found a number for him ages ago, and every day I stare at the phone, but I can't get my fingers to dial."

Eloise began to laugh. "Well, girls, that makes three

of us." She took a long breath. "Do you know why I called you guys to lunch?"

"Our sparkling company?" Nora asked.

"Yes. That, and the fact that I had dessert before you arrived. Not to mention the two corn muffins I had for breakfast and the Big Mac I scarfed down on my way home last night."

"Ah," Nora said, "the mystery is solved. So gospel music may not be that fascinating after all."

"Gospel music is wonderful to listen to," Eloise said, "but the only organ currently working in my body seems to be my mouth. My ears will just have to wait their turn."

Nora turned to Kip. "And you, little missy. What seems to be raining on your parade?"

Kip waited to respond until the waitress laid their appetizers in front of them. She picked at a lettuce leaf as she spoke. "I don't know. I've lost all the natural motion you have when you're a kid. And practicing is agony. I used to love being around other skaters. They would inspire me. The sounds of the coaches and the onlookers, even at practice. Now, the only sound I hear is my butt falling on the ice." She put the lettuce in her mouth and chewed slowly. "Skating used to feel, well, inspirational. I would glide around feeling attached to, I don't know, some kind of God or something. Now, I just feel like a middle-aged klutz."

"That's insane," Eloise answered. "First of all, you're not middle-aged. I'm older than you are, and I don't even think of myself that way." Her voice became urgent. "Besides, it's not *winning* some championship that's going to make a difference in your life. It's the *trying* that matters. And who said that skating would come back so easily? You have to work at it."

"You mean, the way you worked at the Big Mac?" Nora interjected.

Eloise glared at her. "Unlike the Vassar graduate who doesn't know how to dial. You're a fine one to talk."

Kip laughed. "We are a pathetic crew, aren't we?"

The other women nodded.

"This is crazy," Kip continued. "The three of us could easily have died, yet here we are, unable to exert the slightest measure of willpower." She looked at Eloise. "You know what? You're absolutely right. It *is* a matter of trying."

"And maybe something more than that," Eloise said. "If I could just lose a lot of weight, well, I would have done it years ago. I need help." She faced Nora. "And so, obviously, do you."

"And me, too," Kip added. "So, how are we going to do this?"

There was a small smile on Nora's face as the three of them considered the question.

"What are you thinking?" Eloise asked.

"I think you're right about everything. That's what I think." She looked at Eloise. "How about if I help you exercise? We only live across the park from each other. I could run with you every morning."

"You would do that?" Eloise looked impressed.

"Hell, I run almost every morning anyway. Now I'll get to push someone else around. It'll make it more fun." She turned toward Kip. "And I may even have something that will help you."

"What?" Kip asked.

"I don't want to say. It may add up to nothing at all."

Eloise addressed Kip. "How about if I call you every morning, and Nora calls you every night? It won't make practice any easier, but we'll praise you to the skies. That can't be a bad thing."

"Yes, I'd like that very much."

"And," Eloise added, "just to be sure all three of us get inspiration, how about a conference call every week. I could do it from my office after I finish up, let's say Monday nights."

Nora nodded. "That works for me if it's not too early. I get caught up until at least eight or eight-thirty."

Kip turned to Eloise. "How about Monday nights at nine?"

"Good for me," Eloise answered.

"Me, as well," Nora said, lifting her water glass.

The other two followed suit. "To success!" Nora proclaimed.

"To trying!" Kip added.

"To berry bread pudding!" Eloise put in, as the other two laughed.

13

Kip walked over to where J. P. was sitting and refilled his cereal bowl with Mini-Wheats. "You have karate today, remember. Andrew Shane's mom will take you both after school."

"Yeah, I know. Can I have some more milk, please?" he asked.

Across the table from her brother, Lisa was skimming through a textbook as she ate. It was unusual for her to have breakfast with the rest of the family; on most weekday mornings, Kip dropped her off at the pool at six-thirty. But Lisa had an important math test that morning and had decided she would get up at her regular time of five-fifteen and use the hours before school to study instead. If she had given up practice to study, Kip knew she must be far behind in class. But Kip felt it best not to say anything about it. Her daughter knew full well she had to keep her grades up if she wanted to continue swimming.

Lisa took a bite of her whole wheat toast with peanut butter, the same breakfast she had eaten every morning since sixth grade. "Dad," she said, chewing, her eyes still on her book, "you didn't forget you're supposed to come talk to my class tomorrow, did you?"

Peter was tentatively putting his lips to a steaming cup of coffee. He paused, the expression on his face indicating that he had indeed forgotten. Lisa glared at him. He lowered the cup. "Right, of course. What time did they want me there?"

Lisa reached for her glass of orange juice. "I've told you fifty times. Ten o'clock. And bring some copies of your books. It would be kind of cool to show them."

He saluted. "I shall obey. At ten hours precisely, Captain."

"Yeah, sure," Lisa muttered. "We all know what that means. More like eleven."

Peter drew himself up in his seat. "Madam, you cut me to the quick."

Kip had finished adding milk to J. P.'s bowl and was putting away the container. "You know," she said as she shut the refrigerator door, "your father isn't the only one here who might have a topic to lecture about. Maybe I could come in and talk about skating. Now that I'm back doing it, I wouldn't mind. Tell them what's involved, give them a little behind-the-scenes stuff." She zipped J. P.'s lunch bag closed and went to put it inside his backpack, which lay on a low pine bench near the door. "If you want to make it more career-oriented stuff, I could explain how exhibitions and competitions work."

Lisa was staring at her with something near horror. "No thanks," she said emphatically.

Hurt, Kip folded her arms across her chest. "Why is that such a terrible idea? If your father can talk about writing, why can't I talk about being an athlete? They're both interesting career choices."

Lisa made a noise halfway between a laugh and a snort. "Come on, Mom, Daddy's a famous writer. You're a middle-aged mother practicing figure eights. It's, like, insane. I mean, I know you were once a big deal, but that was years and years ago." She made a face at a sudden realization. "I can imagine what the boys would think. I'd be embarrassed to death. Besides, it's not like any of them are exactly considering ice dancing as a career."

Kip felt as if she had been smacked across the face.

"You don't have to be so mean to Mom," J. P. said to his sister.

Lisa didn't wait for him to go on. "Stay out of it, little goody two-shoes. No one's talking to you."

"All right, that's enough," Peter interjected, his tone milder than Kip would have liked it to be.

Kip found her voice. "Lisa, not only was that a nasty little speech, but you're dead wrong. Skating has become big business, and well respected too. Just look at all the televis—"

"Hey, bring me Nancy Kerrigan or Michelle Kwan and we've got a deal." Lisa grabbed her textbook as she got up and strode out of the kitchen. "Tonya Harding would be even better," she added over her shoulder with a laugh.

Wounded, Kip shouted after her. "You didn't clear your dishes. And you're not supposed to read while we're all at the table."

No response. Kip looked at Peter.

He shrugged. "Just keep reminding yourself, she'll outgrow it."

"She'd better," Kip said. Looking at the time, she saw it was twenty after seven. "J. P., you're going to be late."

"Right." He stood up, deposited his bowl on the counter, then dashed to grab his backpack. As he slipped his arms through the straps, he moved closer to Kip. "Mom, I think the kids in my class would think you were neat. Really. Maybe Mrs. Shapiro would let you come in to talk to us."

Kip reached out to help him with the heavy backpack. "Thanks, sweetheart." She mustered up a smile as she stooped down to tie his sneaker laces, which were, as usual, trailing on the floor. "I welcome pity from all corners."

"It's not pity." He bent over to kiss her cheek and smiled. "I mean it. Bye."

Kip started to pull away, but then she held him still for another moment, staring at him with a slight frown. "What's different about you?"

He averted his face. "Nothing."

"Uh-oh." Kip's voice turned pleading. "Don't tell me you lost your biteplate again, please, *please*, don't tell me that."

J. P. looked at her, miserable. "It broke. Then I lost half of it."

Kip sighed. "Shall we get another one with a baseball on it, or something else this time?"

"Doesn't matter." He hung his head. "I'm really sorry, Mom."

Kip ran her hand along his shiny brown hair as she stood up. "What am I going to do with you? I'd like to stop loving you, but that's not possible. I'm stuck here, loving you to absolute pieces."

He grinned as he turned and ran out the side door to catch the school bus.

Kip picked up Lisa's plate and the childrens' rumpled napkins. "I could live without having to replace that biteplate every twelve minutes. But sometimes he's so sweet, I think he must be an alien in human form. It's as if he doesn't know how regular children behave."

Peter nodded, laughing. "Maybe he's on drugs."

"Perish the thought." Kip picked up the children's placemats with one hand and shook them out over the sink. "Although if he is on drugs, I wish he'd share some of them with Lisa."

Peter's smile faded. He picked up his coffee cup and turned to the copy of the *New York Times* at his elbow.

"What did I say?" Kip asked, surprised by his abrupt retreat. She turned on the faucet to rinse the dishes.

"Nothing." Peter flipped through the sections, deciding which one to read first. Kip watched him do this daily; he invariably chose the "Arts" section.

"Peter, come on." She turned off the water. "Give."

He sighed in exasperation. "It's just that the two of you never stop. You're always at each other."

Kip stared at him. "I beg your pardon? We're at *each other*? You mean, like we're equally responsible for things?"

"Well, not exactly. But, maybe. Some."

"I see." Kip could hear her tone turning shrill, but she couldn't help herself. "Our daughter is self-centered, self-important, and obnoxious. She is also, on occasion, downright cruel. I'm not clear about how offering to talk to her class constitutes baiting her."

Peter stood up, shoving his chair back and grabbing the newspaper. "Enough. I'm tired of listening to you two bicker all the time. I'm tired of being in the middle. I'm tired of watching poor J. P. trying to be a peacemaker. And do you realize how shamelessly you favor him? It's gone on far too long. Whatever it is between you and Lisa, work it out, damn it."

Kip watched his retreating back as he headed down the hall to his office. She was too surprised to do anything but stand there. Then, she went over to the counter and poured a cup of coffee into the World's Greatest Mom mug that J. P. had given her on Mother's Day several years before. She set it on the table and sat down. Barely aware of what she was doing, she used one hand to sweep the crumbs off Peter's place at the table into her other hand, cupped just below the level of the tabletop.

It wasn't *what* Peter said that bothered her. She didn't believe for one second that she was responsible for Lisa's adolescent monstrousness. And Peter wasn't about to change her mind on that.

What disturbed her was that he said anything at all about it. They rarely disagreed on how the children should be raised. For him to suggest she was at fault in such a major way didn't make sense. And it was totally out of character for him to bark at her and storm off like that. Peter rarely got annoyed or irritable. He generally said what he had to say and waited for a response. Kip always claimed that J. P. got his father's good nature, and then somehow doubled it. Worse, he had accused her of favoring. It wasn't a matter of *favoring* their son. It's just that it was possible to get along with him, to laugh with him, to still be a mother to him. Kip used to have the same kind of relationship with Lisa when she was little. Peter was perfectly aware of all that.

But today, he had been furious with her. Usually, it was only work-related problems that could get to him. He would get upset about something his editor said or did, or feel misunderstood by a reviewer on some major point. He would rant and rave while she listened, and then it would pass. She could understand it: he was a serious, well respected writer who needed to protect his art. But stuff with the children—no, she thought, that almost never made him lose his cool.

Still, she didn't believe she had deserved that little tongue-lashing. She gave a mental shrug as she sipped her coffee. There were too many other things on her mind to wonder about the deep, dark significance of his flight of temper. Going over to the refrigerator, she pulled out a package of chopped sirloin. Before she left the house, she would prepare a meatloaf and roasted potatoes. Making dinner at eight in the morning wasn't something she enjoyed, but her new schedule made it necessary. If a recipe couldn't be cooked ten hours in advance, her family no longer found it on their dinner plates.

She turned on the oven and started to chop an onion, her mind going back to Peter. Despite her efforts to ignore what had just happened, she was still troubled by it. If something was bothering her husband, she should make an attempt to find out what it was. But if she got behind on her schedule, she wouldn't get any decent skating in before gymnastics class. It was the first meeting of the class, which she had signed up to take twice a week, so she didn't want to miss it. She had joined a twice-weekly ballet class as well, which left her one weekday to work out with weights. Skaters needed both strength and flexibility; one without the other was useless. But making time for these classes, plus five days a week at the rink, was a challenge, to put it mildly. She had known it would be a problem, and it was.

Still, she was managing. Having the cleaning woman

come in four days a week helped keep the house under control. She had signed Lisa and J. P. up for a local van service started by a couple of Rhinebeck mothers who ferried children to after-school activities. Lisa complained bitterly about being the oldest one on the van, so Kip tried to arrange for rides as often as possible for her daughter. She had also compiled a complex chart of carpooling, trading off with other mothers to drop off or pick up at different sports. She had switched to a dry cleaners that picked up and delivered. With the help of her son, who knew far more about it than she did, she was able to order most of the groceries through the kids' computer, filling in at the supermarket once a week.

Kip finished preparing the meatloaf and put it into the oven to cook. It was an ongoing struggle to cope with the guilt she felt about not being there for J. P. every afternoon, as she had been in the past. She was also guilty about having to spend more time in the evening doing paperwork and making calls instead of being with her son; she no longer had time to get those things done during the day. Her attention was diverted further by having to elevate her leg so much after practicing at the rink, keeping moist heat on her aching muscles as she tried to relieve the frequent swelling in her ankle and knee. And even though Lisa barely looked at her, she was sorry she wasn't around more in case her daughter needed her or if she miraculously developed the urge to converse once in a while. Admit it, she said to herself, nothing is running the way it used to. She was moving as fast as she could, but things kept slipping between the cracks, whether it was permission slips that went unsigned, or J. P.'s missing that birthday party for a friend last week. Overwhelmed, she had even canceled her annual Valentine's Day party this year.

As she peeled potatoes, Kip thought about a tribe of people Peter had once described to her. She couldn't remember who they were or very much about them, but she did recall that they actually had no word in their language for *guilt*. That odd fact had stuck with her, but now she was genuinely intrigued by it. Hard as she tried, she couldn't seem to wrap her mind around the idea of not needing the word because no one felt the emotion. Not only did she need the word, but she needed it more and more often lately.

Hurriedly sprinkling olive oil and dried rosemary over the potatoes, she shoved them into the oven, and set a timer so she would remember to turn it off and refrigerate the food just before she left the house. Then she started up the stairs to change into her practice clothes. *"Tonya Harding would be even better,"* she mimicked Lisa in a singsong voice, exaggerating the disdain that had been so evident in her daughter's remark. Despite everything, she couldn't help but laugh.

The ringing of the cell phone startled Kip. She slowed the car down before reaching into the pocket built into the door where she stored the telephone. She had gotten the cell phone just a few months earlier for emergencies. Only Peter and the children had the number. She didn't see the need to have anyone else calling, and she tried to use it herself as little as possible. Cell phones were a pet peeve of hers. She couldn't stand the way people walked around with little black things clamped to one side of their heads, apparently lost in conversation but fully aware of how important they looked—or believed they looked. Hell, she thought, most of the time they were saying, "I'll be home in ten minutes" or "I'll be home in twenty minutes." As if their precise time of arrival was a matter of tremendous urgency. Of course, there might be additional, truly critical information added, such as "I'm at the shoe store, looking at the *most* adorable pair of sandals . . . and I'll be home in ten minutes."

She pulled the car over to the side of the road. Flipping the phone open with one hand, she put it to her ear, assuming it would be a wrong number.

"Hello?"

"Hi, darling."

"Mom? What are you doing calling me on this phone? I didn't even know you had the number."

"I asked Peter for it. I hope you don't mind."

"Of course not." Kip was happy to talk to her mother, realizing it had been nearly two weeks since their last conversation. "How are you and Dad?"

"We're fine, honey. Your father is out in the garage making a marionette for Jordan. He's getting such a kick out of it, planning how to surprise him."

Kip smiled. Her father had taken up woodworking since his retirement from accounting, and he genuinely enjoyed it, immersing himself in projects ranging from benches to figurines. Some of his work was quite good, although he seemed more interested in the artistic flourishes than in measuring and planning. Bob Pierson loved all his grandchildren, but for some unknown reason, he had a special rapport with Nicole's younger son, Jordan. The seven-year-old would doubtless get a huge charge out of a marionette made by Grandpa just for him.

"That's nice."

"Yes, but it isn't Jordan I wanted to talk to you about. That's why I'm calling now." Patricia Pierson hesitated. "I'm kind of worried about something."

"What's wrong?" Kip was growing concerned.

"It's about your sister. I don't feel right discussing this with you, but it's been on my mind."

"What?"

"She seems so unhappy. I don't like to meddle in her life. But I don't understand why she's always so angry, especially at you."

"About what?" Kip asked.

"Not about anything in particular. In a general sense. It's more like—" The older woman searched for the word she wanted. "—she *resents* you."

Kip let out a small laugh. "With all due respect, Mom, you're just figuring this out now?"

Patricia paused. "I guess I hoped you two would work things out somehow. But I can't keep ignoring it. You're sisters. This shouldn't be."

Kip shrugged, even though her mother couldn't see it. "I don't want it to be this way. But I don't see what I can do. She's the one who has to get over it."

"There's nothing between you that could have started this? Something that could be fixed?" Patricia asked.

Kip smiled. That was so like her mother. Patricia Piersen didn't overanalyze. She ignored trouble until the moment it could no longer be ignored. Then she tried to shove it out the door without further ado. The years-old antagonism that Nicole felt toward Kip was obvious to anyone who bothered to watch them together for five minutes, and the causes ran way too deep to be sorted out in a little let's-make-everything-okay-again session. But their mother must have been really troubled by it if she went so far as to make this call.

"Mom, if you have any ideas how to get that chip off Nicole's shoulder, I'm right there with you."

"I don't want Ethan and Jordan to be around that. It's not good for their sense of family," Patricia spoke as much to herself as to her daughter.

"Hey, I've got an idea," Kip said with a laugh. "Tell her the boys are allergic to anger, along with nuts and dairy. That ought to scare her."

"It's not necessary to be sarcastic, dear." It was evident from her tone that Patricia was frowning.

Kip was suddenly struck by the fact that she sounded like her own daughter. Patricia sounded the way Kip herself did these days. The thought rattled her.

"Listen, Mom, how about I call you later and we'll talk about this more?"

"Okay. Sorry to bother you. I know you're on your way to skating, Peter told me. I just couldn't help myself."

"Don't be silly. Any time," Kip said. "Bye."

She tucked the phone back in its hiding place and started up the car. That couldn't have been easy for her mother. She didn't like to meddle in anyone else's business, ever. It was a side of her that Kip had always admired. She never gossiped about people or looked beneath the surface kindnesses she was shown. She took people at face value, with no interest in discovering ulterior motives or hidden agenda.

Kip turned left and then made a quick right into the rink's parking lot. As she pulled into a spot, she couldn't help thinking that taking people at face value might have been easier for her mother than dealing with them in any genuine way. She didn't ask the deeper questions. If someone in her social circle was suffering behind a smile, it wouldn't be Patricia Pierson who discovered it. It went with her personality, Kip realized, when you really thought about it. Patricia was a caring, responsible mother who wanted the best for her children, but she was never especially demonstrative. And she never tried to delve too far into whatever might be bothering the three of them.

Still, she had been there for them in a different way. God knows, Kip reflected, getting out of her car, I have no reason to gripe about her. Patricia had made all the same sacrifices Kip was now making for Lisa's swimming—and far more—year in and year out. She had even taken in bookkeeping work at nights to help with Kip's expenses. Both her parents had struggled to pay the exorbitant costs that went along with training an aspiring skater. She wondered what Nicole and Dirk had gone without so that Kip could get new skates, or more coaching time, or dance lessons, or any of the million things she had needed. Dirk never seemed to notice things like that.

But Nicole . . . Kip was struck by the unfairness of it for Nicole. Not just the glory and attention Kip had stolen from her, but the unwilling sacrifices Nicole had to have made. Nicole hadn't taken any after-school lessons when they were growing up, although Kip could remember her sister being interested in acting and tap dancing, and a bunch of other things she could have pursued. She didn't get much to spend on clothes, either, while Kip brought home new skating outfits and blades and boots on a regular basis.

Kip retrieved her skates and gym bag from her trunk, still ruminating on her sister. Kip was always so busy being defensive, holding up an arm, as it were, to fend off Nicole's attacks, that she never stopped to see things from Nicole's point of view. She really has a damned good reason to be angry at me, doesn't she? Kip asked herself. She found a way to stand out, to be different from their very ordinary family, if one wanted to be honest about it. And she left Nicole behind without a second thought.

She pulled open the heavy door to the rink. So, now there was even more guilt for her to tussle with. She felt guilty about Peter being upset with her, and her not trying to set things right. She felt guilty about Lisa and J. P., just because she always felt guilty about them now. She even felt guilty about those women she roped into taking over for her on the PTA and school stuff, because she knew she was asking the ones like her, the ones who couldn't say no, which was a rotten trick. To top it off, she felt newly guilty about Nicole, someone who wasn't even on her mea culpa list a few minutes before.

She stepped inside the building, into the cold air. Almost instantly, she was absorbed by the sight of the ice skaters, the muffled boom of sounds and voices ricocheting off the high domed ceiling, and the smell of wet rubber and wool. The associations were so powerful, they drove everything else out of her thoughts. She was about to skate again—to fly. To return to the one place where she felt utterly at home and free.

She couldn't believe how much she had missed skating without even realizing it. It was magic. The sore muscles and bruising made it tough, and the exhaustion had her virtually collapsing into bed at night. Her newly healed ankle still hurt and swelled much of the time. But she had persevered, and she could see the improvement. True, it was as if she were starting all over again. Yet her body somehow remembered the basics, carrying her along, her heart pounding at the sheer joy of it. She had devoted hours to skating forward and backward, doing figures on the ice, turning in every conceivable way, forcing herself to start slowly. She had made additions with great restraint, one day adding the bunny hop, then the forward spiral. Today she was going to attempt some serious jumps. She was ready.

In the locker room, she put away her coat and slipped a skating skirt and a heavy sweater over the black leotard and tights she was already wearing. As she put on a pair of thin socks and laced up her skates, she reviewed the moves she was planning. She walked over to the rail, stopping to do some stretching and deep knee bends. Then she removed her skate guards, set them down, and stepped out onto the ice.

The whiteness was like a burst of sunshine surrounding her. She was reminded of a story she had read over and over to Lisa when she was little, about a girl who steps through her attic door into a magical world. That was how Kip felt when she put her blade down on the ice for the first time each day. She was stepping into her own private wonderland.

Gliding along, she looked down at her new skates, happy with the way they felt. It had taken all her courage to buy them. So many phone calls, checking out the best places to order custom-made boots. Then came the blades, and the right person to attach them to the boots and sharpen them properly. There was no point in doing it if she wasn't going to have the right equipment, the same quality she'd been used to. It was well worth it, she thought, as she did a lap of crossovers around the rink, her right leg gracefully curving in front of the left as she leaned in toward the center of the rink. Once she had the skates and new practice clothes, she had finally started to believe she was actually going to go through with it.

She skated for nearly thirty minutes, warming up her muscles, preparing herself. There was only a handful of people skating, so she had lots of space. At last it was time. She was going to start with the salchow. It required switching from forward skating to backward, pushing off her left foot, raising her arms to shoulder height and making a revolution in the air. She would have to land on her right foot, skating backward into the finish.

This was a jump she had performed hundreds of time, and for some reason she could never put her finger on, she liked it better than the other jumps. She took off across the ice, building up speed, her eyes on the spot in the center of the ice.

She turned to skate backward, then pushed off. She was up in the air, for one perfect moment gloriously turning, her arms outstretched, excitement coursing through her. But as she finished the turn, she could feel her balance shifting and knew she had lost control. Her blade wobbled as it touched down, and she fell to the right, smashing her elbow and knee on the ice. Pain shot through her as she slid. As soon as she was able, she struggled to get up. She had heard the gasps of the people watching as she went down, and she didn't want to see the sympathy in their eyes. Eyes downcast, she skated off the ice, the pain intense.

She sank onto a bench. What the hell was I thinking? she asked herself as she clutched her elbow. It had been way too soon to jump. She had succumbed to the most amateurish desire to move ahead when she wasn't ready. You're a hundred years old and coming off an injury, but you're going to do a flawlessly executed salchow, no problem, she berated herself.

She bent over to rub her knee. What bothered her wasn't that it had been too soon to jump. That may have been true. But she knew what that jump was supposed to feel like, every fraction of a second along the way. It had been all wrong from the start. She was light-years away from getting it right. Hell, she would never get it right. It had been too long. She was too old. Only a young girl could skate with the fearlessness necessary to be great.

How could she have thought she could do this? Tears of pain and misery spilled onto her cheeks. It was outlandish, just as Lisa had said, a middle-aged mother trying to recapture her days of youthful glory. She was pathetic, Kip thought. It was absolutely crazy, pretending she could be a real skater again. She could train and practice all she wanted. It was over for her.

She wiped her wet cheeks with a gloved hand, but the tears wouldn't stop coming. At long last, she had gotten back to the thing she cherished above everything else outside of her family. The sorrow she had felt in leaving it had been so great she hadn't permitted herself even to think about it in all these years. Then, she had let herself fall in love with skating all over again. It had been a mistake. She should never have permitted herself to stir up the old feelings.

She sat there, waiting for her tears to subside. Too dejected to limp back to the locker room, she rubbed her throbbing knee as she stared out over the ice. There weren't many skaters, but the majority of the ones there were concentrating on different moves, obviously training rather than skating recreationally. Kip's eyes were drawn to a girl of about twelve or so, wearing a sweater made out of rainbow-colored yarn with a matching muffler. As she skated closer, Kip could see that the sweater and muffler were hand-knit—and not by somebody who was particularly good at knitting. The girl had a delicate translucent complexion, but her eyes were hard with determination.

Kip stared after her as she circled the rink backward. No doubt her mother had made the sweater and scarf, trying to save money as skating ate up every extra dollar in the household. The family might be struggling, but this child was going to skate come hell or high water. So her parents were doing all they could. And the girl was wearing that sweater and scarf, loose ends, uneven stitches and all. Kip almost winced at the thought of what Lisa's reaction would be if Kip ever asked her to wear something that looked like that. But this girl was doing what it took. Kip could see the whole story right there in her face.

Why hadn't Kip's parents been angry when she gave

up skating to marry Peter? The question came to her with a start. It was one she had never asked herself before. Bob and Patricia had devoted so much to helping Kip realize her dream. Then she had dropped it as if the whole business had simply been an amusing diversion. Had they ever wondered how Kip could have been so thoughtless and selfish? Had she repaid their sacrifices with a slap in the face when she took off for Europe with Peter? She had never considered that it must have been a crushing disappointment to them. Yet they hadn't said a single word about it.

Now I'm a crushing disappointment to myself, she reflected. Here I am, vowing to skate, and failing.

She watched the girl pass by again, raising one leg out straight behind her as she bent forward, her arms extending out to the sides, that ferocious concentration still on her face. Kip felt as if she was right there with her, twelve years old and circling the rink in Utica where she practiced. Dedicated, undaunted by setbacks, all things still possible.

Kip stood. The pain in her elbow and knee was easing up. She bent and straightened both limbs several times. Then she went back onto the ice. No more jumps for her today. But no more giving up for her today, either.

14

Kip ran a brush through her hair. She felt disoriented, as if it were the middle of the night. It was hard for her to believe she had slept for two hours. She rarely napped in the afternoon, considering it a luxury reserved for vacations. She had come home from practice at five-thirty and gone straight to her bedroom to change into sweats, intending to do some paperwork for the next half hour. But as she was passing by the bed, she couldn't resist the opportunity to grab a few minutes of rest. She lay down and closed her eyes. The next time she opened them, it was eight o'clock.

Going downstairs, the sound of the television in the family room told her where the children could be found. Lisa and J. P. were seated on the floor beside the coffee table, where they had set up their dinner of waffles and Coke. They were watching a rerun of *Bewitched* as they ate.

"Hello, guys," she said, taking a seat on the couch.

Lisa didn't take her eyes off the screen or acknowledge that she had heard Kip.

"Hi, Mom," J. P. said, taking one of the tiny waffles and swirling it around in the pool of syrup on his plate. As he lifted the waffle to his mouth, syrup dripped onto his shirt. He chewed as he spoke. "You're finally up."

"You made yourself dinner, I see." Kip thought of what she had planned to serve them, the roasted chicken in the refrigerator, the cut-up broccoli in a bowl beside it.

He nodded. "We didn't want to wake you."

"That was nice of you." Kip was touched. She watched Lisa drain her can of soda. "I didn't mean to sleep, but thanks, both of you."

"No big deal," Lisa said, her eyes trained on the television.

"Where's Dad?"

"NYU," Lisa answered without turning around. "He left around six."

"Oh, right," Kip said. She had forgotten all about the literary symposium he was due to attend that night. "Did he eat?"

J. P. popped another soggy waffle into his mouth. "He had a sandwich. He said we should let you sleep."

"Well." She stood up. "You two seem to be taken care of. Homework all done?"

J. P. nodded. Lisa didn't respond.

Kip went into the kitchen and made herself scrambled eggs. She supposed she should be glad that they had worked things out so well. Everyone had had dinner, such as it was. No one seemed to be in a state of shock because Kip hadn't been there to serve a well-balanced meal. So why was she—yet again—consumed with guilt?

When the telephone rang, she was putting her dirty dishes in the dishwasher. Upstairs, Lisa answered it, and shouted down to Kip that it was for her. Kip considered asking her daughter to take a message, but then she grabbed the portable phone from its base on the counter.

"Hello?"

"Kip, are you there? It's Eloise."

"Eloise, hi. How are you?" Suddenly, Kip remembered. It must be nine o'clock. They had agreed to talk every Monday at nine. She couldn't believe she had actually forgotten. "Is Nora on the line?"

"I'm here," came Nora's voice.

"All present and accounted for," Eloise said. "So, what do we do now?"

"Did you have a good week?" Kip asked. "Did anybody do anything spectacular about their personal mission impossible?"

There was silence on the line.

"Nora?" Eloise asked. "Did you find Alex sorry-but-I-can't-remember-his-last-name? Have you set a wedding date yet?"

"Give me a break," Nora retorted. "And it's Fenichel."

No one said anything.

"Okay," Kip said, "how are we going to coax this out of one another?"

Eloise answered. "Kip, tell us something great you did this week. What was the best thing that happened?"

She considered the question. "I guess the best thing was that I skated for longer than usual today. I've had so many bad days—my leg is giving me so much damn trouble. Today was a little better. And I had a good time doing it. I didn't feel like it was a mistake to be out there. It made me happy, and I improved." She paused. "Now that I think about it, unlacing my skates when I was done was the best moment of the whole week."

"What was the worst moment of the whole week?" Nora asked.

Eloise jumped in before Kip could answer. "I thought we were supposed to be positive."

"No," Kip said, "no, it's a good question. Because, you know what? Skating for a longer time also led to my worst moment of the week. I was so exhausted that I came home and took a two-hour nap. I never saw my husband, who drove into New York for the evening, and I left my children to eat a dinner selected from the absolute top of the pyramid."

"Horrors," Nora exclaimed. "I'm calling the cops this instant."

"It may seem silly to you," Kip went on, "but I can't help feeling bad. My kids didn't sign on for this. I didn't even remember Peter was going someplace. It's hard for me not to be the mother who's in control of things. That's my world. So, now, one of you tell. What was your best moment, Eloise?"

She considered the question. "The perfect lemon sorbet at La Place. It tasted great and it had no fat."

"Do you want to tell a worst moment?" Kip asked.

"Take your choice. I missed going to the gym on Wednesday. The next issue of *Metropolitan Woman* is likely to be late. I took the name of the Lord in vain, and I had impure thoughts."

"Very funny," Nora said, "but you have to pick one."

"What do you mean?" Eloise asked. "Why do I have to pick one?"

"Those are the rules." Nora spoke with authority.

Kip laughed. "Since when are there rules?"

"Since right now," Nora answered.

"Okay, Boss Lady," Kip retorted. "So what were your best and worst moments this week?"

"Three-oh-one p.m. on Tuesday was my best moment, and five-thirteen on Thursday was my worst."

"Come on, Nora," Eloise insisted, "we did it. You have to do it too."

"Okay, okay. I chose to work late on Friday night instead of going on a date with some guy who asked me out for dinner. I got a lot of work done. I would classify that as my best moment. You two might think otherwise."

"Damn straight," Kip responded. "That's a worst moment if I ever heard one."

"I promise to do better next week," Nora said without sincerity.

Kip heard the sound of Peter's car pulling into the garage. "I hate to say it, but I really should get off the phone. My husband's back, and I've hardly seen him all week."

"That's fine. It's time I left the office anyway."

"Next week, ladies," Nora said. "And I swear I'll give you a best moment that'll knock your socks off."

"We can't wait," Eloise said.

Kip couldn't have explained why, but she felt an unexpected burst of optimism as they said their good-byes and she hung up the phone.

15

Eloise felt as if her heart were about to burst through her chest. Nora had picked her up in front of her building at six-thirty that morning where she stood waiting with Buster. There had hardly been a minute since that Eloise hadn't wished she were somewhere else. Anywhere else. Doing absolutely anything besides what Nora was making her do. To her left, Nora was running effortlessly, her breathing even, an attractive pink flush across her face. Buster scampered alongside them, delighted by this unusual departure from their morning ritual. There were hundreds of men and women jogging around the reservoir in Central Park, virtually every one of them trim, young, and having the time of their lives.

"Do you think . . . it's unattractive of me . . ."—Eloise was gasping for breath as she tried to get the words out—"to wish that everyone here would suddenly trip on a thousand hidden banana peels?"

"On the contrary," Nora answered, "it speaks well of you as an American. And when you start beating up babies and stealing from homeless people, we're going to award you Miss Congeniality."

"Damn," Eloise sputtered, slowing down to a walk, "I just can't keep this up. I really can't. It's killing me."

Nora slowed down as well. "It's not supposed to be torture. We don't have to run the whole time. In fact, it's better if you walk some and then run some. You'll see, it will get easier and easier as we do it. And after we're finished, I promise you'll feel fabulous."

"Yeah," Eloise said, still breathing heavily, "and I'm going to look like Audrey Hepburn."

Nora scowled. "Why would you want to look like someone else? You're beautiful. Surely I can't be the first person to say that to you."

Eloise shook her head. "I used to be pretty, I suppose, not that I ever felt it. But, now, in my elephant years, it's a little hard to conjure up the memory."

Nora stopped moving, making the runner behind them curse before overtaking them on the narrow track. "What in the world do you think you look like?"

Eloise flushed, but it wasn't the healthy glow from aerobic exercise. "I know exactly what I look like, and if you were being honest, you would know, too."

"Are you kidding?" Nora's voice displayed more anger than sympathy. "If Botticelli were around, you'd be his dream girl. Listen, Eloise, you're not gross and you're certainly not ugly. You're a beautiful woman who could stand to lose fifteen or twenty pounds."

Eloise began to walk once again. "Sweet of you, but one hundred pounds would be more like it."

"If you were a hundred pounds lighter," Nora replied, catching up to her, "you'd be dead. You know, I really like doing this with you, and I hope you lose a few pounds because it will make you feel better and be good for your health and all that crap. But you'd better get some grasp of who you are and how people really see you or all the weight loss in the world won't help."

Eloise looked up at the buildings towering over the park. She and Nora were approaching the east side entrance to the running path at Ninetieth Street, where many more runners were joining the early morning throng. She thought about what Nora had said. In fact, no one seemed to be looking at her, singling her out amid the sea of thin people. She scanned the newcomers. A large number of them were quite a bit older than she was. Now that she thought about it, many of them were just about as heavy. She looked down at the oversize navy blue sweatshirt and baggy sweatpants that she had put on to hide her body when she'd left the apartment an hour before. Actually, she realized, most of the joggers she saw were dressed exactly the same way.

Nora interrupted her reverie. "C'mon. Let's go around one more time, doing the same drill. Walk a few minutes, run a few minutes. By next week at the latest, it'll seem like a breeze."

Eloise lifted her eyes to take in the entire perimeter of the reservoir. "Maybe more like a tsunami than a breeze."

Nora increased her pace so the two of them were jogging at a slow, steady clip. "Let's concentrate on something more important. Tomorrow, you're going to a desert island. You're allowed to take one book with you. What book would you bring?"

"Oh, I don't know. *How to Build a Tent out of Sand,* maybe."

"Yeah, yeah. You can do better than that."

Eloise glared at her, but kept her pace up just the same. "I don't know. Maybe *Pride and Prejudice.* How about you?"

Nora sped up, but the change was so subtle it was hard to discern. "Oh, I guess *Ulysses.* The only way I'll ever get through it is to be somewhere there's absolutely nothing else to read. So, tomorrow, you're going to a desert island. You can take one movie star with you. Whom would you bring?"

Eloise considered the question. If Cary Grant were still alive, the answer would have been obvious. But a living actor? That was hard. Al Pacino? Russell Crowe? Why not Paul Newman at age twenty-five. After all, it wasn't actually going to happen. She could name anyone at all, no matter how impossible.

She knew that Nora was just trying to take her mind off what they were doing, but she found herself enjoying the distraction. She doubted that she'd ever really *like* running, but exercising with Nora was a vast improvement over doing it by herself. And it wasn't so bad to be outside, early in the morning, the sun shining, the air crisp and fresh.

"You start this time," she said to Nora, smiling for the first time that morning.

"Hmmm . . . ," Nora said, beginning a slower jog, "I've always been a sucker for Chow Yun-Fat."

Eloise looked at her knowingly. "Of course, you would choose someone a couple of continents away."

Nora slowed down to a walk. "You can't give me grief about this anymore. I'll have you know that I'm meeting Alex Fenichel tomorrow."

Eloise stared at her, clearly amazed. "How could you not tell me this until now? Were you *ever* going to tell me?"

"I suspect I would have gotten around to it eventually."

"Don't be annoying. This is *huge*. What did you say to him when you called? Was he thrilled to hear from you? Is he actually *single*? Are you excited?"

Nora started to laugh. "Yes, no, no, yes. Or no, no, no, no. Too many questions all at one time."

"Well, tell me any way you want, but *tell me*."

Nora started a slow trot. This time Eloise stayed right with her.

"First of all, I didn't exactly call him. Kelly, the girl who works for me, reached him and set up the date."

Eloise lifted an eyebrow. "Oh, really. Is *she* planning to marry Alex too?"

"Don't be smug. I would have called him myself once Kelly found the number, but she's just superefficient. And she had my calendar right there."

Eloise looked as if she weren't buying it.

"And, okay," Nora said, "I admit it. I'm nervous about it. I don't want to think about what to say until I'm actually there, in a room with the guy. After all, I haven't seen him in over a decade."

"So, where are you meeting him?"

"You won't believe this. He lives only a half hour or so from Rhinebeck. He was from Providence originally, but he teaches at Vassar."

"You're kidding. Our alma mater. What does he teach?"

"Probably something scientific. That's what he was interested in when I dated him. It's so funny. I never thought he'd go back to graduate school, let alone become a professor. Actually, I'm surprised he didn't start up a computer company or something."

"Well," Eloise said, noticing with great relief that they had made it around the reservoir for the second and final time, "I hope it goes really well. Will you call me when you get back from seeing him?"

"If it's not too late. I'm driving up to my sister's house tonight, then staying through my niece's birthday party tomorrow. I probably won't even get to see him until after seven. Then there's the long drive home."

Nora led Eloise off the track, stopping in the open space to stretch.

"He didn't want to come to the city?" Eloise asked, trying her best to imitate Nora's graceful movements.

"Listen, I wasn't the one who talked to him."

"But you must have told Kelly what to say," Eloise insisted.

"Hey, I promised the two of you I'd find him, and I've found him. I'm meeting him in a restaurant in Poughkeepsie, and . . ."

"—you can walk right out the door the minute he gets too close," Eloise finished the sentence.

Nora glared at her. "I assume your dedication to the letter and spirit of our agreement means that you'll be out here again tomorrow morning at six-thirty, despite my absence?"

"Not only that," Eloise retorted, "but when you call me to tell me you've fallen madly in love, I'll give you a calorie breakdown of every meal I had while you were doing it."

"Too much information," Nora responded, holding her

fingers crossed in front of her as if warding off the devil. "Show up here tomorrow morning and go around a couple of times. You can walk the whole thing if you want. Just do it, okay?" She gave Buster a pat on the head, then turned, heading toward her apartment on West End Avenue.

Eloise shouted after her. "How would you feel about calling me on my cell phone around six-fifteen, so you can talk me around the track?"

Nora began to run. "How would *you* feel about driving up to meet Alex and pretending you're me for the first few dates?" she yelled over her shoulder.

Eloise slogged slowly toward Fifth Avenue. An interesting question, she thought: pretend to be someone you in no way resemble, meet a man who's supposed to be the love of your life, but whom, in reality, you've never laid eyes on, and get said man to fall deeply in love with you and marry you; or, on the other hand, wake up tomorrow morning and run around the reservoir.

Why did the former proposition sound more doable than the latter, she wondered as she walked toward her building.

"Thank you, Seth," Tamara said as she removed the paper from one of the gifts on the pile. The wrapping paper tossed aside, she opened the box, pulling out a Magic 8 Ball. She shook it in her small hands and then turned it over, exclaiming, "This says I will have seven children."

The dark-haired girl seated next to her shook her head vigorously. "It can't say that. They never have stuff like that in a Magic Eight Ball."

Tamara answered her with dignity. "I asked it if I would have six children, and the ball said 'only one more time.' That means that instead of six, I'm gonna have seven."

Nora sat on the couch next to her sister. She noted a rare hint of wistfulness on Wendy's face.

"What's the matter?" Nora whispered.

Wendy shrugged her shoulders. "Nothing, really. It's just that she seems so old suddenly."

It was true, Nora thought. Tamara had been acting different all day. Being nice to the other kids, instead of taking part in the occasional fights that broke out, waiting for the others to get their pizza instead of attacking hers immediately. Even saying a polite thank you as she opened every gift, like some twenty-five-year-old at a wedding shower. It was as if the girl's fifth birthday had suddenly evoked the grown-up within Tamara's little-girl body. She was on her way from towheaded, adorable baby to responsible school-age child. And if the change was mostly wonderful, there still was something a little sad about it.

"Maybe it's time for another baby," Nora said, pointedly looking at Wendy.

"Feel free," Wendy answered, refusing to be goaded. She looked down at the yellow pad on her lap, adding the name of the child whose present Tamara had just opened. "I think five is just the right age for her to start doing her own thank-you notes."

"A skill I could still use some help with at thirty-nine," Nora answered. She sat back, watching her niece open yet another gift. "Do you think our parents ever wanted a boy?" she continued, lowering her voice and looking across the room to where her mother was sitting.

"I don't know about Dad, but I doubt that Mom ever gave it a thought," Wendy said just as softly. "I mean, she was great to us and all, but I think, secretly, if she'd had her wish, she would have done nothing but paint all day."

Nora thought about what her sister had said. Certainly her mother had an artistic sensibility. On very little money, Belinda Levin had made the small house they grew up in look beautiful. Unusual, harmonious colors, an array of interesting textures, all the things that made a house a home had been attended to with care. And the watercolors she had occasionally painted over the years were lovely. Even the menus she'd illustrated at

David's restaurant were commented upon almost every day by some new customer.

Both Nora and Wendy looked over toward their mother. Belinda Levin was paying no attention at all to her daughters' conversation. She wasn't even paying much attention to the opening of the gifts by her darling grandchild. Instead, she was sketching on a large white pad, an array of colored markers at her elbow.

"You don't have to worry about Mom overhearing," Wendy said to Nora. "She's much too busy."

Nora watched her mother with affection. It was nice to see her so wrapped up in the afternoon's activities. On the coffee table were the boxes of clay she was going to have the children form into animal shapes. Then she would lead them in baking the clay forms and painting them in the bright array of colors from one of the many tubes she'd brought for them. She had done the same thing for Sarah's fifth birthday, and it had been a big hit with the children.

Wendy watched her daughter open her next-to-last gift. It was a copy of *The Secret Garden,* the second one she'd received that afternoon. Rather than whining about the redundancy, Tamara turned politely to the girl who'd given it to her.

"Thank you, Anya," she said, placing the gift respectfully on the pile by her side.

Wendy smiled at Nora, bringing her hand theatrically to her chest with pride. Then she got up and walked over to her mother.

"Almost time, Mom," she said. "You ready?"

Her mother looked up, beaming. "I'm more than ready. You girls used to love doing the animals with me."

Wendy smiled. "Yes, we did. And Tamara's friends are going to love it too." She leaned down to look at what her mother had been drawing. It was a picture of a dragon, holding four small children on his back. Both the dragon and the children were drawn in colorful detail, the dragon's snarling mouth in midspeech, two of the children holding on to his neck, terrified, the two others

having the time of their lives. The whole picture was
vivid and exotic, illustrated with talent and verve. "Gee,
Mom, that's amazing."

Belinda smiled at her daughter in appreciation. "When
do you want me to start with the clay?"

Wendy checked her watch. "Tamara's opening the last
gift now. If you start right up, we should be ready for
cake by about four. That sound okay?"

Her mother nodded. "Your father should be here by
three-thirty or so. He said he'll be bringing some special
cookies that Jack made."

"Yum," Nora said, coming to stand beside her sister.
She remembered the gingerbread men her father's baked
goods supplier used to give them when she and Wendy
were kids. It was nice to see that the son was carrying
on the tradition.

Belinda beamed at both her daughters. "I have some
wonderful shapes for the children to use for the clay.
There were cookie cutters I'd completely forgotten about
hidden behind some old cans in the pantry. Parrots,
monkeys . . . all kinds of things."

Nora hadn't seen her mother this animated in a long
time. It reminded her of the long afternoons when she'd
been a child and stayed home from school with a cold.
Her mother used to sit with her, painting magical watercolors or finger-painting on weirdly shaped pieces of
heavy paper. There had been so little spare time in the
Levin household, with Belinda attending to everyone in
so many ways, that Nora remembered those sick days
especially fondly.

Wendy picked up the picture of the dragon carefully.
"I'm going to frame this before the hordes get to it."
She looked over at Tamara, who was standing up, clearly
ready for the next event. "Well, Mom, you're—" she
started to say before being cut off by the sound of the
front door slamming.

David Levin swept into the room, going straight to his
younger grandchild and picking her up into his arms.

"Happy birthday, you beautiful girl," he said, kissing her on each cheek before redepositing her on the rug.

Tamara's older sister came over to him and threw her arms around his waist. "Hey, Grandpa, you should see what Tamara got. It's awesome!"

David kissed Sarah as well. "I intend to see everything," he said, smiling broadly at his granddaughters, "although it has to wait until next weekend."

A look of alarm passed across his wife's face. "What do you mean?" she asked from across the room.

"I mean," David said in a jolly tone, "that Grandma and Grandpa have to buy Grandpa some new work shoes this afternoon, but next Sunday we'll be able to play with every single toy you got." He pinched Tamara lightly on the cheek.

Nora and Wendy exchanged glances.

"Listen, Dad—" Nora began, her voice challenging.

Wendy cut in, sounding infinitely smoother and more patient. "There will be plenty of time for shoe shopping, as soon as Mom is finished."

"Finished with what?"

"Finished with making clay animals with the children. They've all been looking forward to it." Wendy's tone was firm.

"Animals, schmanimals," her father retorted. "I've got something much better than animals. I've got people!" He reached into the bag he was carrying and lifted out a mass of gingerbread men, each one decorated with frosting and chocolate chips. With maximum fuss, he started handing the cookies out to the assembled children, oohing and aahing over each of them.

"This guy looks exactly like you," he said to a little boy dressed in brown corduroy overalls. "And this one's almost as beautiful as you are," he added, holding another cookie up to a girl with red ringlets falling to her shoulders.

The children seemed delighted with him. Nora looked at her mother. All the animation had gone out of Belinda's face. Almost robotically, she was moving toward the

closet, taking her handbag from the hook where she'd
hung it, pulling the gray wool coat around her shoulders.

"Daddy, you can't make Mom leave now," Nora pro-
tested. "She was looking forward to this. She spent days
getting everything ready."

David looked at her, his face awash in impatience. "Darling, the children will love the cookies, and this is the only
time I have to get to the shoe store. My feet have been
killing me for weeks, and the store closes by five. If, God
forbid, we hit any traffic, or we don't find something right
away, it's curtains for my feet. And you know how essential
they are." His face assumed an expression meant to be
adorable. "You know, darling, if Daddy can't stand up
comfortably, Daddy can't earn a living."

"But that's crazy!" Nora had the impulse to run across
the room and hold him there by force. She couldn't bear
how cavalier he sounded, or, more than that, how automatically her mother was going along with him. "You can buy
a pair of shoes anytime. And if you have to do it now,
why can't you leave Mom here and do it by yourself?" She
knew she was courting his anger, and she didn't even care.

But her father didn't take her objections seriously
enough to get angry. "Sweetheart," he said, coming over
to put an arm around her, "your mother *always* goes
with me to buy shoes."

Nora pulled away from him, looking first toward her
mother and then to her sister, as if hoping for some
support. But Wendy stayed quiet. Nora could see that
her sister had already gone on to think about what to
do with the party. Her mother, to Nora's eye, looked
resigned. Numb, in fact. Belinda Levin kissed Wendy
lightly, then turned to Nora.

"Don't fret, dear," she said, kissing her as well. "It
doesn't really matter."

She took one last look at the group of children, waving
at her granddaughters tiredly as she pulled her coat
around her and walked to the door.

"It was a lovely party," she said to no one in particular
as she went outside.

16

Nora tapped rhythmically on the steering wheel with her left hand as she drove along the Taconic Parkway. It had been about forty minutes since she had left her sister's house to go to Poughkeepsie, but listening to The Dixie Hummingbirds had made the time fly by. She'd immersed herself in gospel music since her meeting with Will Stanley. The CDs she'd been listening to for the past couple of days contained so much wonderful stuff, she felt as if she'd been visiting heaven. When Will had said that gospel was all he wanted to use in the film, Nora had disagreed. How about the seriousness and depth of Mozart's *Requiem,* she thought, or the voices of prisoners emerging into sunlight in Beethoven's *Fidelio*. But nonstop listening to gospel singing from Paul Robeson to the Abyssinian Baptist Gospel Choir had proved that Will's idea might not be such a bad one.

Unconsciously, she eased her foot off the gas pedal, slowing with the leisurely, almost bluesy opening measures of "When the Gates Swing Open." She wished she could close her eyes and just enjoy the music. Nothing bothered her when she was listening to music. No parents to be angry at, no love life to worry about, no problems of any kind. It was only Nora and the music. And for this project, there had been so much to acquaint herself with. She'd begun by sampling some of the gospel groups; then she'd gone on to the solo performers, Marion Williams, Mahalia Jackson, Sister Myrtle Fields. Al-

most an entire week had been devoted to Paul Robeson.
There was nothing showy about him, not ever. It was the
most beautiful male sound she had ever heard. "Get on
Board, Little Children" would start up and her eyes
would fill with tears. It happened every time she played
it, every single time.

Just ahead, she spotted the exit that would take her
to Route 199. It caught her up short. She'd been so involved with the music, she'd practically forgotten what
tonight was supposed to be about. She was supposed to
be concentrating on Alex Fenichel. In a scant few minutes, she would be walking into The Tin Door, whatever
the hell that was, and seeing the love of her life for the
first time in over a decade. Would he look the same, she
wondered, or would his thick dark hair be covering a
bald spot, or—worse yet—sporting a comb-over.

She pictured the tall, good-looking young man she'd
known with an extra thirty pounds or so, imagined the
start of a second chin and a roll of flab around his waist.
The thought made her smile until she realized what Kip
and Eloise would say if they'd known what she was
thinking. "You're fighting the whole idea of finding a
man to love," they would undoubtedly state, and they'd
be right.

Okay. She admitted it. The notion was terrifying. And
she hated being scared. But more than that, she hated
putting any part of herself in someone else's control.
She'd arranged her entire existence so she could live as
she liked, buy what she pleased, go to bed when she
chose, with whom she chose. To have a man to answer
to . . . why in the world did she think she wanted that?
The whole idea sounded horrible. She thought about the
men she'd dated in the past couple of years, smiled at
the picture that formed in her mind of her last interlude
with Duncan. She liked her life that way, damn it. Everyone knew what was going on and everyone got something
out of it. She played by her own rules, but she'd always
been completely honest about what they were. Nobody
got fooled, nobody got hurt.

True, when she'd been lying on the floor of that store in Rhinebeck, believing that her life was about to be summarily terminated by that psychotic boy, she had suddenly found herself longing for some kind of real connection, someone who'd actually miss her. But right now, a scant five minutes from the restaurant Alex Fenichel had chosen, it seemed the height of folly.

No, she reminded herself, she *wanted* this. No one was making her do it. Except Kip and Eloise, a tiny voice inside her head rejoined.

"No, no, no." She said the words out loud. She must not turn this into a big joke. She'd done that all her life, making light of everything. That was just as cowardly as giving all her power to some man. She wanted to see Alex, wanted it all by herself. Okay, her friends had given her courage, but the longing had been her own.

The CD finished, and the dark silence within the car seemed prophetic. Here she was, in the middle of a cold and empty country road, no one within shouting distance. It was like her life, and, frankly, how much fun was it really in her emotional isolation booth? Walking the streets of New York, she often observed couples strolling hand in hand, laughing at some joke only they understood. Truth to tell, it often annoyed her— how exclusive couples like that seemed, the way they made everyone else feel nonexistent. But at her more vulnerable times, she could imagine how pleasurable it could be. What a relief to have someone to share the joke with, to sit in the car while you ran into H & H for a raisin bagel, someone to understand why the actor is insufferable without having to have it explained, to share the sorrow over the obituary of someone you hadn't even met.

The next CD went on. The truth was, she wasn't even sure that Alex was that person. But she remembered how solid he'd been, how intelligent. He was so different from the other men she'd known. Since the robbery, one scene kept coming into her mind. It was right after they'd first met. Alex had invited her to the house at the New Jersey shore that he shared with some friends. His roommates were guys he'd gone to Dartmouth with, two of them also going to Columbia for their MBAs as he was. It was a particularly hot Saturday afternoon in mid-August. There were six or seven men, plus assorted friends and girlfriends, and everyone was having a good time. The beer was flowing, the same Rolling Stones song was blaring from a boom box over and over, most of his friends were either surfing in the ocean or dancing on the sandy beach.

With pandemonium all around him, Alex might as well have been five hundred miles away. There he was, she remembered, seated on a blue-and-white plaid blanket, surrounded by textbooks, a yellow pad on his lap, a bottle of root beer in his hand. He paid no attention to the friends around him, although he never ignored Nora. Every few minutes, he would pat her leg or push her hair back from her forehead. But he was taking six credits over the summer, and he had to prepare for class on Monday. Nothing and no one was going to keep him from his goal.

If only she'd had his concentration, she thought, once again turning up the volume of the car's CD player, she could probably have scored the music for *Gone with the Wind*. For a few minutes, she tried to focus on The Golden Gate Quartet, singing "Swing Down Chariot." Finally, she gave up and turned the CD player off. Images of Alex floated through her mind. He'd been so handsome at twenty-six, his dark brown hair neatly cut, with the kind of chiseled face she'd seen only in cartoons. He'd come from Providence, second of three boys, all of whom were well behaved, with good grades in school, popular with the other kids. Alex had played baseball in high school and still worked out every other day, rain or shine, while he was in graduate school. His father was an engineer and his mother taught English at a high school. When Nora had met his family, she'd been impressed with how thoughtfully everyone behaved toward each other. Alex's father, Jim, was so solicitous toward his wife, it seemed as if they'd been dating for a month, not married for thirty years or so.

Just like her family, Nora thought, scowling. Oh, how considerate David Levin was of his wife. Nora replayed his behavior at Tamara's birthday party, the fury she'd felt earlier springing back like a rubber band. She pictured her father, passing out gingerbread men as if they were gold pieces. Of course, kids actually liked her father. He'd always had a certain Pied Piper esprit that delighted people under the age of eight. It was grownups who had a problem. But not her mother, she amended. Belinda Levin never put up a fight. She just followed behind meekly, throwing away any chance she had to fulfill her own happiness.

Well, that's her problem, Nora thought, eager to get away from thoughts of her family. Tonight wasn't about them; it was about her and a man who might fulfill *her* happiness.

She felt her body clench in fear and willed herself to relax. What was the big deal, anyway? If it worked out, fine; if it didn't, at least she wouldn't have to cope with Eloise and Kip nagging her about it. Besides, she thought, it wasn't likely that Alex would still be as wonderful as she remembered. She'd probably be ready to leave dinner the minute she got to the restaurant.

Which, she realized with a start, was right now. The entryway to The Tin Door was marked by a tin arrow, leading to a large parking lot, filled with expensive-looking cars. The restaurant itself seemed to be constructed almost entirely of glass, its jutting angles and dramatic curves in no way resembling the wooded country road on which it was located. Nora pulled into a space and checked her face in the rearview mirror. She took a lipstick from the pocket of her coat and applied it hastily across her mouth. She was damned if she was going to go through some big song and dance, trying to make herself into a glam queen. Take it or leave it, she thought as she pushed the car door open.

As the air hit her, she realized how silly she was being. She had called Alex—well, okay, she had had Alex called. In any case, it was *her* choice, so what the hell was she so mad about? Get hold of yourself, girl, she thought as she walked toward the door of the restaurant.

When she entered, she was struck by the smoky aroma of the wood-burning fireplace and the muffled sounds of a happy crowd. Everyone there looked well dressed and well off. The Tin Door was exactly the kind of yuppie haven that had sprung up—and in many cases sprang out less than a year later—all over the Hudson Valley. She peered around the large dining room, wondering if Alex was there, secretly staring at her, judging how she looked, how much older she'd gotten, how well or badly she was dressed. The notion infuriated her. A tall man in tight-fitting blue jeans and a navy blue jacket approached her, carrying menus in his hand, a concerned smile on his lips.

"Is everything all right, ma'am?" he asked.

Nora turned toward him. Of course everything was all right, she felt like snapping. Why shouldn't it be all right? She realized that she'd been frowning. This was the maître d'. He was just doing his job. She was being irrational. Here she was in a nice restaurant filled with contented people and able staff, and she wanted to lash out like a prisoner of war.

"I'm fine, thank you," she answered finally, conjuring up a smile. "I'm meeting Mr. Fenichel."

The man smiled broadly. "Oh, Alex is right over there. Let me show you to the table."

Nora followed his gaze to a table near the back, where a bearded man wearing a houndstooth jacket sat, sipping a glass of red wine. As she approached, she looked for signs of the Alex she knew, but they were almost nonexistent. True, he looked about forty, which was the age Alex would be now, and his hair was brown. But it was wavier than she remembered. She couldn't really see much of his face with the full beard. Yes, she thought, as she came closer. His eyes were the same blue, but it was hard to see the boy he'd been. Now, he wore old-fashioned wire-rimmed glasses. He was still attractive, she realized as he rose slightly and smiled, but utterly unfamiliar.

"Nora!" he exclaimed, grabbing her hand and holding it as she sat down opposite him. "How long has it been? You're looking beautiful!"

She stared at him. She recalled his way of speaking as tentative, halting whenever he started a sentence, gaining in confidence as he went along. But now he sounded as smooth and strong as a politician.

"Well," she answered, "I guess it's been almost fifteen years."

There were so many questions she had wanted to ask him, but they all seemed to have disappeared from her mind. Alex, however, wasn't at all short on curiosity.

"Tell me everything about yourself. What is it you're doing now?"

Nora felt as wooden as a coat hanger, but she pushed herself to describe her business. Alex seemed entranced by her job.

"You know," he said, when she finished telling him about Levin Music, "I feel stupid admitting this, but I can't remember exactly what you were doing when we last saw each other."

Nora was surprised. She'd spent so much time going over the pros and cons of leaving publishing when she'd been dating Alex. Oh, come on, she said to herself. No one pays as much attention as you think they do. Especially an ambitious young man with his own future to worry about.

"I was an editorial assistant," she prompted him. "Remember, you picked me up in my office on Fiftieth Street a few times. I worked for the guy who always wore bow ties."

"Of course," Alex answered, nodding his head.

The man who'd seated them came up to their table once again. Alex caught sight of him and smiled. "Henry Caparelli, this is my old friend Nora Levin." He looked at Nora. "Henry and I play doubles every Tuesday and Thursday, and when I win I get paid off in free dinners."

"You wish," Henry said, smiling at Nora. "What would you like to drink, Nora?"

"Oh, I guess a glass of wine would be nice," she said.

"Red? White?"

"Red, thanks."

"Have the same one I'm having," Alex interjected. "It's a cabernet, and it's a good one."

Nora nodded, and Henry began to walk away. But Alex stopped him.

"Nora, tell Henry how we first met. It's a story he'd like."

Nora felt uncomfortable. Why in the world did Alex want to share that with a stranger? Well, not a stranger to him, obviously, but certainly a stranger to her. It wasn't all that sweet a story, after all. In fact, it didn't speak terribly well for either one of them.

"Well," she said, hesitating, "I was somewhat the worse for wear and Alex rescued me."

Alex began to laugh. "You mean you were clobbered."

"Not clobbered, just slightly more liquefied than I'm comfortable being." She looked apologetically at Henry. "I had just broken up with someone, and I was pretty unhappy." She turned to Alex. "It's not as if you were stone-cold sober. As I remember, you took me back to your apartment and were so hammered you accidentally locked the door. Your roommate walked around the block for about three hours, as he reminded us two hundred times over the next year."

Alex and Henry both laughed loudly, which annoyed Nora. What was so damn funny? She felt like a sideshow attraction. She felt both of them watching her and reddened in embarrassment.

"I'll get your wine," Henry said, clearly picking up on her growing discomfort. "Then I'll take your order. Some of the specials are going fast, I'm afraid, and I'd like you to get the whole Tin Door experience while you're here."

Nora looked around the room. She wasn't sure she was going to enjoy the Tin Door experience.

"Tell me about what you do," she said to Alex.

"Well, I teach a few hours a week, and I do a lot of consulting. In fact, I helped Henry start up this restaurant. Came up with the business plan, helped him establish his bookkeeping operation, and such."

"I have to admit I'm a little surprised," Nora said. "You were always so fascinated by technology. I'd have thought you'd have gone into a computer business or something like that."

Alex didn't respond right away, and she wondered if she'd hurt his feelings. She hadn't meant to; she just couldn't quite relate the man she'd known with the man he'd become.

"How are your parents?" she asked, trying to return the conversation to some kind of equilibrium.

Alex sat back in his chair, finishing off his glass of wine and indicating to a passing waiter that he'd like another. "Well, Dad died a couple of years ago."

"Oh, I'm so sorry," Nora replied. She remembered Alex's father fondly. He was so sweet, so solid in his old-fashioned New England style. "I hope he didn't suffer."

Alex shook his head. "Actually, it happened in seconds. It was a hiking accident."

Nora was astounded. Jim Fenichel must have been in his sixties when she'd known him years earlier. What was he doing on a hiking expedition at what must have been close to eighty?

"Is your mother holding up all right?"

"Oh, yes, she's fine."

Nora noticed that he seemed disinclined to go any further with the conversation. She found herself out of things to ask him about, and was relieved when Henry returned, bringing her glass of wine and setting another one down in front of Alex.

"So, have you two decided on dinner?" he asked, pulling a notebook out of his pocket.

"Nora," Alex said, "do you know what you want?"

Nora looked quickly at the menu in front of her. She didn't take much of it in, but felt too nervous to pore over it. "How about the chicken," she said.

"I'll go with the scallops," Alex said.

Nora stared at him, surprised. "Gee, you never used to like shellfish. You always steered clear of it. I remember trying to get you to try some stone crabs in Miami. You acted as if I were trying to kill you."

"Well, people change."

Nora again felt at a loss. She wished she could ask him what novel he might take to a desert island or which friend he might bring, but that would be really asinine. She decided to stay quiet.

The silence lasted until a waiter deposited two salads in front of them.

"I know you didn't order these, but Henry thought you might like them."

Nora eyed the plate of arugula, slices of pear and some blue cheese deposited prettily at the sides. She started to giggle. If there was one thing Alex wouldn't touch, it was blue cheese. He wouldn't even allow her to eat it when they'd been dating. He claimed he could smell it for the next three days.

She looked across at him, intending to share the laugh, but stopped when she saw him spearing the salad, large chunks of blue cheese at the end of his fork. He took the salad in his mouth, chewing contentedly then washing the bite down with a long sip of wine.

Nora reached across the table for his hand and inspected it closely. Alex's hands had been one of his best features, the fingers long and expressive. This man's hands were wide, with short, stubby fingers. She released his hand and looked him straight in the eye.

"You're not Alex," she said.

A slight smile crossed his face. "Oh, I'm Alex all right."

"But you're not *my* Alex, are you?" She heard the

hurt in her voice and was dismayed at letting him hear it as well.

"I'm Alex Fenichel. Whether I'm *your* Alex or not, I guess is up to you."

Nora stared at him.

"Okay, so we've never met before," he said. "But you're one pretty lady, and I hope we get to meet many times again."

Nora wanted to strike him. She wanted him to feel the abject humiliation she was feeling. "How could you do this to me? What kind of person are you?"

He leaned back in his chair, smiling like a salesman. "Oh, come on, you have to admit this was fun. I mean, you're a nice person and I'm a nice person. So what if I'm not the guy you used to know. I'm a guy you might want to know now."

"Didn't you have any compunctions about lying on the phone? You must have realized how much this probably meant to me, trying to find someone after so many years. I'm sure Kelly made that perfectly clear."

"Oh, sure," he admitted. "But it sounded like fun."

Nora threw her napkin on the table. "So you were just going to go on and on, getting me to fill in the details, to get a good laugh."

"Hey, come on." He grinned. "I think you're beautiful. And you're a hundred times more interesting than most of the women I meet."

She stood up and opened her handbag, pulling out a twenty-dollar bill and laying it on the table. "I recommend you do not get too attached," she said.

"Don't be silly," he said, standing up and coming over to her side of the table. "It's on me."

Of course it's not Alex, she thought, belatedly seeing that he was at least four inches shorter than the man she knew. And thin across the shoulders where her Alex had been broad. His eyes were nothing like Alex's. Nothing at all. How could she not have realized it immediately?

He stood there, his napkin fluttering awkwardly from

where it had attached itself to his shiny leather belt. "C'mon, Nora. Give me a chance."

Without gracing him with a response, she walked away. Henry approached her as she pushed open the door to the outside.

"Is there anything I can do?" he asked.

She shook her head, worried that she might burst into tears if she tried to speak. Henry looked at her with pity, making her realize that he'd known the truth all along. His sympathy made the whole thing even more humiliating. Miserable, she made her way to her car, sitting there for long minutes. How could she have been such a fool? One part of her wanted to strangle that man in the restaurant. But, in a weird way, the entire episode was like a warning sign. This whole notion had been insane from the start. Even if he had been the right Alex Fenichel, it would never have worked out.

She suddenly became aware that someone was leaving the restaurant, headed toward her car. Afraid it was Alex, she started the car and sped out the exit. She followed the road toward the parkway, not even sure where she was headed. New York City was a two-hour drive, which seemed insurmountable given the way she was feeling. But having to go through the whole story with her sister and brother-in-law—or, God forbid, her parents—was a horrible alternative. Yet she needed to talk to someone.

She drove along the dark road, the lights of her car the only illumination for miles. Realizing she didn't even know what time it was, she looked at the clock on the dashboard. She was surprised to see that it was only 9:45. Spotting the sign for the Taconic, she made the left turn, still uncertain of where she was headed. Driving slowly, not really ready to commit to a direction, she reached across to the CD player and turned it on. Quickly, the car was filled with the sound of The Abyssinian Baptist Gospel Choir, singing "Said I Wasn't Gonna Tell Nobody." She listened to the call of the lead singer's full-throated contralto voice, her occasional high-pitched notes reminding Nora of Little Richard, then to the large choral responses, the whole choir clapping through the entire song. The song was about keeping to yourself the things the Lord has done, but Nora wasn't taking in the religious significance. Rather, she was stung by the need to keep things to yourself, the good things, the bad things, the humiliating things like her meeting tonight.

And suddenly, she knew exactly where she wanted to go.

Kip lay on her bed, listening to the voices downstairs. She couldn't imagine who would have rung the bell at ten-thirty at night. Probably some friend of Lisa's. By rights, she should yell downstairs to Eloise not to let the friend in. Teenagers shouldn't be dropping in on each other at this hour. But she couldn't even summon up the energy to object. If Lisa wanted to exhaust herself before tomorrow's practice, that was her problem. Right now, Kip had enough problems of her own. Her daughter would just have to look out for herself for once.

She heard Eloise's laugh and wondered what she and the kid at the door might be laughing about. In her experience as a mother, teenagers weren't all that funny—at least, not when they were talking to parents. Maybe the fact that Eloise had no children called forth some magical recognition and allowed her entry into kids' secret world. In any case, it was a relief to hear Eloise laughing. God knows, Kip hadn't provided much amusement. In fact, she had practically forced Eloise to drive up here this afternoon.

Jesus, Kip thought, a bad day on the ice and she'd turned into a demanding, helpless fool. At this morning's practice, she had fallen coming out of a spin, and the searing pain in her lower leg brought up all the old dread and fear associated with an injury. Sure enough, it was a bad sprain. It would set her back for weeks. Depressed, she'd limped into the house after seeing the doctor only to be set upon by a furious Lisa. Her daughter screamed at her for forgetting the shopping excursion Kip had supposedly promised for the afternoon. Kip had no memory of making such a promise, but she'd tried to hold her tongue, pointing to her bandaged ankle and explaining what had happened. Lisa had glared at her mother's leg with obvious disgust at her mother's bumbling, as if it were more proof of the foolishness behind Kip's return to skating.

"Oh, sure, Mom. You have *all* the problems, don't you," Lisa snapped before stomping off to her room. Eloise had called a couple of minutes later, and Kip couldn't make herself sound cheerful. She'd let Eloise worm out of her the fact that Peter and J. P. were away, at a Boy Scout Father-Son Weekend, and she had gone on to describe the fight she'd had with her daughter. When Eloise expressed concern, Kip had tried saying all the right words, how she'd manage to make dinner and how her ankle would be fine, and on and on. But she knew that she'd done a crummy job of hiding what she was really feeling. When Eloise offered to come up, she said no, but she really couldn't bear the thought of lying there, alone in her room, and Eloise heard it loud and clear.

It was amazing that Eloise had come all this way to take care of her, Kip thought, so grateful and depressed, she felt that she might burst into tears. When she heard footsteps outside the door, she turned her face toward the window so her friend wouldn't see. But when the door was pushed open, it wasn't Eloise's voice she heard.

"I gather it wasn't exactly your day," Nora said, walking in and taking a seat on the end of the bed. Eloise entered right behind her.

Kip gaped at her. "I can't believe Eloise made you come, too. I must be even more pathetic than I thought I was."

"Oh, I'd say you were in pretty good company." Nora reached up for Eloise's hand, which was closed in a fist. As she uncurled her friend's fingers, she revealed the three Oreo cookies that had lain hidden in Eloise's hand. "I'd say we were pretty much Flopsy, Mopsy, and Cottontail in the pathetic department. So, would you like to hear what happened to Cottontail tonight?"

"Oh, damn, I forgot. You had your date with Alex tonight. How did it go?"

Nora rose from the bed and began pacing around the room. "Where shall I start? Let's see . . . How about, *he wasn't Alex Fenichel!*"

Kip was confused. Eloise, watching Nora intently, placed one of the cookies in her mouth, obviously unaware she was even doing it.

"Okay, he was Alex Fenichel, but not the Alex Fenichel I knew and loved and thought I was going out with." Her voice rose as she spoke. "This bastard was some guy with the same name as my Alex. When Kelly called, he thought it would be hysterical to pretend." Now she was almost shouting. "Side-splittingly hilarious, isn't it? I mean, what kind of son of a bitch would go through a charade like that, making me drive a hundred miles from home?"

Her indignation had reached top volume as she continued her furious pacing. "Oh," she said, imitating the fake Alex's tone of voice, "you're such a pretty lady, and I'm such a cool dude. . . ."

As Nora continued her rant, Kip looked at Eloise, who was frowning in concern. Then Kip turned back to watch Nora, and a more thoughtful expression came over her face. Kip sat up straighter on the bed, adjusting one of the pillows higher up behind her head.

"You know what?" Kip said, a smile playing at the corner of her mouth. "I think you're having the time of your life."

Nora stopped walking. "What are you talking about?" she snapped.

Kip stretched her hands out in front of her, as if to frame Nora. "This is the liveliest I've ever seen you. You should see the color in your cheeks. If you ask me, you're so relieved you could jump for joy."

Nora stood there, looking as if she had been slapped. "I don't know," Nora said, dropping down onto the quilt, "maybe you're right."

"What do you mean?" Eloise asked.

Nora lay her head down, crunching the quilt in her hands as if she were a child. "Maybe it's a relief to be good and mad at someone, to experience some emotion other than terror. Half the time I'm scared of somebody trying to love me; the other half, I'm scared of somebody trying to attack me."

Eloise and Kip stayed quiet, and Nora continued her thought.

"I just can't stand it, dreaming about that day almost every night, worrying every time I enter an elevator that some guy's behind me, or somebody's going to push me in front of a car. I never worried about anything before in my life."

Kip placed a hand on Nora's shoulder. "I know exactly what you mean about the fear. When I'm alone in this house, I think I hear noises on the stairs, nonexistent intruders on the gravel outside. I've always loved living in the country. Now, I almost wish I lived in an over-crowded apartment building, with other people around me to make me feel safe."

Eloise sat down on a chair and pulled it close to the bed. "Trust me, there's nothing inherently safe about an apartment. If I checked the locks on my front door any more times a night, the men in the white coats would come to take me away. Not to mention late nights at the office. I used to work till ten, eleven at night and not think a thing about it. Now I start obsessing about having to stay late before five o'clock even rolls around."

Kip moved the pillow up behind her head, causing her leg to twinge. "Do you think all this is ever going to end? Or are the three of us still going to be talking about this when we're ninety."

"I don't know," Nora answered, loosening her grip on the quilt and sitting upright. "Maybe it never goes away, but you find some way to deal with it."

Kip nodded. "God, I hope so." Her brow furrowed as she went on to her next thought. "Maybe we're even using it just a little bit to keep us where we are. To keep me here in bed, to keep you knee-deep in Oreos—" She cocked an eyebrow at Eloise. "—and to make you happy when a date doesn't work out."

"It's not as if we asked to be terrorized," Eloise objected.

Kip shook her head. "Of course not. And there's no question about it. What happened was real, and horrible. And it's going to take longer than a couple of months to get over it. And, yes, maybe we won't get over it completely *ever*. But I still think it's important to question what we're doing. To separate out the stuff we have to go through from the stuff our worst selves might just *want* to go through."

"Zo profound, Herr Doktor Professor," Nora intoned in a German accent.

Eloise gave her a sharp glance. "It's a whole lot easier to make fun of each other than to consider what Kip is saying."

Kip nodded to her gratefully.

The three remained in silence while Nora thought about what Kip had said. "Okay, so keeping our promises to each other isn't turning out to be so damned easy."

"No, indeed!" Eloise agreed.

Now Nora began laughing outright. "So here we are, the three of us," she said, expelling a big breath. She pointed to Kip. "Flopsy's black and blue and bedridden." She turned toward Eloise. "Maybe Mopsy has a few more cookies hidden away?"

Eloise reddened as she put her hand in her pocket and pulled out five more Oreos.

"As for Cottontail, she feels like giving up." Nora's expression grew more serious. "She—that is, *I*—gave it my best shot. If it were meant to be, it would have happened." She was almost frowning. "That's it! I'm done!"

Kip lay back against the pillow. Boy, she thought, how

great it would be to give up, as Nora claimed she was doing. Eloise could eat whatever she wanted, Nora could go on sleeping with men she didn't give a damn about, and Kip could never enter a skating rink again in her life. No more injuries, no more making a fool of herself.

Oh, yes, she thought, closing her eyes and imagining a life with no anxiety and no fear. The image of her daughter swimming to a victory went through her mind, snapping her back to reality. What that kind of life would really mean, after all, would be giving up any dreams she had, and, worse yet, giving in to a lethargy that would damage everyone in her family. She couldn't really delight in the success of her husband and her children unless she also delighted in her own. She could imagine herself at Lisa's swim meets, pretending to cheer for her daughter while secretly resenting her success. And all the while, she'd still be frightened of ghosts on the stairway in the dark of night. Still see violence lurking behind every tree.

Nope, she thought, looking up at Nora and Eloise, I'm not giving up, and, if I have anything to say about it, neither is anyone else.

"Sorry to deprive you of your bliss," she said, staring at the two of them, "but, no, you're not anywhere near done. I don't know exactly how, but I'll be damned if we're going to throw up our hands so easily. My ankle is going to heal, and the cookies are going to run out, and the real Alex Fenichel is still out there, waiting to be found, so don't get too comfortable."

Eloise sank down onto a chair opposite the bed. "Oh, I don't think an excess of comfort is our problem."

Kip met her eyes, her tone defiant. "Maybe there's not that much we can do about the scars we've got thanks to that psychotic kid, but we're going to get you fit, get me skating, and get her—" She pointed to Nora with the back of her thumb. "—dating for real. Even if it kills us."

"Which," Nora said, "I'm beginning to wish it would."

17

Peter Hallman's gaze drifted upward to the wispy clouds streaking across the sky above the baseball field. It was warmer than usual for mid-April, and today was a picture-perfect sunny afternoon. His mood, however, was in sharp contrast to the cheerfulness of the weather.

Behind his sunglasses, he continued to stare at the sky, and imagined an airplane overhead, soaring through the piercing blue brightness. Barely breathing, he waited to see where the thought might lead him. He pictured a man seated in first-class, mid-forties, wearing a charcoal gray suit, with a well-dressed but disinterested-looking woman next to him. Was she his wife? A woman he'd never met? It was to be a short flight. Peter sat, the scene crystal clear in his mind, waiting to see what would happen next.

Nothing happened. The image was completely static.

The crack of a bat, accompanied by encouraging shouts, made him jerk his eyes back to the playing field. One of the boys had hit a long drive to center field. The bases were loaded, and there was a great deal of hollering and scurrying around as the runners rounded the bases. The batter made it home only seconds before the ball reached the catcher's mitt. Peter watched the runners exchanging high fives, saw the batter's exultant father run over to clap him on both shoulders. A perfect moment of high drama, Peter thought, exactly the way you want to see a home run played out. Every boy's dream come true. He turned his head to locate J. P., who was standing at first base and grinning as he casually punched his glove again and again.

Peter shifted his long legs, cramped from his perch in the middle row of the rickety metal bleachers. Kip had always been the one who took J. P. to baseball practice, but her new skating schedule had changed all that. Peter admired her for sitting through this two or three times a week, or whatever it was. Of course, she enjoyed the game, which made it a very different matter. He wasn't quite sure how he was going to get through this now that he was on after-school duty every other day. He wondered if he could slip away to get a cup of coffee somewhere. Would J. P. really care, or even notice?

"You are a genetic mutation," he scolded himself under his breath. Fathers were supposed to be deliriously happy to have sons who were good at baseball. Baseball was the link between fathers and sons, the link, in fact, between every generation of males from the time somebody first dreamed up the game. But Peter had never been much for sports, nor had his father been a fan of any particular game. Their connection to one another came from a mutual love of books.

It might have been nice to share this stuff with J. P., he thought, but he couldn't help it; he wasn't a sports kind of dad. Actually, it went further than that. He had been the worst ballplayer in school, the worst *anything* player in school. His father may have been disinterested in athletics, but Peter was downright terrible at them.

It wasn't a secret. Both his children knew their abilities in sports came from their mother, and he was grateful that it had turned out that way. He had two natural athletes, instead of two fumbling kids playing only because they had to, picked last for every team, hopeless losers of points, wreckers of victories.

He thought of Kip, always so fit and bursting with good health, able to master so many sports, or at the very least become proficient enough to take part in a game with reasonable results. A skater, for Christ's sake. She knew that Peter was no big athlete, but he doubted she was aware of how uncoordinated he really was. He steered clear of situations where it might be revealed, affecting lack of interest but actually praying to prevent discovery. He dreaded her contempt, being hit with the reality that she—such a vibrant person—had married such a physically ineffectual man. He was awed by her athletic abilities, her skating talent, the way she could actually *do* something. What a contrast to the way he lived, totally in his head.

Only the week before, without telling her, he had driven over to watch her skate at the rink one afternoon. Hidden from view, he had watched in amazement as she glided along, as natural on the ice as if it were more home to her than dry ground. Her control of her body had made him feel even more ineffectual, more effete and useless, than ever. And this was after the woman had been hospitalized with brutal injuries.

Still, he was glad he had gone to see her. He had forgotten how astoundingly beautiful the sight of her skating was. She had been so young when they met, so full of promise in her field. He recalled sitting in the stands back then, following her every graceful move, holding his breath with each jump. It had been one of the biggest surprises of his life when she chose to come with him to Europe and give up her career. He hadn't pushed her to do it, but he hadn't tried to dissuade her, either. So selfish of me, he thought now, a mind-boggling level of selfish. But, of course, he had desperately wanted her by his side; he was thrilled by her decision and hadn't chosen to examine it too closely.

He never understood why she cut skating out of her life so completely. She didn't display any resentment toward him for making her give it up, or, more accurately, he reflected, being the catalyst for her giving it up. But the fact that she never even went for a spin on the ice with the kids had always bothered him. He was genuinely happy and relieved when she told him she

wanted to go back to skating. It was an unfinished piece
of business in her life, it *had* to be. Besides, it was high
time she had something of her own, something other
than the massive job of catering to his and J. P.'s and
Lisa's needs. She had been willing to do it, but that alone
couldn't be enough of a life for her.

Peter focused once more on the action before him. He
didn't know the father who was the team's coach, but,
watching him now, he thought the man seemed intensely
serious about the whole business. Which was to the good,
he supposed. He was only glad the man's barked orders
weren't directed at him, as has been those of so many
other coaches in his youth. As was usual, there were
several parents who stayed to watch practice. Peter
could imagine how thrilled that father was, the one who
had been present to witness his son's alpha male performance, hitting a home run with the bases loaded. He
supposed if J. P. hit a home run, he would jump up and
carry on, but at the moment, he hoped he wouldn't be
called upon to do so. It would take more enthusiasm
than he could summon up.

The excitement died down, and the boys resumed their
practice game. Peter was able to retreat into his thoughts
once more. Not that he wanted to. Dear Lord, he said
silently, grant me unconsciousness, save me from the
blackness in my own empty head. If I have ever done anything good in this life, help me now by easing the clutching
panic in my chest.

And please, please, above all else, give me an idea.

Nothing. Nothing for months. He was dry. He was
empty. For decades, his mind had been flooded with
things he wanted to write about. He hadn't thought there
would be enough time given him on earth to get to all
of it. And yet, after he had turned his last book in to his
editor and taken his customary two weeks off to clear
his mind before starting something new, he had sat down
at his desk one morning and faced a blank wall.

At first, he hadn't realized what was going on. It wasn't
as if he came up with a new book plot the minute he

was done with whatever he had been working on. He usually had several ideas percolating in his brain, but deciding on what was worth doing next was a process. He had waited patiently to see what direction he wanted to take, what themes were going to stick as his thoughts traveled over miles of images.

After two months, he was at the same point he had been on the first day. His ideas had deserted him. Whatever he considered struck him as supremely uninteresting. At the time, he would have described himself as uncomfortable with the situation. When four months had passed without a hint of progress, he was anxious, unable to put his concern out of his mind for more than an hour or two. By the end of six months, he was in a state of full-blown panic.

He hadn't told anyone. His next book was to be the third of a four-book contract he had signed with his publisher. When his editor called to ask how things were going, Peter lied with a gusto he hadn't known he was capable of. It wasn't difficult to hide the situation from Kip, because she knew better than to ask about work in progress. Years ago, he had explained that it was hard, sometimes almost painful, to talk about the few pages he might have written on any given day. When he had reached a natural transition point, he might bring it up. She respected his wishes on that. As she respected his wishes on most things, he thought, struck again, as he so often was, by his luck in marrying her.

He doubted that she was feeling so lucky to be married to him these days, though. No matter how he resolved to get a grip on himself, he couldn't prevent his terror about his writer's block from spilling over into his dealings with his family. Lashing out at his wife and children at the slightest excuse was making him feel worse about everything. Kip appeared to be oblivious, but he doubted anyone could miss how short a fuse he now had.

On the other hand, he reflected, she was so caught up in her skating and training and classes, she might be unaware of his foul temper. She seemed to think of little else besides becoming proficient at skating again. She did what she had to do to keep the household running, but she had whittled her participation down to the minimum; it was obvious that her mind was elsewhere. And she was so tired at night, she either went to sleep before him, or she was out the second her head hit the pillow. She certainly wasn't initiating any lovemaking lately, and she didn't seem to care that he wasn't either. They'd made love just a few times in the past month or two. Sex seemed to have taken a backseat, he thought, for her because of her injury first, then because of fatigue, for him, because he didn't find being in a permanent state of panic all that conducive to arousal.

He couldn't bring himself to tell Kip about his writing problem, let alone anyone else. The great Peter Hallman, without a creative idea in his head. He'd heard about writers suddenly shutting down, unable to produce another good line, but he had counted himself among the lucky ones who weren't the type to be stricken with that problem. Apparently, he had counted wrong.

So here I sit, he thought, literally trying to pull ideas out of the sky.

"Hey, Dad, let's go."

The sound of J. P.'s voice startled him. He looked down to his left. His son was standing there, gazing up at Peter, his gym bag slung over one shoulder, his baseball cap on backwards.

"Great playing, champ." *I'm a terrible father, I didn't even watch, but I'm sure it must have been great.*

"Thanks," J. P. said with a small smile. Peter wondered if his son knew the truth about his father's lack of attention. He suspected he did.

Peter got down from the bleachers and threw an arm around J. P. as they started to walk. "Yessirree, old slugger, old batter guy," he said, "Mr. All-Star Game, Perfect Pitcher Man, that was quite a practice. That team would be nothin' without you, and they know it, too."

"*Daaaaaadd . . .*" J. P. said, giving his father a slight punch in the arm. "Cut it out."

"So modest. That's another quality I like about you."
Peter retrieved his car keys from his jacket pocket.

As they drew closer, he pressed the button on his car
key to unlock the doors to his Acura. Maybe, Peter
thought suddenly, a book about a man for whom baseball
is a religion—but baseball fails him utterly, just the way
his religion did, and he . . .

Peter sighed as he pulled open the car door for his
son. Or maybe I just get a job as a waiter.

18

"To Bernini," Eloise said, looking across the table to Kip and raising her glass of wine. The light sparkled through the delicate filagreed stem, making a tiny rainbow appear on the pristine white tablecloth. Tonino's prided itself on serving the finest food within a ten-block radius of the Frick museum, with almost as much attention lavished on the most expensive accoutrements, from their sterling silver flatware to their almost see-through china.

Kip raised her glass in return. "I believe Mr. Tramwell would pronounce it 'Berrrrniyynnni.' "

Lionel Tramwell's discussion of Roman sculpture had been thorough and engrossing, but the expert's erudition had been more than matched by his pretentious manner and obvious self-regard. Listening to him overpronounce every Italian word, extravagantly rolling his *r*s and elongating every vowel, had struck Eloise as amusing in the beginning, but by the end of the hour-long discussion she'd wanted to cover her ears with her hands.

Kip laughed out loud. "If that man's biography hadn't stated that he was born in the Bronx, it sure would have been easier to take." She put her glass down on the table. "Not that what he had to say wasn't interesting. It certainly was. And I do thank you for bringing me."

Eloise took another sip before returning her glass to the table. "Please, it was my pleasure. I've had a subscription to that lecture series for ten years, and if I've made it four times in all, I'd be surprised. I'm usually so bushed by the time I get out of the office, I don't have the energy. And, since John left . . . well, it's hard to go to these things alone." She smiled. "When you told me you were going to be in the city, it was the best news I could have had."

She didn't have the heart to add how badly she needed her friend. She'd thought the worst thing John could have done was walking out on her the way he did. But yesterday's meeting in her lawyer's office had proved, if anything, even more painful. She'd assumed their divorce negotiations would be easy. After all, both of them were lucky enough to be well off, and there were no custody issues. What could they possible fight about?

Oh, how wrong she had been. First, John had laid claim to the Matisse her parents had given her when she'd turned twenty-one, then to the seventeenth-century chest that had been in her mother's family for generations. The *coup de grâce* had been his insistence that both her apartment and the house in Rhinebeck be sold, the money they took in to be shared between them. Her lawyer had assured her that John couldn't possibly get everything he was asking for; in fact he might end up with none of it. But the experience had left her shaken. Did she know this man? Had she *ever* known him? The two of them had been married for well over a decade, and John Kaline might just as well have been a complete stranger.

"So what do you eat here?" Kip asked, raising the menu the maître d' had left.

"I think the fish is what they're known for," Eloise answered, grateful to have her thoughts interrupted. "Actually, I don't come here that often. It's good, and, of course, convenient so close to the Frick, but unless I'm up here I don't think about it much. To tell you the truth, it's filled with the same people I deal with all day long, and at night I usually prefer something lower key.

But the food is justly famous, I assure you." She looked down at the menu, which instantly seemed to signal a nearby waiter to come to her side.

"May I help you with your choices, *mesdames*?" the young man said. "The snapper is superb tonight, and the veal was brought in only two hours ago from our own grazing land upstate."

With his unctuous air and slicked-back pompadour, he looked to Eloise like an extra from a 1930s Fred Astaire–Ginger Rogers movie. Eloise began to be sorry she had brought Kip here. She'd thought her friend might get a kick out of the Upper East Side at its most chic, but the fawning attention and glittery splendor was getting on her nerves. She should have taken her to the burger place on Second Avenue. They could have relaxed into a cozy evening, instead of finding themselves two more performing seals in the crème de Manhattan circus.

Eloise put her menu down in front of her and smiled politely. "We're not ready to order yet. Could you give us a couple of minutes?"

The waiter vanished.

"I'm glad you bought us some time. I can't possibly decide what to have. Everything looks so spectacular. One thing about Rhinebeck, it's nowhere near an ocean. The number of different sea creatures on this menu makes my head spin."

"They all taste like chicken," Eloise answered, smiling. "What are your husband and the kids doing tonight?"

"Oh, at a guess, J. P. is watching *Xena—Warrior Princess,* Peter is engrossed in some book, and Lisa is complaining to her friends about what a bitch I am. She has a meet in Fishkill tomorrow morning, and she has to go with her friend Louise's mother because I won't be there to take her, which means she has to get up half an hour earlier than usual." She expelled a long breath. "Naturally, I'm consumed with guilt about that, but I'm sure all three of them are doing fine."

"Have you ever taken the kids to Rome?" Eloise

asked, thinking back to the image of the Piazza Navona that had appeared in one of Lionel Tramwell's slides.

Kip grimaced. "We certainly did. It was about a year ago. J. P. spent most of his time playing with his Game Boy, and Lisa complained about the food." Her face assumed a sulky expression. " 'Oh, Mom, the gelato has a billion calories, and everything is, like, so oily.' "

Eloise grinned. "I always thought I wanted children. You're making me feel relieved."

Kip looked at her in surprise. "Why didn't you and John have any?"

"Well, my husband had an uncooperative sperm count. I suggested adoption, but he didn't feel he could really give of himself to a child who didn't have his genetic code."

"I'm sorry," Kip sympathized. "That must have been tough for you."

Eloise shrugged. "I guess I was somewhat ambivalent myself."

"Or just a good, good wife."

"How are we going to get our Nora to be a good wife?" Eloise asked, longing to escape the sadness Kip's question had evoked in her.

Kip smiled. "Okay, I won't ask you any more questions. Anyway, we can't make Nora do anything for the next few days. Not while she's in Mississippi."

"Oh, that's right," Eloise responded. "That was this week. I wonder how she's doing with Will Stanley. He's not an easy man to get through to."

"Do you know him?" Kip asked.

Eloise started to answer, but was interrupted by the return of the waiter.

"So, *mesdames*, have we chosen?"

Eloise picked up her menu and made a swift decision. "Grilled tuna rare, please, with broccoli rabe on the side." And French fries and a soufflé, she added in her head, knowing she could never order what she'd really like with Kip right there beside her.

"Same for me," Kip said, closing the menu and handing it to the waiter.

"An exquisite choice," he said, taking the menus and wheeling around toward the kitchen.

"We have made it into the inner circle of fine orderers, and I, for one, applaud our talent," Eloise said, flourishing her fork like a sword.

"Back to Nora's movie guy. You know him?"

"Not really. He came to a couple of parties at my parents' house when he was married to the newscaster." She straightened the napkin in her lap. "She was the friendly one, although in that journalist way. You know, a million questions, in case there was some information you might give her some day. He was more mysterious. Quiet, smart. Attractive as hell. Sat in a corner chair most of the night. Talked to people if they bothered to approach him. Otherwise, just sat there observing everybody." She smiled. "For all I know, he was doing crossword puzzles in his head. He certainly wasn't pumping anyone the way the wife was."

"Did you like him?" Kip asked.

"Well . . ." Eloise considered the question. "I guess you could say I was curious about him. When people are quiet that way, they seem mysterious and fascinating. It's sort of a corollary to the 'who wants to belong to a club that wants me as a member' thing. The more he didn't care about us, the more we all wanted to know what made him tick." She laughed. "It drove my father crazy. Both times they met, Dad spent at least half an hour trying to get him to interact with the people he decided Stanley would find interesting, but the guy couldn't be pushed. Dad would take him up to some diplomat, and this Will would utter a few polite phrases and extricate himself. It was satisfying to watch, I have to admit. I've never seen anyone handle my father quite so deftly."

"Don't you and your brother deal well with your father? I mean, you must. You both work with him all day long."

"Ohhh . . ." Eloise's response sounded almost like a groan. "I'd say the truth would be, he deals with us. It's pretty hard to go up against him. He's so damn charming and filled with good will. It's like fighting Kris Kringle. You know, he's giving you gifts left and right, so you feel like an ingrate if you go up against him. And, frankly, he's right most of the time. In fact—"

Eloise stopped talking suddenly. From across the room came sounds that turned her insides to jelly. She looked past Kip's shoulder, desperately hoping she had been mistaken.

"Hilton, James, you should be proud of yourselves. That Haskell maneuver was a stroke of genius."

John Kaline's booming voice carried across the large room. Horrified, Eloise saw that he and the dark-haired woman by his side were being led to a table, stopping along the way to greet acquaintances. The woman, whom Eloise recognized as the one she had so casually dubbed Schnauzer Lady, looked stunning, dressed in an immaculate white silk suit, her hair swept up into a perfect chignon. She was smiling effusively at the two men John was chatting with, seemingly thrilled to meet them.

Eloise stared so hard, Kip turned around in her chair to see what was going on. Both of them watched the elegant couple as John left that table and stopped at another a few feet farther on.

"Liddy and Bill, I don't think you know Francesca."

Again, the woman beamed in response.

Kip turned back to Eloise. "What is it? Do you know them?"

Eloise nodded. "Oh, yes. Yes, indeed. That's John. My husband. Or my not-husband. I don't know what to call him." She looked at Kip, her eyes full of pain. "My soon-to-be ex. And his new lady love."

She dropped her eyes. She'd been having such a nice time with Kip. Maybe her luck would continue and John wouldn't notice her sitting there.

"Eloise!"

At the sound of her husband's voice, she lifted her head up.

"Francesca Circone, you haven't met Eloise. I'm glad you two are finally getting to know each other. It's about time."

John put one hand on Francesca's shoulder and brought his other hand down on Eloise's. She sat there, frozen, unable to bring herself to pull away. His voice betrayed nothing of their relationship. They might just as well have been people who'd been on a trip together or known and liked each other in the sixth grade.

"John has told me such wonderful things about you," Francesca said, her tone wooden but with the same broad smile she'd brought to their previous encounters as they'd crossed the restaurant.

"How do you do?" Eloise's face felt as if all the blood had rushed out of it, but she managed to sound cordial. "This is my friend, Kip Hallman."

John peered at Kip. "You're one of the other people who was part of that terrible situation upstate, aren't you?"

"How did you know that?" Eloise asked, astounded.

John smiled knowingly. "Bobby Gedalecia. We played nine holes at Wykagyl a few weeks ago, and he told me all about it. He said that Peter Hallman's wife had been in the robbery with you. Tragic, really a terrible thing." His face assumed a mask of sorrow.

Eloise wanted to slap him. Who was he to lay claim to her life, to her friend? But she said nothing. This whole meeting was humiliating enough. What would it serve for her to make a further fool of herself?

She was interested, though, to note that Kip said nothing at all to John, barely acknowledging that he was even standing there. Eloise wished she had the nerve to freeze him out that way. Hell, she'd like not just to ignore his presence, but to do something spectacularly bad. To pour the rest of the bottle of wine over his head. And hers, the beauteous Francesca. How does it feel, stealing another woman's husband, she longed to ask. Are you happy? Do you ever wish you could give him back?

Perhaps John read the ambivalence in her eyes. He

backed away from the table, waving gaily in Eloise's direction. "You look grand," he said by way of good-bye. Francesca offered one more brilliant smile at Kip and Eloise both before allowing herself to be led off.

Left alone at their table once more, Kip spoke first. "Wow."

Eloise took a long drink of water and set her glass down, hard. "Yeah, wow."

Kip was shaking her head. "You never told us any of that."

"Any of what? I did, too. I told you about the fabulous Francesca."

"No, about John." Kip's expression showed her ongoing astonishment. "About how he's exactly like your father."

Eloise stared at Kip. "*What?* What are you talking about?"

"But, he's exactly . . ." Kip trailed off. "Oh, God, you don't know. And now you're never going to talk to me again for saying it."

Eloise sat up straighter in her chair. "Saying what? You think he looks like my father? No, he's—"

"Eloise," Kip broke in, "he doesn't *look* like your father. He *is* your father. I mean, he's exactly the same kind of person. It's as if you married your father!"

"What?" Eloise glared at her. "I married someone I was in love with. He may have turned out to be, well, not all I could have wished for, but . . ."

Kip leaned forward. "I'm telling you, John is exactly like your dad. I mean, speaking of Kris Kringle giving you gifts as he's maneuvering you into doing something you don't want to do—he's right off the same page."

Eloise was stunned into silence. The thought that John was anything like her father had never occurred to her. "I don't know," she said slowly. "When I married him, he was just a poor law student. He was nothing like the glad-hander he's turned into. He wanted his own firm—"

"—and everything his own way." Kip raised her hands, imploring Eloise to listen. "This man just made his girl-

friend stand around making nice to his wife. Not only
did he want everyone to act the way he wants, but he
wanted them to love him for it. I mean, really, he walked
in to this place like he was running for governor!"

And like he wanted to take all my possessions into the
governor's mansion with him, Eloise thought but did not
say. She took a piece of her roll and buttered it.

Kip yanked it out of her hand.

"No wonder you have a problem with food. That's
probably the only part of your life you've ever been in
charge of. No wonder you grab at it. It's all you have
that's *yours!*"

"You think I eat because of my parents?"

Kip gave her a sad smile. "I have a teenager. The
mothers talk about it constantly. Every anorectic child
of every supercontrolling parent has basically the same
story. All they feel in control of is food, so they stop
eating. You've just got it in the other direction."

Eloise sat back in her chair. She thought about all
those weekends in New Hope: "Smile for the Edbergs,
dear. Show the Billinghams the greenhouse."

Even at the magazine, her father was the one in
charge: "That model's way too heavy. No one wants to
read about the ungainly." Eloise blushed with shame.

"You may be right," she said quietly, lifting up the
roll once again and then putting it down.

The waiter returned to their table, bringing with him
two plates of perfectly cooked tuna, resting gracefully
atop a mound of bright green broccoli rabe. Kip lifted
her fork and cut off a tender piece of rare tuna. Eloise
watched her put it into her mouth.

Moments before, Eloise had been famished. Now she
felt strangely detached, poking her own piece of tuna
with her fork and tasting a tiny bite. For the first time
she could remember, her appetite seemed to have deserted her.

19

"Yuh know, Mistuh Stanley, just because Huhdson is a puhblic school doesn't mean that we're invahtin' in total stranguhs, anytahm they please."

Nora had to listen carefully to Eustace McLuhan's sonorous baritone voice, with its pronounced Mississippi drawl, to figure out what he was saying to Will Stanley. Even the slow cadence of McLuhan's speech didn't do much to mitigate the mellifluous slurring of his words. The two men had been fighting, albeit with exquisite politeness, for almost fifteen minutes over Will's desire to film the inside of one of Hallport's elementary schools. Each in turn exhibited perfect manners, plus the absolute certainty that he and only he held the moral high ground.

Nora found it fascinating. She had flown down with Will the night before, although the word *with* was somewhat of an overstatement. They had met at LaGuardia Airport, sat in different rows on the airplane, barely nodded on the hour-long drive to the small but attractive hotel, and exchanged perhaps twenty words at breakfast, five of them *Milk? Sure. Sugar? No thanks.*

Before going to their rooms the night before, Will had handed her an enormous envelope of still photographs that he'd shot, with the promise that after finishing up today he would let her see some actual footage. The photographs were spectacular, but seeing the city of Hallport with her own eyes was a different matter. Will had focused in on many different sections of Hallport society, from the blues hangouts along the winding streets of the downtown area, where the old wooden buildings still stood, to the garish new casinos, which had just about taken over the strip of beach land along the Gulf of Mexico.

In the past few years, Hallport had gone from a small, conservative town, where whites lived on one side of town, blacks on the other, neither group especially prosperous, to an energetic, almost fully employed boomtown. With casinos legalized—just so long as they were on the water—unemployment had almost disappeared. Years before, the overhanging blanket of white magnolia blossoms in their glorious April bloom used to line the roads between the ramshackle buildings in the middle of town to the cotton farms in the outlying areas. Now they led the way to a miniature version of Las Vegas. Nora and Will had walked through one of the largest casinos on the beach that morning, and what they saw at the blackjack tables and the five-dollar slot machines were people of every age and every color taking their shot.

The photographs and film footage Will had amassed from forty years earlier couldn't have been more different. But the question remained, was the easier mix of people today due to changing laws governing integration or simply a manifestation of the economic changes in the state? According to the few things Will had said, most people he'd spoken to in town were much more likely to attribute everything to economics. The Supreme Court under Earl Warren wasn't getting nearly as much credit in Hallport as legalized gambling was.

Nora could see from the photographs he'd given her to look at that the citizens of Hallport had been cordial to Will, enabling him to film courtrooms and clubs, parades and stores. But he was desperate to get his camera into the Hallport schools, and this was something Eustace McLuhan wasn't about to let him do. As head of Hallport's public school system, McLuhan had complete authority, and, clearly, the sudden entrance of a Northern stranger come to pass judgment on a town he couldn't possibly understand didn't seem like a good thing to Eustace McLuhan.

Nora watched Will squirm in a slightly-too-small wooden chair opposite McLuhan's desk. His feet were entangled between the front of the desk and the legs of the chair, while the wet umbrella he'd carried in that morning's on and off rainfall bumped against his knees. His arms, with nowhere to rest, seemed to spill awkwardly onto the spotless surface of McLuhan's desk. Will had taken the trouble to put on a navy blue suit. Before this, she'd only seen him in blue jeans. But his wardrobe didn't seem to impress McLuhan.

Nor did he seem impressed with the gift Will had brought for him. It was a copy of a book Will had written a few years before, filled with beautiful black-and-white photographs of Las Vegas. Nora had flipped through a few pages that morning on their way over in the rental car. He'd shot the parade of tourists in shorts and sneakers, with children in tow, the rash of new communities, their split-level splendor eating up the land, and the neon-lit strip, with its permanent traffic jam and interminable crowds. Inside the huge, flashy hotels, he'd captured the croupiers and cocktail waitresses, the senior citizens pulling at the slots. But, toward the end of the volume, for a few magic pages, he'd gotten what still remained of the desert, its empty, raw beauty unmarred for mile upon mile.

She understood why Will had given the volume to McLuhan. *"I'll be fair to your city,"* it should have cried out to him. But Eustace McLuhan wasn't listening.

"I swear to you, Mr. McLuhan, I'm not some proselytizing fool who's come here to make your city look foolish or backward. I just want to show it as it is." Will's voice was earnest. "I'd be happy to show you a couple of other films I've made. You might find them interesting, and you'd see something about how I do things."

"Mr. Stanley," McLuhan said, the picture of civility,

"I'm sure your movies are just swell. In fact, I'd bet that not since King Solomon has anyone been more fair. But I just don't let strangers into my schools."

"I bet your students would enjoy seeing themselves on television," Will offered.

McLuhan began to push back his chair. For him, the meeting was about to be over. "I'll be happy to tell you everything you want to know about Hallport schools. We have regular neighborhood places, plus four magnet schools, where kids who want something more personal can choose to go. We even have a performing arts complex, not much less grand than the place y'all have up in Manhattan, or so I'm told."

Will stayed firmly in his seat. "I'm sure it is. In fact, the proprietor of the hotel I'm at was telling me that very thing."

McLuhan frowned. "You up at the Charter House?"

"Mmhmm," Will answered.

A look of disgust passed across McLuhan's face. "Belle Hoover wouldn't know a magnet school from a farm animal." He stood up abruptly.

Will had warned Nora to say as little as possible. In fact, she'd practically had to beg to get him to allow her to come along. She knew she wasn't supposed to be butting into his business, but she could hardly make the situation any more difficult than it already was.

"Have you lived in Hallport all your life?" she asked the elderly man.

"No, ma'am. I was born in Montgomery, Alabama, and the wife and I lived in Hartford, Connecticut, for about ten years after I got out of the navy."

Nora smiled. "That must have been a shock to your palate."

Will turned around and looked at her, *What the hell do you think you're doing?* clearly in his eyes. But she went on, paying no attention.

"When I used to come North after my summers in Georgia, my stomach would practically growl at the thought of everything I was leaving behind." She let a small sigh escape.

"Like what?" McLuhan asked, obviously not at all sure she was telling the truth.

"Oh," Nora said, thinking, "like my grandmother's fried chicken." She swiveled around to address Will, as if she were being polite to the outsider in the group. "You know the secret to perfect fried chicken, don't you?"

Will crossed his legs, causing his upper body to twist into an even more awkward angle. "No, I can't say that I do."

Nora smiled at McLuhan. "Well, of course, you soak the chicken pieces in buttermilk for three hours. That's three hours exactly, not one minute more or less, Grandma used to say."

McLuhan grinned at her and sat back down. "My grandmother's greatest triumph was her biscuits."

"Do you know what her secret was?" Nora asked.

"Well, she used to say it was a combination of not working the dough too hard and using ice-cold butter." He deigned to look at Will. "Makes them tough otherwise."

Nora nodded vigorously. "You're absolutely right. In fact, my grandmother used to hypothesize that the best bakers were the ones with the lowest natural body temperature."

"Well, now, that's true!" McLuhan was leaning forward, chuckling with Nora as if he'd known her for decades. "My gosh," he said, leaning back in his chair and casting a derisive glance at Will, "you certainly were no fool when it came to picking a wife. This little lady's a damned good advertisement for you, young man."

"Nora is n—" Will tried to speak, but Nora cut him off.

"Mr. McLuhan, you're making me blush." Nora smiled conspiratorially. She knew McLuhan understood that she was parodying herself, and he enjoyed being in on the joke. It was clear to her that McLuhan was nobody's fool. She was playing a role, and Eustace McLuhan was charmed in spite of himself.

McLuhan was smiling back at her, enjoying her show. "You know, when I was a boy, there was a woman in town who reminded me of you. I remember her because I was her date for the high school prom, which was pretty big stuff back then, I tell you. . . ." He continued with a number of stories from childhood and then began to describe his years in Hartford. ". . . so I told my wife, I give this town fifty more times of 'What's that you're saying?' and then we're leaving. People there couldn't seem to understand plain English. Sure enough, about three weeks later we sold the house and came right down here to Hallport."

Nora laughed with genuine enjoyment. Eustace McLuhan was an interesting raconteur when he wasn't defending his turf. She decided it was time to take the bull by the horns.

"Mr. McLuhan. I know you don't want to give us access to the school, but if you'd change your mind, I'd give you my personal guarantee that you wouldn't be sorry. So much has happened over the past forty years, and so many of my fellow Northerners don't understand how deep the changes go." She raised her hand and pointed at Will. "This guy's a really good filmmaker, and he plays it straight."

She stayed silent, sensing that more would definitely be less. McLuhan shook his head from side to side, finally raising his eyes to heaven.

"Okay now, folks," he said after a minute or two had passed, "how about I give you an hour—that's one hour and not a minute over—inside? You don't rile up any of my kids and you don't get in the way of any of my teachers."

"That would be wonderful," Nora exclaimed.

Will sat there for a moment, shell-shocked. Nora, however, stood up quickly.

"Let's go, honey," she said to Will, offering her hand as if to pull him out of his chair. *"Tempus fugit."*

McLuhan reached for his telephone. "I'll call over to Harvey Briggs, who's principal of Hudson Elementary, and tell him it's okay to let you in. But one thing you got to promise me . . ."

"Yes?" Will responded this time.

"You two have to come over to my house when you're finished. Laura, my wife, is gonna introduce you to flavors I'll bet your grandma never even thought of."

Nora beamed. "Why, we'd love that, wouldn't we, darling?" She turned to Will.

"Wouldn't we ever," he mumbled. Out of nowhere, a sardonic grin appeared on his face. "I hope your wife will let Nora help her in the kitchen. My wife considers a day without cooking a day wasted."

Nora felt a laugh rise in her throat, but managed to control it.

McLuhan's good will radiated toward both of them. "Y'all get back here after you're through, and I'll show you the way. The school's on Whitlaw and Third. I assume you have a map."

"You bet," Will responded as he led Nora out of the office. Together, they walked down the corridor. Grinning, Nora took his arm as they went, knowing that with McLuhan watching them, Will couldn't pull away.

Which was exactly what he did as soon as the doors of the building closed behind them. The spurts of rain that morning had turned to a steady downpour, but Will handed Nora the umbrella, choosing to stride several feet in front of her. It was only when they got into the car, and Will started the engine that he spoke.

"So where does a girl named Levin learn about cold butter and low body temperatures?"

Nora adjusted her seat beat. "My great-uncle Isaac owned a dry goods store in a small town outside Atlanta. He and his wife used to come up for Passover."

Will pulled the car out into the driving lane. After another few minutes of silence, he cast her a disdainful look. "And when Mrs. McLuhan asks you to hand her the buttermilk, you won't offer the sugar by mistake?"

"Why, darling," Nora batted her eyes, "you simply wouldn't believe the things I can do with grits." She was beginning to like this game. Will Stanley was such a pain in the ass. Such a law unto himself, above the common fray. Teasing him was just too much fun.

Will consulted the map of Hallport, looking for Whitlaw Street. "Actually, I would have taken you for an order-in type."

"Gee," she said, "married all these years, and you don't even appreciate my cooking."

Will shifted uncomfortably in his seat, which only made her want to tease him more.

"And what kind of example are you setting for little Wilma and Bill Junior? I believe the twins know more about me than you do."

He didn't even stoop to answer her.

It was over two and a half hours later when they headed back to Eustace McLuhan's office. The children at the school had been lively and interesting. Will used the minicam digital video, with the microphone built in, as he didn't have his sound man along. And the kids had been enchanted when he'd let them watch themselves on the screen in the camera after he'd shot a couple of the classes.

Teeming rain, borne by sudden gusts of wind, made it hard to see even when he'd turned the windshield wipers on. The moisture had soaked through Nora's clothing, and she hugged herself for warmth. Will looked over at her and switched on the heat.

"Can I watch the footage tonight?" Nora asked. "I have a load of music lined up, but I need to see as much as you have, so I know what to throw out and what to keep in."

"Sure," he answered, starting the car. "Actually, the whole thing's almost finished. I can show you a lot of it later. I'll plug it into the television when we get back to the hotel. But first"—he turned and glared at her—"we have to get through dinner with the McLuhans."

Nora knew she should keep quiet, but she couldn't

help herself. "Just in case Mrs. McLuhan asks, what do you sleep in?"

"Raw clam shells and a pound of margarine," he answered, turning on the radio to ward off further conversation.

Three hours later, they were seated at Eustace McLuhan's dining room table, stuffed with redfish and collard greens, accompanied by a homemade punch that tasted like sugar but packed a wallop that suggested massive quantities of bourbon. They had traveled over two different bridges to get to the house, which was on a peninsula that jutted out to the Gulf. The house itself had been a plantation. Large and spanking white, it looked imposing from the long grassy driveway, with a second-story veranda that bespoke centuries of afternoon mint juleps. But within sight was a new clutch of split-level houses, which must have been built over the past couple of decades.

McLuhan's wife, Laura, was a small, bustling woman with bright blue eyes and a quick smile. Easily sixty or so, she did everything at top speed. Also at the table was Terry, their five-year-old granddaughter, whose parents had left her for the weekend. Nora found the child as smart as she could be and adorable besides. Dressed in dungaree overalls and a red blouse with a bow under the collar, she had Shirley Temple curls and enormous brown eyes that seemed to melt into anyone she chose to talk to.

Laura and Eustace were telling a long story about their time in Connecticut, and she could see that the child was becoming restless. Nora decided to play a game her nieces liked. "So, Terry," she said, whispering in the little girl's ear, "tell me, which would you rather be, a bricklayer or a fireman?"

Terry's answer was immediate and definitive. "A fireman, silly."

"Okay," Nora said, "would you be a dining room or a living room?"

"Well . . ." Terry tapped her chin with her fingertip.

". . . a living room 'cause the couches are more comfortable."

"What would you be, a horse or a lion?"

Terry said the word *lion* so quickly Nora almost missed hearing it. By now, the other adults had stopped their conversation and were listening to them.

"So, Terry, what would you be, a dog or a cat?"

"Ummm . . ." The girl hesitated. She tucked her hand under her chin as if she were considering the question with the utmost seriousness. "I'd be a cat, and I'd sit in the window all day long and report robbers!"

Nora began to form another question, but Terry interrupted her.

"What would *you* be, a spoon or a knife?"

Nora grinned. "What a great question," she said. "Knives are incisive, but spoons are so cozy. I guess I'd be a spoon."

Terry giggled. "And would you be salt or pepper?"

Eustace cut in before Nora had a chance to answer. "Would you be sleepy or asleep?" he asked, scooping her up from her chair into his arms.

"Oh, Grandpa, that's so silly. I'm awake." She lifted her hands to her eyebrows. "See," she said, manually widening her eyes, "I'm not sleepy or asleep."

The man smiled. "Well, you're soon going to be." He put her back down on the floor. "Say good night to our guests, and let's go count us some sheep."

"Are there sheep in my room?" the little girl teased, taking his hand in hers.

He guffawed. "Not exactly. Now, say bye-bye to Mr. and Mrs. Stanley."

"Bye, Mrs. Stanley." Without being asked to, Terry put her face up to Nora's, offering her cheek for a kiss.

Nora put her arms around the girl, lifting her up for a quick hug. "Sleep tight, honey," she said, giving her back to her grandfather.

"And Mr. Stanley." Eustace's tone was stern, though there was a hint of a smile on his face.

Terry was a bit more shy with Will. "Night night, Mr. Stanley," she said with gravity.

"Good night, princess," he replied, placing his hand on top of her hand as if he were offering a benediction.

They all watched her leave, accompanied by her grandfather. Nora turned to Laura McLuhan.

"Is she always that well behaved?"

Laura laughed heartily. "My Lord, no. But we told her we'd only let her stay up this late if she went to bed without a single protest. She's a nice child." The words themselves were modest compared with the look of pride on her face. Then her eyes grew pensive. "It's not the easiest time for her. Our son and daughter-in-law have been having some problems. That's why Terry is with us this week. Tim and Carole went down to Barbados for a little romantic getaway." She sighed. "I hope it helps."

It seemed to Nora the better part of tact to stay silent, but, surprisingly, Will touched Laura's hand for a sympathetic couple of seconds. The woman smiled at him, grateful for the support.

"How did you two get together?" Laura asked.

Nora stiffened. She'd gotten to like Eustace and his family. Now, the notion of perpetuating the lie seemed indecent. She looked at Will, tempted to blurt out the truth, but he started to speak before she had a chance.

"Nora picked me up at a country and western bar on Bleecker Street, right in the middle of New York City." Will kept a straight face, but his eyes twinkled with evil pleasure.

Laura McLuhan looked fascinated. "Well, imagine that!"

Nora thought she would faint from shock. What a puzzle Will Stanley was. She'd been certain that Will would have her head for this fiction she had created. It never would have occurred to her that he would take it over and give it wings.

"She was there all alone in a pretty little black skirt and a suede vest. And cowboy boots! Red leather cowboy boots."

The sincerity in his tone was stunning, but more surprising was the fact that he was clearly enjoying himself. Nora found herself staring at him, wondering what he would come out with next.

He did not disappoint. "She'd been there with a bunch of friends, and they'd all disappeared, and I looked like a guy who'd give her a free ride home."

"Will!" Nora said, equally outraged and entertained. Oh, well, she thought, in for a penny, in for a pound. "But, sweetheart, you forgot to mention what you were wearing." She turned to Laura. "Leather pants. Skintight black leather pants."

"I believe you're mixing me up with a man you once picked up in Chelsea, sweetheart," he answered, almost laughing out loud.

Nora took a long sip of the punch. She'd had several glasses by now and was glad.

"I don't think you two mean a word of this," Laura said, her blue eyes crinkling in laughter. "I bet you two were fixed up by your minister or maybe by your mothers."

Will reached across the table and took Nora's hand, holding on to it tightly. It was all she could do not to jump out of her seat. "You're not far wrong, Laura. Nora and I are just about the most conventional couple you'd ever want to know." He interlaced their fingers, softly stroking her wrist with his thumb. "Chatted like a couple of magpies from the moment we met at the zoo."

Nora could only stare at him.

"That's right, Laura," he said, now looking Nora straight in the eye. "If it weren't for the monkeys throwing the banana peels at us, we'd never even have met." He ruffled Nora's hair and smiled at Laura.

Eustace walked back into the dining room. "You folks got a little trouble, y'know."

They all turned to look at him.

"The bridge to town is rained out. It's not gonna open until tomorrow morning, at the earliest. I believe you two are going to be our guests for a little bit longer than you meant to."

Nora looked at Will. His good-natured spell seemed to be over. She could imagine what he was thinking: Take this woman and get her a thousand miles away from me. That would probably be the gist.

"We've got a spare bedroom on the third floor," Laura said, jumping out of her chair. "Let me just run upstairs and pull some linen out for you."

"Don't go on up yet," Eustace said, taking his seat. "It's early." But his wife had already left the room.

Will pushed his chair back. "You're sure there's no other way to get back to the hotel?" he asked, all his former playfulness gone.

"Not a prayer," Eustace answered. "They're pretty good about getting in shape quickly. By eight or nine tomorrow morning, they should have it all set to go." He reached for the glass of punch in front of him and drank a greedy sip. "Happens all the time here on the coast."

Nora watched Will resign himself to the situation. But he'd once again turned into the silent, brooding man she'd been used to. She wasn't sure the McLuhans were ready for the real Will Stanley. She heard Laura coming back downstairs.

"You know, we have some prep work to do for tomorrow's shooting," Nora said to Eustace. "I think maybe we'd better go on upstairs, if you don't mind." She rose out of her chair.

Will frowned and stood next to her.

Eustace smiled. "You two go on now."

Laura called to them from the bottom of the stairs. "Come on, I'll show you where everything is."

There were several rooms on the third floor. Though the air was slightly musty, the curved ceilings and wooden floors made for great charm. Laura led them to the room farthest from the stairs, opening the door to a modest-sized but beautifully appointed guest room. They saw a large maple bed covered by a flowered cotton canopy. There were two windows, slightly too high to see through, covered by curtains of the same fabric as the canopy. Next to the bed were two small end tables, one holding a stack of Reader's Digest Condensed Books. At the foot of the bed was a large oak chest, on top of which sat a white ceramic washing bowl with a tiny cornflower pattern around the rim. A matching pitcher sat in its center.

"This room is lovely," Nora gushed.

Laura smiled. "It's nice to have people taking advantage of it. Especially youngsters as nice as yourselves." She walked over to a doorway on the right. "You have your own bathroom. I put out some towels and soap. Yell down if you need anything."

She waved to them as she went out. They stayed quiet as they listened to her footsteps descending the stairway.

Will didn't say a word to Nora. Nor did he look at her. They both stood there, neither one knowing what to do. There wasn't even a chair in the room, and opening the ancient, squeaky door so one of them could find another space in which to sleep would likely be heard downstairs.

Nora felt nervous, and more than a little guilty. This really was her fault. She considered apologizing to Will for allowing this business to start in the first place, but one look at his face stopped her. He was in full retreat, very much like the first time they'd met, giving nothing, getting nothing. Then, it had intimidated her. Now, it got under her skin. She had the uncontrollable urge to goad him, to make him react. It's the bourbon, she thought. But she realized she was lying to herself.

She walked over to the bed, sat down, and removed her shoes. "So, sweetheart," she said, pushing her skirt up to her knees and rubbing her legs suggestively, "do you think we're gonna last or did them monkeys pick the wrong couple?"

She didn't expect him to answer. He did cast a disdainful eye at her before going to the other side of the bed, taking off his shoes and socks, and sitting up against the headboard. She looked at his face, gray with exhaustion, and almost felt sorry for him. But his refusal to respond to her ended any sympathy she might have had.

As far as she was concerned, he was begging for trouble. "Well, darling," she continued, stretching out beside him and nudging his leg with her knee, "at least you didn't mention the night in the Mexican motel."

As she heard the words come out of her mouth, she knew it was time to stop. There had been something so outside of real life about this trip. Here she was in this unfamiliar place, pretending to be a wife, pretending to be intimate with someone she didn't even know. Will Stanley was a client. An important client. She'd never conducted business this way, and this certainly wasn't the time or place to start. No amount of bourbon justified this level of irresponsibility.

She turned over and faced away from him, intending to close her eyes and attempt sleep. Not that it was likely to come very easily, but it was what she should have done the minute they'd entered the room. Her eyes flew open when she felt his arm come over her shoulder. He pulled her close against him, the hardness of his chest cushioning her back, his legs coming up behind hers, as if they'd embraced hundreds of times before.

"So, Nora—"

The sound of him saying her name made her blush.

"—what would you rather be, a knife or a spoon?" He took his other arm and brought it around her from underneath, enfolding her thigh and then traveling up to trace her hipbone.

Suddenly, it was Nora who was speechless. This wasn't supposed to happen. She'd been teasing him. She was grateful for the darkness as she felt a flush of heat spread all the way up from her chest through the roots of her hair. She pulled away from him, forcing a few inches distance between them, praying he would turn over and go to sleep. After all, he'd had his turn making fun of her, punishing her for her ill-conceived teasing.

But instead of turning away from her, he once again

leaned into her, his closeness all-encompassing. His knee rose between her thighs, and his arms reinstated themselves around her, his left hand stroking her neck, his right much too close to her breast. She felt engulfed in his embrace, the warmth of his body intoxicating. Again, she thought of pulling away, but she had trapped herself by edging so close to the end of the bed. Another inch or so and she'd be on the floor.

She shouldn't be encouraging this, she knew, but her fear of falling off the bed made her relax back against him, fitting herself into the seat he had made of himself. She felt his hands making their way inside her blouse, one from the open neck of her shirt collar, the other coming from beneath; he'd freed the fabric from the band of her skirt without her even feeling it. His long fingers crept underneath her bra, gently but firmly taking possession of her breasts. His caresses were slow and sure, making her nipples harden, making her long for more.

He seemed to intuit her acquiescence as one of his hands moved down toward her center, setting her on fire. Unable to resist, she felt herself giving in to his embrace, making their connection even closer.

"You don't have to do this," he murmured, brushing his lips along the nape of her neck, then tracing his tongue along her shoulder blade.

And I'm not going to, she thought, fighting for self-control. Nothing had ever felt as wrong as this. As dangerous. But her body seemed to have a mind of its own. Instead of pulling away once more, as she meant to do, she felt herself melt into him, her body aflame. Without intending to, she covered his hands with her own and wandered past them to the strength of his wrist, the muscles of his forearms. His fingers tormented her as they slipped inside, opening her to waves of pleasure.

"I mean it, Nora," he said, his voice hoarse. "I'll stop right now if you want me to."

She shivered at his touch, feeling his hardness pressing against her back. Oh, yes, stop, she said inside her head as she allowed her legs to widen even farther.

20

Kip stepped back to appraise her placement of the vase of irises on the sideboard. Satisfied, she turned to the dining room table for one last inspection, moving around it, pausing to straighten out an errant fork and refold one of the oversize plaid napkins.

She yawned as she headed back into the kitchen. By most Fridays, the week's activities had caught up with her, but she was especially exhausted today. J. P. had awakened in the middle of the night with a fever of 103. Hearing his distressed call, she had gotten up and gone to his bed at the exact moment he vomited, splattering the bed, his pajamas, the carpet, and her. It seemed like forever until she finished giving him medicine to bring down his fever, cleaned him up, stripped and remade the bed, and got him back to sleep. Then she had to clean herself up.

When her alarm went off in the morning, she could barely pry her eyes open. Making this luncheon was about the last thing she wanted to be doing. But there was no way on earth she would have backed out. Months before, she had offered to make Nicole a birthday celebration. Her sister had been talking about it for weeks. It would have taken a life-or-death matter for Kip to cancel now.

J. P. was upstairs, napping after a few hours of watching television, which was all the activity he could handle. Peter could have stayed home with him, but Kip was planning to skip ballet class and skating practice anyway. She needed the morning to cook and set up for the party. So different from her usual style, she mused, which consisted of doing most of her preparation for company days before. There wasn't enough time for that in her life anymore. Peter had gone off to have lunch with his editor in New York, and Kip was just as glad she was around to look after her son.

Still, she had to admit to a bit of secret relief about having the excuses of a party and a sick child for taking the day off. Until today, she had been sticking to her schedule—God knows she was running roughshod over the rest of the world to make it to her classes and practices. But something wasn't quite right. She had to face it. She didn't feel as if she were getting anyplace. Her skating felt so—uninspired, she guessed was the only way to put it. Over time, she had relearned so much, the jumps and moves that she feared were forever lost to her. But she wasn't progressing beyond simple technical ability. The artistry was missing; she could feel it in her bones. Try as she might, she was going through the motions and not much more.

Don't think about it, she instructed herself. Today was about Nicole and her birthday, not skating. She yawned again. "Stop it," she said aloud, lightly slapping her cheeks in an effort to wake herself up. With a sigh, she went outside to check on the vegetables, which were softening on the grill.

She hoped her sister would be pleased with the menu. Nicole watched her weight relentlessly, and would rather die, she often said, than touch red meat. In deference to that, Kip had flipped through her *Well-Seasoned Appetite* cookbook the week before, choosing a fruit soup with shortbread croutons and an herb-crumbed roasted chicken with watercress, along with the grilled vegetables. Dessert would be a hazelnut chocolate cake that Kip had baked, along with store-bought mango sorbet. Nicole wouldn't eat any cake, of course, but Kip believed everybody should have a birthday cake. Besides, maybe some of the other women would partake.

She was turning on the coffee machine when the doorbell rang. As Kip walked to the door, she pushed the sides of her mouth up with her fingers. "Smile, baby, smile," she urged herself. Damn, she thought, she wanted this to be nice, and she wanted to do what she could to improve her relationship with her sister. She didn't want to be tired, her eyelids heavy, her only wish that everyone would leave her the hell alone.

Nicole stood at the front door, dressed in a red suit and high heels. Kip knew that the suit was the most expensive item of clothing her sister owned.

"Greetings." She smiled at Kip. "You did remember today was the day, didn't you?"

"Very funny." Kip ushered her in. They had spoken the night before, when Nicole filled Kip in on the personalities of the six guests and her concerns over what the dynamics among them might be. Only two of the guests knew each other well, and some of the rest hadn't even met any of the others before. Kip tried hard to listen, but she was washing dishes and eyeing a stack of papers sent to the parents from school that she had yet to read through. The truth was she didn't actually care; she just wanted Nicole to feel good about her birthday. "I did forget, but the birthday fairy stopped by to remind me."

"Good." Nicole appeared uncharacteristically cheerful. She peered into the dining room. "Oh, the table looks beautiful. As always. It's like a French country thing."

"I'm glad you like it," Kip said, surprised by her sister's effusive praise. Nicole must really be trying to keep the peace between them. "Hey, you know, you look great," Kip added sincerely. "That suit is so nice on you."

Nicole ran her eyes up and down Kip, taking in her tailored beige gabardine slacks and silk blouse, her honey-colored leather belt and suede flats. The cheerfulness seemed to be leaking out of her. "Thanks. But

looking at you, I feel overdressed." She pursed her lips.
"Of course, if I came in wearing what you're wearing,
I'd look *under*dressed. Somehow, no matter what you
wear, you always look just right. Amazing how that
works."

Her sister's last words were spoken in the put upon
tone of voice Kip knew so well. Before she could respond, the doorbell rang again.

"Let me get it." Nicole turned and strode off.

Kip sighed. So, she said to herself, we're going to have
Nicole sniping at me while I serve lunch in a stupor of
fatigue to a bunch of people I don't know. It promises
to be a glorious afternoon. She rubbed her eyes. Given
a choice, she believed she'd rather be cleaning up vomit
at 3 A.M.

"You're very welcome. It was lovely to meet you,
too."

Kip shut the door behind the last guest. She leaned
her forehead against the door, relieved beyond words
that the luncheon had gone as well as it had and that it
was finally over. All the women seemed to have gotten
along, despite her sister's trepidation, and everyone appeared to have had a good time. Nicole's mood had lightened as she basked in being the center of attention. She
was actually giggling, something Kip rarely associated
with her sister, when she opened the present of a black
cut-out bra and panties from one of her friends. And she
thanked Kip graciously for the gift certificate to a "Day
of Beauty" at a nearby spa.

So, it's done, Kip thought with satisfaction. She went
upstairs to check on J. P., as she had several times during
the party. Quietly, she opened the door to his room and
peered in to see the lump under the red comforter gently
rising and falling. Poor thing, she thought. Sleeping again.
She headed back downstairs to clean up.

As Kip was walking from the dining room to the
kitchen, dirty dessert plates in hand, she glanced into the
living room. Her sister was over by the window. She had

refilled her wineglass, and was sipping at it, gazing out at the front yard.

"There you are," Kip said, going toward her. "I was wondering why it was so quiet down here." She moved closer, still holding on to the plates. "I think it went pretty okay," she said. "That Mona is funny. I liked her a lot."

Nicole fixed her gaze on Kip. Her voice was flat when she spoke. "And she liked you, too. That was obvious."

Warning sirens went off in Kip's head. For some reason, Nicole was upset that her sister and her friend had gotten along; apparently, she would have preferred mutual dislike. Although the demands of hosting the luncheon had given Kip the adrenaline boost she needed, her exhaustion suddenly returned, settling over her like a cloak. Is it my imagination, Kip wondered, or is Nicole becoming really crazy? Negative, yes, she always was, and a world-class complainer. But lately it was as if everything were some big conspiracy to make her miserable.

I don't have the patience for this, Kip thought. I really don't. She turned to go to the kitchen as she had originally intended.

"Would you like her phone number?" Nicole asked. "You two are welcome to get together on your own."

Kip kept going, pretending she hadn't heard. The intent behind her sister's pleasant words was laced with something ugly, and Kip didn't feel like dealing with it just then. She deposited the plates in the kitchen sink. Don't tangle with her, Kip told herself. Let Nicole drink her wine, and then she'll go home. She herself might even get to lie down for twenty minutes before J. P. woke up again if she was lucky. Wouldn't that be heaven.

She started to retrace her steps to the dining room to retrieve more dishes.

"You didn't have to do that, you know." Nicole moved closer to the doorway as Kip passed by. "A normal lunch would have sufficed."

There wasn't going to be any getting around Nicole

today, Kip thought, either literally or figuratively. She walked over to her sister.

"I didn't have to do what, Nicole?" she said, hating the way her temper was rising. "Make you a party? Give you a present? Be nice to your friends?"

"I appreciate that you wanted to make me a party," Nicole answered sharply, not sounding appreciative in the least. "But you couldn't just make me a normal party. No, everything had to be so far beyond what a regular mortal would do. A simple salad, some cheese and crackers, that would have been fine for my friends." She drained her wineglass and set it down on the piano. "*Herb-crumbed* chicken with watercress. *Mostly cherry* soup. I mean, what are those?"

Kip stared. "Your friends asked me what everything was. I just told them what the recipes were called."

Nicole continued as if she hadn't heard. "*Hazelnut* cake, not just chocolate cake, but *hazelnut* chocolate cake. Baked by you, naturally. Steamed milk for the coffee. Jesus."

"Let me get this straight," Kip said. "You're displeased because I made too nice a meal?"

Nicole glared. "Yes, damn it, yes. Because you do everything so over the top, so much better than anybody else. You just *had* to show off for my friends, show them how much of a better hostess you are than I am, a better cook, how you can entertain like a professional caterer. And you had to give me the most expensive present of anyone."

"Excuse me?" Kip asked in disbelief.

"No one there could afford a whole day at a spa, and we all know I certainly can't," Nicole snapped. "It was you doing your charity number. Let the poor sister enjoy a peek into the way the better half lives."

Kip's voice rose to a yell. "I thought you would enjoy it. It was as simple as that."

"Oh, nothing's ever as simple as that with you," Nicole spat back. "I feel like a stupid little hausfrau, bringing my friends to this fancy house with Grace Kelly as hostess. I'm sure they were all intimidated, you made certain of that. And now they know I'm just the poor relation in the family."

The bile was rising in Kip's throat. "You have said some terrible things to me, Nicole," she said, "but you are crossing lines now that I don't think you want to be crossing."

Nicole turned away in disgust. "Even when you're supposed to be angry, you're so poised and well spoken. Look at you, in your neatly pressed clothes, with your Cartier watch and your pearls. You have it so damn easy."

Kip felt herself losing control. *"What do you want from me? Why is your dissatisfaction always my fault?"* She yanked the watch off her wrist. "You want my stuff? You think that'll make you happy? Here, take it!" She threw the watch down on the piano, then unhooked the earrings from both ears and slammed them down next to it.

Nicole stared, too surprised to say anything.

"Take these, too." Kip was shouting, the anger she had held in for so long finally bursting through as she pulled the strand of pearls she was wearing up over her head. "Wait, what about my shoes? Maybe the secret to happiness is in them. They cost plenty." Kip knew she sounded hysterical as she yanked off her shoes, but she didn't care. "What else? This bowl? This box?" She moved around the room, grabbing at things and adding them to the growing heap on the piano.

"Stop it," Nicole yelled.

"Oh, wait, what was I thinking?" Kip shouted back. "Of course, it's what's in my purse that you want. That's what'll buy you everything you need to become a happy woman. The credit cards, the checkbook. Silly me, not realizing."

Nicole clenched her fists as her sides. "How dare you!"

"How dare I? I'll tell you how I dare. Because I'm fed up with your contemptuous attitude, that's how."

Nicole's words were almost a whisper. *"I hate you."*

Kip grabbed her by the shoulders. *"Why? Why do you hate me so much? What did I ever do to you?"*

Nicole began to cry.

"I'm sick and tired of your jealousy," Kip yelled. "I'm sorry, I'm truly sorry, for what you had to deal with when we were kids."

"You don't have any idea. Kip this, Kip that. It never stopped."

"I understand," Kip said, "or, at least, I'm trying to. But I'm done letting you blame me for accomplishing something."

Nicole shook her head, covering her hands with her face. "That's not it," came her muffled reply.

"Then what? I'm entitled to know. You've never set foot in my house without telling me that I don't deserve what I have. That my life is too easy and yours is too hard."

Nicole sobbed, but she turned away and didn't answer.

"What the hell is so hard about a husband who loves you and two great, healthy kids? Why is your life such a disappointment?"

Nicole's crying made it difficult for her to get the words out. "Be-because you're so wonderful and I'm such a n-nothing."

Kip was having trouble making out what her sister was saying. She was certain it couldn't be what she thought she had just heard. "What? Because I'm so what?"

"You heard me." Nicole turned back to her, misery in her voice. "Don't make me repeat it."

"Nicole . . ."

With a loud sob, Nicole seemed to let go of the last remnants of her restraint. "Because you do everything right and I do everything wrong. You're a better wife, a better mother. And you can do anything. I can't stand it."

Nicole flung herself into Kip's arms, holding on tightly as she buried her head against Kip's shoulder, and cried as if her heart would break.

Kip felt as if the wind had been knocked out of her.

She wrapped her arms around Nicole and closed her eyes, overwhelmed with emotion.

"Does what I do matter that much to you?" she murmured in sad wonder.

Nicole was struggling to compose herself. She pulled back to face Kip, wiping at her eyes. "It's all I ever thought about," she whispered. "Since when we were kids. Don't you know that?"

"No," Kip said. "No, I didn't."

Nicole smoothed her hair and took a deep breath. "Well, that's the sorry truth." She pulled down on the hem of her jacket and stood up straighter. "It's embarrassing. But, yes, you, my little sister, have been my idol and my tormentor for my entire life."

"I—I don't know what . . ." Kip was at a complete loss for words.

"I think it's time I was going." Nicole seemed to have suddenly shifted gears. She walked out to the entryway and retrieved her purse from the bench, speaking as if nothing unusual had happened. "I have to get back to the boys."

Kip followed her. "Wait." She put a hand on Nicole's arm. "We should talk more."

"There isn't much to say, really. My problem. Nothing you can do about it, is there?" She gave Kip a forced smile as she unlocked the front door.

"Nicole, don't be so proud," Kip begged.

"Thank you for making the party for me. I'm sorry I was such an ingrate. It was beautiful, truly it was."

Nicole went down the three stone steps to the walkway. Kip stepped outside, one hand on the doorknob. "I wish you'd stay. Anytime you want to talk—"

Nicole gave a small wave. "Thanks. Bye." She walked to her car, her back straight, not stopping to look at Kip again before she got in and turned on the ignition.

Kip watched her sister pull out of the driveway. She was feeling so many different things, she couldn't even begin to sort them out. But more than anything, she realized, she was feeling ashamed. She was ashamed of her own insensitivity, her inability to see what was so obvious, not only recently but over their entire lives together. When she thought about all the horrible things she had just said to Nicole—she winced.

She couldn't think straight right now, that was certain. She was too upset and tired. Later, she would try to sort it all out.

As she turned to go back inside, Kip noticed a FedEx envelope propped up against the house right next to the door. She reached down for it, scanning the label for the return address as she went in. It was from Nora. Kip wasn't expecting anything from her, and certainly nothing by overnight mail. She tore off the paper strip to open the hard white envelope then decided it would have to wait while she checked on J. P. She left it on the table in the entryway without looking inside. Coming back downstairs, she was about to pick it up once more when the telephone rang. Whatever it was, she thought as she hurried to get the phone before the answering machine picked up, it would have to wait a bit longer.

The next time Kip was able to return to the envelope was just after eleven o'clock that night. What was left of the afternoon had slipped through her fingers in a rush of taking care of J. P., answering the constantly ringing telephone—she had struggled unsuccessfully with herself for years to let the answering machine pick up while she was there—and the preparation of dinner.

Peter had returned from the lunch with his editor in one of the worst moods she could ever recall, and sequestered himself in his office the second he got home. He reluctantly emerged for dinner, and Kip tried to keep the conversation light. Still, she was unable to stop Lisa from getting into an enormous blowup with her father over her request to sleep at a friend's house after some upcoming school dance. Kip was surprised at the vehemence of his refusal, particularly since he usually left Kip to deal with these issues. When her attempts to get them to calm down failed, Kip finally retreated, eating her meal in silence as they yelled at each other. She was unhappy to see them arguing, but she had to admit she was taking a small, guilty pleasure in not being the one fighting with Lisa for a change.

Peter disappeared into his office again for the rest of the evening, while Kip dealt with the rituals of getting things prepared for the next day. Then she sat with J. P. until he was asleep for the night. At last, Kip was able to flop down on the couch in the family room, envelope in hand, to see what Nora had sent her.

It was an audiotape, labeled simply FOR KIP. The note wrapped around it read "I hope this is helpful. Love, N." Kip went over to the tape deck and put it on, settling back down on the couch to listen.

The first strains of Aaron Copland's *Appalachian Spring* filled the room. How beautiful it is, Kip thought, closing her eyes and letting the music flow through her. She felt the tension draining out of her as the Quaker melody built in volume. Then, the music flowed into the "Maple Leaf Rag" by Scott Joplin. It was lighter, more playful, she reflected, listening to the lively piano. She envisioned herself doing some shorts hops along the ice, then some swift turns with her arms moving quickly, up and down, up and down.

Kip's eyes flew open. It wasn't just any music. It was music for a skating routine. Of course. Nora was a professional in the business, and she had put together a tape specially for Kip. The piano music segued into Kate Smith singing the rousing version of "God Bless America" for which she was so famous. Kip shook her head in amazement at the cleverness of the choice. It was totally unexpected, yet exactly right. Somehow, Nora had put her finger on the critical issue of how to keep things interesting while breaking up the elements of the simpler moves and more difficult jumps. Each piece spoke in such a completely different way about America. Yet, together, they were even greater than the sum of their parts.

"*Wow,*" Kip whispered. In a million years, she thought, she never would have dreamed of using that old

Kate Smith recording. She smiled as she listened to the soaring notes and voice, her fatigue forgotten. Wonderful. She felt goose bumps on her arms and legs. Incredible.

When the music was over, Kip took the cassette out of the tape deck and just stared at it. She would get Peter to watch J. P. for a couple of hours tomorrow, bad mood or not. She *had* to get on the ice with this tape in her Walkman. Hell, she thought, if the rink were open, she would go over right now.

She felt the surge of a special sort of excitement, a sensation she instantly recognized from years before. It was the thrill of knowing she was about to do something fantastic, that she had the skill and the drive to create magic. She hadn't felt it for a very long time, certainly not since she had resumed skating. But she was drunk with it now. She would choreograph a routine for this tape. Already, her mind was flooded with all sorts of possible moves. With that, she would get a coach, a good coach to push her to the next level. She was on her way.

"Nora, what can I say?" she asked aloud in the empty room. "Thank you."

21

"It's a little too hot," Nora said, listening intently to the sounds of the Golden Gate Quartet. She peered up at the images on the large screen at the front of the studio. "If we bring it under, it won't take so much attention away from the kids."

Will Stanley nodded. "Yeah, you're right. It's important to hear their voices, even if the words themselves aren't completely comprehensible."

Curt Woods, the sound engineer, sat between the two of them in the studio's dim light. "God bless Pro Tools," he said, adjusting various components on the mixing console. "In the old day, I would have been sitting here with a razor blade and a floor full of tape. Now, the tweaking's a cinch."

He played the section one more time, both Nora and Will paying close attention as it flashed on the screen.

Will looked at Nora. "Okay with you?" he asked.

"Yes, much better," she answered.

She kept her attention on the images as Curt moved to the next section of tape. For the past five days, she'd been working with Will and Curt at the postproduction studio high up in a building on Madison Avenue, not far from Grand Central Station. They'd averaged fifteen hours each day, poring over the film footage, taking quick naps on the leather couch at the back of the room, ordering in countless Chinese meals. By now, Nora was used to the dimness of the studio, the particular odors of leftover moo shu and Curt's cigarette smoke, and even the normally taciturn Will had taken to saying "Honey, I'm home," every morning as he arrived. It did feel familial to Nora, working with the two men whose talent and focus were proving to be impressive. They were courteous to each other and to her, all three of them respectful professionals doing a job they did very well indeed.

Which would have been apt if Nora hadn't been plagued by a discomfort she didn't want to think about. She knew it had to do with Will, but that was about as far as she was willing to go. Since their trip to Mississippi a few weeks before, he'd been solicitous to her. In fact, more than solicitous. He'd been friendly, attentive even. Not that he'd pressed her on anything. Not that she'd exactly given him a chance to, she acknowledged to herself. After spending the night together at the McLuhans', she awakened early the next morning, crept out of bed, making sure not to wake Will, and hurried downstairs. Over breakfast, he'd touched her hair a couple of times, taken her hand as they walked toward the car. Nora found herself almost frozen. She couldn't respond to his touch, terrified of what she'd set in motion, and Will had quickly picked up on her unwillingness to respond. He'd searched her face that morning as he let her hand go, not asking in words, yet obviously waiting for an explanation.

But there was no explanation. All Nora knew was that what had taken place never should have. And the truth was, *she* had made it happen. Worst of all, she thought, making love with Will had been the most pleasurable experience she'd ever had. She couldn't imagine what had possessed her, but whatever it had been, it couldn't happen again. Since then, both of them had acted collegial but distant. She'd caught Will looking at her several times, his expression seeming to be one almost of amusement. But he never said a word.

She heard the opening measures of Mahalia Jackson's rendition of "My God Is Real," and looked up to the screen. This was the most satisfying job she'd ever worked on. Will had a lot to say about how it all should sound, but he was attentive whenever Curt would comment on the music or even the film itself. Once or twice, the sound engineer had made a suggestion about the placement of a song. As Will had directed, Nora had selected fifteen different gospel numbers, with everyone from The Dixie Hummingbirds and Paul Robeson to The Staple Singers and Marion Williams, which were played in their entirety throughout the film. She'd also chosen sections of other old blues recordings as musical undercurrent.

The film Will had put together was an amalgam of live scenes, both from the sixties and from this year, old and new photographs and narratives from a series of experts, from historians to random citizens of Hallport. When Nora had first viewed the rough cut he'd sent her, she'd been overwhelmed by how beautiful it looked. He had managed to capture the inherent fascination of the town and of the people, without romanticizing the very real problems. Usually, selecting the music was the part of her work she liked best, but on this project the work she was doing with Will and Curt was even more exciting. Maybe she didn't wish to be intimate with Will Stanley, but he was a phenomenal colleague.

She watched him out of the corner of her eye. Although Curt was the person who performed all the mechanical tasks on the mixing board, Will was taking in every small movement on screen, his hand hovering above the machinery like a conductor who's about to quiet a string section or lengthen a fermata. He knew his business inside out, and he knew how to trust the people who worked for him. She watched as he pushed the cuffs of his white cotton shirt up to his elbows, his forearms still tan from the hours he spent filming out of doors. There were strands of blond in his hair, lightened by the southern sun, making his blue eyes even bluer. Okay, she said to herself, so he's attractive. Big damn deal.

Maybe in another lifetime, she would figure out why, despite his appeal, despite his talent, she was so stymied by the thought of sleeping with him again. God knows, it had never been a problem before. She'd had her share of professional entanglements over the years, although they had always been with sound guys and other people who worked *with* her. Never clients, never anyone who could hire or fire her.

And the men she'd slept with had never left her nearly immobilized, as this one had. Why is that? she began to ponder. She stopped herself. Not important. Doesn't matter. Not going to happen again, *period*.

"That's it for today." Will's voice interrupted her reverie. "I've got a meeting with the PBS people this afternoon."

"Okay," Nora said.

She watched as he stood and stretched, his head thrown back, his long body a graceful arc.

"See you back here tomorrow at nine," Will said, picking up his brown leather book bag and slinging it over his shoulder.

Nora and Curt both nodded, but Nora stayed seated at the console. After Will had walked out of the room, she turned to Curt.

"Can I steal you for another couple of hours?" she asked.

He smiled. "Sure. What'd you have in mind?"

"Well," she said, turning to look behind her, making certain that Will was gone. "I had some other ideas about music for a few spots, and I thought maybe we could put it together so I could show it to Will tomorrow."

"What are you doing, Luuuccy?" Curt asked, employing a terrible Desi Arnaz imitation.

"Nothing," she said. "Well . . . something. I just wanted to broaden it a little." She reached under her chair, where she'd left the music she hadn't wanted Will to see. "If he doesn't like it, I'll throw it in the garbage, but at least I want to give it the tiniest try."

"Hey," Curt said, grinning. "It's your funeral." He yawned. "How about if we do it in a couple of hours.

This is the first afternoon break I've had in weeks, and there are a couple of things I need to do."

Nora nodded. "Okay if I get back here at four?"

"Great," Curt answered, standing up and walking out of the studio.

Nora looked at her watch—1:30. There wasn't really time to go back to her office, nor were there any particular errands she had to do. A thought popped into her head, and she reached out for the telephone, dialing a number she'd come to know by heart.

"Eloise Bentley's office," an efficient voice answered.

"Hi. This is Nora Levin. Is Eloise in, by any chance?"

"One moment."

Nora waited only a few seconds before Eloise came on the line.

"Oh, Nora, how great to hear from you. I thought you'd still be buried in the studio."

"Actually I am, but I have a couple of hours to kill. I'm right near you. You haven't, by any chance, time for a late lunch, have you?"

Eloise seemed to hesitate, but then responded. "I'll tell you what. I'm expecting a call from Hong Kong sometime in the next hour or so, but if you come up to my office, I'll bring in a lunch fit for a queen. How's that?"

"I'm on my way," Nora answered.

Fifteen minutes later, Nora was seated across from Eloise at the small round table in her office. An array of sushi, plus a large platter of cut fruits and vegetables lay in the middle, with two bottles of San Pellegrino.

"Is this okay?" Eloise asked, unwrapping the plastic wrap from the sushi.

"Magnificent," Nora answered. She reached for a piece of the tuna roll, and added some ginger. "Yum. I expected American cheese on whole wheat at best. This is a feast."

Eloise bit into a floret of broccoli. "So how was Mississippi? I've hardly even spoken to you since you got back."

Nora blushed, thinking about Will. Then she realized

that Eloise was asking about the documentary. "It was fascinating. Hallport is this weird amalgam of glitzy and folksy. We got great footage."

"What was working with Will Stanley like? You know, I've met him once or twice."

Nora took another piece of sushi into her mouth and chewed it. "He's an excellent filmmaker."

Eloise looked at her. "Thank you, Roger Ebert. I mean, what kind of man is he? I always thought he was attractive."

"We were working, Eloise." Nora couldn't keep the testiness out of her voice.

"Excusez-moi," Eloise responded, smiling. "Is it just about finished?"

"Yes. Well, sort of yes." She leaned forward. "Actually, we're going to be done by tomorrow afternoon at the latest, but tonight I'm putting together an alternate cut, with music that's a little different from what Will's heard. I'm dying to add some different sounds. I guess he'll either love it or fire me."

"Seriously?"

"No, not really. I mean the regular one's almost done, and it's just fine. But I think the one the sound guy and I are putting together will be much more interesting. I just hope Will doesn't shoot me for trying."

Eloise put down her chopsticks. "Okay, so dead or alive, you'll be finished with this project within about twenty-four hours. Which leaves only one question. What are you doing about finding Alex Fenichel?"

Nora scowled. She hadn't even thought about that subject lately. And it wasn't like she wanted to start thinking about it right now. "Oh, please. The imitation Alex Fenichel was quite enough. Besides, I've been so busy."

Eloise raised an eyebrow. "I believe the three of us made a pact. I'm eating sushi. Kip is on the ice forty hours a day."

Nora smiled. "You know, now that you mention it, you look great!"

She very much wanted to change the subject, but, in

fact, Eloise did look thinner. The fitted brown suede
jacket she was wearing hugged her body, and it looked
damn good. Nora gazed at her friend, noting the emer-
gence of cheekbones that hadn't been there before.

"I've lost a few pounds. Nothing to write home about,
but I'm in there trying." Eloise waggled a chopstick
toward Nora. "Which brings us back to you. I'd say you
were not precisely 'in there' and—" she smiled wryly.
"—more than a little trying."

"Har har har," Nora answered. "Listen, Alex has
waited this long. I think he can wait another week or so."

"Or perhaps a month, or maybe a year," Eloise said.
"Or maybe you've decided that Will Stanley is a more
fruitful direction than Alex."

"That's insane!" Nora said. She felt her cheeks redden
in embarrassment. "Okay, fine, I'll find Alex Fenichel.
I'll fall in love with him. I'll marry him, goddammit."

"Mighty romantic," Eloise commented. "You know,
my assistant is a whiz with the computer. I bet Kara
could locate the real Alex Fenichel before lunch is over."

"I'll find him," Nora answered, reaching for her glass
of sparkling water. "You have important things to do."

Eloise smiled. "Nothing more important than this."

Nora found herself almost angry. She didn't want to
meet any more men. She'd had enough of sex and romance and uncontrollable urges. Will's face flashed
through her brain. Oh, shit, she thought. She'd be with
him again tomorrow. One more day of feeling like a
child.

"Oh, come on, Nora. Let me help you with this. It'll
be fun," Eloise wheedled.

Nora sighed. Right now, she could barely remember
what Alex Fenichel looked like. Yet, somehow the notion of finding Alex was fifty times less unsettling than
having Will in her mind all the time.

"Okay," she finally said to Eloise. "Let's see what your
staff can do."

Within twenty minutes, Eloise's assistant had found
him. Kara had gone into Yahoo, and within just a few

keystrokes, had homed in on Alex Fenichel. And this time, there was little doubt that he was the Alex Fenichel that Nora had known. Just as she had originally guessed, Alex was president of a company called Allydyne, which did some kind of work with connectors—whatever the hell they might be—and had had its first public offering only a year before. According to the Internet sites, Alex had worked his way up the ladder at a large electronics company in Chicago and then left to form his own business.

"Let's see how the company's doing," Eloise said, tapping her assistant on the shoulder.

Nora gaped at her. "What are you—my mother?"

Eloise was unapologetic. "I'm curious. Besides, don't you want to know if you have to bring your American Express card with you to dinner?"

"What dinner? I haven't even spoken to him!"

Eloise pointed to the computer screen. "Well, you're about to. He got divorced last year."

Nora looked as well. Kara had uncovered an interview in *Crane's* from two months before. There it was, right in front of their eyes. Alex had married someone named Nancy Firth, and they were divorced three years later. Nora read down the page. There wasn't very much personal information besides that fact. He had two children. His company was located in Boston. And his office telephone number—hell, Nora thought, there it was, right there.

Eloise gave her a significant glance; then she lifted the receiver from the telephone on the table. "Shall I dial the number for you?"

Nora took the telephone from her. "Is there an empty office somewhere? If I'm going to make an ass out of myself, I'd like to do it without people watching me."

Eloise gestured to Kara. Together, they stood and walked to the doorway.

"Take as much time as you want," Eloise said, pulling the door closed behind her.

Nora sat there for a few minutes. She thought about getting up and leaving. Eloise might be annoyed, but so what? She'd get over it. That's what she would do, she decided, standing up and reaching under the chair for her bag. As she picked up the black leather pouch, she felt the weight of the CDs she'd been carrying around. Without thinking, she found herself sitting back down in the chair. This time, she reached for the phone and dialed the number in Boston that Kara had copied down. A man's voice answered on the second ring.

"Alex Fenichel."

Nora recognized his pleasant baritone immediately. It hadn't occurred to her that he would answer his own phone. Why hadn't a secretary picked up? Anything to give her time to think.

"Um, Alex." She paused, trying to come up with something to say. "This is Nora Levin."

"My God!" Alex's voice rose in obvious excitement. "After all this time. How are you? Where are you?"

Nora laughed. "I'm in New York. I was thinking about you, and I had the impulse to call."

"That's great. I can't tell you how glad I am to hear from you. You know, I was thinking about you just last month. Actually, my father asked about you."

"How are your parents?"

"They're fine. Living in Florida since about a year ago."

Nora found herself smiling. "Well, that's wonderful. You have to send them my regards. I remember them so fondly."

"Wouldn't they love to see you," he enthused. "And wouldn't I love to see you. In fact, I'll be in New York on some business next week. Maybe we can get together. That would be terrific!"

"Absolutely spectacular," Nora answered, putting as much life in her voice as she could muster. Inside her head, all she could think was, please, please, let me wake up and realize this has only been a dream. But, as Alex buttoned down the details of their meeting—dinner, Wednesday, eight o'clock, she knew it was absolutely real.

"We did it!" Will said, leaning back in his chair, a huge grin on his face.

He turned to Nora, grasping her hand for a triumphant moment.

Nora smiled. "It's great, Will. Really, I think it's spectacular."

"Time to celebrate," Will replied. "The beer's on me." He began to rise from his chair, but Nora touched his elbow.

"Listen, Will. I hope you won't be angry. . . ."

Will sat back down, his eyebrows furrowed. "Angry about what?"

"Well . . ." Nora was having trouble deciding exactly how to phrase what she had done. "Last night, I tried something. It would mean a lot if you'd just listen to it."

Will rubbed his eyes. He was obviously exhausted. "What exactly do you mean by *something*?"

"It's an alternate musical track. Please," she implored, "give it one chance. That's all I'm asking."

Will leaned back in his chair. "Okay, folks." Then he turned to Curt. "I guess you must figure in this, too."

Nora answered for him. "He did it strictly as a favor to me. And I paid for it out of my own pocket."

"Okay, let's go."

Nora slipped out of her chair and went to the couch at the back of the studio. She couldn't bear monitoring his reaction minute to minute. But that didn't stop her from registering every move he made, every inclination of his head whenever a song had been replaced. His back was taut as he listened to Billie Holiday singing "Do Nothin' Til You Hear From Me," which she'd put in place of "What You Gonna Do?" by The Staple Singers. When the voice of Louis Armstrong came on, singing "Struttin' with Some Barbecue," she could see him relax back into his seat.

It was the sound of the "Pie Jesu" from Gabriel Fauré's *Requiem* that elicited a glance back from him to where she sat. She'd put it in during one of the few outright racial confrontations Will had captured between black men who lived in downtown Hallport and the mostly white police force. *Lord, I pray in thy mercy, grant them rest.* To her, it seemed more than fitting. But she couldn't read the expression on his face, didn't know if he was pleased or unsettled or plain disgusted. As far as she was concerned, the alternative music filled out the images on the screen. The undercurrent of Bach's Unaccompanied Cello Suite, which she'd added toward the end, gave the streets of Hallport a seriousness that felt appropriate to everything Will seemed to be saying.

When the film had ended, she stayed where she was, too scared to go back to the men. But Will got up and came to where she was sitting.

He stared down at her, his eyes aflame.

"So, your rules are I get to spend a solid year planning a film, raising the money to make it, obsessing about every detail until four in the morning. And you get to waltz in, give it ten minutes' thought, and . . ."

He seemed unable to continue, his cheeks flushed with fury. Without another word, he left the room. Nora saw the pity in Curt's eyes, felt the stamp of humiliation in her stomach.

"Hey," Curt said, "it was worth a try. Actually, I thought it was kind of terrific."

Nora tried to smile at him, but she couldn't quite make her mouth work. "Thanks," she said, the word a whisper.

"Listen," Curt said, standing up and holding out his hand to Nora, "how about you help me with some of the stuff I'm doing for Stella Kiefer. She has a sound she wants, and I bet you're just the person who's gonna know what she's talking about. I've been going through everyone from Laura Nyro to Petula Clark, and I can't put my finger on it."

Nora allowed him to pull her out of the chair. She followed him to the studio office, knowing he was just trying to make her feel better. Besides, even though Will hated her version, Curt had done her a big favor. She owed him. It was hard to stop dwelling on Will's reaction as she and Curt worked. She felt embarrassed and angry at the same time. She wasn't some entitlement queen, she wished she could have explained to him. Just someone who wanted the movie to be great. She tried to explain that to Curt, but, as he made clear, he already understood it.

At least, she was relieved to see that he did really need her help. Together, they slogged through dozens of snatches from old records. She found herself enjoying the feel of vinyl in her hands. It made her feel as if she were fourteen years old, discovering Ella Fitzgerald or Sarah Vaughan for the first time. After a while, she managed to isolate the sound Curt was looking for. Then Curt mentioned a recording of a studio session Otis Redding had done years before. Every time Will's voice would come into her head, she would do her best to drown it out with the sounds of Otis.

Suddenly, from behind her chair, Nora felt a hand on her shoulder.

She looked up to see Will looming over her. His face no longer looked angry, as it had before. He just seemed exhausted.

"Okay," he said.

"Okay?" Her voice was uncertain.

He sat down on a chair next to her. "Okay, meaning your way is better." He smiled. "In fact, it's great."

"Oh, wow," she cried in relief.

She wondered how he'd gone from absolute rage to calm acceptance in about an hour and a half, but she wasn't about to ask him. After all, there wasn't much she really did understand about Will Stanley. And maybe it was better that way, she acknowledged to herself. Knowing him too well could be dangerous.

Curt stood and raised his fist in the air. "Good for you both. I think the film's amazing." He turned a beseeching glance to Will. "Don't forget me on the standardization piece, okay?"

Will smiled at him. "Don't worry."

Curt sauntered toward the door. When he walked out, Nora turned to Will.

"What standardization piece?"

Will sank back into the chair. "If I ever move out of this chair, I'm planning a documentary about the way everything is becoming the same in America—mall stores, television, on and on." He looked at Nora. "You interested?"

"You bet," she responded, grinning.

Will got up and moved across to the brown leather chair facing the couch. "So we'll be working together, no matter what." Suddenly, he reached across and took her hand. "Now, tell me what's going on."

Nora felt her grin freeze. "What's going on with what?"

Will said nothing, but again his face registered that ironic smile Nora had come to recognize.

"What's so damned funny?" she asked.

He stopped smiling. "Actually, it's not funny at all. Here you are, outspoken, honest, fun-loving Nora, lying to the one person you most need to be honest with."

"I don't need anything from you," she snapped, pulling her hand back.

He shook his head. "I didn't mean me. I meant you." He got up. "It's okay. I'll speak to you next week about the new film. And thanks for today. I'm picking up the expenses for Curt. Your work was sensational."

With that, he left her there. She tried to think about the fact that she'd gotten another movie, a project that would be incredibly interesting. And, besides, she was meeting Alex Fenichel for dinner next week. Who cared about what Will Stanley thought or said or did or felt?

Yeah, she sighed, sitting there in the near darkness. Who cares?

22

As the closing garage door rattled behind her, Kip unlocked her car trunk and carefully removed the large bubble-wrapped painting.

Only took me five years, she said to herself as she went in the house, headed toward the hall outside Peter's office. There was a long wall there, blank since the time it had been retired as the site for the children's artwork. Somehow, Kip could never find the right thing to hang there. It was a mystery to her how she had suddenly known that this painting was the answer the second she saw it in the window of a small art gallery. Without another thought, she had swung the car around. Less than ten minutes later, she was loading the landscape into her car.

She paused at a spot about two feet away from the closed door to Peter's office. *Bucolic,* she thought, as she peeled away the plastic. She wasn't exactly certain what the word meant, but she knew it was the right description for this painting. Holding it up against the wall, she experimented, shifting it up, then down, a little more to the right. Peter would see it every time he went in or out of his office. God knows, she thought, he could use a little bucolicness in his life. She liked the idea of his getting a jolt of tranquillity when he passed by.

"Peter?" she called out softly, not wanting to disturb his writing, but letting him know she was there.

There was no answer. She called his name again, louder.

It was unusual for him to be out at this time; he always said he did his best work in the early afternoon. Which meant he wasn't even sticking to his schedule anymore, the schedule he had followed without exception since before J. P. was born.

If only he would tell her what was bothering him. With a small sigh, she set the painting down, leaning it against the wall. In all their years together, she had never seen him behave the way he was behaving lately. He was chronically tense and upset, ready to bite off the head of anyone who intruded on his private misery. She had begged him to tell her what was going on. His answers varied from a sullen "Nothing" to a dismissive wave of his hand, as if she were imagining things. Her protests, pointing out that he had dark circles under his eyes, that he was losing weight, that he barely looked at her and the children, elicited disinterested shrugs or baleful glares.

Even Lisa and J. P. had taken to avoiding him, once they had been reassured by Kip that Daddy was temporarily in a bad mood and would snap out of it soon.

"You know how it is when you're feeling rotten, right?" she had said to them. "You want the world to leave you alone." J. P. had nodded sympathetically, while Lisa just said, "Ahh" in a knowing way, as if she understood Peter better than Peter did himself. Since then, they had steered clear of their father, but seemed unconcerned.

Kip, on the other hand, was growing more concerned every day. Peter was coming apart. But how could *her* Peter, the rock, the easygoing guy that he was, come apart? If he were unhappy—or in trouble—surely, he would come to her with his problem. If he didn't feel he could, then they didn't have much of a marriage. She brought herself up short. What a ghastly thought.

She went back to the garage to get a hammer from the pegboard where the tools hung in neat rows. The hammer tucked under her arm, she sifted through a small jar of picture hooks to find the one she needed. In her

mind, she ran through different scenarios to explain her
husband's troubles. He had lost everything they owned
in the world in a poker game and couldn't bring himself
to tell her. He had killed someone. He was being black-
mailed. Nothing she came up with seemed even remotely possible.

The question, she thought as she returned to the hall,
is how long has whatever this is been going on? Thinking
back, she could recall a few incidents that might be inter-
preted as signs of distress. She had been too consumed
with skating to notice anything out of the ordinary, or
bother to do something about it. Her focus on her sport
had left her no time or energy to contend with anything else.

It was a little different now. She had calmed down
enough to see what was going on around her again. No
doubt, she reflected, because things were going so well
for her these days. Her skating had been transformed as
soon as she had begun working on a routine to go with
the music Nora had sent her. Practicing was no longer
work. It had become a glorious exercise, hard but infinitely rewarding. Tomorrow, she would start training
with Dimitri Gordonov. By some miracle, the man she
considered the best coach in the area had agreed to take
her on after watching her new routine. He remembered
seeing her perform years before, and told her she was
still capable of doing strong work. From a stern and quiet
man like Gordonov, that was high praise indeed.

What good was all this, though, she wondered, if she
let her husband go to pieces because she was too damn
busy when it mattered?

She set the hammer and hook down, deciding she
should put a piece of tape on the wall to keep the paint
from cracking. About to go to the kitchen, she realized
Peter would have tape in his office. She turned the glass
doorknob and went in.

Kip rarely had an occasion to go into Peter's office, a
masculine-looking writer's haven of dark woods and
leather. He never actually asked her to stay out, but she

had long ago sensed that he considered it his private sanctuary. It was perfectly understandable to her. He did his thinking and writing here, and he didn't want people traipsing in and out. Once or twice a month he allowed their cleaning lady in to vacuum and dust, but he stayed there pretending not to watch to make sure she didn't accidentally move anything.

Today, however, it was evident that the cleaning lady hadn't been in the room for well over a month. Unhappy surprise on her face, Kip took in the scene before her. Typically, her husband's office was a bit messy, papers and books in low piles, folders here and there. But this was another matter altogether. Books and crumpled papers were everywhere, and file folders lay strewn haphazardly around the floor. A plate with a half-eaten sandwich rested on his leather armchair along with an opened magazine, and she saw an empty bag of potato chips and a crushed box of cookies on the floor. Not only did Peter rarely eat junk food, but, as far as she knew, he had never brought food into his office before.

Most disturbing, though, was what she saw on his desk. She crossed the room to get a better look. Right next to his computer was a bottle of Chivas Regal with three smudged glasses next to it, one still a quarter-full. She picked that glass up and sniffed, her head jerking back slightly at the powerful smell of the Scotch. Replacing it on the desk, her gaze went to the yellow pad nearby. The front page was covered with Peter's handwriting, notes and lines all crossed out with large *X*s from his black pen, the Mont Blanc she had given him on their first wedding anniversary. She flipped through the pages, but it was only more of the same: notes, ideas, lines of dialogue started, some stopped in midsentence, everything crossed out with savage slashes.

Kip put down the pad, thinking. She moved to the left side of the desk and reached for the handle on the top drawer. Peter would have been furious, but she didn't care. This was where he kept the computer printouts of whatever he was working on. He printed each chapter as soon as he completed it, never fully convinced that it would survive a computer mishap. He also liked to read his chapters on paper, get the feeling of them in print, he had told her; it was different from reading the words on the computer screen. But he didn't want anyone even glancing at his pages before he was finished; he was extremely superstitious about that. So he stashed the chapters here, out of sight. When he was done with a book, he filed all the printouts in a cabinet in the basement and started fresh.

Kip pulled open the drawer. It was empty.

"Something I can help you with?"

At the sound of Peter's voice, Kip gasped and slammed the drawer shut, her heart pounding with startled fright. She turned her head to see her husband leaning against the doorjamb, his arms folded. The sarcasm in his tone was matched by the displeased expression he wore. His hair was uncombed, and he hadn't shaved that morning, Kip noted, both of which were totally uncharacteristic of him. In fact, she was upset to realize that he looked worse than she had even admitted to herself.

"I thought you were out," she said.

"Evidently," he said. "I was. I came back."

She turned to face him more fully. "Why didn't you tell me?" she asked.

He shrugged, coming over to the leather chair and carelessly depositing the magazine and plate on the floor before sinking down into it. "What's the point? There's nothing you can do."

"This has been going on . . . not since you started on this book?"

"Yup." He nodded wearily. "Haven't written a word."

It was difficult for her to take it in. Peter wrote, he always wrote. He never had trouble. "But you've always said you had so many things you—"

"No longer," he interrupted.

They were silent. Kip was reviewing all the signs, so painfully obvious now, signs that practically shouted that

he was having difficulty with his work. She had simply
been too self-absorbed to see them.

"Do you have any idea why this is happening?"

His tired eyes met hers. "I wish more than anything
that I did."

"You've spent so many hours locked up in here. All
these months." She wanted to cry for him.

"But nothing. Not a page, not a thought."

She started to go to where he was sitting. He stiffened,
so she stopped, trying not to let him know how much
his reaction hurt her.

"Is there anything I can do?" she asked, knowing
the answer.

He shook his head. "I'm alone in this big, black hole.
I have to find my way out somehow, but nobody can
help."

Suddenly, she felt a jolt of anger. Why now? she
asked herself.

"Peter," she said, trying to keep her tone neutral,
"does this have anything to do with my skating?"

"What?" He glanced at her uncomprehendingly. "Why
on earth would it have to do with that?"

She went on, feeling more tentative. "Are you upset
because I'm gone so much?"

He laughed, an odd, low sound she didn't like. "Oh,
Kip, if only it were that. No, you're entitled to do something else with your life other than make lunch for me.
Besides, I'd like to think I'm not so pathetic that I would
sabotage my career to get my wife to stay home with
me more."

"Oh." She was embarrassed for having had the
thought. "I'm sorry."

"It doesn't matter, don't worry about it." He leaned
his head against the back of the chair.

She stared at him, feeling helpless. "Well, let me get
this place cleaned up a bit." She moved to the desk,
starting to collect stray papers.

"Kip, no." Peter's sharp words stopped her almost immediately. "This isn't something we can fix with a good attitude and some elbow grease. Please."

She set down the pages she had been holding. "Okay, Peter, you tell me what you want me to do, and I'll do it. Anything."

"Thank you," he said. "But right now, all I really want is to be left alone."

"You want me to leave the room?" She couldn't remember Peter's ever shutting her out of a problem this way.

"Yes, please." He closed his eyes. "I'm sorry, honey."

She nodded, even though he couldn't see her. Quietly, she crossed the room and left, pulling the door shut behind her.

Dear Lord, she thought, standing in the hall, immobilized. Writing was everything to Peter, his air and water. No wonder he was in such wretched shape. It must be six or seven months since he had started his new book—or since she believed he was starting his new book. All that time, and nothing. What was he going to do? And what was she going to do for him? Because there had to be something she could do. Something.

23

Eloise inhaled the aroma of the scallops she'd ordered. Eating fish instead of meat, and adding enormous amounts of fruits and vegetables to her daily fare was helping her to gain control of her weight, but at Picholine, not even the fish could be considered dietetic. Exactly how much butter is in this sauce? she wondered, imagining that the answer was closer to a cup than to a spoonful. Oh, well, she thought, pushing most of the viscous liquid to the side of the plate, it still looked delicious. She'd lost about twenty-five pounds in the past couple of months—not enough to get into a bikini, but enough to make her hate herself a little less.

And in this room, not hating herself was a priority. Picholine was one of the few upscale French restaurants on the Upper West Side of Manhattan. With an expensive menu and a celebrated wine list, it tended to attract an older and more refined crowd than the other places near Lincoln Center. The waiters were more formal than at The Saloon up the street, and out-of-work actors were unlikely to be hanging around the bar, unlike at O'Neal's, a few doors away. This was an elegant atmosphere for well-heeled diners.

And here they all are, Eloise thought, looking around the large table. On one side of her was her brother, George, whose chiseled face showed unusual signs of fatigue. Yet again, his wife Bettina was a no-show. He'd said something about a headache. On her other side was her father's special guest, Nigel Henderson, the editor of a British magazine that was like *The New Yorker* in content and tone. Medium height, with unruly salt-and-pepper hair, he had a rumpled quality that made him seem comfortable and appealing. In addition, the party included Eloise's parents; Jim Goldenstein—the attorney general of New York State—and his wife, Reva; Cal Betscher, a popular television reporter and his silent but very beautiful girlfriend; and last—and, in her mind, absolutely least—Bob Allard, the publisher of the *New York Journal*. As always, Grey Bentley was keeping the group alive, working the overcrowded table so no long silences ever came to be. And Eloise was grateful. It was Friday night, and she was exhausted. The magazine had been a madhouse, and her workday was lengthened by the hour she spent in the gym every afternoon between two and three.

It still amazed her that she could make herself exercise so regularly. Nor had she been indulging in the kinds of food binges that had kept her so depressed and uncomfortable. Since Kip's comments about John's similarity to her father, Eloise had applied herself to the task of making every decision her own. And, as if by magic, it had actually cut down on her need to binge. How could it be, she often wondered, that one day you were in thrall to potato salad and chocolate bars, and the next day you weren't? A mystery. Of course, she reminded herself, at any moment, her mysterious willpower might go right back to where it had come from. But at least for now, the mystery was working in her favor.

She'd thought long and hard before agreeing to come tonight. No longer did she say an automatic yes to every request for her appearance at family events. But she knew tonight was important. In truth, she found it energizing—almost, if not quite, fun. However, after a long workday and the star-spangled, two-hour AIDS benefit concert across the street at Avery Fisher Hall, which was what had drawn all of them together, she was dying to go home and get in bed. Besides, she mused, even with her father charming the crowd, this dinner was proving to be work. Jim Goldenstein was a decent, intelligent man. The son of wealthy parents, whose home in Scarsdale Eloise and her family had visited several times over the years, Jim had served doggedly in the state legislature before running for attorney general. Unlike most of his legislative colleagues, Jim had been admired by both Democrats and Republicans, and was enjoying almost universal high marks in his newest career. Regardless of his previous accomplishments, however, he was spending most of the evening defending the policies of the state's less than acclaimed governor to Bob Allard.

Thus far, they'd touched on capital punishment, tax abatement, gun control, and abortion rights. And on every subject, the two had almost come to blows. It was clear that Bob Allard had no real agenda except to disagree with every word the attorney general said. When Goldenstein talked about raising the minimum wage, Allard countered with fairness to employers. At the mention of Goldenstein's second-in-command, Allard threw out a salacious—and most likely made up—story about the man's behavior toward his ex-wife.

Eloise would have bet that if Jim had asked for ketchup with his rack of lamb, Bob would have slammed him for eschewing mustard. As far as she was concerned, that was about the level of discourse. Bob Allard was a professional provocateur. His newspaper called itself "the voice of outrage," but to Eloise it was the voice of insincerity and idiocy. If the *New York Times* was known for "all the news that's fit to print," the *Journal*'s slogan might as well read "all the garbage that's in your face."

Cal Betscher, the television reporter, who was seated to her brother's left, had stopped trying to put his two cents in at least an hour before. Instead, he would occasionally comment on his meal to George or whisper in his girlfriend's ear. Tina the Silent—as Eloise had begun to think of her—didn't seem to have much more to say to her boyfriend than she did to the crowd at large. She would simply stare up at him, her face a lovely, unreadable mask, and then return to pushing morsels of food around her plate.

Eloise had enjoyed some pleasant conversation with Nigel. He had written an article on the Walker Evans exhibit at the Metropolitan Museum for *Vanity Fair,* a piece she had liked very much, several months before. In person, he was intelligent and well spoken. And, of course, she realized, with no stake in American politics, Nigel had no reason to care terribly about all the dissension at the table.

"Well," Reva Goldenstein enthused, as Jim and Bob finished up yet another nasty dialogue, "one thing we can all concede—tonight's show was spectacular!"

Her husband shook his head in agreement, as did most of the others.

"I could have done without the magician," Bob Allard argued. "Frankly, I don't see what pulling rabbits out of hats has to do with raising money for disease control."

Jim Goldenstein smiled at him. "The duet from *The Marriage of Figaro* isn't directly related either, but that doesn't bother you?"

Allard gave him a wave of annoyance. "None of it really has anything to do with curing AIDS. In fact, the only thing that would take care of AIDS is if people would keep their goddamn hands to themselves."

Unexpectedly, Tina the Silent spoke up. "So, basically, you blame the people suffering from this disease?"

Allard glared at her. "You're damn right I do."

Eloise's brother, seated across from Allard, put down the fork he had in his hand and looked incredulous.

"In other words," George said, "in the African countries that have been completely decimated by AIDS, not to mention in the Far East, and, of course, here in North America, you see all this as everyone's own fault."

Allard nodded. "You betcha." He looked pleased to have gotten the whole table riled up.

"And, presumably," George continued, "during the Black Plague in the Middle Ages, it was everybody's own fault for being self-indulgent enough to go outside."

"Well, going outside isn't the same as doing it like bunnies, with everything that moves." Allard was grinning.

"Why, in that case, would you bother with a thousand-dollar ticket to tonight's concert?" Eloise contributed, angry with herself for allowing the man to engage her in his narcissistic exercise, but nonetheless unable to stop herself.

Allard laughed out loud. "Why, your father was nice enough to pay for that ticket. And I'm mighty grateful." He picked up a slice of grilled tuna and placed it in his mouth, sliding his fat pink tongue over his lips after he swallowed. It reminded Eloise of the Labrador retriever they'd had when she was ten.

"Frankly," Allard went on, spearing another piece of tuna but leaving it on the plate, "I think the fairy boys should be taking care of themselves." He turned toward Jim Goldenstein. "Even you must agree with me, Jimbo. You Jews have always put up the cash for your people. You've got your UJA and your ORT. You don't lay your troubles on everybody else."

Jim Goldenstein had maintained as pleasant a demeanor as possible for most of the evening. Clearly, that had now become impossible. "Do you rehearse your lines, or do they just spew right out of your mouth?" he asked, any pretense of fellowship gone.

Eloise was watching Bob Allard. His eyes were shining. This is heaven for him, she thought, deciding then and there not to say another word. He probably didn't even believe his own spiel. It was the drama he liked. But, as Cal and Tina stood up, she could see that no one else was having anywhere near as good a time.

"Sorry, Grey," Cal said to her father. "We've had a long week."

Grey Bentley smiled, but his disappointment was plain to see. "Oh, stay for dessert, you two. You know we're just exercising our rights as Americans here." His tone was jocular, but there was an edge to it.

Eloise knew that her father could barely tolerate it when events got out of control. He liked to gather people around him, to be at the center of a happy band. Tonight's group was definitely not in the happy-band category. And Grey Bentley was not in control.

His weak attempt at a smile faded as Jim Goldenstein and his wife stood up as well. "We have a big day tomorrow. We have to get back up to Albany early in the morning." He reached out to shake Grey Bentley's hand. "It's been terrific."

Within seconds, almost everyone had left the table, with the exception of the Bentley family and Nigel Henderson. Eloise felt sorry for Nigel. Obviously a polite man, he was a guest of her father's, and as such didn't seem to know what constituted the proper thing to do. The five of them sat there, plates of half-eaten smoked trout and salmon en croute pathetic witnesses to their discomfort. Finally, Nigel rose.

"I promised my assistant I'd call him early in the morning, and in London that would be just about now. I'll be right back."

He walked away from the table. Grey Bentley stared after him for a few seconds and then threw his napkin down. "I don't see what the heck everybody was so upset about," he said, his patrician face flushing. "Who gives a damn what people say in the privacy of a dinner. X says one thing, Y says another. It doesn't amount to a plate of potatoes as far as I'm concerned."

It might not have been worthwhile to say anything to Bob Allard, but this was Eloise's own father, and that was a different matter. "Honestly, Dad," she said, "what people say means quite a lot. How can you buy up fifteen thousand dollars' worth of tickets to a benefit concert and listen to that kind of crap?"

"Oh, for Christ's sake," her father answered, "Bob Allard doesn't mean a word of what he says. Besides, maybe he has a point."

Eloise blanched. "You can't mean that."

"No, no," he responded. "I'm all for finding a cure for the disease, but I can't say I'm crazy about the way certain groups have taken over half the city."

Felicia Bentley threw a hand over her husband's. The

message was clear: Stop talking. But it was lost on Grey Bentley.

"I swear, there were always fellows who preferred other fellows, but at least, in the old days, they had the courtesy to keep it to themselves. They weren't imposing their ways on a whole population. I mean, hell, your mother and I once had an apartment on West Twenty-fourth Street. Nowadays, I'd be frightened that some guy would jump me. And I don't mean for my wallet." His entire face was red now.

George spoke up. "In other words, you actually agree with Bob Allard. Gay men should hide themselves away, so as not to offend the other fine citizens."

"I'm not saying I agree with Bob. He's an asinine jerk. I'm just saying that society has become a little too self-indulgent. It wouldn't hurt if people kept their impulses to themselves. A little discipline and a lot of hard work might solve a few of life's problems rather than a roll in the hay with a stranger from some filthy bar."

George's cheeks were turning the same color as his father's. "So, gay men are not only self-indulgent, but lazy."

Eloise turned to her brother. She noticed that his hands were trembling. She wished there were some way to end this discussion before it turned any nastier. But there wasn't anything to say.

"Do you think *I'm* lazy?" George asked, his voice a hoarse whisper.

Suddenly, Grey Bentley looked frightened. "I'm not talking about you, son. I'm not talking about anything. Let's just get out of here. We're all tired."

"I'm not tired, Dad," George responded. "And I'm neither lazy nor self-indulgent." He took a slight pause. "But I am gay."

Grey Bentley's mouth opened, but no words came out. Eloise turned to face her brother. She said nothing, but took his hand. George squeezed hers in return. Then he looked at his mother. Felicia's expression gave away nothing. She seemed to be rooted in her seat.

"I know you're trying to make a point, George. You don't mean a word of this. You're a man with a lovely wife and a prestigious career. There's no way you would destroy all of that with something so ridiculous." The words came out bellicose, but the look on his face was pleading.

George lay his napkin on the table. "As you can see, my wife is not with me. In case you haven't noticed, she's hardly been with me for a long time." He ran a tired hand down the side of his cheek. "I finally came clean with Bettina a week ago. As for the prestigious career, I doubt that I have any less talent now that I'm being honest than I did all those years I was lying to you."

Grey Bentley stood up, dragging his wife up with him. "This is repulsive. I don't want to hear any of this."

George's shoulders slumped. "But I guess you have to. I'm your son, and this is who I am. It's who I've always been. I'm sick of pretending otherwise to you, and I'm even sicker of pretending to myself."

"Fine," Grey snapped. "Do whatever you want. But don't expect me to listen to it. Don't expect me to listen to anything you have to say ever again."

Eloise watched as her father pulled her mother toward the front of the restaurant. She observed him taking the waiter aside, shoving his credit card into the man's hand and hurriedly signing the credit slip. Within a minute or so, Grey and Felicia Bentley were out of the restaurant.

George turned to his sister.

"You're not surprised, are you?"

Eloise gave him a sad smile. "No, I guess I'm not."

"So, do you hate me, too?"

"Oh, George," she said, "I couldn't hate you. In fact, I'm proud of you. It took a lot to do what you just did."

George looked rueful. "I'd guess it took my next twenty or thirty years at Bentley Communications."

Eloise thought about what her brother was saying. It wasn't precisely a shock to find out that Grey Bentley was homophobic. Men of his generation and background almost always were, she'd found. But could he be foolish enough to break up a family over it? She hoped not.

"You know," George went on, "it's ironic. I always thought you'd be the one to escape from the family business. I've always been happy to think of myself as Dad-in-training. I actually was looking forward to running the company when he retires. I guess it's time to evaluate other options."

Eloise put her arms around him, hugging him hard. "Don't jump to any conclusions. He's just in shock, that's all. He'll come out of it."

George didn't look convinced.

"How is Bettina holding up?" Eloise felt indelicate pushing the subject any farther, but her sister-in-law had been part of the family for so many years. It seemed indecent to not ask.

"I couldn't believe it," George answered, relaxing slightly. "Speaking of people who were *not* surprised. She carried on as if she'd been shot for maybe two minutes. Then, she got this expression on her face like she'd been let out of jail." He looked contrite. "I've put her through hell, and no way did she deserve it. Although, truly, I think she's much happier already."

The sudden reappearance of Nigel Henderson took both Eloise and her brother by surprise.

"I gather I missed saying thank you and good night to your parents," he said, taking note of the empty chairs.

"They said to apologize for having to leave so abruptly," Eloise explained. She felt sorry for poor Nigel. He had no idea what he'd stepped into the middle of.

"Can I ask you a favor, Nigel?" George stood suddenly. "I feel the need for a walk. Do you mind seeing my sister home?"

"Oh, that's not necessary," Eloise demurred. "I'm a big girl, and I'm happy to get myself home."

"No, I'm pleased to do it," Nigel responded, looking down at her. "Shall I get your coat?" he asked.

Eloise didn't know what to do. What she really needed

was to think about everything that had just happened. Although she felt 100 percent supportive of her brother, it had been a lot to take in. She wasn't shaken so much by George's coming forward. Rather, it was the idea that the fabulous Bentley family might be a thing of the past. Left to her own devices, she'd have sat right where she was for a while, at least long enough to calm herself. She sighed. That was not to be. She reached into her purse, removing the ticket for her coat and handing it to Nigel.

"Thank you," she said, rising out of the chair.

Together, they walked to the coat-check area. The maître d' gave her a sharp, questioning look as she passed him. She saw Nigel take it in, but he had no comment to make. Of course, he knows that something monumental happened, she realized. At least he was polite enough not to ask what it was. Within a few minutes, she and Nigel were walking toward Central Park West. There were no taxis in sight, so they began to stroll uptown. The streets were empty and silent, save for the occasional doorman at the front of one of the large, weathered buildings facing the park.

"I wondered what enticed you to write for an American magazine," she said to him. "I really enjoyed that piece on Walker Evans, but I was surprised to see it in a magazine other than your own."

Nigel smiled. "Oh, I met the editor—through your father, in fact—a couple of years ago. He knew I had an interest in photography, and he thought it would be fun to have a Brit comment on such an American phenomenon."

"Do you do much photography?" she asked.

He nodded. "I started out at the magazine as photo editor. I guess you wouldn't know that. My rise to power—" He gave the words an ironic edge. "—was unusual at best."

"That must have been difficult, going from the picture side to the word side."

He chuckled. "Difficult would be an understatement. It took about ten years of twenty-hour workdays, not to mention proving myself over and over again to people unwilling to believe that both sides of the brain can be engaged at one time."

"And was it worth it?" she asked.

He stared at the sidewalk, seeming to be making his mind up about something. "Well," he finally said, "I love my job, but I no longer have a wife, and I see my daughters twice a month, plus Christmas and a month in the summer."

"I'm sorry," Eloise said. "I'm not usually so nosy. Tonight's been difficult."

They both spotted a taxi coming east on Sixty-fifth Street. Nigel put out his hand, and it stopped in front of them. "Where do you live?" he asked as he ushered her into the cab before him.

"Just across the park," she answered, "on Fifth Avenue and Seventy-fifth Street. Where are you staying?"

"Around the corner from you. At the Carlyle."

"In that case, I'll drop you off on Madison. The driver has to go that way anyway."

His glance toward her was almost shy. "I wonder if you would stop in for a drink with me. Not if it's an imposition, but I would love to unwind."

She surprised herself by saying yes. And, an hour later, in the attractive Carlyle bar, she was glad she had. Nigel was such a nice man. He hadn't even mentioned the events of that evening, but he displayed genuine interest in *Metropolitan Woman,* in the subjects that worked in the United Sates versus those that were effective in England. When it came to the business of publishing a magazine, she could see how good he must be. His insights were fresh, untinged with the sniping and hyperbole that marked many of his American counterparts.

She even found herself talking about her personal life. Her separation from John was something she rarely discussed with anyone, but speaking about it with Nigel proved oddly comforting. For one thing, she was stunned to realize that she wasn't in such horrendous pain any longer. Not that it didn't smart; it likely always would. Yet she found herself describing the evening she'd run into John and his new love in the restaurant, and being able to joke about it. Nigel's separation was, in a way, sadder than her own. According to him, he had been fully responsible for the break with his ex-wife. Ambition and drive had replaced family responsibilities years before he had been willing to acknowledge it. By the time he'd known enough to try to put the family back together, it was already gone.

Glancing at her watch, she was shocked to see that it was past two in the morning. "I have to get home," she said, reaching for her coat, which she'd flung over the back of an empty chair.

"Let me walk you," he said, pulling a few bills out of his wallet and leaving them on the table.

As they were walking through the hotel lobby, he stopped and touched her elbow.

"I don't know quite how to say this," he said, "but I've enjoyed this evening tremendously."

"Thank you," she said, smiling.

"What I'm trying to say is, well, is there any chance you would come upstairs with me?"

Her eyes widened in surprise.

Nigel's hands rose to cover his face. He was scarlet with embarrassment. "I'm sorry. I must sound insane, but I haven't felt this longing since Nina and I split up. I know it might just be too much solitude talking or the fact that I'm abroad, but I would give anything to go to sleep with you beside me."

Eloise could hardly believe what she was hearing. She'd met this man five or six hours earlier. She didn't know him, didn't love him, wasn't certain she would recognize him if she met him again in five years. Yet, she wasn't insulted by his offer. His words were more moving than outrageous. Nigel Henderson was a nice man, and a lonely man. As lonely as she herself was. But she wasn't about to sleep with a stranger. For goodness' sake, she said to herself, you don't go to bed with a man you just met at your parents' dinner table.

She was about to turn him down gently, when he

reached out and touched the side of her face. It was a tentative caress, a question rather than a statement. And it left her breathless. How long had it been since any man had desired her? Long before John had left, certainly. No one had even bothered to look at her in years, let alone to want her. Then she thought about what her father would say if he knew what she was contemplating. He'd be horrified. And would that be a good thing or a bad thing? Was the woman who didn't take comfort from an attractive stranger Eloise Bentley or Grey and Felicia Bentley's daughter? A shocking question, she realized, but one that made her consider her next words carefully.

"We barely know each other," she said, not brushing his hand away.

"Yes," he said. "That's right."

He didn't amplify his response, but his fingers went from her cheek to her neck, slowly, seriously, seeming to study her, to learn her.

He smiled at her and then reached out with his other hand, clearly hoping she would take it in her own. And, with some hesitation, she did. She couldn't deny the trembling she felt inside, the fear that she was making an awful mistake, but she also couldn't deny the excitement that was impelling her forward. She followed him to the elevator, stood silent as he indicated what floor he wanted to the attendant, walked behind him to the door of his room.

"You are an exceptionally beautiful woman," he whispered to her.

No, she wanted to answer. I'm middle-aged and overweight and have no idea what to do right now. Blessedly, she managed to keep the words to herself.

Instead, she allowed herself be led by him as he took her hand and entered the room. There was some illumination from the windows, but all she could take in was the large bed in the corner. He didn't go there, stopping instead near a couch and chair that were across the way. He sat down, pulling her after him. She thought she would evaporate from nervousness. It had been so long since she'd been with any man but John. Then, he kissed her, running his tongue around her lips, exploring the inside of her mouth. He was in no hurry.

She'd forgotten how intimate a kiss could be, how satisfying it felt to be enveloped in an embrace. He kissed her for what felt like hours, the sweetness of his mouth erasing the pain of all that had happened that night. And when his lips moved down her neck, his hand taking gentle control of her breasts, she found herself drawing closer to him. Even when his hands roamed down to the waistband of her black skirt, she didn't pull away. It was as if she'd entered another time, another planet. Where the rules were all suspended. Where she was a vibrant, sexual woman, rather than loathsome and invisible.

When he reached for the zipper on her skirt, she didn't stop him. She felt it slide to the carpeted floor, felt his fingers stroking her, bringing her senses alive. She heard herself gasp in pleasure as he continued his caress, sensed his own pleasure build. And she found she couldn't hold back, didn't want to. The excitement was exquisite. She wanted to bask in it, to have it go on and on.

They moved to the bed. She was ready as he pulled off his own clothing and entered her. For the first time in so very long, she knew again what it was like to feel as one, to connect.

Later, as they lay side by side, she could hardly believe what she'd done. She doubted that she'd even see this man again. Yet, she felt no regret. No, she thought as he reached out for her hand, she wasn't sorry at all.

24

Nora grinned as she saw Alex at a wrought-iron table near the back of the public space. The builders had been forced to provide open seating space when they'd built the combination office and residence a few years before, and any number of people were sitting around, some reading a book, others staring into space. Several of them seemed to be working, but none so intently as Alex. This time, there was no mistaking him. Alex Fenichel had not changed a bit. He was hunched over a pile of papers, fountain pen in hand, the twin lines that had always indicated intense focus across his forehead. True, he was now resplendent in a navy blue three-piece suit instead of the chinos and T-shirt he'd sported when she'd seen him last, and there were a couple of random strands of gray in his hair. But, without a doubt, it was the Alex Fenichel she'd known and cared for. When she reached him, he looked up, standing eagerly at the sight of her.

He hugged her and held a chair out.

"Nora, you look spectacular!" he said, taking his seat once again.

Nora beamed. "And you look wonderfully like you."

"What does that mean?" he asked as he placed what he'd been working on into a folder. She watched with amusement as he tapped the folder on the tabletop sharply three times, so the papers would line up precisely. It reminded her of what he used to do with his

dinner napkin. He'd fold it exactly in half, then smooth
it twice across his lap, perfectly centered above his thighs.

"It means I'm glad to see you."

"You need something to drink," he said. "There's a
snack bar over there." He stood up and smiled. "Vodka
and tonic for the lady, right?"

Nora held her hand up. "Well, actually, these days I
prefer a glass of red wine."

"Of course," Alex said. "I'll be back in a second."

She watched him walk toward the back of the space
and order two drinks from a bored-looking waiter behind
the bar. She could see that in addition to various bottles
of liquor, there were premade sandwiches and a few
cakes, with slices already cut. Alex took the two glasses
the man handed him, plus a stack of paper napkins,
quickly returning to the table. As he approached Nora,
his face bore the same grin she recognized from all those
years before. And she bet he'd ordered Scotch on the
rocks with a twist for himself, just as he always had.

"Dewar's, right?" she said, laughing.

He nodded and sat down, also smiling.

"You haven't changed an iota."

He scratched his head. "Not much, I guess. But I'm
older. And grayer."

"Oh, please. You look terrific. Tell me everything
that's happened."

He gathered up the folder he'd been working on and
put it into a leather briefcase; then he placed the briefcase on the floor, leaning it against the side of his chair.
"Well, let's see. Everything. That's a tall order."

He took a sip of his drink.

"I started up a company a few years ago in Boston,
which I'm pretty proud of. And I have two fabulous
children."

"Do you have pictures?"

"I guess," he said, pulling out a wallet and rifling
through it. He drew out two color snapshots and pushed
them across the table to Nora. "The blond one's
Heather, and the big one's Keri."

Nora studied them. The girls must have been around eight and ten. Heather looked a great deal like Alex, the same clean features and high forehead. She had the look of someone who greeted every day with a smile. Keri was darker, more anxious looking, staring into the camera as if something might leap out of it at her. "They're beautiful," she said, handing the photographs back to him. "What are they like?"

He looked surprised. "Gee, what are they like? . . . They're nice and they're sweet. They're great kids. . . ." He paused. ". . . My wife and I got divorced about a year ago, and that was kind of tough on them, but they've bounced back completely."

Nora laughed to herself. Another thing about him hadn't changed. He was such a *guy*. Alex wasn't the kind to roil around in darkness, searching for trouble. She found it restful.

He went on. "What about you? Are you still in publishing?"

She smiled at the fact that he'd bothered to remember what it was she was doing when they'd last seen each other. It once again reminded her of the horrible man she'd met in Poughkeepsie. Thank God this man was the real Alex Fenichel. Someone who honestly remembered who she was. She didn't even have the terrible nervousness she'd experienced with the first one. It was amazing, really, how comfortable she felt.

"Actually, I'm a music producer. I started up a company a couple of years after you left New York."

"What exactly is that?"

Nora started to tell him about Levin Music, and he listened with interest. After she was finished with a description of the business, he even asked a number of questions concerning the kind of digital equipment she used.

"What about your business?" she asked.

A sparkle came into his eyes. "It's called Allydyne, and it's worked out exactly the way I hoped it would. I planned it out for years when I was working for TemCo in Chicago, and it's even better than I thought it would be. We started off with fiber optics, and the rest of it grew out of that."

He continued with a technical dialogue, of which Nora understood little, but she appreciated his enthusiasm. Alex had always been that way. He worked very hard, expected everything to work out, and just about every time it did. She had never been sure which was the greater asset, his intense concentration or his sheer optimism. What a relief it was to be with someone who looked for the best and then found it.

"Tell me about the movie you did," Alex said.

Nora had mentioned the documentary in her description of her job, but talking about Will Stanley and the complexities of the new South was the last thing she wanted to do. She shivered inwardly. If Alex was a sunny day, Will was murkiness incarnate.

"It was a nice project. I'll tell you when it's going to be on television, and you can judge for yourself."

The answer seemed to satisfy Alex. "What do you say we go and get some dinner. I'm in the mood for steak and a Caesar salad."

Nora began to laugh. "You're still eating the same meal!"

"When I like something, I like it." He lifted his Scotch and took a long sip; then he looked straight at Nora. "When I like something, I like it."

She couldn't stop herself from laughing. His seriousness brought back so much about their time together. It was touching, really, that he would be so direct, but somehow it made her want to tickle him, or to dip his elegant silk tie into his glass of Scotch.

"The end of your marriage must have been tough for you," she said, forcing herself to focus on weightier issues.

"I don't know if *tough* is the right word."

"What do you mean?"

He thought about it. "I guess it wasn't so much tough as it was mystifying. One day we were going about our business and everything was fine, and the next day my wife was telling me it was over."

Nora was reaching for her wine, but her hand stopped in midair. "That was it? You didn't fight? She didn't give you any explanation?"

He shrugged his shoulders. "Not really. At least not anything that made much sense. I thought we were happy."

"Wow," she exclaimed. "That must have hurt like hell."

"I guess," he said, taking another sip of Scotch. "But it's all right now. We've made our peace with it, and she's good about letting me see the kids. Actually, it's pretty amicable."

Nora shook her head. "You're amazing. I've never known anyone with that kind of fortitude."

"You know, I'd like it if you came up to Boston and met the kids. They'd love you."

Nora felt a clutch of fear. It was the first time tonight she'd been grabbed by the emotion that had stopped her so many times before. Going to meet his children was so, well, *real*, for God's sake.

She caught herself. This was precisely the moment Kip and Eloise were daring her to get past, damn it. She wasn't going to stand in her own way this time. She was going to move forward, even if it killed her.

"That would be nice," she answered, getting the words out without missing a beat.

Nora's cheeks were red, both from exertion and from the cold. Boston was having an unusual cold spell, so her afternoon of ice skating with Keri and Heather Fenichel had left its mark on her. When Alex had met her at Logan Airport earlier that day, he had surprised her with a pair of size seven skates. She was grateful that he'd thought of an activity that would make their meeting so much more natural than sitting in some restaurant would have been. And the fact that he remembered her shoe size was damned impressive besides.

The day had been fun. Alex had picked up the girls and then met Nora at the pond, which was only blocks from his apartment. Nora hadn't skated in years, so for the first few minutes, Alex had held her hand, leading her around the pond until she found her sea legs. She'd laughed at her own awkwardness, telling him a little bit about her friend Kip, who she imagined would have been amazed at Nora's hesitancy about the simple act of skating forward. Alex had been reassuring, and Nora had gotten the knack back within a few minutes. The four of them had skated for about an hour. Afterwards, they'd gone for hot chocolate and sandwiches at a family restaurant not far away.

Alex's kids were delightful, although Nora was not so certain they were getting through the divorce with quite the ease he imagined they were. They were polite girls and very beautiful to look at. Heather, who was eight, was a delightful child, curious, easily pleased, although she had what Nora found to be a little too much eagerness to make certain everything was okay, that everyone was happy. Keri, the older one, was nine and a half, and she was the opposite of her sister and, for that matter, her father. Alex was someone who thought things would always turn out well. Keri, on the other hand, seemed frightened of everything. Would the pond be frozen enough to hold them? Would there be enough bread left for a grilled cheese sandwich at the café they'd gone to when they'd finished skating? Was that man on the other side of the pond laughing at her?

She also seemed suspicious of Nora, which wasn't all that difficult to understand. Why should a child necessarily indicate happiness watching her father skate around holding hands with a woman who was not her mother? But the child had warmed up a little by the end of their time together. When Alex dropped them off at his old house, each girl had given Nora a dutiful "nice to meet you," which she appreciated. Alex had walked them inside while Nora waited in the car. It didn't seem appropriate for her to meet Maura, Alex's ex-wife, although he would have been willing to bring her inside. The house itself was in Newton, right outside of Boston. Large and elegant, it was one of a cluster of well tended, lovely homes. It seemed a classic example of the kind of neighborhood that was almost an advertisement for happy families. Nora was again struck by how painful the separation must have been for Alex.

When they got back to his apartment, she said as much to him, but he demurred.

"I'm happy now. Everything's fine." He took her hand and led her to a couch in his living room. "In fact, everything's more than fine," he said, putting an arm around her and gazing into her eyes.

Nora knew he was going to kiss her, and it made her uneasy. It wasn't as if she didn't know him, she chided herself. She'd known Alex for over fifteen years. Yet, he was in some ways a stranger, or at least a new incarnation of someone from the deepest past. He pulled her down beside him on the couch and put both arms around her.

"Oh, Nora," he breathed, "I'm so glad you called me." Then he ran his hand down the center of her spine and kissed her.

The caress down her spine was familiar, as was his kiss. Solid and strong, it was Alex's kiss, as it had always been. When they drew apart, he lifted her legs into his lap, removing her shoes and rubbing first one foot and then the other. It made her smile. He had done that hundreds of times. She knew exactly what he would do next. His hand would travel up her leg, and then he'd kiss her again, and soon they'd leave the couch and go to the bedroom. Leaning back against the cushion, she relaxed into his caress. This was territory she knew by heart. There was nothing, *nothing*, to be nervous about in this room.

25

Kip and Peter filed out of the performing arts center with the rest of the crowd, not speaking until they were in the lobby.

"I'm really sorry you didn't enjoy that," Kip said as they reached the doors leading out to the Bard College campus. "I shouldn't have dragged you here."

"It wasn't your fault." Peter held the door open for her. "I just hope I didn't ruin it for you."

"No, no. That's not important."

She managed to muster up a smile for her husband. When Kip had suggested coming here tonight, she thought the music might distract Peter from his problems, at least for a couple of hours. He had been reluctant, but finally succumbed to her urgings, only to shift in his seat the entire time. Whenever she looked over at him, she saw his troubled expression growing darker and darker, his mind clearly elsewhere. Instead of distracting him, the Mozart only served to focus him so that he could suffer without interruption. Good move, she berated herself, giving him a solid two hours in the dark to think about how he *still* can't write. Lately, he had begun to talk about facing the fact that his writing career might be over for good.

Upset for him, Kip had sat there feeling miserable, spending the second half of the concert debating whether or not to ask him if he wanted to leave. She kept hoping he would somehow get caught up in the music of one of his favorite composers, but Mozart failed utterly to reach her husband.

Peter took a deep breath of the warm night air. The moon was bright, illuminating the paths connecting the school buildings. "How about a little walk?" he asked, extending his hand.

"Great." Kip slipped her hand in his.

They had always liked strolling the Bard campus. Situated in Annandale-on-Hudson, the college was a wonderful resource for the people in neighboring towns as well as for its students. The school's physical beauty asserted itself anew with every season, and the buildings and grounds evoked the spirit of old New England, whether in the quiet, blanketing snows of winter or the lushness of summer.

Kip especially loved it now, in spring, bursting with life. It surprised her, though, that year after year she was invariably struck by sadness when the students packed up and left for the summer; the passing of time, people scattering and abandoning their happy routines, some going for good—she couldn't avoid feeling a slight mournfulness in June. On the other hand, there was September, with its mad bustle and anticipation. Kip felt a bittersweet combination of excitement and envy watching the students unpack their cars as they returned or arrived for the first time, shouting out to one another, going in and out of their dormitories staggering under computers and tennis racquets, books and bedding.

"Get a life," Kip muttered under her breath, the phrase she imagined her daughter would use if Kip ever confided these mental wanderings to her.

"What?" Peter glanced at her. "Did you say something?"

Kip shook her head, then decided to tell him. At least, she thought, it will give us something to talk about besides the subject they were ignoring.

"I was ruminating," she began grandly. "Thinking

deep thoughts about youth. Being around a college keeps you connected to your youth in a strange way. You get older, but the college kids are perpetually nineteen."

"Makes you want to kick their tight little butts, does it?" Peter asked, his smile gratifying to Kip.

She hurriedly continued, not wanting to lose his momentary good cheer. "I like them, but I feel both happy and sad for them. Happy because they have their whole futures ahead of them. Sad because they're only going to get middle-aged like everybody else."

Peter drew her closer, putting an arm around her. "Oh, my darling, down that path lies existential despair. Not to mention a sudden longing for expensive cosmetic surgery."

Kip laughed.

"Besides," he added, "you look better than all these kids. Like a real woman. Not cute or pretty, but beautiful. That's so much better."

"Thanks. I think."

"And you have things of real import in your head."

Kip drew back slightly, surprised. "Real import? What do I have that's so important in my head?" Her tone turned wry. "You mean, like what date J. P.'s history project is due?"

"Of course not." He sounded equally surprised. "What kind of thing is that to say? I meant you're smart, and you have thoughts of significance."

"Wow." Kip was silent, reflecting. "I guess I never thought you regarded me that way. I sort of believed you saw me more for my physical skills. And I know you appreciate that I'm good at getting things done."

Peter turned to her as they stopped beneath the glow of a streetlight. "Do you view me as such a jerk, thinking that's what I care about? I love all your skills, I admire them more than you could possibly imagine. But that's one little part of you. 'Getting things done'? You've got to be kidding. When have you ever known me to give a damn about that?"

She looked into his eyes and saw the concern for her

there. "I love you," she answered, putting her arms around him.

They kissed, the longest and most heartfelt kiss they had shared in months, she realized as she pressed against him and felt his hands moving along her back.

He pulled his face away just far enough to whisper to her. "You have no idea how grateful I am to you for what you've put up with. I know I haven't said anything, but I'm well aware of how difficult it must be to live with me."

"Difficult doesn't come close," she whispered back with a smile.

He laughed as he cupped her face with his hands and planted a few quick kisses on her lips and cheeks. "Don't surgarcoat it like that."

"I don't mind, Peter. This is a big deal, and it's not about me. I only wish I knew what to do for you."

He put his arm around her as they started to walk again. "So, you were thinking about your lost youth?" He wasn't attempting to be subtle in changing the subject.

"Not mine in particular, no. Just youth in general." She paused. "If you could go back to being a kid, what age would you go back to?" It was such a Nora question, she realized in amusement.

"What age in college? Junior year, definitely. Not on the bottom of the heap anymore, but not having to deal with the real world yet. That was a great year."

"Never having gone to college myself, that doesn't ring any bells for me," she said. "What about younger? I don't imagine I'd want to do adolescence again. Too much angst."

"Weren't you too busy with skating for that?"

"I doubt anyone's too busy with anything to escape that. I had all the insecurities of any teenage girl, plus the pressure of performing." She considered her question. "It would be nice to go back to being seven. I liked seven, or maybe it was eight. I could skate, I had friends, I didn't worry about anything. I remember feeling good about myself and the whole world. Eight was kind of a perfect year for me." She looked up at him. "Do you remember as far back as those years, seven or eight? Would you want to repeat them?"

His arm still around her, Peter stiffened. "No."

"Well, that didn't seem to require a lot of consideration," she said, surprised by his curt tone.

"You asked, I answered. No."

"What's so terrible about being seven or eight?"

"Nothing," he said.

She waited, but he didn't go on.

"What did I say?" She was bewildered by his reaction.

He gave her the same terse reply as before. "Nothing."

"I always thought you were a pretty happy kid. You had both parents, everybody got along. You've never told me otherwise."

His tone was sharp. "I wouldn't want to repeat those years, no. Does that answer your question?"

She pulled free of his arm. "What's going on? You're acting weird."

He glared at her, his voice growing louder. "Enough, Kip. Drop it, okay?"

"Drop what? What did I say?"

"Okay, okay. If I could go back, I'd like to go back to being six months old. That was probably a swell time, one long party."

"*Hey*. Don't be like that."

Peter's lips were tight. "What's it going to take for you to move on to another topic?"

She was genuinely annoyed. "We're supposed to be able to talk about things. That's what married people do."

"No," he said, his voice growing even louder in anger, "married people do not talk about *all* things. They talk about *many* things, perhaps even *most* things. Which we do."

"Listen, if there's something I should know about, I wish you'd tell me instead of dismissing me. It's—"

The words seemed to explode from him. "Gee, Kip, I don't know if my being molested as a child is *something you should know about.* Do you think it is? Do you want to know about every Thursday, regular as clockwork, me and Mr. Carroll?"

Kip stood still, her eyes open wide. *"What?"*

"That's right." He spoke quickly, with controlled fury. "Our next-door neighbor, a nice old man who watched me one afternoon a week, when my mother taught a writing workshop. He didn't even charge my mother, said he was only too glad to do it. A lovely man, as everybody knew." His voice got quiet and bitter. "Except what everybody *didn't* know was that he was fondling me in his living room every goddamn Thursday. And making me fondle him."

"Oh, my God," Kip breathed.

It was suddenly so obvious. The nightmares, his nervousness about letting the kids go to the house of someone he didn't know, the way he scrutinized the kids' teachers and coaches—any adult who had control of their time or might be alone with them. Even when the children were little, she recalled with a start, he had always been so reluctant to leave them with a sitter, insisting she check in by telephone when they were out at least twice during the evening. It all fit together now.

Peter went on. "He said if I told anyone, my mother might not understand and might not let him baby-sit anymore. Then, if she quit her Thursday job, my family wouldn't have enough money. He was a crafty old bastard, I'll give him that. He explained how my father didn't make much at the magazine, and he would be so ashamed if we couldn't get by on his small salary." He paused to take a breath. "He understood that a little boy would rather die than embarrass his father that way. What the hell did I know, I was *seven freaking years old.*"

"Oh, Peter—oh, my God." Kip was too overwhelmed to find any words. Without realizing it, she clutched her arms around herself.

"An entire year," Peter spat out. "For an entire school year, until my mother finished her course. I remember counting down the weeks until her teaching would be over,

when I could stop going over to Mr. Carroll's." He gazed
off into the distance, lost in the past. "We went away for
the summer, to a beach house, I don't remember where.
The whole time I was terrified that he would come there.
That he would be in one of the houses near ours, and,
somehow, I would have to spend Thursdays with him again.
When we came home, I found out he'd died in July." Peter
paused. "That was the happiest day of my life."

He turned away from Kip, a wrenching sob bursting
from him, a terrible, animal sound that tore at her. She
reached out to him, putting her hands on his back, but
he shrugged her off and moved farther away.

"Don't touch me."

She could barely make out his muffled words. He
dropped down to his knees, his hands covering his face,
and wept with horrible grunts. Kip knelt beside him, saying nothing, not daring to move closer, his sobs making
her feel as if her heart would break. She had never seen
him cry before, never even seen tears in his eyes. Now
it seemed he had unleashed a tidal wave of pain. His
guttural moans were unbearable in their anguish. Tears
spilled down her cheeks as she watched him.

He dropped even closer to the ground, resting on his
forearms; then he raised his tear-streaked face to her.
"Oh, Kip, oh, God." He buried his head in her lap, his
arms encircling her legs.

She held on to him as tightly as she could, rocking
him, stroking his head. "It's okay, sweetheart," she
soothed, "it will be all right. I'm here, we're together.
Everything will be okay."

Swallowing, she wiped the tears from her own cheeks.
She wasn't at all sure everything was going to be okay.
But she continued to murmur words of comfort as he
wept in her lap, his hands gripping her as if she were
the only thing in the world left to hold on to.

Kip stood by the bed, a blue mug of steaming coffee
in one hand, watching Peter until he somehow felt her
gaze and opened his eyes.

"Good morning." She extended the mug. "I brought you this."

He eased himself up on one elbow with a groan. "Bless you, my child," he said hoarsely as he reached for the coffee.

She sat down on the edge of the bed. "Good sleep?"

He made a big show of how hot the coffee was as he brought the cup to his mouth, his lips trembling in apparent fear. She laughed, waiting as he took his first sip.

"Yes, a fine sleep," he said, sitting up against the bed's headboard, "the sleep of the dead. Or the useless."

"Come on," she admonished him. "Useless is when a man won't get up from the dinner table to get the butter for himself. You're not useless."

He took another sip of his coffee. Neither one of them wanted to mention the night before.

They had finally managed to pick themselves up off the ground to drive home from Bard, only to spend two more hours crying and talking. It had left them drained of both emotions and words. The story of Peter's molestation as a child was so vile, Kip felt as if she had been injected with a poison, and it would take some time before she could expel it from her system and examine it rationally. She didn't know how she could make peace with something so terrible being done to him. Her Peter, as a little boy, having to endure such ugliness. Her heart hurt.

There was one positive note to their discussion, though, she realized. He had apparently found some relief in getting his secret out at last. After all the shouting and sobbing and suffering, he had fallen asleep on their bed, exhausted. Kip took off his shoes and managed to get the covers over him without waking him, and he had wrapped his arms around her lovingly as he turned over, nuzzling her neck. He even smiled at her in his sleep, his slightly swollen eyes still closed. She gazed at him as she put on a nightgown and slipped under the comforter. There was this strange peacefulness about him all of a sudden. But she guessed it made sense. Living with a secret like that had to eat away at you, even if you had shoved it as far away from your consciousness as you could manage.

She wondered why everything had happened now, but she doubted she would ever figure it out. For whatever reason, the horror of his past had reasserted itself, attacking him at the point of his greatest vulnerability, his writing. She had no doubt that his writer's block was connected to this, and she could only hope that getting the secret out into the open would signal the end of his paralysis. Whether Peter would agree with that was another matter.

She herself was far too upset to sleep. She sat up in bed, staring into the darkness before dozing off around four o'clock. Nonetheless, she had awakened at seven. After straightening up downstairs, she had sat down with some coffee and stared out the window, turning things over in her mind.

Peter's voice interrupted her thoughts. "The kids up?"

Kip nodded. "In their rooms." She reached for his hand. "I'm going to make breakfast for everybody."

He nodded. "I'll be right down."

Back in the kitchen, she went to the refrigerator for the eggs and milk to start making French toast. Her mind was on Peter as she pulled a large frying pan from the cabinet beneath the stove. If only she could think of some way to help him.

Peter appeared, wearing his bathrobe, as she was dunking bread in the egg-and-milk mixture, butter sizzling in the pan.

"Smells good," he said, coming over to put his coffee cup in the sink.

"Want some orange juice?" she asked, placing a slice of bread to one side of the pan.

He didn't answer. She turned around to look at him. His eyes met hers.

"I had a thought." He stopped, fingering the sash of his robe. "Maybe it's a stupid thought."

"And maybe not," she said.

"When I was upstairs just now, I started wondering if I should try to write something shorter. Something different from what I usually do."

"You mean like a short story?" She reached for more bread.

"Actually, I was thinking about nonfiction. Like a magazine article or something. Something with less riding on it than a novel."

She nodded. "Sort of like getting a jump start."

"If it works." He moved to get the syrup from the pantry. "I was actually thinking of calling your friend Eloise to see if her magazine would be interested."

Kip grabbed a spatula to flip the French toast. She didn't want Peter to see how excited she was that he had come up with a plan, that he was showing enthusiasm for something. She glanced at him, keeping her tone casual. "I'm sure she'd be thrilled. It would be a coup for her magazine to have Peter Hallman writing for them."

"Well, I have to think on it awhile." He seemed reluctant to commit himself. "See if it actually is a good idea."

Kip forced herself to remain silent. She wanted to jump up and down, to yell that of course, it was a good idea. Anything that stimulated his mind would be a good idea, anything that took him away from the horror that held him would be a miracle. Instead, she adjusted the burner and turned to get plates.

"I can see it, kind of getting your feet wet again," she said at last. "I'll give you Eloise's number."

"I guess you may as well." He shrugged as if the matter wasn't particularly important.

"Would you grab the placemats?" Kip asked, her manner indicating the topic was already forgotten. Inside, she was cheering. Please, God, she begged, let him find something to write about and let it come out great for him.

She went to the bottom of the stairs. "Kids," she called, "breakfast is ready."

"Mom," Lisa shouted back down, "where are my socks with the fish on them?"

"If they're not in your drawer, they're probably still in the laundry," she answered.

Her tone grew irritated. "But I *need* them. Nobody takes care of anything in this house anymore."

Kip decided to ignore the unsubtle reference to her new less-than-perfect housekeeping.

A sleepy J. P. practically stumbled downstairs, still wearing his pajamas. "Another tragedy for Lisa?" he asked Kip.

She nodded gravely. "Socks. It's too sad to talk about it."

He grinned. They listened as Lisa complained loudly to herself on her way down the hall to the bathroom. "Nothing is ever ready when I need it. Everything takes forever."

"Come on, sport," Kip said, putting an arm around her son's shoulder. "Your morning fare is waiting."

She settled J. P. at the table, keeping an eye on Peter, who was sipping a glass of orange juice and looking out the window. At last, he turned to her.

"Maybe something that involves going someplace." He picked up their earlier conversation as if they were still in the middle of it.

"Mm-hum." Kip didn't want to interrupt his train of thought. She watched J. P. pour syrup over his French toast and set the bottle down.

"A trip might be good. You know, get away from things, get a fresh perspective on it all. Maybe do a piece on something in Europe. Some aspect of change in Asia might be even better." He nodded, still thinking. "Yeah. I'll call Eloise tomorrow morning."

Kip picked up the syrup, twisting the cap closed as she walked back to the stove, her heart sinking. She didn't want Peter to go away. It was too lonely without him. Managing both kids and the skating would be next to impossible. But, mostly, she would miss him too much.

"Sounds great," she said brightly. She picked up a spatula and held it over the griddle. "French toast for you, darling?"

26

Eloise looked at the array of photographs that Priscilla Seidner had brought with her. The fashion editor was sorting them into piles as she kept up a running commentary on their quality. According to Priscilla, they ranged all the way from "revolting" to "heaven."

"I mean, really, Eloise," she said, holding up the image of a blue-and-red plaid blouse, "some of this stuff belongs in a tag sale at my grandmother's nursing home. Honestly, this is *dreck*."

Eloise consulted the master list the designer had enclosed. "That particular example of what you call *dreck* will be retailing for nineteen hundred dollars."

"My mother-in-law dropped a fortune on a silk muumuu a couple of months ago. That doesn't make it fashion." Priscilla ran through the photographs quickly, only a very few making it to the possible pile. She turned one photo around to face Eloise. "I saw this outfit in Milan. It's completely spectacular."

Eloise examined the photograph. The garment could, she supposed, be called a dress, although it was actually a series of thin silver chains, held together at three strategic points by strings of more closely fitted chains. "How many of our readers are going to be buying this?" she asked.

"None," Priscilla tossed back. "But the fantasy factor will be through the roof."

Eloise picked up a pile of rejects and began leafing through it. Priscilla looked at her with alarm.

"Don't get sentimental on me, Eloise. This is our fall fashion issue, and the ladies want to see the cream of the crop."

Eloise smiled at the notion that a garment presumably made expressly for an evening of sadomasochism could be thought of as cream of any crop at all. But she held her tongue. She knew that Priscilla was brilliant at what she did, and, in fact, women who read the magazine did want to see the outrageous, the clothing that would never appear at the Macy's in their local mall. But that was not all they wanted to see.

She continued going through the pictures, finally coming upon the one she was looking for. Priscilla had passed it by without a second thought, but Eloise knew there was something there. It was a long-sleeved, black silk evening dress. From the top of the bustline to the round neck, the fabric was replaced by sheer black netting, through which a fair amount of cleavage was apparent. Tapering at the waist, the dress fell to the floor with a wide, swooping skirt. She could almost hear the material make a swishing sound even in the inanimate photo.

"I'll give you the chains if you'll give me this one."

Priscilla reached over for the photograph.

"Gee, do you think we could pick something that was designed some time after 1956?" Priscilla squinted at the image. "Besides, our crack team of bulimic models are practically going to disappear in this thing. This thing is tailor-made for women who gained twelve pounds when little Tiffany was born and were never able to take it off." She glared at Eloise with sudden insight. "That's the whole point, huh?"

"No," Eloise said. "Well, maybe a little. But I love this dress. Okay, so maybe it does harken back to our mothers' era, but you know everything comes around again. I think our ladies will do a dead stop at the Marquis de Sade number, but they'll go out and buy my guy by the thousands."

"Okay, okay," Priscilla agreed. "But who are we going to put in it?"

Eloise's eyes gleamed. "I know just the model." She got up and walked over to one of the bookshelves, pulling out a catalog from a department store in Chicago. She turned the pages until she came to the image she was looking for.

"Here she is."

Priscilla reached out and took the catalog out of her hands. "Did they take her right from her grazing area to the photo shoot?" she sniffed.

Eloise snatched the catalog back from her. "Pretend you're human and look more closely." She held the page up. It showed a tall, blond young woman, with even features and wide-set eyes. Her body was shapely and full.

"I know her," Priscilla sneered. "She's the illegitimate daughter of *zaftig* and heifer."

"On the contrary," countered Eloise, "she's the actual human who's going to model this gorgeous dress in our fall fashion issue."

Priscilla shook her head, her disdain plain to see. "Your father's never going to go for this."

Eloise closed the catalog and held it against her chest. "My father is not the editor of this magazine. I am."

"But I'm the fashion editor." Priscilla's voice had gone very quiet.

"Yes," Eloise agreed, sitting down once again.

"There's something I don't understand. You'd think that now that you've dropped a ton of pounds, you wouldn't want to align yourself with the Lane Bryant set."

"Your flattery is going right to my head," Eloise retorted, frowning. She didn't especially mind the inelegant phrasing Priscilla had chosen. What bothered her was the fact that she and Priscilla—or was it she and the rest of the world—seemed to be living on two different planets. In fact, Eloise thought the model was beautiful. And there was no question in her mind that the dress would look perfect on her. This was not the dress a beanpole would wear. It called for someone curvaceous and womanly. And, for goodness' sake, she thought, the model was not an ounce overweight. She probably wore a size ten. Eloise herself was down to a size twelve, and she was feeling good about it.

"Do you find this notion really offensive?" she asked, her tone a challenge.

Priscilla did not answer right away. Eloise observed her, swearing she could almost see the wheels turning. Priscilla was snobbish and fiercely protective of her turf, but she was also a thorough professional. If an idea was good, she could generally find her way to it.

She reached out for the catalog, taking it from Eloise again. Then she held it next to the picture of the black dress. "Okay," she finally said. "So this woman will probably look smashing. But"—she looked up at Eloise—"I do think your father is going to yell bloody murder."

"Speaking of my father," Eloise answered, "he and my mother were due here ten minutes ago."

Priscilla nodded. "Ah, the birthday surprise."

"Well, not exactly a shock. Given that we've gone to Lutèce on my birthday for the past twenty-five years or so, it's not all that unexpected."

Priscilla smiled. "That's all right. I don't think Dad needs any more shocks. When he sees the black dress in the big-gal fall issue, that will be all the surprise a man of his age should have in one year."

"I'll tell him when the time is right," Eloise said, her tone casual. She caught the sharp look of questioning Priscilla threw her way, but pretended not to notice.

They both heard the sounds of Grey Bentley's arrival from outside the office.

Priscilla stood up. "We can finish this after the birthday celebration, assuming you still work here."

"The issue won't even be printed until July," Eloise responded. "Then I'll ready myself to go on welfare."

Priscilla walked toward the door, meeting both of Eloise's parents on the way.

Grey Bentley gave the fashion editor an enthusiastic

hug, while Felicia Bentley's greeting was more measured. Eloise's mother always left the theatrics to her husband.

"Priscilla, that Calvin spread in April was beautiful. I loved the dark-haired girl in the pantsuit."

"Thank you, Mr. Bentley," Priscilla responded, her tone sweeter by far than it had been a minute before.

"She had a study session with her trigonometry tutor right after the shoot," Eloise threw in. "Soon, we're going to recruit them right from preschool."

"Oh, sweetheart," Eloise's father retorted, "you look just as young as all these models. And I admit it, I'm glad. There's nothing wrong with wanting to be your best self."

She could only imagine what her father would consider her "best self," but she didn't feel like getting into an argument. It was her forty-first birthday, and she was beginning to enjoy *acting* like an adult, instead of screaming on the inside and stuffing herself with food. Forty had been the worst year of her life, and she was perfectly happy to leave it behind. And she *had* left it, she was pleased to realize. Okay, maybe there were still pitfalls coming up, but she could hardly believe how much more in charge she'd been feeling. Getting on top of the food issue had led to so many other changes.

And sleeping with Nigel had helped more than she could have imagined. She'd left the hotel feeling as if she'd shed twenty years. Just two days before, she'd received an e-mail from him, telling her that he was going to try to convince his ex-wife to give things another go. "The pleasure I felt with you that wonderful night is what's given me the courage to try harder," he'd said. And Eloise was happy for him. As far as she was concerned, the encounter had been a special gift for both of them. She smiled at the thought and then looked up to realize that Priscilla was staring at her.

"Happy birthday, Eloise," she said, her eyes puzzled. She waved toward the Bentleys. "Have a lovely lunch." She glanced toward Eloise once more. "We'll reconvene later this afternoon, and you can tell me everything about your birthday lunch," she said, an ironic twist to her voice.

Eloise knew the code for "and you can tell me what that smile is about when your parents aren't around."

Grey and Felicia watched Priscilla as she walked out.

"That's one smart cookie," Grey said, striding over to his daughter and giving her a hug. "Getting her away from *Glamour* was one of the best things you've ever done."

Eloise pulled back from him. "That was nine years ago. What have I done lately?"

Felicia Bentley stepped forward, offering her daughter a cheek to be kissed. "You know what your father meant, dear. It was a compliment."

Eloise smiled. "I know, Dad. I was only kidding." She went to her desk, taking a seat. "Actually, I have done something lately. Guess who's going to write an article for me?"

"I don't know, sweetheart. Who?" Grey Bentley checked his watch as he spoke.

"Peter Hallman!" Eloise announced.

Her father looked impressed. "That's terrific. What is he going to write about?"

Eloise leaned forward. "I'm sending him to Brazil to do a long essay on the new rich in Rio."

"Gee, that's a terrific idea," Grey said, leaning back against a file cabinet, "but with a writer of his talent, why not extend it to all of Brazil? There's all that business going on with the street kids. He could do a two-part series, or even a three- or four-part."

Eloise looked uncertain.

"C'mon kiddo," her father said, his eyes bright with excitement, "Peter Hallman's known for his grip on society. His novels are famous for all that sociological depth. Imagine what he could do in essay form."

"But, Dad," Eloise countered, "he's a novelist. I don't know how comfortable he's going to be with something that's practically book length."

"Better still," her father responded. "He can make it

into a book after it appears in the magazine. Good for him, good for us!"

Eloise thought about what her father was saying. Maybe it would be good to give the assignment more breadth. It was much more demanding, but it could provide a whole new window for his writing. In fact, the more she considered it, the more she realized that it might be a blessing in disguise.

"What are the Brazilian street kids?" her mother asked, sitting down in the chair that Priscilla had left vacant.

Grey Bentley began to explain the situation to his wife, his face assuming the serious, knowing expression it always took on when he presented in public. "There's been a terrible problem in Brazil with gangs of poor kids congregating in the big cities, especially in the tourist spots. They steal, they loot. And they're as young as they are dangerous."

He went on at some length, outlining several situations in which the American ambassador had to intervene all the way from the capital in Brasília. As she had hundreds of times before, Eloise had to admire the depth of knowledge her father carried around in his head.

"Why is it happening in Brazil?" Felicia asked.

Eloise's father hesitated. "Truthfully, I'm not sure." He smiled suddenly, alight with the anticipation of his plans. "But that's what Peter is going to tell us." He turned to his daughter. "Do you know if he speaks Portuguese?" he asked.

Eloise nodded. "That's one of the reasons we decided on Brazil. It turns out he's spent a lot of time there. He had lived in Rio for a number of months just before he met Kip. He said that that was where he wrote *Winter Deep*."

She didn't tell her father that that was probably the main reason he had wanted to return to Brazil. She knew how desperate Peter was to get his voice back. Maybe going by himself to a place that had once before provided him with such creative energy would do the trick.

"I'll suggest your idea to him, Dad. I can't promise he'll say yes, but I'm sure he'll think about it."

"Why don't I call him?" Grey suggested.

That's all he needs, Eloise thought. Grey Bentley, the eight-hundred-pound gorilla, sitting on his head and pressuring him. "That's all right, Dad. I think he prefers to go his own way. Frankly, his doing this for *Metropolitan Woman* is a huge favor, thanks to my friendship with Kip. I don't want to do anything that will rock the boat."

"Really, dear, I think you're underestimating my persuasiveness."

Eloise sighed. "Oh, no. I know exactly how persuasive you are."

"Well, you don't have to make it sound like a curse."

Eloise could see that her father's feelings were beginning to be hurt. That was the problem with him. He wasn't some classic bully, thwarting everyone in his path. If he'd been some horrible cartoon bastard, it might not be so difficult to be independent from him. But in many ways, her father was a very nice man, wishing the best for those he loved and trying to make everything come out all right. The problem was, she no longer wanted anyone else to make things all right for her.

"Dad, I know that Peter would love you, but he's a solitary writer type. I think I'd rather tell him your idea and let him decide for himself." She smiled with genuine warmth, a little guilty about how she'd been feeling about him lately. After all, without her father's charisma, she wouldn't be seated in this beautiful office, doing a job millions of women would envy.

He returned her smile as he held out his hand to his wife. "We'd better get going if we're going to hold on to our one o'clock reservation."

Eloise started to gather her things. "I'm sure George is already there."

She saw her father's eyes go cold.

"I didn't know George was coming."

"Of course he's coming," Eloise said, her softer feelings evaporating. "He's been at my birthday for forty years. I see no reason for him not to be there this year."

For a moment, it seemed as if her father wouldn't move. His mouth was tight and his posture rigid. Finally, he began to walk toward the door in measured steps, his usual garrulousness gone. He said nothing as they left the office, did not respond to greetings from several people on Eloise's staff as they walked down the corridor. When they rang for the elevator, he kept his face down.

Eloise didn't know what to do. She'd spoken to George several times that week. He'd shown up at the office each day, but his father hadn't spoken a word to him. She knew that her brother was in a terrible limbo, not knowing whether he even *had* a job anymore. Even more tragic, she thought, was her brother's assumption that with or without a job, he certainly no longer had a father. George had tried to get out of coming to her celebration. He was afraid he would make it awkward. He'd urged Eloise to go to the restaurant alone with Grey and Felicia. At least, he'd said, she'd have a real birthday celebration, one that was about *her*.

Eloise wouldn't hear of it. Maybe George was ready to give up, but she was not. There had to be a way through this morass, and providing an occasion Grey Bentley couldn't back out of seemed a good start. But, when the elevator stopped on the third floor, where George had his office, Eloise realized the confrontation was likely to come even before the celebration. Sure enough, as the doors opened, her brother was standing right there.

"George!" Eloise cried out.

She didn't dare look at her father.

"Hello, Mother, Father," George said with formal courtesy as he stepped onto the elevator.

Felicia Bentley looked from her husband to her son. She seemed to be waiting for something to happen. When it did not, she turned to George, reaching over to offer a slight peck on the cheek. He smiled, grateful for the hint of warmth. Then, he caught his father's hostile gaze. The smile disappeared.

This is going to be some celebration, Eloise thought as the elevator doors opened to the lobby. As they proceeded down the street, they might as well have been strangers. Eloise found it unbearable. She longed to break the silence, to get her brother and her father to acknowledge each other, to fight. Anything would be an improvement over the four of them marching along as if they were going to their deaths. But she couldn't find the words to use. Her father was in high gear most of the time. Yet, when he switched off, as he had upon encountering his son, he was implacable. Her brother just looked miserable. No, she corrected herself, miserable and also very angry. But it didn't seem as if George were going to direct that anger toward his father. In fact, she thought with some panic, her brother might well veer off from the group before they even got to the restaurant. She could almost see him weighing his options as they moved along. And she would understand, she really would. After all, what was supposed to happen once they were seated? Two hours of silent indifference might be the most benign result to be hoped for.

Their destination was only a short distance from the Bentley offices. The Midtown street was crowded with workers on their lunch breaks, people jostling each other for space on the sidewalk. Yet, curiously, everyone left them alone. It made Eloise feel even more isolated. Again, she wished she could think of some solution, some easy fix. But it wasn't Eloise who broke the terrible stillness. Instead, Felicia Bentley stopped suddenly.

She turned to her family and, without saying anything, led them to a tiny space between office buildings. It was one of the city's many "pocket parks." She took a seat at the only empty table and stayed in it until her husband and her children joined her. Grey was glaring at her, while George seemed surprised.

"So, what are we going to do?" Felicia said, her voice breaking with emotion.

Eloise stared at her. She had never seen her mother

so overwrought. If her father had always been the live wire, her mother had perfected an air of cordial near-warmth that covered nearly every situation, whether amid a crowd of strangers or with her immediate family.

Neither Eloise nor her brother seemed to have any answer to their mother's question, but Grey Bentley spoke up, his expression still immobile.

"It's my daughter's birthday, and we're going to a nice place to celebrate."

"And that's what you think a father's role is?" Felicia asked. "To buy a pricey meal and offer a lovely toast?"

Eloise looked at her mother, amazed. She'd never heard her like this.

But her father seemed intractable. "I think being a father, like being a son, implies taking responsibility for your actions."

His wife bored in on him. "By which I assume you mean that George's actions are reprehensible."

Grey turned to his wife, seeming to stare her down. "Yes, frankly, that is what I mean."

"Well," Felicia responded, tears springing to her eyes, "I think it's reprehensible to want everyone else to be in your own image. Your son is an accomplished, intelligent man. You've said thousands of times how smart he is, how good in the corporation—damn it, Grey, how proud of him you are."

Her son regarded her with awe.

"And he is homosexual. Which, if you have any kind of honesty, you know is not a big surprise. It's just what *is*. It's what always has been. And it's what Leonard Bernstein was and what Plato was and, according to the newest biography, what Abraham Lincoln was." Her voice had gained strength. "It's what *my son* is, and it's going to be good enough for you!"

Grey Bentley seemed to be breaking down inside. His vigorous coloring had turned mottled and spotty. His eyes were wild with fury. "But he lied to us! And to Bettina." He turned to George. "How could you do that for all those years?" he demanded.

George looked back at his father. "You're right. It was a terrible thing to do, and I'll be sorry about it for the rest of my life." A spark of anger came over his face. "But what the hell else was I supposed to do? If I had admitted it, you would have stopped loving me twenty years earlier."

Grey Bentley's mouth fell open. "Son, I will always love you." His breath was ragged. "But I don't know if I can live with this."

It was a genuine admission, Eloise recognized. Not a pretty thought, not a generous one, but an honest statement. Her mother, though, was not about to let it stand.

"Think about it this way, dear," she said, wiping at her tears with her hand, "how could you possibly consider living without it? George is our son. Every part of him bears a part of the two of us. To be without him is to be without yourself."

They all stared at her. Eloise couldn't believe what she was hearing. George reached over and clasped his mother's hand. She entwined their fingers, holding on to him so tightly that her knuckles whitened.

George eyed his father. "You know, Dad, I've always been proud to be your son. That will never end, no matter what."

Eloise stole a glance at her father. Clearly a battle was being fought. Finally, Grey stood up. He walked behind George and laid his hand on his son's shoulder.

"I haven't had a bite to eat since seven o'clock this morning. I'm famished. Let's get going."

Eloise watched her brother relax into his body, as if a huge weight had been removed from his shoulders. This wouldn't be the end of it, she was certain of that. But at least it was a beginning.

27

"If you could be anybody you wanted for a year, who would you be?" Nora was seated in her sister's living room along with the rest of her family, plus Alex Fenichel. They had spent the night before playing Monopoly and had just eaten a lunch that could easily have fed a group four times as large. "Come on, girls, you can pick anybody you want." She sneaked a look at Alex, who sat next to her on the sofa, but she addressed the question to her nieces.

Sarah, who a moment before had been pulling her little sister's hair, claiming to be playing beauty parlor, lay back on the rug and thought about the question. "Does it have to be somebody real or can it be, like, Goofy or Peter Pan?"

"Hmmm . . . ," Nora said, "it has to be a real person, but it can be a historical figure—" She noted confusion on the faces of both of her nieces. "—someone who isn't around anymore, but used to be real. You know, like Beethoven or George Washington."

"I wanna be Tweety Bird," Tamara yelled before her sister could answer.

Sarah regarded her with contempt. "Aunt Nora said *real,* not a cartoon. And it has to be a *person,* stupid."

"*You're* stupid," Tamara replied, throwing a piece of popcorn from a large bowl that sat between them into Sarah's lap. "People are animals and birds are animals, so people are birds."

Nora began to laugh. "That's not one hundred percent true, but it's brilliant anyway. Okay, honey, so you'd be Tweety. How about you, Sarah?"

"Wellll . . . I think I'd be Madame Curie, 'cause she was the first smart woman."

Nora's father entered the room, licking the spoon he held in one hand, holding a half-eaten bowl of chocolate mousse in the other. "And, some would say, the last smart woman."

"Daddy, that's terrible," his daughter Wendy said as she came in from the kitchen carrying a large tray laden with seven more bowls of mousse.

It was obvious to Nora that her sister had overheard the whole discussion, and it hadn't actually bothered her one little bit, her protest notwithstanding. Of course, it hadn't, thought Nora. Wendy was so blissed out at having Alex in the house, it probably wouldn't have bothered her if the garage had exploded.

Wendy kept one of the heavy bowls for herself, handing the rest of them around the room.

"So, Dad," Wendy kept the game going, "who would you be?"

David Levin shrugged his shoulders, as if to say the question was beneath him, but eventually came up with a response. "I would be Henry the Eighth. He did *what* he wanted *whenever* he wanted."

In that case, Nora mused, you already *are* Henry VIII. With good grace, she kept the thought to herself. "And Mom, how about you?"

Belinda Levin stopped her knitting needles in midair. She'd been working on a blanket for Sarah, which was about half finished. As she considered the question, she smoothed the large red-and-white woolen rectangle over her lap. "I'd be Carole Lombard," she said, with a sigh of contentment. "She was so beautiful and so funny and charming."

"And she got to kiss Clark Gable so many times," Nora said, grinning.

"So, how about you, smarty pants?" her mother replied, once again taking up the needles.

"Let's see. . . ." Nora pondered her choices. It was so much easier to be the one asking the questions than the one answering them. There was Mother Teresa or Billie Holiday. Or Lena Horne or Eleanor Roosevelt.

Suddenly, she knew whom she'd pick. "Robin Hood," she said. "I'd be stealing from the rich to give to the poor, and wearing tights and riding horses, with lots of fresh air and no one to tell me what to do."

"But Robin Hood's a man," Sarah objected.

"Sure, but I said we could pick anyone."

Wendy turned to her husband. "Well, in that case, Andy, you could be Heather Locklear. You'd enjoy that."

"And here I was thinking of becoming Einstein," he said. "How about you, Alex? Brilliant world leader or busty starlet?"

Alex didn't wait a second. "I would be me. Right now. Right here." He reached over and took Nora's hand.

She blushed, her awareness of the pleasure on the faces of her mother, sister, and father making her even more embarrassed. "Enough of this. I have a meeting to get to by six-thirty."

She jumped up from the couch, but was stopped temporarily by her nieces, who practically flew up into her arms.

"It's too soon," Tamara cried, her mousse-covered fingers winding around Nora's neck.

"You haven't even read the books you brought us," Sarah added, hugging her aunt around the waist, daintier than her sister, but no less insistent. "You were going to do *Pippi Longstocking*."

"And so I will," Nora replied, tearing the girls away from her and walking toward her parents. "The next time I'm up here, I'll read the whole book."

Her father stood up. "I don't see why you have to have a meeting on a Sunday night. It's supposed to be the weekend." He kissed her and sat back down.

"Things aren't on a routine schedule in my business,

Dad. The person Will Stanley wants me to meet with is only in town tonight." She bent down to hug her mother; then she blew a kiss toward Wendy and Andy. "This was great, guys. Thank you for a terrific weekend."

Her sister put the bowl of mousse she was eating down on a small table and came to join Nora and Alex. "It was barely twenty-four hours, Nora. Not even a whole two days. Next time you have to do it for real."

Alex answered this time. "We'd love to. And thank you for such a great time." He turned to the children. "Next time, I'll bring my girls. You guys would love each other." He spoke to Nora. "Have you got everything, or is there anything I need to run upstairs for?"

Nora's mother looked up, amazement on her face. Nora could imagine what her mother was thinking. Had her father ever made any offer of help? She doubted it. Nora could feel the maternal stamp of approval toward Alex. The entire family had loved him. Not that he was a stranger. When they'd first dated, they'd spent several nights with Wendy and Andy, long before the two were even married. And Nora's parents had met him once or twice. Then, he had been one of a string of nice boys Nora dated, none of whom had seemed special to the Levin family. Now, he might as well be the second coming.

"I put everything in the car before lunch," Nora said to Alex. She went over to her nieces one more time, giving each of them a big, smoochy kiss. "I love you guys. And I'll see you very soon, I promise."

It took several more kisses and promises to get out of the house and into Alex's car. By the time they actually got to the end of the driveway, it was nearly three, and Nora began to get nervous about making it to the city on time.

"It only takes about two hours," Alex reassured her as he drove. "Besides, how much of an ogre is this Will Stanley? If you walked in five minutes late, surely he'd understand."

"If I walked in five minutes late, he'd probably fire

me," she replied, only half meaning it. "Actually, he'd give me the silent treatment. That's more his style."

"Why would you work for someone like that?" Alex asked.

"We don't all have the luxury of working for ourselves," she said, trying not to sound as irritated as she suddenly felt. "Besides, Will may be brooding and rude, but he does terrific work."

Alex reached over and caught her hand. "The truth is, you don't really have to work at all."

Nora looked at him. "I believe you have me confused with someone named Rockefeller or Gates."

Alex looked into the rearview mirror and pulled over to the side of the road. "Listen, Nora, you must know what I mean." He turned in his seat, bringing her toward him and putting his arms around her. As he spoke, he rubbed his face against hers as gently as a butterfly. "As far as I'm concerned, we've wasted the last fifteen years. Marry me. Marry me and move to Boston. You can produce music up there as easily as you can here. And we can have the life we should have been living all this time."

Nora was stunned. She sat there, enfolded in his embrace, almost numb. She couldn't believe he was saying this, here, now, just like this. They'd only gotten together a few weeks before. How could he possibly have decided this so quickly? She tried to get some words out of her mouth, but she couldn't bring herself to answer him. Alex held on to her, steady and sweet, as he always had been.

Nora didn't know what to say. Being there with him all these years later, being proposed to like this . . . the whole thing felt like a dream. But it's not a dream, she realized. It was exactly what was supposed to happen. It was the precise scenario she'd told Kip and Eloise she wanted. Here it was, just as if she'd planned it herself. Which meant that there was only one possible answer.

"Okay," she breathed.

Alex's arms tightened around her. Then he kissed her, his happiness warming her.

"My daughters are going to be thrilled," he said, turning back to the wheel, and once more pulling out onto the road.

Within minutes, they were on the Taconic, Alex going on about how excited his parents were going to be, how large or small a wedding they should plan, how soon it could take place. But Nora couldn't concentrate on what he was saying. She was aware of the sounds from outside the car—the wind rushing past her open window, the booming radio from an oversize Jeep as it passed them. Nora felt as if time had almost stopped, although Alex was keeping to his constant speed of fifty-eight miles per hour. Her mind started going back over the days she and Alex had spent together since she'd phoned him.

She'd gone up to Boston for a second weekend. Again, they'd spent one afternoon with his daughters, playing with their Barbies and listening to Britney Spears. And they'd had dinner at the home of his best friends, Don and Barbara Millar. Don was the chief financial officer for a computer company on Route 128, while Barbara stayed home with their three children. Barbara had cooked a lovely meal of grilled flank steak and corn, and the evening had been pleasant. "They loved you," Alex had said when he'd called her during the week.

She guessed that was nice, although she had no idea what had been so lovable about her that night. The men had discussed business deals they were involved in, while she and Barbara struggled to find a single thing they had in common. After that, Alex had come to New York several times. In fact, it was because he had business in Manhattan the next day that they'd decided to meet in Rhinebeck and drive back to the city together this weekend.

She'd found it a little odd to be on her home ground with Alex. His New York was very different from her own. With him, she ate in expensive restaurants and attended Broadway theater. He'd managed to get tickets for a sold-out musical imported from London and for a

Eugene O'Neill revival that was considered the hit of the season.

Left to her own devices, Nora tended to socialize in smaller jazz clubs and ethnic restaurants. But it was nice to give herself up to his care. Alex was the most considerate man she'd ever known. When she'd gotten a migraine on a night they were supposed to go to dinner with business contacts, he'd canceled the evening without a second thought and then stayed in the living room of her apartment, bringing her a fresh ice pack and a cup of tea every half hour or so. And he'd been wonderful to her parents and her sister's family. She could read the expression in her sister Wendy's eyes all the time they were up there: He's the one, Nora. You finally caught the prize!

Even her brother-in-law, who often seemed some combination of dazed and outraged by the way Nora lived her life, didn't seem to worry about her with Alex in tow. The men had bonded in her brother-in-law's toolshed, like something out of an episode of *Father Knows Best.*

"So what do you think about July?"

Nora realized that Alex was asking her something.

"July is nice," she answered, wondering what the question had been.

Alex looked at her with affection. "You're not even listening, are you? Your mind is on your meeting." He reached over and ruffled her hair. "I love how much you care about your work. It's the same way I feel myself. I'm really proud of what you've built."

Nora took in the neatly pressed chinos he wore, the blue broadcloth shirt neatly tucked in, the brown leather loafers polished to a high gloss. Alex was the nicest man she knew. She'd been right to call him, right to say yes to his proposal. He would be good to her. He would be faithful and kind, and if they had children, he would be a loving father. He was everything she could hope for.

"So, what's happening at this meeting?" he asked.

"He's got some expert coming he wants me to meet."

"Will must be an interesting guy. I certainly enjoyed the Mississippi film." He grinned. "Of course, that was because of the music."

Nora had shown Alex a rough cut a couple of weeks before.

"He's a talent, for sure," Alex said, making a slight adjustment to the rearview mirror.

"He's a major pain in the ass," Nora grumbled. "Just about as flexible as Mussolini."

"But nice to you, right?"

Nora laughed. "If you call barely speaking *nice,* I guess. To a guy like Will, *nice* means the absence of horrible. When he doesn't display complete contempt, you know you've done all right."

Alex took his eyes off the parkway for a few seconds. "You know, in the movies, when a woman talks that way about a guy, she usually turns out to be interested in him." His tone was bantering, but his eyes were more serious.

Nora was horrified. "Will Stanley is one man you definitely don't have to worry about. His work is great, but his humanity is practically nonexistent."

Alex smiled. "Good, then that's settled." He reached for her hand once again. "So, what do you think, July or October?"

She tried to picture herself walking down some imaginary aisle. She could see the full bloom of a July Sunday, outdoors in some garden, or maybe down at the Jersey shore, where they'd spent so much of their time while they were dating years before. The trees would be twenty shades of green. Pink and red flowers would line her path. All the guests would wear T-strap sandals and sundresses. Or it might be a brisk October day. They'd be up in Rhinebeck, or maybe in the Dairy in Central Park. Fall colors would be in full display, leaves would be in enormous piles on the ground, glorious in yellows and oranges. Her nieces would be dressed in pinafores with white blouses and Mary Janes. The air would smell of apples and cinnamon.

She could see the scene, envision her parents sitting proudly in the first row of whatever setting they were in. Her nieces and Alex's daughters would be flower girls, with big bows in their hair. Her sister would be her matron of honor, beautiful and elegant beside her, while Andy could be an usher. Alex would look handsome in a navy blue suit or maybe even a tuxedo, if he chose. She could practically see the glow in his smile for her as she came down the aisle, the look of unmitigated joy on his face. Standing in front of the guests would be a judge, or perhaps a rabbi.

Something is missing, she thought as the scene passed through her mind. Suddenly, she realized what it was. There was only one thing she couldn't conjure up.

It was herself. She couldn't put herself in the picture, couldn't envision herself as a bride, dressed in white, or, for that matter, dressed in fuschia. She couldn't conceive of standing beside Alex, making sacred vows, ending her life as she understood it. There was no bride in her picture, and no matter how hard she tried to place herself in the scene, she couldn't do it.

They had reached the West Side Highway, and Alex was peering at the signs. "Should I take Ninety-sixth Street, or is it better to go to Seventy-ninth?"

"It doesn't matter," she answered.

Alex must have heard something in her voice. He turned off the highway at Ninety-sixth Street, but instead of pulling onto the exit ramp, he turned into the parking area just off to the right of the highway.

"What's going on?"

If I knew what was going on, maybe I could do something about it, Nora almost snapped at him, knowing how unfair it would be.

"I'm not sure exactly," she said, her voice breathless and soft.

"You're going to chicken out on me, aren't you?"

Alex turned off the motor, but kept his body in driving position, his eyes straight ahead.

Nora could barely stand to respond. She knew she was making the mistake of her life. Yet . . . yet . . . in the depths of her soul, no matter how wonderful he was, no matter how good to her he would be and how happy she would be making her mother and her father and her sister and her friends, she just didn't love him. It wasn't fear of commitment or marriage phobia or any other fancy-sounding concept people had thrown at her.

She wasn't in love with Alex. She should have been. She was supposed to be. Goodness knows, she thought, he was deserving of her love. But it didn't matter. She did not love him. It was that simple. And she knew, despite how very much she wished it weren't so, that it would always be true.

She took her hand and slid it down his arm, overwhelmed by affection for him, grateful for all he'd offered her.

"I'm sorry. I'm so very sorry." They were the only words she could think of to say.

What the hell have I done? Nora asked herself as she approached the door to Will Stanley's building. There had been little left to say before Alex had dropped her off, her pathetic little overnight bag in her hand, once again venturing solo into life. As it's always been, as it always will be, she thought, wishing she didn't have to face Will this very night.

Alex had been so nice, so generous, especially given how selfish and cruel her actions had been. First, she looked him up and went about seducing him; then she put a stake through his heart. She caught her reflection in a mirror on the wall of the stair landing and scowled at her own image. Don't be so dramatic, kiddo, she said to herself as she continued to climb the stairs. Alex wasn't even particularly surprised by her refusal, and he would most assuredly get over it within days, if not within hours.

She hesitated as she came to Will's front door. Inside, she heard the sounds of lively conversation, Mick Jagger singing something in the background. The person she was supposed to be meeting was from an organization called MarketScan, but the noises she was hearing sounded more like a party. At the burst of raucous feminine laughter, she finally rang the bell, waiting a good minute or so until Will answered the door.

"Hey, Nora," he said, waving her inside without really looking at her.

She followed him through the work area to the small den beyond. On the couch was a sandy-haired woman, perhaps thirty-five or so, wearing hiking shorts and a tank top, her long legs already tan although it was only May. In front of her was a half-empty bottle of red wine and two glasses, plus a platter of crackers and cheese.

"Claudia, this is Nora Levin. Nora, Claudia Ostreicher. Nora's the one doing the music," he said, sitting down next to Claudia, leaving Nora to sit opposite them on a sturdy wooden chair.

Will, too, was in shorts, his muscular legs less tan than Claudia's. He was wearing a threadbare yellow T-shirt, which, despite having obviously seen some better days, was bringing out a healthy glow to his face. He also sported well worn hiking boots. Between the two of them, Nora thought, they looked like a page from an L.L. Bean catalog.

"We walked the Palisades this afternoon," Will said, observing Nora's glance at their attire.

Nora found herself annoyed. What business is it of mine? she had the urge to respond. For all she cared, they could have been swimming the Atlantic or camel driving through the Gobi Desert. Hold on there, she said to herself. Her annoyance was irrational, not to mention unprofessional. She sat in her chair quietly, trying to calm herself. After all, she thought, she was here for a job, and tearing two people to shreds because they happened to look good didn't seem like an especially fruitful choice of business activity.

"So, Ms. Ostreicher, you're with MarketScan?" Nora asked, after a minute or so.

"It's Claudia," she answered. "And, yes, in my real life, I'm with MarketScan." She looked at Will as if her answer had been some kind of private joke between them. Which it must have been, since he looked back at her, returning her smile in force. She turned back to Nora. "It was kind of fun today just to think about nothing but getting up and down the sides of a mountain, but I guess it's back to business."

She smiled at Will, appearing to Nora like a cat after the canary has been fully digested.

"Will and I haven't had a day like this since . . ." Claudia hesitated. ". . . maybe, 1988 or something."

He nodded. "I know it was post Jimmy Carter, but I'm not sure of the exact year. Remember the kids on Half Dome?"

Claudia began to laugh uproariously. Then, she seemed to realize that they were being rude, and addressed herself to Nora once again. "We were hiking in Yosemite, going about a quarter of an inch a minute on this slippery stretch of rock, and these children, these little babies, start running past us—"

"—about eighty miles an hour . . . ," Will interrupted. "They looked too young to be alive, let alone to be running up a mountain. It made us feel about a hundred and eight years old."

Nora watched him as he glanced at Claudia with an easy affection she had never seen him display. He looked like a kid himself instead of the serious adult he had always presented to Nora.

Nora felt uncomfortable. What was she doing here, in the middle of what seemed to be a date? She thought that Will was getting her together with an expert on the market economy, who would help them decide how to structure a film about industrial standardization, but this felt like a college reunion.

Will must have noticed her discomfort. "Claudia and I were at Michigan together," he said in explanation.

Oh, great, Nora thought. It really *was* a college reunion.

"Well," he continued, "I guess we'd better get down to business." He picked up his glass of wine and took a sip. "Gee, Nora," he offered as an afterthought, "would you like a beer or something?"

She shook her head, but he got up anyway, bringing a glass for her, plus another bottle of wine.

"Maybe you guys want to do this tomorrow," Nora said as Will sat back down on the couch.

"Of course not," Claudia said with enthusiasm. "I've been waiting all day to meet you. Will played the Mississippi film for me, and I was so impressed with your work."

Nora thanked her. "Tell me about MarketScan. Will hasn't really explained much about what you do."

"We study the marketplace, the financial trends, the commercial trends," Claudia explained. "We can basically tell you everything you need to know about how businesses are set up within the United States."

She went into further details about location, mall sizes, urban renewal areas versus exurban settings, but Nora found herself concentrating on Claudia herself. She seemed intelligent. No, she corrected herself, she seemed actually brilliant. And she looked like the kind of woman Nora usually liked—down to earth, pretty without much makeup, her hair a wavy tangle that seemed not just natural but uncombed. But what set Claudia apart was her air of utter confidence. This was not a woman given to "Does he like me?" or "Will I succeed?" And it didn't seem to come from arrogance. Claudia was sharing her ideas with Nora in a way that radiated equality, not superiority. She seemed absolutely at ease with herself and with the world. Nora knew she should find this admirable, but somehow she didn't.

She's too perfect, Nora decided, knowing how unfair she was being. Unlike Will, who had hardly looked at Nora since she arrived, Claudia was going out of her way to make Nora feel part of things. Yet, as the minutes

wore on, Nora felt increasingly hostile. She tried to make
herself concentrate on what Claudia was saying, instead
of evaluating her like a bitchy high school sophomore in
gym class.

"So, what The Gap and Banana Republic and Crate
and Barrel have come to mean in terms of centralization
of product placement is akin, in MarketScan terms, to
the industrial revolution. If a hundred and fifty years ago,
virtually everyone was forced to leave their own pocket
of land and go to centrally organized work areas, now,
instead of the independent drugstore or the independent
bookstore, everyone is being shoved into the same
seventy-five outlets. Standardization has replaced diver-
sity, and you wouldn't know if you were visiting Miami,
Florida, or Boulder, Colorado, except for the humidity
index."

"Which is not all negative," Will interjected. "You
now have full employment in places that used to have a
third of their populations on some kind of welfare, not
to mention wide availability of everything from books
to hairbrushes. Traditional mail-order businesses may be
suffering, and of course individual business owners, but
people in Topeka, Kansas, can buy a pair of jeans without waiting three weeks for delivery from the Sears
catalog."

Claudia picked up the conversation. "The question is,
how has this affected society at large? MarketScan is
trying to evaluate the effects on the country as a whole,
not just on the small business owners who are being
squeezed, but on school kids who are all wearing the
same outfits, and adults who watch the same television
programs and shop in identical malls. To what extent has
capitalism come to mean exactly the kind of unilateral
power communism tried and failed to bring about for all
those years."

Nora began to sip the wine Will had poured for her.
She took in most of what Will and Claudia were saying,
but found herself distracted by their glances back and
forth, their obvious fondness for each other. This was an

aspect of Will she'd never seen. Not even when they were making love that night in Mississippi. Not that she had thought to miss it. The thought of their passion that night made her squirm in discomfort.

She willed herself to follow the conversation once more. Will was saying something about a film they'd worked on together in South America, the months they'd spent in Argentina and Brazil in the early nineties. She couldn't take her eyes off his long fingers and strong forearms as he sketched an idea in the air he was trying to get across. It made her remember how his hands had felt on her body that night, how completely they'd taken possession of her, how completely she'd let them.

Jesus, she chided herself, knowing she was flushing with embarrassment. She *had* to get hold of herself.

"So, outside of Pete Seeger singing about ticky tacky houses, I don't have a clue about what music you might want to use." Claudia's amused gaze was focused on Nora.

Belatedly, Nora realized the woman must have been asking her some question, but she had no idea what the question had been. She hesitated, wondering what response would sound least stupid.

"Listen, guys," Claudia continued when an immediate reply from Nora was not forthcoming, "I've got an early plane to catch tomorrow morning, so it's time to get back to the hotel."

Nora watched her pull herself up from the couch, the picture of long-limbed grace. Will got up as well, so Nora did also.

"No, Nora, if you can stay, there are another couple of things I'd like to go over with you," Will said, walking out of the room with Claudia, not even looking to see whether Nora was doing as he asked.

She sat back down, finishing her glass of wine and pouring half a glass more. She needed it, she thought, though she didn't feel like exploring why that might be true. She listened as Will let Claudia out of the apartment, heard the sounds of their affectionate good-bye.

Will came back into the den, still smiling from something Claudia had said. "We've had some good news," he said, taking his seat once more on the couch.

"You and Claudia?" Nora asked, wishing the moment the words came out of her mouth that she hadn't.

He looked at her as if he could see right through her. "No, you and I."

Nora stayed quiet this time.

"*Mississippi* has been chosen to close DoubleTake."

"Wow," Nora said. That *was* great news. The documentary film festival in Durham, North Carolina, was the nonfiction equivalent of Sundance. "Well," she said, raising her glass, "here's to you."

"And to you," he answered. "You know, I watched it again with Claudia last night. Your music really made it what it is."

"Are you drunk?" Nora asked.

Will leaned across to where she was sitting. He reached out to her, pushing the hair back from her forehead. It was the first time he'd touched her since their night together, and it left her stunned. She had no idea why Claudia had gone and she had been made to stay, not a clue why Will was suddenly concentrating on her with an intensity he usually reserved for a camera. She prayed he would take his hand away, then, perversely, longed for it to snake around her neck and draw her near.

The sound of the telephone ringing was a shocking intrusion. Will did not pull his hand away. Instead, he slid it down her cheek, his fingers leaving her skin tingling. His eyes bore into hers, as if he were asking her some question. She couldn't bring herself to look back at him. She sat perfectly still until the loud ringing managed to interrupt his concentration. He sat back in his seat, seeming to decide whether or not to answer the telephone, but then he got up. She watched his back as he went into the next room. Nora stayed in place, unable to move a muscle. Two opposite emotions were at war inside her. Deep in her belly was a chasm of fear, that he might come back into the room, that he might touch her again. But, also within her was a longing for him, a loneliness so profound, it threatened to burst out of her chest.

She felt as if her entire body was composed of nothing but nerve endings. Miserable, she stood up and walked over to the small window. The view was a concrete backyard, a few pots of plants and a small metal tray table the only ornamentation. Seeing a scene so mundane made her feel slightly more tranquil.

She waited for Will to finish on the telephone, not knowing what was going to happen when he returned. What do I want to happen? she asked herself, the fear once again pounding away at her. As bad as the feeling was, she couldn't lie to herself. If Will walked back into the room right now, what she really wanted was for him to take her in his arms and carry her to his bed. She wanted him to kiss her, to make love to her so she could forget how frightened she was. She hugged herself. No, she thought. What she wanted was for him to disappear forever.

She walked back to the couch and sat down. She glanced at the bottle of wine, but the thought of drinking more of it made her almost ill. This was no time to give up control of her faculties. A hurricane of thoughts started racing through her head. For one thing, she had no idea what Claudia was to Will. The thought nagged at her. That was just like a man, to start cozying up to her one moment after he'd been with another woman. No wonder he scared her. Besides, she thought, growing angry now, where the hell was he? He'd been on the phone for at least ten minutes. Did he even remember that she was in here, waiting for him?

As usual, he thought only about himself. That she was taking her weekend to work with him, that she was sitting here without a damn thing to do meant nothing to him. He was probably chatting about the weather, for God's sake. Or, for all she knew, there was some other woman. Maybe they were planning a bike trip to Zanzibar or a trek up Everest. She rose from the couch and began to pace around the room. It was so typical, this kind of behavior. The image of her father suddenly came into her mind, and she knew why. It never mattered to these guys whether you were busy or harried or had other things to do. Whatever suited them was supposed to suit you.

She didn't even hear Will when he came back into the room.

"Sorry it took so long," he said, coming up behind her and putting his arms around her.

She evaded his grasp, moving beyond his reach. "Listen, Will, I'm really sorry, but I've got to get going. We'll have to talk about everything Claudia said later in the week, okay?"

He stared at her, surprised, then grinned. "You betcha, ma'am," he said, raising his hand in a kind of salute.

He walked toward her, though she noticed he did not hurry. It was as if he wouldn't give her the satisfaction of urging her to stay. And I wouldn't stay even if he did, she thought, furious now for reasons that even she was not sure of.

"I've got to get home," she insisted, despite the fact that he didn't seem to be stopping her. "There are a thousand things that have to get done by tomorrow." She picked up her suitcase and strode out of the room. At his front door, she forced herself to slow down.

He's a *client,* she thought, making herself turn around. "Thank you for the meeting tonight. It was very interesting." With that, she opened the door and fled down the stairs.

Although she didn't hear any sounds from behind, she had the horrible feeling that if she looked back, she'd find Will standing there, laughing at her.

28

Eloise twirled the telephone cord around her left hand as she listened to Kip and Nora. It had been a couple of hours since she'd watched the photo shoot for the fall fashion issue, but she found herself smiling still at the image of Hermione Sinclaire in the black dress. The size ten model had looked as stunning as Eloise knew she would. Even Priscilla had offered a grudging compliment as the model was on her way out. Now, Eloise was on the weekly conference call with her friends, which usually energized her. But she found herself shifting in her chair, not quite comfortable in her own skin, not really focused on the conversation. She knew she should be feeling great, reveling in her accomplishment, but something was nagging at her. For God's sake, she thought, impatient with herself, she was down to 132 pounds and she'd had a great day. When was she going to let herself relax and enjoy it?

"So, I guess my best moment is . . . well, it's hard to say," Kip was explaining.

Eloise was startled to realize she had tuned out the last few minutes of the conversation. She willed her attention back to the Monday night call. "Why?" she asked, hoping neither Kip nor Nora had noticed her absence.

"Actually, the whole week was really good. Peter will be working for *Metropolitan Woman,* and that's certainly all to the good. And my practices went pretty well. Oh, and J. P. got mostly A's on his report card."

"And Lisa?" Nora asked.

"Hmmm . . ." Kip thought. "Well, my daughter didn't club me to death with a baseball bat while I was sleeping."

Nora's answering laugh echoed through the telephone lines. "How about you, El?"

Eloise thought about voicing the sense of dissatisfaction that seemed to have enveloped her, but the feelings were so blurry. She might as well stick to the facts. "I guess my best moment and my worst moment are the same. I just came from a photo shoot where the model is a size ten."

"And?" Nora responded.

"And that's five sizes larger than any model has worn in at least ten years."

"Jeez," Kip said. "That's amazing. Are they really all size zero?"

Eloise frowned into the receiver. "No, some of the elephantine girls sport a size two. Premenstrually, a few of them even slip into a four!"

"Well, then, good for you," Nora said. "But why is this also your worst moment?"

"Because I've had to apologize for the damn picture to everyone from my fashion editor to the girl's agent. Honestly, you'd have thought the woman's job was to talk me *out of* hiring her client instead of *into* hiring her. 'Are you sure you're talking about Hermione Sinclaire? Maybe you're confusing her with Helen Settler.' I mean, really, you'd have thought I was asking to photograph Godzilla."

Kip's reassuring voice answered her. "Then you should be even more proud of yourself. And even happier to be turning the anorectic tide in a national forum."

"You sound like someone running for office," Nora teased.

"Oh, yes? Well then, little missy, what were your best and worst moments?" Kip asked, unwounded.

Nora stayed quiet for a few seconds, which Kip picked up on.

"Had yourself a complicated week?" she asked.

"Oh," Nora sighed. "I don't know that complicated quite covers it."

She hesitated yet again, and this time Eloise was the one to nudge her.

"With all the things we've gone through, I doubt that anything could be that terrible," she said. "Why don't you just spill whatever it is and let us wipe up the mess."

"I'm not so sure you're going to be that happy about the mess when I tell you what happened." Nora's voice had become almost inaudible. "Well, okay, so, here it is. I guess you might call it a best moment—Alex proposed to me."

Eloise began to congratulate her friend when she realized that that had to be only part of the story. "And," she prompted, "your worst moment?"

"I said no."

There was a small silence. Then Kip picked up the conversation. "When did this happen?"

"Sunday night. We had been at my sister's house and Alex was driving me to a meeting with Will Stanley."

"Interesting," Kip said. "And you said no because—?"

"Would it make any sense if I said I said no because he was driving at exactly fifty-eight miles an hour?"

Kip stayed quiet, but Eloise found herself responding. She knew Nora expected her to be disappointed, but that was not at all how she felt.

"You know what, Nora? You said no because you said no. You don't have to apologize to us any more than I should have been apologizing to my fashion editor." Eloise didn't know where her certainty was coming from. For months, she and Kip had been pushing Nora into a relationship with Alex. Yet, all her instincts were telling her that Nora had done something she had to do. In fact, something about what Nora said resonated within Eloise, but she couldn't put her finger on quite what it was. All

she knew was that Nora deserved to follow the path she
and only she had chosen.

Kip entered the fray. "You're absolutely right, Eloise.
Nora, no one, least of all your friends, is going to make
you do something you're not ready to do. That's the
whole point of friendship, to love the things that *are,* not
the things that *might* be or *should* be."

Nora started to laugh. "Do you guys really believe a
word of what you're saying? I mean, don't you actually
want to disown me?"

Both Eloise and Kip began to laugh along with her.

It was Eloise who finally answered the question. "Let's
face it. The real act of friendship is buying the bullshit
of those you love just as readily as you buy your own."

"Amen, Sister Bentley," answered Nora, hanging up
before the others forced her to say another word.

Kip giggled. "She sure couldn't wait to escape from
us, could she?"

"Whew!" Eloise said in agreement. But she thought
about Nora's quick exit. Maybe there were things her
friend wasn't so eager to discuss. Or maybe, like Eloise
herself, there was something nagging at her that was so
vague, there wasn't even a way to start talking about it.

29

Kip supported a small pile of folded laundry in the crook of one arm, while she used her free hand to open the top drawer of Lisa's bureau. The cleaning woman invariably confused Kip's and Lisa's clothing, so swapping misplaced underpants and socks was a weekly ritual after laundry day. It amused Kip to think that the woman believed she might be the one who owned the red thong panties or the spaghetti-strapped camisole that looked as if it were designed for a large doll. She supposed she should be flattered.

Surveying the array of folded shirts in Lisa's second drawer, Kip was struck yet again by the disbelief that she herself had ever dressed that way back in high school. Everything Lisa wore looked so . . . *tiny*. Hell, she could remember really short skirts and close-cut tops—it wasn't as if she were a dinosaur. But she couldn't envision putting on these tight little knit numbers and walking outside.

"You are old, Father William . . . ," she intoned, aware that she was quoting something, but having no recollection of what.

Her eyes traveled over the items littering the top of the bureau: lipsticks, Q-Tips smudged with eye shadow, hair gels, perfumes in sample bottles, assorted hair brushes and a large comb. Why Lisa's short hair required three brushes was a question Kip knew better than to ask. Typical teenager stuff . . . and so much better than syringes or plastic baggies full of pills and other illegal who-knows-what, Kip reassured herself.

She turned to go, trying not to see the clothes strewn all over the unmade bed and floor, the sneakers smack in the middle of the rug. She stepped over schoolbooks, a backpack, two swimsuits and a pair of goggles, a plastic water bottle, and a balled-up bath towel from Lisa's shower the previous night—no doubt still wet, Kip couldn't help thinking. Over on the desk, a messy pile of clothing buried the numerous framed pictures of Lisa and her friends, scattered papers and assorted odds and ends, probably lost to mankind forever. It must have been four years since the desk had been used for its intended purpose of homework.

Long ago, Kip had decided that the clean-your-room battle was not worth waging. It was too high a price for too small a victory. In fact, she was rather proud of herself for being so enlightened on this issue. It worked for her, she knew, only because she ventured into the room as rarely as possible, and, whenever she passed by, she pretended that behind the closed door was a sparkling model of cleanliness and order. Every thousand years or so, Lisa cleaned it up without being asked, Kip reminded herself, and that was in itself a major victory.

"Breathe deeply," she told herself in a soothing voice. "Do not see the horror that is before you." She pressed her palms together, fingertips up, as if in prayer. "Remember your mantra. This, too, shall pass. This, too, shall pass."

Unable to resist, she picked up the bath towel, which was indeed damp, and took it with her into the children's bathroom. It was so quiet in the house, she thought as she spread the towel over the shower rod. Deadly quiet. She hated it.

With a sigh, she went downstairs. It wasn't as if Peter made a lot of noise during the day when he was locked away in his office writing. Or not writing, she added to herself with a wince. But there was no question, his absence was sorely felt. She recalled him once commenting on how different the atmosphere in the house was when one of the kids was out. She thought back to that night, the two of them curled up next to each other on the sofa, he with a book, she hemming a pair of pants for J. P. She could see herself nodding in agreement, liking that he was the kind of man who would feel the absence of his children that much.

This was the first time Peter had been away for more than a night or two at a time. His idea to go away someplace to write a magazine article had translated into a trip to Brazil. He was in Rio de Janeiro, doing an in-depth look at the lives of several people at either end of the economic continuum there. The rich and the poor coexisted practically side by side in the beauty of Rio, but might as well have been living on different continents. Peter would use profiles of individuals to personalize the bigger issues. Everyone seemed delighted with the plan, and Peter was on a plane to Rio just a week later.

Kip was happy for him, although she wished he had been drawn to write about some other topic, closer to home. There was a pervasive sense of emptiness in the house. She dreaded going to bed at night, lying there wide-eyed, unable to sleep without him beside her, feeling the length of his body pressed against hers, the weight of his arm draped across her. She needed to smell his skin and hear his voice whispering in her ear. She wanted to make love with him, looking into his eyes as they moved together until their passion took over, the way they had made love the night before he left. That night had been beautiful and sad and sexy all at once. She was missing him even as she wrapped her arms and legs tightly around him, feeling his lips on her lips, her forehead, her neck, having him and knowing she soon wouldn't have him at all.

The days were utterly flat without him. There was no one to talk to when she got home and the kids were off doing the millions of things they did. She did her best to enliven mealtimes, but Peter's vacant chair constantly reminded them all that things were out of kilter. Even

Lisa had asked this morning when Dad would be coming home. And J. P. had told her several times he wished Peter hadn't gone away for so long, and could she please ask him not to do it again?

What amazed and puzzled Kip was that she suddenly felt so incompetent. Here she was, the woman who could reduce her own sister to tears with her supposed perfection, the superwoman who was always improving everything—feeling useless and helpless. Where was that old rah-rah, take-charge gal? It wasn't that she was too busy. She was the same level of impossibly busy that she usually was. It was that ever since her husband had left, she was feeling overwhelmed by the smallest things. Like the fact that the bank mistakenly debited a three-hundred-dollar withdrawal twice on this month's statement. Or that she had discovered yesterday that one of the small windowpanes in the dining room was broken, and a chunk of it had fallen out. Lately, her Lexus was making a funny noise when she accelerated. She didn't want to deal with any of it. Stupid little things that never bothered her before. Now the effort to take care of them was more than she could manage. What was worse, she silently admitted, was the growing sense of panic she felt about it all. But *why* was she so panicked? No answers had come to her.

Without Peter, she thought, she was drifting in space by herself, flailing, ready to drown. Not that that made any sense.

"I'll mix my metaphors if I damn well want to," she retorted to no one.

She picked up her gym bag from a chair near the door to the garage, checking to make sure it contained everything she needed. What was hardest to believe was that Peter would miss her first competition the following week. Okay, it wasn't a big deal competition, just a small one on the way to her goal of skating in the Nationals. But it was her first since she had started skating again, and it might as well have been the Olympics, given how nervous she was about it. She wasn't ready, she knew she wasn't, she didn't care what her coach said. On the other hand, she soothed herself, Gordonov wasn't one to let a skater compete prematurely. Still, Kip couldn't imagine how she would get through it. And today's crisis was that her skating routine for the competition had turned out to be six seconds too long for the music. That meant she had to rechoreograph everything. After her Pilates workout, she would head over to the rink to struggle with it.

"Peter, I *nneeeed* you," she wailed as she slung the bag over one shoulder. Wow, it feels so good to whine, she thought.

The telephone began to ring as she was almost out the door. She glanced at her watch. Damn. She would barely make it to her workout on time as it was. But she couldn't help herself. She ran back to the kitchen.

"Hello?"

"Kip? Hi, it's Edna Pyne. From Pyne Travel."

"Edna, hi." Kip spoke pleasantly but quickly. "What's doing?"

"A spot opened up at the hotel you wanted in Venice for that week in September. Should I grab it? It's for one of their better rooms, so it'll be a couple of hundred more per night."

Kip tried to think. Months before, she and Peter had discussed going to Venice, just the two of them, for their wedding anniversary. She had researched hotels, and discovered a small, romantic place that seemed perfect, but which turned out to be fully booked around the time she wanted. After that, she had dropped the project, taken up with all her new activities. She had completely forgotten that she asked Edna to see if anything opened up at the hotel. Would Peter still want to make the trip, given all that had been going on? She wasn't sure if it would be a good thing for them, at least not at the moment.

"The opening won't last, will it?" she asked Edna.

"Heck, no. And they want a nonrefundable deposit."

Kip had no idea what to say. She needed to talk to Peter. The panic that had been creeping up on her lately was making itself felt once again. She couldn't think. Why couldn't she just make a decision?

"Edna, I'm sorry, I'm running out, and I can't give you an answer right now. I'll call you back later, okay?"

"Okay, hon. Up to you."

Kip hung up and raced to her car. It was next to impossible to get Peter on the phone to discuss this with him. He was never in his hotel room, and she had missed two of his calls to the house. They had spoken only twice so far, and there had been a delay in the transmission so they were always stepping on each other's sentences. She needed to deal with this situation herself. The room cost a fortune. Maybe they should go somewhere else, a different hotel. But everything would be booked for September. Maybe a different city altogether would be better anyway. Frantically, she rummaged around in her purse for the car key and her sunglasses. It was stupid to be worrying about this now when she had the competition coming up. Her panic was worsening. It's not such a big deal, she told herself. Why was she getting so upset?

Her eyes were welling up with tears. Jesus, what was wrong with her? She stopped what she was doing and put her purse on the seat next to her, taking slow, deep breaths. There was something weird about the way she was feeling. She waited, somehow certain it would come to her.

It was familiar, that's what, a familiar sense of having something important coming up in skating, and taking a trip with Peter. The two things together. Closing her eyes, she let her mind drift.

In a few moments, she realized what she was remembering. It was back when she had left skating, when she had decided Peter was more important to her. She had been scheduled to go on a yearlong skating tour, her first long-term commitment. Also the first time she would have been without her parents for such an extended period. Instead, she had run off to Europe with Peter—the week before the tour was to start. She had never consciously thought about the tremendous relief that accompanied having a reason to back out of the tour. Of course, she loved Peter, there was no doubt about that, but she had also been quietly terrified by the prospect of being on her own, traveling across America. She had found a way out of it, going straight from her parents' house to Peter, from her strictly supervised life to marriage.

Kip cleared her throat, calmly reached for her purse, and looked inside, spotting the ignition key. She pressed the button to open the garage door and started the car, backing out into the bright afternoon. Her movements were slow and deliberate, as if she were fragile.

I never believed I could be on my own.

There, it was out. That was the truth. No, the sorry-ass truth, she corrected herself. Miss Perfect-Can-Cook-Anything-Sew-An-Evening-Gown-Plant-A-Garden didn't really believe she could make it alone in the world. All that motion, running around, doing a million things at the same time. It was just a smoke screen to hide her terror of being responsible for herself.

She pulled out of the driveway. Peter and she always acted as if he were the distracted one, the intellectual who couldn't do anything practical. But it was *she* who was the weak one, she who needed to lean on him. There hadn't been a day in her life when someone else wasn't taking care of her. Knowing he was there freed her to tinker with her projects, to be class mom extraordinaire, or social director for the school fund-raiser. But that was all busywork. It was the big stuff she was afraid of. The stuff where you were the one responsible for your family, for everyone feeling they had a place in the world. And that it was a safe, secure place. She was only playing house, playing at being a mom. It was Peter who made their lives real. He was the grown-up. While he was away, she had to be the grown-up for real. And she didn't like it one bit.

She turned on the radio and twisted the volume knob way up.

*   *   *

Kip put her hands on her hips and arched her back, stretching as she glanced at the ice on the television monitor yet again. The monitor was set up to allow everyone behind the scenes to observe how each skater was doing during her turn. Some chose to watch, while some studiously avoided seeing what was going on. Right now, the ice was empty, pristine and readied for the first skater. Kip and the rest of the competitors were waiting in a large, bare room to go on. They all wore their skates with the rubber guards still on, observing the unofficial rule of silence as they paced or stretched. Some talked to their coaches and some talked to themselves, raising an arm, turning this way or that. A few exchanged slight smiles, but most kept their heads down or stared at nothing as they reviewed their routines in their heads.

Kip was startled to recognize Nora and Eloise on the monitor, sitting together in the second row. She had known they were coming, but she hadn't seen them that day, having driven herself to the rink much earlier. She moved closer, glad to distract herself with the sight of them, their heads together, whispering, excited. She took comfort in the sight of Nora's thick, dark curls and Eloise's bright, hopeful eyes. What had she done before she knew them? Then she felt a stab of anxiety. She didn't want them to see her make an idiot of herself.

No, wrong. Don't talk like that, she instructed herself. She turned away from the screen, running her hands over her stomach, feeling the smooth powder blue satin of her costume. A seamstress in Manhattan who worked with a lot of skaters had made it for her. It was a simple design with a short, chiffon skirt and tiny seed pearls scattered across the shoulders and down the arms to catch the light. Her hair was pulled up into the old tight bun she knew so well. Just the sensation of brushing her hair up and wrapping it into the small knot transported her back to when she was seventeen. As she inserted hairpins and tried not to inhale the cloud of hairspray she released to keep everything in place, it was as if her hands remembered the motions all by themselves.

She did a deep knee-bend, wishing her coach were there. Gordonov had been admitted to the hospital the day before with a severe case of food poisoning. Only something that serious could have kept the man away, but, sure enough, something that serious had happened. Kip resisted the "Why did this have to happen to me?" tirade she was tempted to indulge in, and reassured herself repeatedly that she could do this, that she *had* to do this to show Gordonov that his faith in her hadn't been misplaced.

The first skater was up. Kip watched just long enough to note her orange costume and watch her initial moves as the notes of Vivaldi's *Spring* filled the air. A beautiful piece, she thought, but so overused.

She turned away, not liking her need to be critical. Yes, and you're using an original classical piece composed by Paul McCartney exclusively for you, she chided herself. If only. Focus on what you have to do. Nothing else.

She wondered if she might actually throw up. So many years since she had last skated in front of an audience, even if it was such a small one. This was a minor competition, and most of the people were friends and family of the skaters. Kip could have won this in her sleep in the old days—which might as well have been in the Dark Ages, she mused, if you want to compare the form of a teenaged skater to a middle-aged one.

Orange Lady was done, skating off with a look that said she knew she hadn't performed well, but she was nonetheless thrilled that it was over. A girl with a long black swinging ponytail took over, her moves crisp and sharp as she skated to the strains of Abba's "Dancing Queen." She was good, Kip thought, unable to resist watching the routine, although the choice of music made her cringe. She liked the next skater's selection far better, Frank Sinatra singing "One For My Baby," but the skater fell early on, and she couldn't recover her concentration after that.

Then it was Kip's turn. Her stomach heaved as she stepped onto the ice. Aware of Nora and Eloise visible in the periphery and audible in their cheering, she tried to ignore them. She skated directly to the center of the rink, the old habits of so many years before being automatically exercised again as she tuned out everything around her.

She waited, in position, her left foot behind her right, her arms extended upward. Somewhere inside her was the feeling she would explode with fear, that she had to get away from here, just get the hell off the ice. But her hard-earned discipline was still in control. She took a deep breath. *Now.*

The first notes of Cole Porter's "So in Love" began, and she was alone with the music. She moved across the ice, feeling the power of her connection to it, aware of nothing else but the music, the cold whiteness beneath her and the movements of her body.

There was applause. For a split second, Kip remained where she was, astounded. She had actually done it. One misstep, yes, but no falls, and, most important, no falling apart. Her hands on her waist, she glided to the exit point, exultant. She glanced over to Eloise and Nora, who were jumping around in their seats, calling her name and clapping wildly. She shot them a grin.

"Attaway, baby!" shouted Nora.

Kip laughed, stepping off the ice onto the rubber floor. As she put the guards back on her blades, she noticed that her hands were trembling. Dear God, she thought, this little routine has meant more to me than anything I ever did when I was so successful. She wanted to cry, her heart aching with the full realization of how much she had missed skating. But she was overjoyed to know that she was back, that it wasn't lost to her forever, that she had reclaimed it for herself. I'll never let it go again, she resolved. It was part of her, always.

She returned to the back room, awash with relief and

happiness. She gulped down more than half a liter of water and resumed her earlier pacing. This time it wasn't brought on by tension, but by the fact that she was too overwrought to sit, too excited to stand still. She watched the other skaters on the monitor, but she was distracted now, not appraising, not concerned with anything but the feeling of coming home.

Nora and Eloise appeared only moments after the last skater was done, extending a bouquet of roses, nearly as happy for her as she was for herself.

"Oh, what you did," Eloise said, her eyes misty. "You said you would, and you made it happen."

"And look at what *you've* made happen," Kip said, gesturing toward Eloise's fitted silk shirt, tucked into a pair of black pants. "You look incredible. Since the last time I saw you, you've developed killer cheekbones."

"Sure." Eloise's tone was sarcastic, but her pleasure in the compliment was evident from her expression.

"I can't believe you know how to do that stuff," Nora put in, hugging Kip again. "I still can't get over the idea that regular people can just lift up like that, sail into the air. You were so wonderful. It was fantastic, unbelievable."

Kip looked at them, her expression serious. "But we all know that there was no chance in the world I would have been here if it weren't for you two. I don't know how to thank you."

Eloise waved her hand. "Oh, *pshaw*. Any time."

"No, wait," Nora said, "I want to hear this. Please continue with the compliments."

Kip laughed. "You are beyond friends to me, I hope you know that."

"Friends that are more like sisters," Nora suggested. "But not exactly like sisters. More like . . . *fristers*."

"Right." Eloise shook her head at Nora's silliness.

"Look," Kip interjected, intent suddenly. She gestured across the room. "The results."

A woman in a gray suit was posting a piece of paper on the nearby bulletin board. People were crowding

around to get a glimpse. Kip made her way through the
throng. Not daring to breathe, she searched for her
name, starting from the bottom of the list. Not there, not
there, not there. She found it, Katherine Hallman, in the
number-two slot. She had won second place. Behind her,
Nora and Eloise saw it as well.

"Wow," Kip exclaimed to them as they moved away
from the crowd of people.

"You're happy?" Eloise asked, unsure of whether Kip
was relieved, or disappointed by having lost out for first.

"I believe this is the sweetest victory of my career,"
Kip said. "At least, that's the way it feels."

"Ladies," Nora announced, "I believe we have done
a good thing. Good for ourselves, good for each other."

The three women regarded each other with affection.

"Okay." Kip broke the silence at last. "One of us
down. Two more to go. Who's next?"

30

Nora walked up Fifth Avenue with her sister on one side and her mother on the other. Belinda Levin was dressed in a brown corduroy coat that Nora recognized as having been her own when she'd been in college. Her sister, however, was wearing a brilliant purple sweater that came down to her knees, its intricate cable-stitched pattern lending it the vertical sweep that made Wendy seem taller than she was.

Nora stared at the garment, smiling. "You made it, right?" she said.

Wendy dug her hands into the garment's deep pockets and looked right back at Nora. "Yes, and I cobbled my loafers and milled my cotton briefs."

Nora laughed, but she knew she'd been correct about the sweater.

"It's so great having the two of you to myself," she said, stopping at the bottom of the enormous sweep of marble stairs leading up to the Metropolitan Museum of Art. "You ready?"

She addressed the question to her mother, who nodded with enthusiasm.

"Culture, here we come," Wendy said, already starting to climb the stairs.

As they made their way up, Wendy looked around at the crowd of people seated there. There were throngs of schoolchildren, led by teachers and parents, young couples eating sandwiches out of paper bags, several homeless people, many with cups of loose change in front of them, and hordes of individuals, looking up into the bright sun or reading paperback novels. "I'd guess that the number of people in front of this museum must equal three-quarters of the population of Rhinebeck," she said, awed. Then her voice brightened. "And not one of them is my child."

"Nice talk," Nora said. "You love being a mother more than anyone else I know.

"Absolutely true," Wendy agreed, her voice breathless from climbing the stairs. "And today, I love being a mother whose children are in school a hundred miles away. Who will be fed and tucked in by their father."

Nora smiled at her as they entered the museum. After a quick perusal of the list of exhibits, they went to the second floor. They began to saunter through the rooms, the sounds of their steps echoing off the high ceilings. Nora's mother stopped in front of a painting by Goya called *The Countess of Altamira with Her Daughter*. It was a portrait of a woman holding a small child in her lap, both of them looking at the artist, neither displaying any connection to each other.

Nora reached out for her mother's hand. "Chilling, isn't it?" she said, beginning to walk on.

Wendy stayed in place. "I can't imagine either of my daughters sitting that long for a portrait. Sarah would have the artist in the kitchen making chocolate chip cookies, and Tamara would be applying his oils as house paint."

Belinda Levin laughed. "Oh, I think you underestimate my grandchildren."

"On the contrary—the cookies would be delicious and the orange-and-pink house would look like a million bucks."

Nora strolled alongside, enjoying their conversation. This was such a treat. None of her family came to Manhattan very often. Now that she thought about it, she realized that her mother had not been here for at least five years. Only Wendy's nagging had succeeded in pry-ing her loose from Rhinebeck, and Nora was certain her father had not made it any easier. Nora could imagine what her mother must have gone through to get permission for her day with her daughters: "What will I do for dinner? What if my car conks out and I need a ride home from the restaurant? What if you break down on the highway?"

But Wendy's appointment with an oral surgeon at ten that morning had provided the perfect excuse. She'd needed her mother as a backup driver, just in case she still felt ill after the procedure. Nora's father couldn't put up much of an argument. And the three women had taken perfect advantage of the opportunity. They'd met and had lunch at a small, elegant restaurant on East Ninety-second Street, where they'd even shared a bottle of red wine. And they'd sat there for two hours, relaxed, enjoying each others' company.

Today was so different from the family days, where the demands of the girls made real conversation almost impossible. Nora had worked until half past twelve the night before in order to make time for the afternoon with them. And she was glad she had done it.

"Now, this I can see my girls doing!" Wendy said, halting in front of a sculpture by Bernini. It was a fawn, being crawled over and taunted by several children.

"Your daughters would never tease an animal," Nora said in defense of her nieces.

Wendy sighed. "You're right. They save it all up for Mom."

Nora looked at her. "Are you meaning any of this?" she asked.

"Oh, Nora. Sure I mean it. And I also mean it when I tell you that I can't wait to get home tonight and kiss them and tell them all about my day. You know I love my kids more than anything in the world. If I had it to do again, I'd make exactly the choices I made."

Nora felt relieved. "You don't usually express anything but the purest contentment."

Wendy thought about it. "Well, I suppose I don't usually feel anything but contentment, although the word *purest* is overkill, wouldn't you say? I guess I'm one of the happiest people I know." She grinned. "But that doesn't mean I can't enjoy a day strolling through the greatest museum in the world."

The three women sat down on a bench in the center of the room, all of them gazing at another Goya. It was so nice, Nora thought, to be in the museum on a weekday, when they could take their time and not fight crowds of thousands. They stayed there, looking around the room, content and quiet for several minutes. Then Nora's sister turned to her.

"So, how's the movie going?"

"Well, the new one's just starting up. I met with Will Stanley the other night. He had this expert from a place called MarketScan."

"Was he helpful?" Wendy asked.

"Actually, 'he' was a 'she.' I guess she was okay. Not that she gave me any ideas about what kind of music to use. But I have the next few months to figure that out."

"It's nice that this Stanley guy is giving you so much work," Wendy said.

Nora felt her face tighten. "Yes," she said. "It's nice."

Wendy must have heard something in her tone, because she turned around, staring at her sister as if searching for something. "I sense a story." She smiled. "And I sense it's a story I'm not going to hear."

Nora had no intention of going into the subject of Will Stanley. But she knew how to avoid it. "Actually, something terrific happened on *Mississippi.*"

Nora's mother had been gazing at a large canvas, seeming not to be paying much attention to her daughters. At Nora's heightened tone, however, she turned to listen.

"There's this important documentary festival in North Carolina, and the people there have selected *Mississippi* to be the closing film." Her tone turned shy. "It's kind of a big deal."

Wendy beamed. "That's fabulous. Andy and I can't

wait to see it. Can you get a copy of it and bring it up the next time you come home?"

"Maybe in a few weeks," Nora answered, grateful for her sister's enthusiasm. "I think it's time we returned to our travels."

She rose from the bench and was joined by her sister, who stretched her arms as she stood.

"I think it's time for some of the Impressionists. I'm from the country and I want me some pur-ty flowers," Wendy said.

Nora extended her hand to her mother, who remained seated, her face turned away from them.

"C'mon, Mom," Nora chirped. "Matisse and Bonnard are calling your name."

Belinda Levin finally turned around and got to her feet. But, as she did, Nora was struck by the expression on her mother's face. It was one she had never seen before. Before she could say anything, tears started streaming down her mother's cheeks. Clearly embarrassed, she sat back down.

"Hey, Mom, are you okay?" Nora asked, as her mother mopped at her face with a clump of tissues from her handbag.

Both Nora and Wendy sat down as well, one on each side of Belinda.

"What's going on, Mom?" Wendy asked, patting her mother's back as she might have one of her own daughters'.

"Oh, nothing. Really, it's nothing." Belinda's voice was strained.

"If it's making you cry, it's not nothing," Nora insisted.

Belinda blew her nose quietly and wiped at her eyes once more. At least the flood seemed to be abating. But Nora was unsettled. In all the years she'd lived under her mother's roof, the only time she'd ever seen Belinda cry was when Wendy had first left for college. Even then, her mother had hidden her tears behind a rush of dish-washing.

"Is there something you haven't told us? Are you sick?" Wendy's voice was anguished.

"I'm telling you girls, everything's fine." Now, her mother was starting to sound testy.

Nora knew her mother wanted them to leave her alone, but she just couldn't do it. "Please, Mom, you know we love you. We need to know what's going on."

A fresh spring of tears erupted. This time, Belinda couldn't seem to stop herself. There were several other people walking through the room. Until they had gone, Nora and Wendy maintained a silence. But the moment they'd left the room, Nora turned to her mother.

"You have to tell me what's wrong, Mom," Nora demanded.

"I *have* to tell you?" Belinda snapped.

Nora could hardly believe the hostility in her mother's voice. Belinda walked away from them, toward a painting that seemed to catch her attention. But she turned back to them almost immediately.

"I *have to* take care of your father. I *have to* wait in front of the restaurant for an hour, two hours, every day of the week. I *have to* monitor his health and pay his bills and keep his house just as he likes it." Her voice broke. "I don't *have to* tell you girls anything at all."

The two sisters looked at each other, stupefied. "You're right, Mom," Wendy said softly, "you don't have to do anything at all."

Belinda suddenly looked shamefaced. "Oh, sweetheart." She raised her hand to include Nora. "What have I done?" she cried, her voice carrying in the high-ceilinged room. She might have said more, but she noticed that she had attracted the attention of a young couple walking by.

"Let's get out of here," Nora said.

Neither of them objected. When they were once more on the steps of the museum, Belinda sat down on one of the side walls. Both her daughters were watching her, wondering what would happen next. But there would be no more explosions.

"I'm sorry, Nora," she said in a whisper. "It's just so

overwhelming . . . being here . . . spending the day at the Met . . . hearing about your movie." She stopped to gather herself. "It was all I ever wanted, to do paintings that would be hung in a place like this," she indicated the museum, "to produce works of art, to live a creative life."

Nora's mouth opened involuntarily. "This was what you wanted?" she asked, incredulous. She felt stupid as soon as the words were out of her mouth. After all, her mother had always been talented. There were paintings she had done scattered around the house, and they were beautiful. Why shouldn't she have wanted that to be her life's work?

"When I was a girl, it was all I ever thought about."

"What in the world made you give it up?" Wendy asked, sitting beside her mother on the wall.

"Oh," Belinda sighed, "you have plans, and then they seem like dreams . . . and your father . . . Well, after a while, dreams become phantoms."

Nora looked over at her sister. She could see that Wendy was shocked. It had been clear, all through their lives, that Wendy was doing what she'd wanted to do. No matter how much she might like a day apart from her kids, or even from her husband, Wendy was living the life she liked. It had never occurred to her that her mother's feelings were so different. Belinda's words came as a total surprise.

Nora was puzzled to realize that she herself was not at all surprised. Sad, maybe. Guilty even. But she was feeling something else, a pain that seemed to pierce right through her soul. She had no idea what the pain was about, but it wasn't unfamiliar. Without realizing it was even happening, the pain Nora felt was replaced by something more familiar. She couldn't have defined it as anger until she heard the words come out of her mouth.

"So why the hell did you stay? Did you really imagine you were doing it for us?" Nora could hardly believe what a shrew she sounded like. And a look at her mother and her sister assured her she wasn't the only one who thought so.

Wendy spoke up right away. "Leave Mom alone, Nora. Haven't you ever heard the rule about kicking a person when she's down?"

"I'm sorry, Mom, really I am," Nora said, though her voice was still more angry than apologetic. "I just, well, I don't understand why you didn't do something with all your talent. Other mothers managed to do what they wanted, even if it was only to go to the gym or work at a department store. Why couldn't you have at least tried?"

Wendy once again tried to intervene. "Really, Nora, you've got to stop this. Things are as they are. Mom was wonderful to us. You know she was. What do you want her to do? I mean, we're practically forty years old!"

Nora wished she could explain all that she was feeling, but that would have been impossible. She didn't even understand it. But there were a few things she did know, and as long as they were in the middle of it, she figured she might as well get them off her chest. "I'm sorry if I'm making you mad. I honestly am. But it's sad having a mother who's clearly powerless. It might have been good for Dad—although, frankly, I doubt it. But it wasn't that much fun to watch." She knew she was risking infuriating her mother still more, yet she couldn't stop herself. "It's not that much fun to watch even now!"

But her mother's glance back at her wasn't one of anger. Nor was it of jealousy or sadness or any of the emotions that had been so strong just minutes before. Instead, Nora thought with wonder, her mother looked *guilty*.

Wendy's eyes had been on Nora, but now she, too, stared at her mother.

"What are you thinking about, Mom?" she asked, her voice gentle but insistent.

Belinda looked from her older daughter to her

younger daughter. Her body seemed to sag in on itself, her crossed hands holding her elbows against her chest, as if she were suddenly freezing cold.

"I suppose I can't make it any worse by telling you, can I?" she said, looking at neither of her daughters now.

Wendy was the one to respond. "Telling us what, Mom?"

"I stayed with your father because . . . I owed him."

"What?" Nora responded.

Belinda shook her head back and forth, back and forth, as if she were trying to keeping back voices she heard in her brain. "When I married your father, I thought it was right. He was attractive and hardworking. My parents were thrilled I had found someone so steady and so smart. But within the first year of our marriage, I knew it had been a terrible mistake." A burst of alarm lit her face. "Not that your father ever struck me or treated me badly. I promise you, nothing like that ever happened." Her voice got quieter. "Maybe it would have been better if he had."

"What does that mean?" Nora asked.

"It means I wouldn't have exposed myself to a lifetime of shame, that's what it means."

Belinda's face filled with an emotion neither of her daughters even recognized. Her cheeks were red, her eyes were almost glassy. She made Nora think of how Anna Karenina must have looked just before she leapt to her death. It took a moment for her to go on speaking, but this time neither Nora nor Wendy said anything until she herself continued.

"We'd been married for thirteen months when I took the art class in Albany. I loved it, being surrounded by people fascinated by art, by culture. And I loved it because my teacher thought I was talented. He showed such an interest in me." Now, as she looked up at her daughters, there was something new on her face. A fraction perhaps of the rebelliousness she must have felt at the time.

"He showed an interest, and I showed an interest, and

then one day your father heard us talking on the telephone."

"You mean you were having an affair with your teacher?" Nora was incredulous. Loyal, beaten-down Belinda Levin, sleeping with another man!

"Is that so impossible for you to believe?" Belinda retorted, anger mixing with her shame. "Well, here's something else that you won't believe. Your father never said a word. Not one thing. He knew, all right, but he treated me exactly as he had treated me for over a year. No better and no worse. He acted as if nothing had happened."

Nora looked at her mother, openmouthed. How had her father lived with the knowledge that his wife was sleeping with someone else? Had he tolerated it because it would simply be too inconvenient to find someone else? Was he arrogant enough to know it would end and Belinda would be grateful to him for the rest of her days?

"How did it end?" she asked.

Her mother gave a mirthless laugh. "I'm sorry, darling, but you ended it. I became pregnant with you."

Nora was startled. "Do you mean I'm not Daddy's daughter?"

"Oh, no, darling," her mother replied. "Nothing that dramatic. In fact, I hadn't seen . . . well, I think I'll keep his name a secret." She smiled. "At least something should remain secret, don't you think? Anyway, you are definitely your father's daughter. But the notion that I could sleep with another man when I was carrying your father's baby. That I could do it all the while knowing what pain your father had to be in . . . There was no choice. I had to stop seeing him. I had to be a good wife. That was all."

The life went out of her face.

Nora and Wendy shared a glance. Neither one knew what to say. Everything about this story seemed so uncharacteristic. Her father so understanding, so decent. Her mother, clutching at a penance that seemed to have left her a life so devoid of everything she had hoped for.

Nora didn't know what it all meant, but the pain inside her let her know that whatever had happened to Belinda and David Levin hadn't only happened to them. Somehow, the decisions her mother had made years before had left their indelible mark on her daughter.

31

Eloise looked around her office, sickened by what she saw. On top of her desk were the remains of her dinner. No, she admitted to herself, the remains of what should have been her next ten dinners. An empty pizza box, a pint of Ben & Jerry's butter pecan, a large, flattened cellophane bag, which used to contain potato chips, and a rectangular cardboard box with small white doilies, which had so recently held a napoleon, a chocolate eclair, and two lemon squares.

She could hardly believe what she'd done. After all these months of temperate eating, after a weight loss of over forty pounds, she'd convinced herself that this kind of bingeing was a thing of the past. Hah, she thought, with an ironic swagger, I guess I showed them, realizing the minute she thought it that the "them" was, in fact, herself.

She looked at her watch. It was almost nine, and it was her night to place the call. It's a good thing phones don't have cameras, she thought, looking at the mess that lay in front of her. Wouldn't Kip and Nora be thrilled to see the detritus of her food orgy? Jesus, she thought with abject self-hatred, all their care, all their cheerleading, there it was, wrestled to the ground by . . . by what? she wondered. By gluttony, by lack of control, by an infantile hunger that they would insist had nothing to do with food. And the damned thing was, she knew they were right. She eyed the conference table across the room. There, scattered like spent bullets after a sniper attack, were the items that impelled her to order and then consume everything in front of her. They were the pages her father had removed during the close of the fall fashion issue.

He hadn't interfered with most of the issue. In the past, he'd never interfered at all. But yesterday, as a special Father's Day gift, she thought, not quite certain whether she was mocking her father or herself, he'd pulled the shots of the large-size model she'd picked to pose in the black dress. That was it; they were out of the issue. He was, as he reminded her, the head of the company. Pulling something from any magazine that bore his name was well within his rights. No, she reminded herself, he didn't bother to generalize about what he was choosing to pull. Pulling something *distasteful* was what he actually said. And he'd used the word with a special twist in his mouth, as if the syllables themselves were utterances to be avoided.

She'd begged him to step back and then went so far as to order him to take his hands off *her* magazine. He hadn't even given her the satisfaction of getting angry. He was as endearing as he was over a country weekend or a dinner party as he explained, in the most reasonable—the most condescending—tone how in tune he was with her readers. How he had enough distance from the subject of *indulgence,* as he so tactfully put it, to understand how her subscribers would react. He was doing this for her own good. He said those precise words. It made her furious. And, of course, left her powerless.

There was no way to go up against him. After all, he was right. It was *his* magazine. He was the one who paid the rent and the electric bill, who underwrote the insurance costs and the carpet cleaning. He was the emperor and *Metropolitan Woman* was but one jewel in his empire.

And so, she'd ordered dinner for ten—and proceeded to eat every last drop.

She took another glance at her watch and reached for

the telephone. It was already a couple of minutes after nine. Kip and Nora would be worried. She dialed Kip's number up in Rhinebeck; then, when Kip answered, put her on hold and dialed Nora's. As the three of them said hello, Eloise swept the cartons and boxes into the trash basket under her desk. By the magic of building maintenance—paid for, she thought with grim satisfaction, by her father—none of the evidence would be left when she got to the office the next morning.

"So," Kip said, "how's everybody?"

"Just fine," Eloise said, almost wishing she had the courage to tell them the truth. But she didn't have the heart for it. Undoubtedly, Kip and Nora would be nice about it, and that would make her feel even worse. Somehow, a sin of omission seemed like the better choice.

"I'm okay," Nora said.

"You don't sound very enthusiastic," Kip responded. "Is something wrong?"

"Well, no," Nora answered. "In fact, something pretty exciting has happened. I went up to Will Stanley's office the other night, and he told me that *Mississippi* had been chosen to close the DoubleTake Film Festival."

Eloise was impressed. "That's huge," she said. "One of our photographers had a film in it last year, and they got an amazing amount of attention from being shown there."

"Wow, Nora," Kip interjected, "that's a darn good best moment."

"So, how about your best moment, Kip?" Nora asked.

"Oh." She stopped to think for a few seconds. "I guess practice yesterday. It went really well. And, by the way, I played that Holst march you sent me for my coach. He thinks we can make it into a dynamite ending for the next routine we design."

"Great," Nora answered, pleased. "Add a little John Philip Sousa to it, wear a little red, white and blue, and you'll have the entire audience on their feet, I promise. So, Eloise, we haven't heard yet from you. Best moment?"

Eloise couldn't imagine what to say. If it were worst moments they were asking for, that would be a cinch. Too many to choose from. But best moment? "Gee . . . maybe my run yesterday morning. It was cool and sunny, and I did the bridle path instead of the reservoir, which makes it a couple of tenths of a mile longer, and it took me only about twenty minutes, which means I was doing an eleven- or twelve-minute mile."

"Don't strain your muscles," Nora advised. "Better to run more slowly for a longer time. Less chance of injury."

"Okay, Dr. Scholl, so what was your worst moment?" Kip inquired.

Eloise and Kip waited nearly a full minute for Nora to answer the question.

"Frankly," she finally said, "this hasn't been exactly a bonanza week, the film festival news notwithstanding."

"Yikes," Kip said, "when you use a word like *notwithstanding* in normal conversation, that means your week must have been pure hell."

Nora laughed. "Not so pure, I assure you. Actually, I went from being a hostile bitch right straight through to breaking my mother's heart."

"What?" both Eloise and Kip answered, practically in unison.

"I'm going to skip over the first part," Nora said, " 'cause it doesn't mean anything at all. It happened before our last phone call, but it was too silly to talk about. Suffice to say, I'm not as nice as I thought I was."

"Hold on a minute," Eloise said. "What do you mean by that?"

"Oh," Nora said, clearly not wanting to get into it. "There was this woman at the meeting with Will, who was . . . I don't know . . . just so perfect. She just got on my nerves."

"In-ter-es-ting," Kip said, with a whisper of a Viennese accent meant to suggest a Freudian psychiatrist.

"Oh, shut up," Nora retorted. "Not interesting in the least. Actually, it was the other thing that maybe I need some help with. The thing with my mother."

"What happened?" Kip asked, serious now.

"I took a day off because my sister and my mother were going to be in the city, and we all went to the Met and were having a wonderful time. And then I told them about the film festival, and suddenly my mother as in tears."

"Why?" Eloise asked.

"She said that she was happy for me, but she was jealous," Nora answered. "I don't know if I've ever talked about it, but my mom was a pretty good artist. I mean, she's done stuff around the house and in my father's restaurant, and it's really nice. If she'd had a chance to develop her talent, she might have done a lot with it. But my father was a demanding guy, and he needed her to be there for him, to help him out in a thousand ways. And, when we were growing up, my sister and I took a lot of her time."

Eloise was struck by the part about Nora's father. She knew it was because of her own problems that day, but something was nagging at her. Her father was nothing like Nora's father, yet somehow the two seemed linked in some way. For one, they both drove their daughters crazy.

"You know, Nora," she said after thinking it through. "There's something to this."

"Hell, yes," Nora answered. "I'm the daughter who made her mother regret her whole life. I'd say that's pretty important."

"No," Eloise said, impatient at the interruption. "Something else. You claim that your biggest regret was not marrying Alex. Yet, when he asked you again, you turned him down flat."

"I know. I'm a jerk," Nora said.

"That's not my point. In fact, I think he bored you silly, and had you said yes it would have lasted about a month."

A wry laugh came from Kip. "Don't feel you have to hold back," she said.

Eloise ignored her. "The problem is, if Alex *hadn't*

been wrong for you, if he'd been everything you could ever have dreamed of, do you think you would have said yes to him even then?"

"I don't know," Nora admitted after giving the question some thought. "I'd like to think I would have, but maybe I'm lying to myself. Maybe I'm just nuts. Or maybe I don't deserve to love someone."

"Slow down," Eloise said. "You're getting way ahead of yourself. What I'm trying to figure out is *why* you feel so ambivalent about marriage."

"The big question," Nora said.

"I'm beginning to think it's not such a mystery," Eloise continued. "The marriage you know best was made up of one person who got everything he wanted, namely, your father, and another person, your mother, the *female* person, getting just about nothing she wanted. I know it sounds simplistic, but sometimes the simplest things are the truest. Maybe, in your heart of hearts, you believe that if you got married, if you really really loved somebody, you, too, would have to give up everything you ever wanted. You'd pattern yourself after your mother, which, by the way, is pretty much what we all do, and become an adjunct to some overbearing guy."

"But that would be a ridiculous assumption," Kip said. "My husband couldn't be more supportive. Not every husband is a demanding, selfish oaf."

Eloise cut in. "I know that, and intellectually, I'm sure Nora knows that, too. But it's amazing what we feel on the inside even when our logical selves know better." Little did her friends know just how intimately familiar with this concept she was, Eloise thought, eyeing her wastebasket.

Nora had been quiet, listening to the two women. When she responded, her voice was softer than usual. "It's a lot to think about."

"You sound shell-shocked," Kip observed.

"Well, actually, I feel a little shell-shocked," Nora answered.

"Speaking of shell-shocked," Eloise interjected, wanting to take the heat off Nora, "Kip, you haven't told us your worst moment."

Now it was Kip's turn to hesitate.

"Did you not have a bad moment?" Eloise teased. "Was this, at last, that perfect week we've all dreamt of for so long?"

"Yeah, perfect," Kip retorted. "It was a good week in a lot of ways, but the truth is, with the exception of the skating interlude, I haven't enjoyed this week in the least. I know I'm going to sound like a baby, but I hate it when Peter's away. I feel at loose ends. Really, like a helpless infant."

"You're being too hard on yourself." Nora's voice was gentle. "It's unnerving to be on your own when you're used to having someone around."

"You seem to manage without constant help," Kip came back at her. "I'm hopeless. Just pitiful."

"You deserve to be shot," Eloise said, laughing.

But Kip wasn't about to be comforted. "You know, you two can joke about it and try to make me feel better, but it's pathetic, it really is, to be so dependent on your husband. Jesus, El, your husband walked out, and yet you manage to have a whole life. You run your magazine, and you face up to your social responsibilities. And, Nora, you may eventually want to get married. I honestly hope you do, because I think you'd really be happy. But until then, you have one of the most fascinating lives I know of." She paused for breath. "Speaking for myself, since Peter left, I've been wandering around the house like a ghost. Frankly, I hardly feel capable of getting out of bed. Whatever the secret to independence is, it certainly ran right past me."

Eloise was dumbfounded. Kip was the most competent, together woman in the world. Hearing her so critical of herself was indecent. On the other hand, she thought, once again looking at the pile of cartons in the wastebasket, maybe it was a relief to know that other people let themselves in for the same self-loathing she herself felt.

"You know what," she said, "maybe we should all

lighten up. Maybe it's time for you guys to see yourselves the way I see you. And, maybe"—she smiled as she went on—"it's even time for me to see myself the way you guys see me."

Nora was the first one to respond. "Amen," she said.

Followed by Kip's, "I second that."

"I believe Reverend Bentley has come to the end of her service," Eloise intoned. "I look forward to next week's episode of the self-actualization hour, same time, same station, next Monday night at nine."

She listened to a chuckle from Kip and a muted, "Love you," from Nora. Then she hung up the phone and began to pack up her belongings. Her stomach ached from the damage she'd done earlier that night, but her spirit felt somehow lighter.

"And so, Miss Scarlett," she said to herself as she rose from her chair and started toward the door, "tomorrow is another day."

32

"*P*eter, it's that time again, son." Mr. Carroll smiled broadly, patting the cushion beside him on the couch. "Our special time together."

Peter stood before him, trembling. He wanted to run, to shriek, to sob. Instead, he took a step forward and sat down.

"Good boy." Mr. Carroll tousled Peter's hair. Then he unzipped his pants. His stroked himself as he looked directly into Peter's eyes. "I think you know what to do next."

Silent screams filled Peter's head. He couldn't move.

Mr. Carroll's eyes were starting to appear glazed as he continued to touch himself. "Come on, boy. Don't make me wait."

Peter opened his mouth, but no words came out.

"Need some help getting started, do you?" The older man placed a hand on the back of Peter's head. He pulled him forward, slowly but forcefully bringing the boy's face toward his lap.

"No, please," Peter cried out as he shut his eyes.

"Yes, oh, yes . . ."

"Unnnhh . . ." The sound burst forth in a loud groan as Peter brutally forced himself awake. His eyes flew open in the dark. He was gasping for air, his heart pounding. Sitting up in bed, he realized he was drenched in perspiration.

He threw back the covers and stumbled into the bathroom, fumbling until he located the light switch. The brightness made him wince as he turned on the faucet and bent over to splash cold water on his face. His tongue felt thick, and his head ached.

"Jesus," he muttered, grabbing a towel to dry his face. *"Jesus."*

He took three aspirins followed by two full glasses of water. The night he'd spent was coming back to him, the quantity of *caipirinhas* he had consumed the night before, stumbling from club to club, convincing himself that the potent drinks would put him into a sleep so deep he wouldn't be able to dream.

"Weren't you wrong about that?" he asked his unshaven, puffy-eyed reflection in the mirror. As he stuffed the towel partway into the rack, he located his watch on the bathroom counter. It was a quarter to five. He turned off the bathroom light and felt his way across the hotel room to the bed. Slipping beneath the covers, he lay back, waiting for his eyes to become accustomed to the darkness again. Every night, the same damned thing, no matter how much he drank, no matter what he did. Mr. Carroll was back, as real as ever. Sometimes, the dreams replayed what had actually happened, as this one had. Other times, Mr. Carroll chased him down an endless corridor or smothered him with a pillow. Peter was having two, three nightmares every night, often awakening in tears.

He had suffered from nightmares for years, but even though his terror always woke him he could never remember what he was actually dreaming about. He wondered if they had always been about this, locked away back in his subconscious the instant he awakened. These nightmares, the ones he could recall, had started as soon as he got to Rio, and by now, six days later, they had left him utterly exhausted. It wasn't just the lack of sleep but the nightly horror, as well, that were wearing him down. Even during the day, he wasn't immune. Yesterday, he could have sworn he saw Mr. Carroll coming toward him on the street. His heart had started thumping, and beads of perspiration had broken out across his forehead. He stopped, staring, until the man came closer and Peter realized he had been mistaken. In fact, the man bore no resemblance at all to Mr. Carroll.

Incredible, he thought, that the minute he left Kip and the children, it was as if some dormant beast inside him found the opportunity to attack. Was it only his family that had stood between him and this private horror show? He knew that if he didn't do something to stop the dreams, he would go to pieces. But he had no idea what that something should be. One thing was certain—he had to get home, back to Kip. He had told her about the nightmares the last time they talked on the telephone two days before. She had been upset for him, and of course, he'd appreciated sympathy and comfort. But what he really needed was to hold her close, to bury his head in her hair and listen to her soothing whispers.

Still, he couldn't allow himself to go home until he was done with this assignment. He needed to put all his efforts into the work here, to focus on something other than himself. This felt like his last chance to unclog his writing arteries. But his brain had apparently decided that there were more important things to attend to, like tormenting him to the brink of insanity.

At six o'clock, he gave up all attempts to go back to sleep. After a near-scalding shower, he shaved and dressed; then he went over his notes to occupy himself until the rest of the city woke up.

He was writing about both the rich and the poor, and Eloise had provided him with the names of two couples to contact, both of whom were at the top of the city's economic pyramid. He had already telephoned to introduce himself, but he was putting off the meetings until he had reacquainted himself with the city. It was pointless to waste the contacts by interviewing them prematurely.

Mostly, he walked the streets, going in and out of the stores, making feeble attempts to brush up on his Portuguese with the salespeople. He meandered through the street markets that sold fruits and vegetables and tropical flowers. All the while, he was observing the people, an astoundingly varied mixture of shapes and sizes and skin and hair colors. Standing near the Christ statue on Corcovado Mountain, hypnotized by the view, he decided that Rio, nestled between the ocean and the mountains, was the most mysterious combination of beauty and ugliness he had ever seen.

It was the poverty and the situation of the children that made it ugly. When he had taken on this assignment, he had already heard a little bit about Brazil's street children. A good many were homeless. They were the lost souls who roamed the streets begging for food or money. The poverty of the *favelas,* the slums of Rio, was gut-wrenching. The dwellings themselves were falling-down shacks of anything from brick to concrete to wood, most without water or any form of garbage collection or sewage. Rain flooded the hillside paths. The dirt and disease were horrifying. Yet the children who lived there were considered the lucky ones, the ones with homes to go to, such as they were.

The street children inhabited a world of sickness, violence, and death. No wonder so many of them stayed drunk or stoned, their young eyes dulled. They had the souls of the old, yet would sleep in doorways with their thumbs in their mouths. Some ten years before, attention had been drawn to their plight when it became known that corrupt police officers were killing them on behalf of business people anxious to protect their economic interests by "cleaning up the streets."

Peter tried to imagine his own two children in these circumstances, forced to fend for themselves. Impossible. They were tucked away in a different universe, or might as well have been. Their concerns seemed so petty from this distance, the carrying on over schedules and who got to do what. When he got home, he was really going to have to find a way to impress upon them how tough the world was. They needed to understand where they stood in the scheme of things. But first he wanted nothing more than to hug and kiss them. How lucky he and Kip were to have a happy, healthy family. Their kids were wonderful, and all the phases they went through, pleasant and unpleasant, were a luxury in a world where some children struggled in misery and torment merely to survive.

Peter jotted down a few more thoughts on his way to breakfast. *Metropolitan Woman* had put him up at the Othon Palace, a luxury hotel in the Copacabana area. It was the perfect place from which to observe the monied class, but he would have liked to stay someplace closer to the *favelas* when he was trying to write about the other side of Rio. Of course, he thought with a small sigh, it was a romantic fantasy to think that a tourist could stay in one of the grittier areas and blend in.

He sat in the restaurant booth, nursing cup after cup of what had to be the strongest coffee he had ever drunk. At eleven o'clock, he was supposed to meet Mauricio, and he wanted to be able to talk to the boy without his head feeling as if it were encased in cement.

After signing the bill, he went outside. The usual swarms of people and cars flooded Avenue Atlantica. On the other side of the wide street was Copacabana Beach, a crescent-shaped stretch of sand adjoining Ipanema Beach. It was warm, in the upper seventies, despite July and August officially being the winter months in Brazil. Not too many snow days for the kids in school here, he reflected idly. He could only imagine how crowded a scene it was in the hotter months of December and January, when tourists from the northern countries came here to escape their cold weather.

He strolled out onto the sidewalk and looked for a spot to cross the street. He was well aware that the drivers would have no interest in stopping or even slowing down for unexpected pedestrians. The whole city moved to its own beat, one that he would never fully understand. In Rio, whatever happened, happened. *When*ever. Down here, an eight o'clock appointment might mean ten o'clock—if it meant anything at all. People showed up, they didn't show up. They made five dinner dates for the same night and decided where they were going minutes before they actually went. And nobody ever seemed to get upset about it, he mused as he seized an opportunity to sprint across the wavy mosaic pattern of the sidewalk and the six lanes of traffic.

He didn't see how he could ever live here. He thought back on conversations he'd had at cocktail parties back at home, neighbors complaining about the difficulty of getting their kitchen remodeled or their landscaping improved, how the workmen didn't show up on the appointed day, dragging their heels when they finally did come. That was warp speed compared to the time it took to get anything done in this city. He couldn't even imagine how much time would be needed to build an entire house in Rio—decades, probably. Presumably the people who lived here, the ones with money and influence, had ways of making things happen when they wanted them to. It was a mystery to him.

Yet the same laissez-faire attitude translated into the famous Brazilian friendliness. That part he enjoyed. And he liked eating dinner at 10 P.M., hearing the bands playing the sounds of samba, feeling the excitement of the night. He had been in the suburbs too long, he thought; he had gotten used to considering the day as over once it got dark.

On the other hand, his nights at home weren't torture sessions with the past.

Frowning at the thought, he stopped at the edge of the sand and looked around. At ten-thirty on a Thursday morning, the beach wasn't too crowded, at least compared to the wall of humanity that populated it on weekends. Still, there were plenty of people around, strolling, lying on blankets, most of the women in skimpy thong bikinis. He watched a beautiful girl of about twenty on a red towel about ten feet away. She had one knee up and her eyes closed, and she was playing with her hair as she talked to a man on a towel beside her. The girl was well endowed and wearing the smallest bathing suit he had ever seen, stark white against her dark skin. The intense sexual aura she gave off seemed completely natural. Sex was much more in the air here than in the United States, that was for sure—at least, than in Rhinebeck, New York, he amended.

He sat down, watching an all-male volleyball game in progress, not minding that sand was getting into his sneakers. From his back pocket, he withdrew his notebook and pen. He made a few additional notes on the people around him going about their business.

About thirty feet down the beach, he caught sight of a small group of teenagers—or maybe they were boys in their twenties—straggling in his direction. He lowered his sunglasses on his nose to watch them more closely. They were barefoot, in ragged pants and dirty T-shirts, nearly zigzagging as they walked, their eyes taking in the scene around them. It was obvious that they were looking for something worth stealing. Peter watched, thinking that the Rio natives, the Cariocans, who inhabited the beach that morning, were unlikely to have anything of value lying unprotected next to them. They were all too familiar with the sight of a kid speeding away with the purse or camera that had been right within reach of its owner a moment before. Slimmer pickings when there were fewer tourists, Peter reflected. But these were the least brazen of the gangs who were part of the ongoing crime problem in Brazil. There were plenty of street criminals who used knives, razors, and any other weapon they could get hold of to persuade their targets to part with their belongings. Actually, he was surprised that some uniformed somebody hadn't ushered these teenagers away.

He checked his watch. He might as well start walking to where he was supposed to meet Mauricio. Peter couldn't afford to be late and risk losing contact with the boy. He was the most important source he had found down here.

They had first met when Peter was out walking on the day after his arrival. From the corner of his eye, he noticed movement in a narrow alley behind a bakery. He stopped to observe a boy rummaging through a garbage can. The child had glanced up from his work to see the tall American watching him, but wasn't the least bit interested, and returned to what he was doing. Peter remained where he was. He observed the boy, reed-thin and barefoot, wearing a torn, yellow, short-sleeve shirt and dirty black pants that were a good two sizes too small for him. The child murmured slightly as he spotted something; then he reached in with one hand to scoop it out of the trash can and wolfed it down in a gulp. Seeing Peter still there, he flashed him a wide grin and winked at him, rubbing his stomach with pleasure. Peter was startled and ashamed, knowing the boy was teasing him for staring. He made an apologetic face and smiled back, appreciating that the boy still had a strong enough spark of childhood inside him to want to do that. Then, as Peter started to speak, the boy darted off and was gone.

The next day, Peter returned to the spot about an hour earlier. He was rewarded by the reappearance of the boy, arriving at precisely the same time he had been there the day before, only moments after an employee had emptied the bakery's trash into the can outside. Clearly, the child knew exactly when the bakery discarded its garbage. Peter admired his resourcefulness in beating others to this prime food source. This time, Peter smiled and held out a handful of Brazilian coins. The boy approached slowly. Peter saw the big eyes and generous lips, a sweet face that should have been the picture of childhood playfulness. As he got closer, he reached out and snatched the coins from Peter's hand then quickly backed up.

"Boa tarde," Peter said softly in Portuguese. *"Voce fala ingles?"* He fervently hoped he had said *"Good afternoon, do you speak English?"* but he wasn't certain.

The boy gave him a cynical look and laughed sharply.

"Eu quero . . . I want . . ."* Peter pulled some bills from his pocket and extended them. It was the equivalent of five dollars. The child's eyes lit up at the sight. He grabbed them and tucked the money into his pants pocket then ran off without a backward glance.

"Aqui, depois . . . ," Peter shouted after him: *"Here, later."* "Please, five o'clock. Just to talk."

The boy was out of sight. Peter cursed. He hadn't handled that well at all. Walking on, he resolved to make real contact with a child, although, as he acknowledged to himself, God knew how he should do it. He went back to the same spot at five, with little hope but no better plan at the moment.

To his astonishment, the boy was waiting for him. He flashed his wide grin as Peter came into view.

"So, you want to talk?" he asked with sarcasm in his heavily accented English. "How much you pay to talk?"

"My God, you speak English," Peter blurted out.

The boy drew himself up, his eyes narrowing. "You think I'm stupid."

"I'm sorry," Peter responded. "I didn't mean . . ."

The boy was getting impatient. "Whaddaya want, mister?"

"I'm a writer, an American," Peter began.

"An *American*," the boy echoed, his admiring tone practically dripping with sarcasm. "No shit."

Peter couldn't believe how badly this was going. "Look," he said, "I want to write about you and put it in a magazine so Americans will know what's going on here in Brazil. That's all."

The boy cocked his head.

"Could you help me, or should I talk to someone else?"

"Yeah, yeah, but why should I talk to you?"

"I'll pay you for your time. I want you to tell me what your life is like."

"How much you gonna pay me?"

They went on like this for a while, the boy continually pressing for financial guarantees. Fifteen minutes later, Peter had handed over the equivalent of three dollars, in return for which he had learned only that the boy's name was Mauricio and that he would be back the next morning.

The next day at eleven, Mauricio kept his word by

showing up again. He agreed to answer questions on the condition that Peter take him to a restaurant and buy him lunch while they talked. Peter readily agreed, realizing that the boy was not only getting himself fed, but protecting himself by insisting on a public place. Mauricio chose the spot, a small and dirty café, where he ordered a virtual mountain of food plus three pastries for dessert. As he ate, he told Peter about his life. About how his father disappeared right after the birth of his fifth sibling, his youngest sister. About how one of his brothers died from some disease no one was able to name when he was four. About how his mother lived in a tiny house in one of the *favelas,* but had arthritis that left her hands and feet all twisted, so she couldn't do much. All his remaining brothers and sisters were out on the street now, although they did return to their mother's house most nights to sleep.

Peter was stunned by the boy's apparent lack of self-pity. Mauricio ordered espresso and sipped at the hot liquid as he informed Peter that he wanted to live in one of the expensive houses in Barra da Tijuca when he grew up, and own a Mercedes. His wife would be the most beautiful woman in Rio. When Peter inquired if the boy ever thought about leaving the city, or perhaps leaving Brazil altogether, Mauricio looked at him with contempt for even considering such a notion. To be successful in Rio was to be on top of the world. Peter watched the boy's eyes light with interest as he leaned across the table to feel the soft cotton knit of Peter's shirt, then peer down to inspect his sneakers. When Mauricio asked to try on his baseball cap and sunglasses, Peter handed them over and told him to keep them. The boy acknowledged the offer with only a slight nod, leaving them on for the rest of their talk.

Mauricio's stories got sadder, though he told them with no more expression than when he had informed Peter of what his name was. He talked about other street kids, whose parents had abused them in every way imaginable. There were drugs everywhere, used by the children to forget their misery and fight their boredom. Mauricio explained that people were out there to kill or abduct the street kids for all sorts of reasons. He was proud of himself for staying off drugs and for escaping most of the horrors, save for getting beaten up now and then.

Peter stayed focused on Mauricio and his world for the next few days. He wondered how he would manage the transition between the poor and the wealthy, not only while he was here in Rio, but when he was back at his computer writing about all this. One of the women Eloise had referred him to had called the day before to insist that she and her husband have a dinner party in Peter's honor. The woman was nice, and Peter had been grateful. Still, he wondered if he could sit through such a dinner without leaping up and shouting. They should be out doing something about the misery in their city instead of sitting around being waited on hand and foot by servants. Mauricio and the children like him had taken up so much of Peter's thinking, he had to force himself to remember that his assignment was about more than that. Besides, he thought, it's not as if there wasn't any suffering in the United States, yet he himself was perfectly capable of sitting at dinner parties without the urge to rush out to the street and donate his plate of salmon or prime rib to some hungry person passing by. Honest to God, he was a hypocrite. He sighed, knowing he would have to write about that as part of the piece.

And no matter how enmeshed he was in Mauricio's world, the horrible nightmares never stopped coming.

Peter approached the agreed-upon street corner for today's meeting ten minutes early, as he was surprised to see Mauricio already there. The boy was wearing a filthy red T-shirt and the same too-small black pants as always, along with Peter's baseball cap. He appeared uncomfortable, as if he were on the lookout for something, his eyes darting in every direction, refusing to light on Peter's face even after Peter greeted him.

"You okay? What's the matter?" Peter reached to put a hand on his shoulder, but Mauricio stepped away.

"I'm fine, no problem," the boy snapped. "You ready?"

"Listen, we don't have to go if—," Peter started.

Mauricio shook his head. "No, man, it's no problem, really. I have a little fight with a guy today. But it's okay. I mean it." He started walking briskly.

"You think he's going to come after you?" Peter asked as he fell into step beside him.

Mauricio waved his hand dismissively. "Nah. And if he does, I can beat him. He's chicken."

Peter nodded. "May I ask what happened?"

"We have a little argument, that's all. Over something that was mine, but he says it's his."

"What was it?"

"Nothing, man. Forget it." Mauricio's tone was irritable. "Let's eat here."

He went into a restaurant, not bothering to see if Peter followed. Peter didn't press the boy for details of what was bothering him. There was so much about this boy's daily life that was unknown to him. Still, Mauricio was quiet as he ate, answering Peter's questions with as few words as possible.

Finishing his food, Mauricio wiped his mouth with a napkin. "Ai, dirty," he muttered as he looked at what had come off his mouth onto the paper napkin, grime along with bits of food. "Always dirty."

Peter was struck by a thought. "Would you be interested in a bath or a shower? There's a pretty nice bathroom in my hotel. Lots of hot water, soap, shampoo. I could take you there."

Mauricio stared at him suspiciously. Peter could imagine what he was thinking.

"Really, you have a shower, by yourself. When you're done, you'll tell me, and we'll go back out. That's all. A shower."

Mauricio continued to size him up. He made a decision. "Okay." He stood up, ready to go.

Peter saw the eyes of the hotel employees upon him as he walked Mauricio through the lobby, but he ignored them. Inside his room, he turned on the shower and pointed out the shampoo, soap, towels and the big bath-robe on the back of the door.

"Enjoy yourself," he said as he shut the door. "I'll be out here when you're done."

Peter sat down in a small armchair with a book to wait, hearing the shower run for the better part of an hour. He tried to imagine what it was like to take a hot shower with a fluffy white washcloth and sweet smelling soap and shampoo if you hadn't had one in months, maybe years, maybe ever.

When Mauricio emerged from the bathroom, he was wrapped up in the white terrycloth robe, far too big for him and dragging on the floor. His face and hair were scrubbed clean, revealing a stunningly good-looking boy. His expression was one of pure joy. Peter looked up from his book and smiled at him, feeling a pang of sadness. That a simple shower should be such a big deal . . .

"It was okay?" Peter asked.

Mauricio nodded excitedly, his words tumbling out. "It was great, like a waterfall. The soap made all—" Suddenly self-conscious, he sat down on the edge of the bed, adopting a more nonchalant expression. "So," he said, pointing, "what's that you read?"

Peter closed the book in his lap. "A story. It's called *Portrait of a Lady*. By Henry James."

Mauricio tilted his head. "Can you read it to me?"

"Read it to you?" echoed Peter in surprise. "Well . . ."

"Never mind." Seeing Peter's hesitation, Mauricio gave a shrug. "I didn't mean it."

"You know," Peter said, "I don't think you would enjoy this book. But I do have one here that you might like. I read it over again sometimes because I enjoy it." He got up and went to the desk where he had a stack of novels he had brought along to fill his spare time. The one he wanted was on the bottom.

"Here," he said, sliding it out and holding it up. "*Hawaii* by James Michener. I always read Michener when I fly in an airplane, I don't know why. Anyway, Hawaii is a beautiful, tropical part of the United States."

Mauricio sat up straighter on the bed. "I want to hear."

Peter opened to the first page and scanned the beginning. He closed the book. "This may not be such a good choice either. If we're going to read a book in English, it should be one that will be fun for you." He saw Mauricio's shoulders sag slightly. "What do you say we go get a book right now. I'll buy it and we'll bring it back. Okay?"

"Really?"

"Sure. C'mon, go get dressed."

Peter was amused by the speed with which the boy readied himself, eager to get going. They took a taxi to a store that sold books in English, where Mauricio leafed through everything he could while Peter made his selection. Back in the hotel room, Peter sat down in the armchair while Mauricio settled himself on the bed, his head propped up comfortably against the pillows, his legs outstretched.

"This story is called *Charlotte's Web,* and it was written by a man named E. B. White." Peter opened the book. "Chapter one. *'Before Breakfast.'* "

The reading went slowly, Mauricio frequently stopping Peter to ask what something meant. Peter tried to anticipate what words or ideas would be difficult in English, and offered definitions and simpler equivalents as he went along. When Peter felt his voice tiring, he waited until he got to the end of the chapter then closed the book.

"Wait," Mauricio said, alarmed. "It's the end?"

"No," Peter said with a smile. "But how about we do some more tomorrow?"

Disappointed, Mauricio nonetheless nodded. "I come right here tomorrow morning. At nine o'clock. We read. Then we talk."

The boy had never been willing to meet Peter before eleven. "Okay, chief," he said with a salute to the child. "You got it."

It was only after Mauricio had gone that Peter noticed

the empty spot where the small glass hotel ashtray had been. He went into the bathroom. The shampoo and soap were also gone, along with Peter's hairbrush and toothbrush. Peter opened the drawer next to the sink where he kept his traveling drug kit, a slim waterproof bag with a zipper. Gone. Where the hell had the boy stashed it all? Somehow, when they went in and out to get the book . . . Peter started to laugh.

It was a quarter to nine the next day when he heard the boy's knock on the door. Letting him in, he wondered how he had gotten past the lobby staff, but he knew Mauricio would have his ways of getting wherever he wanted to go. Barely glancing at Peter, he went directly to the bed and stretched out on it, ready to listen.

"Good morning to you, too. Thank you, I'm very well," Peter said as he shut the door to the room and went to get the book.

"Read, please," was all Mauricio said.

They picked up the story where they had left off. After more than an hour, Peter stopped. "This seems like a good place to put it down for today."

"That spider is smart. More smart than the other animals," Mauricio said.

"Yup."

Mauricio sighed. "My mama told us stories, but no books. She made up some. She knew some."

"How is your mama?" Peter asked.

Mauricio's face darkened. "Ai, he is back. Big trouble for my mama."

"He?" asked Peter. "Who is he?"

The child looked away, apparently deciding whether he wanted to continue the conversation. When he turned back to Peter, he seemed ready to tell his story.

"My mama lived with a man. The worst man. José. He is big, really big, tall and strong. He has a long ponytail and blue eyes, but they are like ice, not nice blue. Scary to look in his eyes. He is mean." The boy shook his head. "You don't know how mean. He beat her. And me and my brothers and sisters, too."

Peter hoped his horrified reaction wasn't showing on his face. "Oh," he said softly. "I'm sorry."

"He did sex with my sister," Mauricio went on, "but my mama didn't know. She hears him one day with me. He says he is going to do sex with me. He grabs me. I scream, and get away, I don't know how. We don't think Mama is there, but she is. She hears. She is afraid of him, but she is so angry. She tells him we are going." He stopped for a breath. "José believes I tell my mama what happened. I didn't, I swear. He don't believe me. When Mama is getting our things, he tells me he is going to kill me. We go, but he beats her first." He shook his head, remembering. "She had two black eyes, and her mouth was so big, like this." His gesture indicated swollen lips.

Peter could only nod. "What happened to your family?" he managed to get out.

Mauricio shrugged. "We live with my uncle; then we go someplace else. José goes away, but my mama is always afraid he comes back. She doesn't want no one to tell him where we are."

"Wait a minute," Peter said, remembering. "Did you just say that he was back?"

"Yes. I see him last night, sitting outside a house as I am walking. I ran as fast as I could. He is sitting in a chair, playing his flute."

"His flute?"

Mauricio nods. "He has a flute, wood. He plays it all the time. I don't like. How you say—scary music. No . . . *spooky*. Yes."

The mental image of this man made Peter wince. "But he didn't see you, right?"

Mauricio shook his head. "He saw me. He ran after me. Almost caught me." The boy's eyes showed his fear of the night before. "He yelled at me. Said he would kill me. But first . . ." He trailed off.

Peter got up and sat down on the bed next to him. "What will you do about this?"

Mauricio held up both hands in a helpless gesture. "I

run fast, I stay out of his way, I keep my mouth shut. Maybe he goes away soon."

"Christ," Peter muttered.

Mauricio suddenly pointed an index finger at Peter. "You want to meet my mama?"

"Yes, I would, very much. Do you think she would want to meet me?"

"You going to ask her lots of questions, right?" Mauricio grinned. "So you bring money for her. She will meet you."

"Ever the negotiator," Peter murmured, smiling, although he was still trying to take in the tale Mauricio had told him. He wondered how the boy could shift gears so quickly.

"I gotta go." Mauricio jumped up onto his knees on the bed, gave Peter a quick, unexpected hug, and hopped off. He was at the door in an instant. "Today, later, around three o'clock. I call you here, tell you when. You come meet me at her house." He disappeared into the hall, slamming the door shut behind him.

Peter was too startled to move. It wasn't just the frightening story Mauricio had told him, or the overwhelming sense that he couldn't comprehend what it was like to live in this boy's world, and never would. It was the realization that the boy had hugged him. Peter put his head down and covered his face with both hands. He was overcome with sorrow.

Peter walked at a moderate pace, not wanting to attract attention either by dawdling or walking too fast. Mauricio had kept his word and telephoned Peter with instructions on when and how to come to the *favela* where his mother lived. Having taken a taxi to the bottom of the hill, he was hiking up, past broken-down houses surrounded by garbage, the metal skeletons of cars, bicycles, and numerous other items Peter couldn't identify, ragged laundry hanging on clotheslines and discarded household items that were beyond use. Men and women stood around talking, smoking, working at some task, shouting at one another, engaged in the business of getting through the day. Children of various ages, mostly barefoot, many of them partially naked, played together, running in and out of the houses. His mind was reeling from the sights and smells he was trying to capture in his memory.

As Peter walked on past them, going higher into the hills, a number of the people paused to stare at him. Some muttered under their breath to one another. Children ran up to him, chattering frantically, their hands out. Mauricio had warned Peter very specifically not to give anyone money, so he only shook his head.

He was getting closer now. Mauricio said he would meet him there. Peter knew this was a tremendous opportunity, getting to talk to this woman in her own surroundings. Mauricio's point of view, his mother's point of view—it was a sensational combination. But he wasn't concerned anymore with just getting the job done, as he had been when he arrived. He wanted this story to be something that resulted in some action. It wasn't about a lucky contact with a poor kid, and some further exploitation to get the really gruesome quotes from his abused mother. Something had to be done about this place. He had to write a piece that was so gripping, so powerful, it would influence somebody to get moving on it. He thought about the woman who had called him a second time, only two hours before, the one who wanted to make the dinner party for him. They had agreed to do it the following Saturday night. Peter dreaded it, but he was anxious to hear firsthand what the upper echelons of Rio had to say about their poor. Damn, he admonished himself, you better get all the material you need from them before you get on your high horse about this, or the interviews will be a total waste of time.

Lost in his thoughts, Peter was barely aware of the music floating down from a point higher up along the path. Slowly, it infiltrated his consciousness. It was a sequence of notes, odd, haunting. Beautiful in one way, but somehow chilling. Peter stopped, frozen in his tracks. It was the sound of a flute.

He ran. Up, up, he pushed himself to go faster, panting now, perspiring, though whether from exertion or fear, he wasn't sure. The music was closer. It *was* spooky, that was exactly the right word for it, it was—

He whipped around the corner of a dilapidated house. There was Mauricio, some thirty feet away, backed up against a wall, his hands and feet bound with gray rags, his eyes wide with terror. The man before him was large and stocky, wearing a dirt-streaked white shirt and gray pants. Before he saw the man's face, Peter saw the long, greasy black ponytail that hung halfway down his back.

Peter backed up around the corner of the house, leaning forward just enough to be able to see. This José must have been waiting for Mauricio, Peter realized, must have grabbed him as he was on his way to his mother's house. Jesus Christ, he thought, he had tied the child up and was playing the flute in front of him, toying with him. José said something to Mauricio in Portuguese and then roared with laughter at his joke as he dropped the short brown flute to the ground. There were other people there, Peter saw, an old man and a younger woman, both of them standing off to the side watching, expressionless. It was then that Peter first noticed the knife stuck into a leather sheath on José's belt, some sort of hunting knife, he guessed. That was why they weren't interceding, he thought, although he wondered if anyone was going to interfere with this man regardless of whether he had a knife or not.

José started to advance toward Mauricio, reaching to unzip his pants as he walked. Mauricio's face was wet with tears, but he said nothing.

A roaring filled Peter's head.

His mind flooded with images of himself and Mr. Carroll, the sickening feelings instantly overtaking him again, as if it had all happened hours before instead of decades. The terror was so profound, it was a whirlpool sucking him almost out of consciousness. *No, no.* Peter fought back, struggled to hold on.

Then it struck him. He had come to this city to test

himself. Little by little, he had narrowed his focus, ignoring his research to concentrate on this boy's world. He was in real danger now, and he had deliberately put himself here.

But he had to help Mauricio. About to move forward, Peter thought about the knife. He stopped abruptly, filled with a fear beyond anything he had ever known. This was the legacy of Mr. Carroll, he thought bitterly. I don't know if I'm any kind of a man or not. I've never known. Is this my own little test? At the thought, a powerful rage swept over him. He thought he might suffocate on it, choke on the bile of his anger.

"You bastard!" It was as if the words were ripped from his throat, a shriek of agony. *"I'm going to kill you!"* He didn't know if he was screaming at the man in front of him or at the man who had haunted his life since he himself was Mauricio's age.

José's head jerked to the right. He turned, caught off guard. Peter lost all control, all sense of thought. He lunged, hurling himself against José. They fell back to the ground, Peter moving quickly to get on top of the other man, aiming punches at his face, knowing only that he had to stop him. José was yelling, roaring like a wounded bull, as blood poured from his nose. He struggled to get his hand around Peter's neck. But even his bulk and strength couldn't overcome Peter's howling fury, his punches driven by the demons that had been locked up for decades, now unleashed to do their worst. Screaming from the darkest spot within his soul, Peter slammed the man's head against the ground again and again. He could see the light in his eyes dimming, could actually feel the life draining from the struggling mass beneath him.

He was so intent it took several extra seconds for him to feel the pain in his side. It was a stinging sensation that moved from beneath his left arm into his chest. He was ignoring it—but then he wasn't, he couldn't. He involuntarily slid off onto the ground, not understanding what was happening, but somehow sensing that the warmth he felt spreading out on his chest and stomach was his own blood. As José was dying, he had managed to reach his knife. And he had used it well.

Peter let out a small sigh. It was dark, and then light. He was home, lying in his bed. Kip was standing before him, holding his hand, leaning down to kiss his lips. To stroke his cheek. Lisa and J. P. were right behind her. It was spring, and the bright sunlight filtered in through the trees outside their window, making dancing patterns on the ceiling.

33

"Mom," J. P. called out as he came into Kip's bedroom, "I don't have clean stuff for tomorrow."

Kip was in the walk-in closet, changing out of her clothes into a lightweight yellow robe, a Mother's Day present from Peter the year before. She never put it on without thinking of him, but as she tied the sash, she quickly pushed the image of her husband from her mind. Any thoughts of him now were so tinged with apprehension, she was trying to eliminate them as much as possible. She rubbed her neck, which was stiff with tension.

She emerged to see her son standing next to her bed. Dressed in his pajamas, J. P. was in the process of getting his camp uniform ready for the next day before he went to bed. Long ago, she had taught both children to put out their next day's clothes at night, and she was always amazed that they stuck with that one particular habit.

"I can't find my shorts," he told her.

"Did you look?" she asked, forcing a smile for him.

"Yeah. I have a shirt, but no shorts."

"Why don't we check it out together. There should be a couple of clean pairs."

Kip put an arm around his shoulders as they went down the hall to his bedroom. Though he would have died of embarrassment at such a display of affection in front of his friends, at home it was perfectly acceptable.

J. P.'s day camp required that the boys wear uniforms. Kip doubted that he was out of clothes because experience had taught her to order extras of everything. She went to his bureau and opened the bottom drawer. Bending down, she flipped through the garments to find two pairs of the Camp Greenacre shorts. She extracted one and held it out to him.

"Oops," he said. "Sorry, Mom."

She got to her feet again. "No big deal. Did you brush your teeth?"

He shook his head.

"Give me a yell when you want me to come in to say good night."

She went back to her bedroom to put the clothing she had just taken off into the hamper, determined to keep busy. When the telephone rang, she felt the knot that had been in her stomach tighten even further. It would be Nora and Eloise for the weekly call. Grabbing the telephone receiver, she sat down on the edge of the bed. She had a pink T-shirt in one hand, and she realized she was gripping it as tightly as she could.

"Kip? It's us."

"Hi, Eloise," Kip answered, somehow finding a modicum of comfort in the sound of her friend's voice.

"Hey, *us* she said. Us. I'm here, too," Nora chimed in.

Eloise laughed. "Nora, you're a big baby."

"So maybe I am," Nora said good-naturedly. "But just for that slight, I'm making Kip go first. Worst moment of the week, please?"

"Jeez, give her a break," Eloise said. "Can she at least start with the best moment?"

"Actually," Kip said in a deliberate tone, "I need to talk to you both about my worst moment. But it's more than a moment. This is serious. I haven't told you until now, because I hoped it would resolve itself, and I wouldn't have to bring it up at all. But it doesn't seem to be going that way."

"What is it?" asked Eloise.

Kip wished more than anything that she didn't have to make the situation real by voicing it to her friends.

Once it was voiced, her worst fear might actually turn out to be true.

"I haven't head from Peter in six days. He hasn't returned any of my messages, even the last couple where I asked him to call immediately. Yesterday, I got hold of the manager at the hotel he's staying at. He said Peter hadn't been back there since Wednesday. His room hasn't been touched and there are a bunch of phone messages he hasn't picked up." Kip knew she was beginning to sound hysterical, but she couldn't help it. "Then they asked me if they should check him out, and could they expect his credit card imprint to be good for the room bill."

"Whoa, whoa," interjected Nora. "Hold on there a second. Didn't you tell us it was hard to get in touch with him?"

"Not like this. Maybe a couple of days would go by before we could connect. That's why I didn't worry at first. I thought he might have gone on a trip somewhere, where there wasn't a telephone, down the Amazon or something. He wasn't planning to, but maybe an opportunity came up. But he wouldn't have done that without letting me know. And there are telephones in other towns. He wouldn't just disappear for so long without a word."

"Is there any chance he really did go somewhere on the spur of the moment?" Eloise was doing a poor job of trying to hide the concern in her voice.

"I even called *your* office this morning," Kip went on, "just to see if they might have heard from him. You were out somewhere. But they asked everybody, including your secretary. Nobody had."

"No," Eloise said, "but he doesn't have any reason to call here, unless he needs something arranged. He doesn't account for his time with us." She sighed heavily. "Actually, Kip, I was going to reach him after this phone call. About a half hour ago, I put in a call to one of the women I know in Rio. She had told me early last week that she would be giving a dinner party for Peter on Saturday night. I figured I'd hear the story later from Peter, but I was curious to hear her side of the evening. Well, she gave me quite an earful. It turns out he never showed up. She had a bunch of big shots sitting around waiting for him all night."

"Oh, my God," Kip breathed, "Peter would never do that."

"I didn't think so. I was hoping he would have told you why he didn't go."

There was silence on the phone.

"Now wait a minute," Nora said. "What are we getting at here? The man is in a foreign country and could be busy doing a million things."

"But it's *Peter*," Kip said, her voice rising. "He's not like that. He tells me what's going on. He's responsible. He doesn't stand people up and he sure as hell doesn't disappear for days on end."

"Take it easy, Kip, try to stay calm. Let's figure out what to do," Nora said.

"I've done one thing, the only thing I could think of," Kip said. "I called the Brazilian consulate in New York. Yesterday."

"And?" urged Eloise.

"So far, nothing. They said they'd look into it."

"That's not good enough," Eloise said, more to herself than to the others.

"What am I going to do?" Kip was growing frantic. "I know something is wrong. I know something is really wrong." Her throat started to close as tears stung at her eyes. The terror she had been holding back for the past several days threatened to overwhelm her.

"Wait a second," Nora said. "I've got a thought. Will Stanley once did a project on Brazil. He spent a lot of time down there. Maybe he'll know somebody with some clout who can get answers."

"Please call him, Nora." Kip was trying to keep herself together, afraid she would break down sobbing. "Please try to find out if Peter's okay." She almost whispered her next words. "If he's even alive."

"Don't *say* that, Kip. Of course, I'll call right now. Let's get off. As soon as I reach Will, I'll let you know what he says. But, Kip, honey, try not to drive yourself crazy. You don't have any reason to think all these terrible things."

But Kip didn't answer. She was crying in earnest.

"Nora," Eloise instructed, "hang up and call your guy. I'll stay on with Kip."

"Right. Kip, please try not to worry, please, please."

"Yes," Kip barely got out. "Thanks."

Nora hung up, disconnecting her phone from the conference call. Oh, God, this was weird, this was bad. She didn't like this. A shiver ran up her spine as she dialed Will's number. She heard the phone ringing in his apartment. What if he couldn't help her, she thought, or if he just refused to? After all, he didn't know Kip and Peter from a hole in the wall. But, no, he couldn't be that uncaring.

"Pick up, come on, damn it," she muttered into the phone.

Another ring. Then another.

"Hello?"

"Oh, thank God. Will, it's Nora. Didn't you once do a film about Brazil?"

"Well, hello there, Nora. Had a sudden interest in my résumé, did you?" he asked. "My career has confused many a person."

"Listen, this is not a joke. This is about my friend Kip. She's married to Peter Hallman, the writer. Her husband went to Brazil on assignment for a magazine and no one knows where he is now. He seems to have disappeared."

Will was instantly serious. "Christ, what happened?"

Nora filled him in as best she could. She explained how Peter had been working for *Metropolitan Woman,* which led her to the story of how she had met Kip and Eloise.

"That's really something," Will said when she was finished. "You never mentioned you'd been through anything like that."

As if you would have cared, she wanted to respond. "It doesn't generally come up in conversation," was what she said instead.

"So we have to find out what happened." Will got back to the point.

"Can you help? Do you know anybody down there? These people mean the world to me. If anything is really wrong . . ." Her voice made a funny cracking sound. God, she told herself, don't you start crying, too.

"Listen, can I get back to you tomorrow? I want to make a few calls now. Then we'll find out what comes next so we can track him down."

"Oh, Will, thank you so much." Nora's shoulders sagged with gratitude and relief. "I know it's a big favor and I'm putting you out, but it's really—"

"Don't be ridiculous," he said sharply. "I'll be in touch in the morning."

"Thank you," she said. "That's—"

He had hung up.

Nora called both Eloise and Kip to report on her conversation. She spent a while on the phone with Kip, trying to find some words of comfort. But both of them knew there would be no comfort for Kip until she learned where her husband was. Upset for her friend, Nora had a hard time getting to sleep that night. She stared at the ceiling, wondering what it must be like to be stuck in a state of limbo, when the answer you're waiting for might turn out to be nothing, or the realization of one of your worst fears in life. But she couldn't imagine it, not really. Poor Kip was having to live it.

When the alarm went off at seven-thirty in the morning, Kip was Nora's first thought. Throwing off the covers, she cursed as she realized that no one had called her with any good news. It wasn't that she expected an answer by now, but it sure would have been nice to end this quickly and happily. She got into the shower, racking her brain for people she could contact who might be able to help. She couldn't think of a single one.

When she was finished dressing, she went into the kitchen to make coffee. Over on the desk in the next room, she could see the red light on her answering machine blinking. Someone must have called while she was in the shower.

Hurrying over, she played the message back:

"Nora, it's Will. Phone calls were taking too long. People were out, or they had to get back to me, and so on. It just wasn't going to work. So I'm calling you from the airport. I'm flying down there to find out what's going on." There was a pause. Nora could make out a muffled announcement in the background. "That's my flight. Talk to you later."

The machine stopped. Nora stared at it. Will was flying to Rio himself. Right now. He had dropped everything to look into the whereabouts of a total stranger. Simply because she had asked him if he could help.

In a tone of wonder, she spoke aloud to the answering machine. "What I don't understand about that man is pretty much everything, isn't it?"

Will shut the door to the room behind him and went over to the bed. He was staying in Peter Hallman's hotel room, now his, acquired through quick payment of the outstanding bill. He stuck out the large, dirty paper bag he was holding and turned it upside down, spilling its contents onto the bedspread. Then he sat down and stared at the objects before him.

A hairbrush and a toothbrush, a bulging traveling bag, a glass ashtray, loose change and three twenty-dollar bills, a Mont Blanc pen, an English paperback edition of a biography of Benjamin Franklin and a hotel hand towel. The boy had said that he couldn't keep the things, to please take them back.

Will wondered how he had managed to lift all of it from Peter without his noticing. He picked up the book, intrigued that the child had chosen to include the biogra-

phy in his collection. Staring at the cover, it occurred to
him that Peter might very well have noticed. This was
all little stuff; there probably wasn't much in the room
worth stealing anyway. What the hell difference would it
make if the kid took a couple of things, a kid who had
nothing in the world?

Will got up and went into the bathroom to wash his
face. He had to call Kip Hallman now. He owed it to
this woman not to delay, this woman he had never met
whose life he was about to destroy. Maybe it would be
kinder to wait, give her another day. No, that wasn't his
decision to make.

He felt as if he weighed a thousand pounds as he
walked toward the telephone. Nora had given him the
Hallmans' number when he spoke to her three days before, a few hours after he had first arrived. It had taken
him this long to reach his contacts and find out what had
occurred down here. Pulling out his wallet, he extracted
the scrap of paper he had written it on and unfolded it
with a deep, sad exhalation of breath.

A woman answered on the third ring.

"Kip Hallman, please," he said.

"Speaking." Her voice was pleasant, but he could hear
tension in it.

"This is Will Stanley, Nora's friend."

"Will, yes, of course," she jumped in. "Oh, I can't
believe what you're doing for us. I'll never be able to
tell you how grateful I am. You're just—there are no
words for someone who—"

"No, please," he said almost brusquely. He paused,
unsure how to say what he had to. "Mrs. Hallman—
Kip—I did find out what happened to your husband. I
found out today."

"Yes?" she asked breathlessly.

"I don't know how to say this. . . ."

"Oh, God."

The panic in her voice made him shut his eyes with
despair over what she was about to be put through. He
spoke gently.

•

"He had befriended a child here, a poor twelve-year-old boy named Mauricio. I don't know his last name. They spent a lot of time together. Peter was interviewing him, and it seems they got very friendly. Peter helped him, from what I gather. I spoke to the boy today, and he told me how Peter would read books to him."

"Books, yes, of course, that's so like Peter," she said, the words coming quickly as if she weren't even aware of what she was saying, as if she were trying to draw out the story to avoid getting to the end. "He mentioned the boy to me."

"Yes," Will said sympathetically. "It seems your husband was a wonderful man in many ways."

"Was?"

He winced. *Damn.* "I'm afraid you were right to be concerned. Your husband did an incredibly brave thing to save this child. But he died doing it."

There was silence.

"Kip?"

"He died?" she asked in a small voice.

"Yes," Will answered.

"You're sure? You're absolutely sure?" Her tone begged that he correct himself, admit he had made an error.

"I'm sorry. Yes."

There was a pause.

"Excuse me a moment."

He heard her put the receiver down and walk a few steps away from the phone. Then there was what sounded like gasping, as if she were choking for air. Listening, he shut his eyes, tighter this time. It brought him back to the moment he learned that his wife had died. Kip Hallman's world had just been yanked out from under her, the way his had been that terrible day. It had been as if someone had punched him so hard he couldn't catch his breath. That's how it was for her right now.

He waited, lost in her anguish and his own. After a minute, she came back and picked up the receiver.

"Are you there?" Her voice was ragged.

"Yes, I'm here."

"Can you tell me what happened?"

"He was meeting this boy at his house so he could interview the child's mother. They live in one of the slums in the hills here. There was a man the mother had been living with at some point. The guy beat her, raped the little boy's sister—this was a real bad guy. He was after this boy Mauricio. He blamed the boy for his mother's walking out on him. It seems that Peter came upon this guy with Mauricio just as he was about to rape him. Mauricio has no doubt the guy intended to kill him."

"Oh, Peter," Kip whispered.

"The boy told me the story himself. The man had a huge knife. Other people were around, but they were all too scared to do anything." Will began pacing back and forth as he talked. "But Peter did something. He attacked the guy with his bare hands, I don't know how, but he did. He gave him such a beating, the guy died. But first he managed to stab Peter."

A moan escaped from Kip.

"I know." Will clenched a fist, wishing he could think of words that weren't so hopelessly inadequate. "The boy said he was incredibly brave. He saved this child."

"Peter saw . . ." There was wonder in Kip's faltering voice, as if she were realizing something. "You don't know what he . . . That would have meant so much to him, saving that boy."

Will didn't have any idea what she was trying to say. He waited, but she didn't continue. "I hate to tell you this, but his . . . body was . . . disposed of. I can't recover it for you."

"Oh, my God," she groaned, clearly not having thought this far until he mentioned it.

He silently cursed his stupidity in bringing it up. He recalled how he had focused on his wife's body and the funeral, as soon as he was told of her death. It was a distraction from dealing with anything else, from the horrible truth. But that didn't mean this woman was going to react in the same way.

"I'm sorry, but I can't hear any more right now," she said so quietly he could barely make out the words.

"I wish I didn't have to bring this terrible news to you. I don't know what to say . . ." He trailed off in misery.

"Thank you," she whispered. "Thank you for finding out. I can't imagine how you did it. How would I ever have known what happened without you?"

Will was filled with admiration for her. She was stronger than he had been under the same circumstances. "I'm flying back tomorrow. May I come and see you at some point?"

"Yes, certain—" She broke off, dissolving into tears. "I have to go," she sobbed.

He heard her hang up, and he did the same. Then he sat down on the bed, lost in the pain he felt for her and for the old wounds he found had just been wrenched open inside himself. He pictured Kip Hallman, three thousand miles away, her heart breaking. So alone. Just as he was.

34

"I won't come down. *I won't!*" J. P.'s voice was muffled by his locked bedroom door.

Standing in the hallway, Kip felt she might just collapse into a heap on the spot. How appealing the thought was. She could curl up into a ball and pretend the world didn't exist.

"Sweetheart, it doesn't have to be for long. It might make you feel better to be with everybody." Her effort to persuade him sounded feeble, even to her own ears. The truth was, she didn't blame her son for wanting to stay in his room.

There was no answer.

"Okay, honey, I'll come back up in a bit with something for you to eat." She waited. Nothing. "I love you, J. P."

As slowly as she dared, she went down the stairs. The house was filled with people, all of them no doubt hungry after sitting through the memorial service for Peter. Everyone had said she was crazy to have a crowd come back to her house; she should be taking it easy while other people took care of her. But she had insisted. It would give her something to do.

Well, that takes care of today, she thought as she reached the bottom step. Now I just have to figure out how to keep busy for the rest of my life.

"There you are." Kip's sister, Nicole, came toward her,

a basket of rolls in one hand. "Please sit down and get off your feet."

Nicole had rallied to her side from the moment she heard about Peter. Even through the fog she now seemed permanently to inhabit, Kip was aware that Nicole had genuinely come through for her, bringing over hot meals, calling repeatedly during the day, running errands for the household without anyone having to mention what had to be done. Kip only wished she could appreciate it.

She gave Nicole a tired smile. "Actually, it's better to keep moving." Drawing herself up, she tried to clear her mind. "Let's see. Do we have enough ice?"

She ignored her sister's protests and went into the kitchen, straight to the refrigerator. Her brother's wife, Sue, was there. She and Dirk Pierson had flown in the day before, leaving their daughters back in Seattle with their next-door neighbors. Sue and another woman Kip didn't recognize were removing plastic wrap from the platters of cheese and meats that Kip had arranged that morning.

She had had plenty of time to make the food look attractive, since she had awakened at three-thirty in the morning instantly knowing there was no chance she would fall back asleep. What the hell, she had decided, predawn is as good a time to work with cold cuts as any other.

The kitchen had been totally silent, so quiet she could hear the humming of the lights in the ceiling when she turned them on. As she folded the slices of rare roast beef and Swiss cheese, and fanned them out around a pale blue platter, she had stared at Peter's chair. It was at an angle, pushed away from the kitchen table. That was strange, she thought, since it hadn't been touched in days. No, she caught herself, she wasn't going down that road, believing Peter was visiting in some spectral form. She would lose her mind. But she could envision him so clearly, sitting there, sipping at his coffee. He would smile, toss out a comment to her, point to something out the window. She ached, thinking that she would give anything for a few of those simple moments with him.

The pain she had felt in the kitchen was bittersweet, sadness mixed with loving memories. The memorial service was a different matter. That was torment, the tearing out of her heart, the gutting of her soul. She had been kept so busy with planning the service and contacting people who had to be told. Now there was nothing standing between her and the emptiness of a good-bye.

There was no casket, of course, just flowers everywhere. They were so right, Kip had thought with detachment as she first entered the hushed room. The natural-looking arrangements of magnificent wildflowers were exactly what she had wanted, what Peter would have liked. She was grateful to Eloise for taking over that task, ordering from her own florist and paying the bill, refusing to listen to any argument from Kip. Nora had provided music as well, a tape of classical pieces whose soaring beauty made Kip tremble without understanding why. Still, the whole scene seemed unreal, more a dream than anything else.

Since Will Stanley's phone call, she had been swinging between sadness and numbness, between acknowledging, at least in words, that Peter was gone, and half believing he would come back one day soon from his trip. It was the speeches at the memorial that made it a little more real. But she knew she didn't believe it yet, not really. What would happen to her when she did?

A long line of family and friends had gotten up to speak about Peter. His father, his favorite cousin, his publisher, his best friend from college, a novelist friend whose career had risen alongside Peter's. They kept coming, people who loved him or admired him or had a funny story to tell about him. Kip didn't think she could stand it as she sat, her arms around Lisa and J. P., her head bowed as she listened to the praise. You don't know the half of it, she wanted to jump up and shout. He was so much better than you even know. And he loved me so much. He was mine, he was mine, my only love. Instead, she gave tissues to her daughter, who sobbed beside her, and stroked her son's hair as he sat rigid and dry-eyed.

She had escaped with the children as quickly as possible when it was over, not caring if she were doing the proper thing or not. She rushed them past the rows filled with a sea of faces. She caught sight of Nora sitting with a man in a navy blue suit whom she knew instantly had to be Will Stanley. Eloise and her parents were beside them. She almost couldn't bear to look at Peter's parents, Vivian Hallman's head on Art's shoulder, her swollen, red eyes hidden behind dark sunglasses, just as Kip's were. Emerging into the hot August sunshine, she had been shocked to find a large group of photographers, waiting to snap pictures and shoot videotape of the crowd at the famous writer's funeral service. She nearly shoved the children into the limousine to get them away from the cameras and shouted questions.

Now there were some fifty people milling around the house. She dreaded the moment when the door shut behind the last one, and she was left with only herself.

"Don't think about it," she muttered. She grabbed a bowl of olives from the refrigerator and took it out to the dining room.

Her brother was standing at the table, fixing a sandwich. When he saw her, he set his plate down and came over to her.

"Oh, Kip, what can we do for you?" Dirk put an arm around her.

She raised her face to his. "Nothing. But, thank you, if I come up with something, you know I'll ask."

"No, I don't believe you'll ask, not at all." He tightened his lips. "I wish we lived closer so I could keep an eye on you. You always have to do everything yourself."

Kip laughed sharply. "You'd be amazed at how I've learned to be able to do absolutely nothing at all lately. So we'll see." She ignored the puzzled look on his face. "I'm really glad you guys came to be here today. It means a lot to me."

"Are you nuts? Of course we came. Are you sure you don't want us to stay a few extra days?"

She shook her head. "You have to get back to the girls. And to your work. I'll be fine."

He peered into her eyes. "You aren't fine now. You can't be. But one day you will be again. I'm sure of it."

Kip felt her throat closing. She nodded, refusing to let herself cry, and pulled away from him. She walked into the living room. It was crowded, and people were talking but their tones were hushed, their expressions somber. She saw Nora's sister Wendy by the window, talking to the man she assumed was Will Stanley. Wendy had come by several times in the past few days, once to drop off shopping bags of food, twice to offer her help. Kip liked her, and understood that the similarities of their lives was touching a nerve in the other woman.

She saw Lisa sitting on the sofa, huddled against her grandmother. It was Vivian Hallman's turn to be the one providing the comfort, and she was holding Lisa's hand tightly, kissing the top of her head. When Lisa saw Kip, she got up and came over to her.

"Mommy, are you okay?" she asked, anxiety in her voice.

"I'm fine, honey." Kip tried to smile as she put an arm around Lisa's waist. "How are you holding up?"

Lisa put her arms around Kip's waist and nuzzled her face against her mother's shoulder.

Kip wouldn't have believed it if she hadn't seen it herself. Ever since they had found out about Peter, Lisa had been almost afraid to leave Kip's side. It had been at least five years since Lisa had called her Mommy, but the words *Mom* and *Mother* suddenly vanished from the girl's vocabulary, and Kip was back to Mommy full-time. All Lisa's anger and teenage nastiness had vanished, but so had her spirit and independence. Kip had spent so long wishing she could have her adorable little girl back. All she wanted now was to see some evidence of the rotten adolescent who had given her so much trouble.

"Sweetie, go see if you can get Grandma Bess something," Kip urged.

"Okay, Mommy. I'll be right back," Lisa said dutifully.

Kip sighed as she watched her daughter go. It would be almost funny if it weren't so terribly sad. The girl bent down over Vivian Hallman's elderly mother and spoke loudly into her ear. "Can I get you anything, Grandma Bess?"

Art Hallman was sitting next to her. "That's all right, Lisa. She's fine," he said wearily, patting his granddaughter on the arm. Kip watched Lisa smile at him and lean over to kiss his cheek. Art clutched her hand for a brief moment, and Kip saw that his was trembling. Peter's father's appearance could only be described as ghastly, she thought, his eyes haunted, his skin waxen. His tall frame seemed to have shrunk. It was incredible that he had gotten through the eulogy at the service earlier. What would it take for him to recover from his beloved son's death? she wondered. He probably never would.

Kip's parents appeared beside her.

"Dear, it was a beautiful service." Patricia Pierson put a hand on Kip's arm.

"Yes," Bob Pierson echoed. "Yes, it was."

"The flowers were exquisite. And so many lovely things were said about Peter."

"He was a good man, a damn good man," her father said forcefully.

"Thank you." Kip loved her parents, but she understood that she couldn't expect much emotional support from them. That had never been their strong suit, and she no longer expected them to change. Even the death of their son-in-law wasn't going to bring on any sudden surprises. Kip envisioned them dropping to their knees, sobbing with grief. She actually came close to giggling at the near-impossibility of the image.

"I made you that cinnamon-raisin coffee cake you like so much, Dad," Kip told him. "Can I get some for you?"

"Thanks, honey. That would be great with a cup of coffee."

She was almost out of the room when Nora and Eloise caught up with her.

"Where are we going now, may I ask?" Nora said. "You haven't sat down for a second."

"I don't want to," Kip said. "I'm getting my father cake and coffee."

"We can handle that," Eloise said.

"It was nice of your parents to come today," Kip said to her.

"No, it wasn't." Eloise made a sour face. "It was the least my father could do." She seemed to realize how she sounded. "I'm sorry, Kip, this isn't the time or place for my carrying on. Forgive me."

Kip smiled affectionately at her. "Eloise, I could forgive you anything. But nothing needs forgiving."

"I . . ." Eloise's expression was pained. "I blame myself for Peter," she got out. "I blame the magazine and my father. But most of all, I blame myself."

Kip was shocked. "You can't be serious. You didn't have anything to do with it. You gave him a job. He asked you to. He chose his own assignment. What happened down there wasn't your fault or anybodys else's." She grabbed Eloise's hand. "Please tell me you'll stop thinking that. I couldn't bear it. Really, it will make me so much more unhappy to have that attached to his—" She stumbled slightly over the word. "—death."

Eloise looked at her doubtfully. Then she took a deep breath. "Well, let's not dwell on this now. It's selfish of me to burden you with my guilt." She paused. "Honestly, Kip, you've done enough here. Let us take you upstairs, and you can lie down and take a little rest."

She was about to refuse, but it dawned on her that she was exhausted. In fact, she wasn't sure she could take another step. "That's not a bad idea," she said.

"I'll take her," Nora said. "El, why don't you get her father's cake and coffee?"

Eloise nodded and walked away. Nora ushered Kip upstairs and down the hall toward her bedroom. It was then that Kip noticed the door to J. P.'s bedroom was slightly ajar.

"Wait a second," she said to Nora.

She took a few steps in the direction of his room, intending to knock. But she stopped as she heard voices coming from inside. Kip had told Nora and Eloise what a hard time J. P. had been having, how he had hidden behind an invisible wall that, so far, nothing had been able to penetrate. He had barely spoken to Kip in the past three days; she couldn't imagine whom he would have let into his bedroom today.

"Who's in there with him, do you suppose?" she whispered.

Nora shrugged, tiptoeing behind Kip to get closer to the door. They heard J. P.'s voice, not the deadened tone he now used when forced to speak, but his old voice, the voice of an eleven-year-old boy.

". . . teacher liked my idea a lot, but we never got to do it. And you wanna know why? The kids couldn't keep it together. I mean, before I could videotape, they had to rehearse, right? Or it would have been awful. But they were always joking around, acting goofy. Man, it made me so mad, I just dropped the project."

A man laughed. "People don't necessarily do what the director wants, do they?"

"Good grief," Nora whispered, "that's Will."

"Your Will?" Kip whispered back in surprise.

J. P. spoke again, his tone indignant. "You would think they'd want to be in a good movie."

"You know what I've learned?" Will said. "I've learned that you have to stick with what you want, what you believe is right, even if it seems as if people are never going to understand it. If the first batch of people don't get it, you move on until you find the ones who do get it. They might be the second batch or the fiftieth. But sooner or later, you'll find people who'll want to be part of something good."

"Yeah," J. P. agreed, his voice filled with admiration.

"What do you say we go get something to eat. I want to hear more about this."

"Okay."

At that, Kip and Nora retreated down the hall to Kip's room, not wanting to be discovered eavesdropping. Nora made it inside, but Kip was still visible in the doorway when Will and J. P. emerged from his bedroom.

"Oh, Kip, you're up here," Will said. She froze on the spot, feeling somehow guilty, as if she had been caught stealing. "J. P., can you go on and I'll catch up in a minute?" he asked the boy.

J. P. saw Kip and frowned. He started downstairs.

"Excuse me, Kip, I was just hoping to talk to you for a minute." He came toward her, extending his hand. "I'm Will Stanley."

She stepped into the hall to meet him and took his hand in both of hers. "Of course I know who you are. I owe you so much. Thank you for coming. And thank you for getting my son to come out of his room."

"I didn't realize I was getting him to do anything. The downstairs bathroom was getting pretty popular, so I came up here to look for another one. He was just leaving it, and we got into a conversation."

"Well, that was a small miracle. I owe you my thanks for that, as well."

"You owe me nothing at all. I'm glad to get a minute alone with you. I would have come to see you before, but I understood from Nora that it was fairly chaotic, people coming and going. You didn't need any more company, I'm sure."

She smiled. "People try to cheer you up, keep you going."

He smiled back. "It doesn't work though. I know that."

She leaned against the wall and examined his face. There was an expression in his eyes that seemed to go deeper than mere consolation.

"It sounds as if you know what you're talking about," she said.

He seemed to hesitate before answering, but then he looked right into her eyes. "I lost my wife a few years ago."

Without thinking, she reached out to touch his sleeve.

"It was the same when she died. Casseroles, phone calls. All I wanted was to be left alone to crawl into a big hole and die myself."

Suddenly, it came back to her. Eloise had once mentioned that the man Nora was working for was a widower. His wife was Theresa Stanley, the reporter she'd seen any number of times on television.

"It was several years ago. She was killed on assignment in the Balkans."

"I'm so sorry." Kip's expression was pained.

"Funny thing, though," Will went on, his tone making it clear that it wasn't funny at all. "She had been diagnosed with leukemia eighteen months before. She had finished the chemo, but it was too soon to find out if she was cancer-free."

Kip didn't know what to say. "That's . . ."

He nodded. "The irony, right? All the doctors, the horrible treatments, the mental anguish—then, boom."

"So you had the worst of both worlds. The pain of a long period of suffering and a sudden loss."

His eyes showed appreciation of her understanding. "That's exactly right. Strange, but the worst part, the really hardest part, was never finding whether she would have beaten the disease. I so desperately wanted to know."

"And how is it now for you?" Kip asked.

He looked way from her. "I went crazy from losing her. I got angry. I got sad. I got a lot of things. But I feel like a person again. And that will happen for you, too."

Kip didn't want to think about his last comment in terms of herself. She recalled Nora's talking about a girlfriend of his, and focused on that instead.

"Surely you've had relationships since then? Nora mentioned someone, in fact, a woman she met who was your girlfriend."

He seemed puzzled for a moment. "Claudia, you mean? That's who you must be talking about." He gave a short laugh. "She's not a girlfriend. A friend, a long-time good friend. That's all."

"Oh."

"Listen, I didn't mean for this to be a trip down my own sorry memory lane. I just wanted to tell you how bad I feel about your husband. I wish I had had the chance to meet him. He must have been a wonderful guy."

Tears filled Kip's eyes. "He was."

"But he did an amazing thing for that little boy in Rio. Truly brave. Very few people would have had the guts."

"Thank you."

They exchanged a long, silent look of understanding. Then Will headed down the stairs. As she turned to go into her bedroom, Kip felt she might pass out from exhaustion. It was all too much.

She found Nora sitting at the end of her bed, staring down at her hands, which were clasped in her lap. Kip stretched out on the bed behind her, sinking with relief into the soft pillows, at the same moment realizing she wouldn't be able to sleep.

"You heard?" she asked Nora's back.

Nora nodded.

"Sad, about his wife."

Nora shifted around on the bed to look at Kip. "Very."

Kip gave a wan smile. "The girl you were so jealous of is just a friend."

"I wasn't—" Nora started to protest, but quickly realized this wasn't the time. "Guess I misread that one."

"Hmmm." Kip closed her eyes.

Nora got up to go. "I'll check on you later."

Kip was alone again. The day will never end, she said to herself, putting her arm across her forehead. This terrible, terrible day is going to go on forever.

A frightening thought occurred to her. This day *would* never end. Outside, the sky would get dark, then light, then dark. The seasons would change. But the rest of her life was going to be one, long, terrible day. A day in which Peter was dead.

35

"What a shame!"
Grey Bentley's voice carried across the green as Eloise watched the golf ball she had just hit plop down thirty yards or so from where she stood. The hole she had been aiming for was at least 180 yards farther on, but she couldn't have cared less.

How did she let her father talk her into this? She watched the caddie pick up her bag and start to lead the way to the seventeenth hole of the Wykagyl Country Club. Here it was, Labor Day weekend, and instead of going up to Rhinebeck to be with Kip, she was playing a game she loathed with a bunch of people she didn't especially like for a reason she couldn't even identify. No, she admitted, the reason was clear enough. Because her father had asked it of her. He had asked nicely, as he always did. And it was a business event, or, at least, was in that realm of business where the private became public and vice versa.

"You know how they love to see the family together," he'd said, smiling at her assumed agreement. "Your brother is coming and he so needs your support." No, Dad, she longed to say. He needs *your* support."

God, she was ungrateful, she thought. Her father had, after all, invited George to his event. Grey Bentley was making a genuine effort to accept her brother for who he was, rather than who he wanted George to be. How much did she expect from one elderly guy? she asked herself. But she couldn't help it. The whole thing rankled her. A weekend golf tournament at a country club in Westchester was the last place she would have chosen to be. And enforced smiling at her father's various cronies—influential, even charming though they were—was wearing her down. Of course, she acknowledged, these days, everything seemed to wear her down.

As she walked along the green—at least she'd gotten her father to agree to let her walk the green instead of using the stupid cart—her father came up behind her and put his arm around her shoulder. She saw the admiration in his eyes and knew what it was about. In her short khaki golf skirt and tucked in white blouse, she looked as slender and lithe as her current weight of 127 pounds allowed. She ought to be glad she was looking attractive. After all, she'd spent enough years hiding half again as many pounds. But she didn't feel glad. She felt enraged. And it wasn't exactly free-floating anger. It was directed squarely at the person next to her.

"You'll get stronger as we go along, darling," he said as he beamed his jovial professional smile toward Chip and Marilyn Wardwell, the airline president and his wife who made up the rest of their foursome.

"I don't want to get stronger," she answered, sounding even to herself like a petulant four-year-old. "Listen, Dad, do you mind if I don't play tomorrow?"

Her father pulled his arm away and looked at her. "Oh, dear, everyone stays till Sunday night. That's when they present the awards. It's considered bad sportsmanship not to show up."

"Honestly, Dad," she said, "nobody will even notice that I'm not here. Except you and Mom. And I imagine you'll still love me if I play only one day."

Her father chuckled. "Darling, I would still love you if you never played at all."

To Eloise he sounded as if he were indulging an untrained puppy. She wanted to stalk off the grass and bury her woes in a martini—no, in a big, fat peach melba. Instead, she found herself standing above her ball. There was the caddie, holding out the three-iron for her. She tore it out of his hands then apologized to him for her rudeness. It was wrong to take her foul mood out on some college sophomore who only wanted to earn a few bucks for the fall semester. She raised the golf club back and tried to concentrate. This time, she got a better pull at it, the ball at least nearing the area of the hole.

"Excellent," her father said. Again, he walked beside her. She took a peek at his face. He seemed relaxed and happy, but she couldn't imagine that that was how he felt. Surely, he must find all this back-slapping bonhomie as wearing as she did. True, corporate executives the world over had to engage in it, but nobody could actually enjoy it. For the past forty-eight hours, they'd all been on a kind of stage. The Bentleys *en famille*. Aren't we just swell? she thought. There was Kip up in Rhinebeck, trying to get her son and daughter to understand why their father was never coming home, and here she was, trying to get a country club full of rich people to appreciate how adorable the Bentleys were.

Her father seemed to intuit her thoughts. "You know, your friends Kip and Nora would probably love to be doing what you're doing this weekend. This tournament is quite famous."

Eloise scowled. "My friend Nora wouldn't be allowed in this tournament, Dad. Wykagyl doesn't allow Jews to be members."

Her father's face darkened. "I believe those restrictions ended many years ago, Eloise. Frankly, you're being rude."

"I'm sorry if I'm being rude. Perhaps I shouldn't have come."

"That's foolish," he insisted. "We've been doing this as a family for years. It's expected of us."

Eloise wanted to scream. "Dad, nobody cares."

Her father resorted to his formal tone. "The people who run this care a great deal, as do our colleagues in the industry. I don't see Harold Pierce's children whining."

Harold Pierce was the publisher of one of the weekly

news magazines. As far as Eloise could see, his two sons were too robotic to even think about whining. And that seemed to her a real shame.

"You know what, Dad? Since I seem to be such a failure as a daughter, maybe it's time to stop trying so hard." She heard the nasty tone in her voice, but she continued anyway. "Let's perform a test. I don't show up at these shindigs for a year or so, and you get back to me with the bottom line on exactly how much Bentley Communications has lost because of it."

Grey Bentley stood still, seemingly not caring when their golfing partners stared at them. "What's eating at you today?"

When she spoke, she was as shocked by the words that had come out of her mouth as she was by the tears that were suddenly spilling from her eyes. "We killed him! We made him go there and we arranged it so he could never come back."

Her father stared at her, his mouth agape. "You're talking about Peter Hallman?"

"Yes," she answered, her voice smaller this time.

The play of emotions across his face went from outrage to shock to a terrible sadness. "You mean, of course, that *I* killed him." It wasn't a question.

Eloise felt as if a boulder were lodged in her chest. It was horrible to accuse her father this way, yet she couldn't help but nod her head.

He didn't seem to have an answer. He walked away from her, not toward the hole, but away from it. She watched his back as he moved. Usually, it was straight and sure; now it was slumped. She suddenly realized what she had said. It was neither accurate nor was it fair. In fact, it was cruel.

She raced after him, stopping him before he got too far.

"I'm sorry, Dad," she said, throwing her arms around him. "That was terrible of me. I'm feeling guilty and awful, and it's convenient to blame you for it. You didn't force Peter to do what he did, and I guess I didn't either."

Her father patted her back awkwardly. She looked up at his face. It was clear that he wasn't over what she had said. He looked five years older than he had mere minutes before.

"Don't fret, honey," he said. "We'll all get through this."

Dispirited, she walked beside him, back toward their companions. Chip Wardwell was warming up with his putter. Neither he nor his wife gave Eloise or her father more than a cursory glance, which was a relief. Chip swung at his ball, and all four of them watched it slide neatly into the hole. His wife grinned, as did Grey Bentley. Eloise was glad to see that her father looked a little more normal as he selected a club.

But she still felt awful. Guilty about her accusation. Miserable about Peter's death. But that wasn't all, she realized. It wasn't just what had happened to the Hallman family that made her unhappy. It was her own life. Arguing with John and his lawyer about who bought what and who deserved to keep it. Going to work each morning with a vague sense of discontent, not quite knowing what was wrong, but suspecting that it was something important.

Yet, she knew that, in a way, all of that was beside the point. What made her so unhappy today wasn't about any of that. It was about being here, literally on her father's turf. Working on *his* passion. Getting recognition as *his* daughter. As editor of *his* magazine.

My God, she thought, she was forty-one years old. She wasn't stupid, she wasn't impoverished. She wasn't even ugly anymore! It was time to grow up. Time to do something on her own.

No. The thought stopped her in her tracks. It was time to do *everything* on her own.

She stayed where she was, digesting what she'd just told herself. She realized she felt relieved. More than that, actually. It left her feeling strong. Strong, and satisfied for perhaps the first time in her life. She could still be a daughter and a sister. Maybe, someday, she could even be a wife. But first she had to be herself.

36

Holding a container of cottage cheese in one hand, Kip pulled open the silverware drawer to extract a spoon. She went over to the kitchen table and sat down. As she took her first bite, she reached for the local newspaper, which she had left there earlier in the day. She couldn't remember when she last had time to do more than flip through to see if there were any important announcements about the kids' schools or special events. Now was the time to catch up on reading. After this, she could go through the pile of catalogs and old magazines, and finally clear them out of the house.

She scanned the front page, but her mind was on the silence in the house. In these past three weeks since Peter's death, she had been so busy, she had barely even been alone there. The children had to go back to school, which meant buying new clothes and shoes, and a haircut for J. P. Then there were the last-minute appointments with the dentist and the eye doctor before the kids' afternoon schedules filled up, and the endless filling out of forms and check writing to register them for what seemed like every activity in the world.

All the action was a godsend, of course, she reflected. It kept her mind off Peter. She cried, but mostly she was able to hold off until she was alone in her room at night. At first, she had lain in the center of the bed, her arm extended to Peter's side, as if she could hold on to some connection between them. She could clearly see him there, the bulk and substance of him. It was too sad to be borne. Now she stayed on her side of the bed, and went to sleep facing away, toward the wall.

At least she was hiding most of her grief from the children. She forbade herself to cry in front of them, reminding herself over and over that she had to be strong for them. It was her obligation. She kept them busy as well, trying to maintain their normal routines.

J. P. wasn't doing as well as she would have liked. He had withdrawn into himself almost from the minute he found out about his father. Her sweet, easygoing son had been transformed into a sullen, angry boy. Ever since the first day of seventh grade, he had been misbehaving in class and refusing to do any work. His new teacher told Kip she would give him all the time he needed to adjust, but she did have to draw the line when he became so disruptive that she couldn't go on with the lesson. Kip thanked her and said she was grateful for her understanding.

She was worried about him. Every night, she would sit on the edge of his bed, hold his hand, stroke his hair, and try to get him to open up, or even talk about his father at all. He only turned away from her, silent. Time, she would tell herself, he needed time and lots of it.

Lisa was a different matter. After she got into her nightgown in the evening, she would ask Kip to come into her room. Then they would sit on her bed together, talking about Peter, and within minutes, Lisa would be sobbing with Kip's arms around her, the two of them rocking back and forth. During the times when she was home, Lisa stuck close to her mother. Kip noticed that the girl appeared almost frail, a shocking change in her usually robust, confident child. Kip found it hard to believe, but she had to admit once more that she would have been only too glad to have her obnoxious, argumentative teenager back instead of this lost, uncertain girl who seemed so without spirit.

How strange, Kip thought, as she scanned the newspaper, that Lisa had needed convincing to spend the weekend with Peter's parents. J. P. had accepted the notion with an indifferent shrug, but Lisa's eyes showed panic at the thought of being away from Kip for so long. Art and Vivian Hallman had offered to take the children so that Kip could have a break; they insisted she must need one and they wouldn't take no for an answer. Kip accepted with profuse thanks, but she understood that the Hallmans needed Lisa and J. P. more than she needed a break. The children were their only link with Peter. It was easy to understand the comfort they would take in having them around, although it would no doubt be mixed with a terrible grief.

Lisa had eventually agreed to go. That meant Kip was able to take care of a long string of errands during the day and plan a hot bath and a few hours of reading in bed for the evening. The cottage cheese she was eating now was dinner, which suited her just fine.

She turned the page to the local movie listings. It's Saturday night, she said to herself, date night. She ran her eyes up and down the listings, wondering under what circumstances she would ever find herself at the movies again. With the kids, she realized, or maybe with a friend. Maybe next time Nora was visiting her sister, Kip could steal her away for two hours.

Kip stared into her cottage cheese container as she continued to eat, an idea forming in her mind. Why couldn't she go to a movie by herself? It's not as if there's a law against it, she thought. Hell, just because she always went with Peter didn't mean her muscles wouldn't work if he wasn't by her side. She could drive to the theater by herself, open her wallet, and pay for a ticket, even buy popcorn. Popcorn would make it fun.

"People go to the movies alone every day," she announced as if she had just made an incredible discovery. "Millions of them. Perhaps billions."

She stuck the spoon into the container and set it down on the table, returning to the paper with a sense of purpose. All right, here was something—a new movie that had opened the day before. She hadn't heard anything about it, but the ad showed two middle-aged people in Elizabethan dress. That seemed safe enough. The next show was at 8:30.

Kip twisted in her chair to look at the clock on the kitchen wall. Twenty after seven. "There you go. It's fate," she pronounced. She was ready to go, dressed in presentable enough black pants and a pale pink blouse. No reason she shouldn't just do it. Forget the bath and the book. Time to get out into the world and be part of the human race. She was beginning a new life whether she had intended to or not, a life she would be living on her own. Might as well get started now.

It took her ten minutes to brush her hair and put on some fresh lipstick and blush, but she was in her car with plenty of time to get to the theater. She felt almost giddy. Her fears of dealing with life without Peter had been understandable, but basically unfounded. The worst had happened, and she was going to be able to get through it.

As she drove, her excitement started to diminish. She saw herself walking into the theater, standing there searching for a seat, a single seat. People would be watching her, wondering what this poor woman was doing there alone on a Saturday night. By the time she pulled into the theater's parking lot, Kip was feeling distinctly uncomfortable.

"You're doing this. Don't argue," she instructed herself.

She got out of the car. It was getting dark, and the air was thick with humidity. She had forgotten the forecast was for rain that night. Walking around to the back of the car, she opened the trunk to get the umbrella she always kept there. Maybe she would need it when she came out. She clutched it as she headed toward the glass doors at the entrance. Good, she thought, I have a little security blanket here to hang on to.

There was a small crowd at the box office. She tried not to look, noticing only a women in a blue halter top, and a middle-aged man in a Red Sox cap. Her head down, she waited until it was her turn. When she got to the window, she met the gaze of the teenage boy on the other side.

"One, please." At that moment, she wished she could sink into a hole. *One, please.* That was going to be her new theme song, her motto, her mantra. She had better get used to it.

The boy said nothing. He only took the ten-dollar bill she slid toward him and slid back a ticket with her change. She thanked him, but his expression didn't alter. Bored, he waited for her to get out of the way so he could attend to the next customer.

Okay, so far so good, she told herself. She summoned up a smile for the man who tore her ticket in half and ushered her inside. As she passed him, she felt his eyes on her. Yes, I'm by myself, she wanted to yell at him, nobody's here with me. She realized that perspiration was running down her back. You're going to a movie, not the electric chair, she silently chided herself.

Opening the next set of doors leading into the theater, she was seized with a fierce desire to go back to her car. She could forget this whole thing, just go home; the bath would still be waiting for her. She glanced around. Many of the seats were taken. What felt like hundreds of pairs of eyes turned toward her, checking out the newcomer. Her heart was pounding, and she felt herself flush with embarrassment. As fast as she could, she located an empty seat on her right and slipped into it. She was still clutching the umbrella, and had her hand tightly on her purse. She realized she had forgotten to buy popcorn.

Out of the corner of her eye, she saw the man with the Red Sox cap, the one she had noticed outside, enter and pause, surveying the room. He was alone.

He was scanning the center section of seats, but she turned her face in the other direction, not wanting to make eye contact when he looked her way. Finally, he sat down across the aisle from her. Kip shifted uncomfortably in her chair. Somehow, she sensed that he was watching her. She put one hand up to the side of her face, hiding it, pretending to scratch her temple. Why was he watching her? Why didn't he stop?

The lights were going down. Thank God. She gave a fleeting glance in his direction. Her heart seemed to leap in her chest. She was absolutely right—he had been staring at her, and he was *still* staring. Had he noticed her buying her ticket, her *one* ticket, when they were both outside? Yes, of course, a woman alone, such easy prey. No one would notice if she vanished, not for hours, maybe not for days. The children wouldn't be home until the following night. If she were to disappear, no one would miss Kip for nearly twenty-four hours.

Her throat felt as if it were closing up. No, there were other people here, she should just sit still and watch the movie. She noticed how shallowly she was breathing, and made a conscious effort to slow it down.

The man got up and moved to the seat right behind Kip.

She bolted from her chair and ran toward the exit, shoving her body against the door's metal bar, and practically spilling out of the dark theater. Running as fast as she could, she ignored the stares of the employees and the people still coming in, and fled to the outside.

It was pouring, a torrential rainfall that made it difficult to see anything. The sky was nearly dark. Unwilling to stop, Kip ran to her car as she struggled with her umbrella. By the time she got it over her head, she was already soaked, her hair plastered to her head. She barely noticed. Stopping short at her car, she cursed as she realized she still had to retrieve the car key from somewhere inside her purse. She tried to balance the umbrella between her neck and shoulder as she opened her bag and began feeling around inside. The umbrella tipped back, leaving her completely exposed to the rain. Frantically, she glanced back at the theater entrance to see if the man had followed her out.

It was then that she noticed the purple pickup truck parked near the entrance. Her hand closed around the key as her mind registered the significance of the truck, that it was the one that belonged to Carleton Avers, a longtime resident of the town, and a widower. He lived a few streets over from hers. Kip hadn't had much contact with him, but he was considered to be an old-fashioned gentleman who happened to drive a bright-purple truck for reasons known only to him. That's who had been watching her. He might have been staring because he was having trouble placing her. Or he was uncertain if he should speak to her or not.

Hot tears stung Kip's eyes. The umbrella slid off her shoulder onto the ground just as she yanked the key out of her purse. Thrown off-balance, she took a step back into what turned out to be a deep puddle. Water filled her shoes and spilled back out as she stumbled to get away. For a long moment, lightning illuminated the sky, followed immediately by a boom of thunder sudden and loud enough to make her jump. She tried to fit the key into the lock, but her hands were shaking too violently. Her whole body was shaking. The rain was coming down even harder, beating her, pounding her. Kip hurled the key to the ground. She put both hands on the top of the car and raised her face to the night sky, letting the rain pelt her.

Somewhere inside her, she had always understood that she couldn't be on her own. And here it was, the unspeakable, for real. She couldn't take care of two children, bring them up, be responsible for them and all their needs. She couldn't even take care of herself.

Small sounds were coming from deep in her throat, gasps that turned into cries, which grew louder and louder. Then, she was screaming, agonized shrieks at the top of her lungs, the terrible sounds drowned out by the noise of the downpour. Lightning lit up the sky again, and there was more thunder, roaring all around her.

"I hate you!" she screamed. *"I hate you, Peter! How could you, you bastard!"* She let out a piercing shriek, an animal's howl of pain. *"You son of a bitch, you said you would never leave me. But you fucking* lied *to me!"*

She pounded her fists on the car's roof. "I HATE YOU, I HATE YOU, I HATE YOU!"

She sank down, letting out a long, low wail, until she was in a heap on the ground. As the rain made contact with the blacktop, it splashed back up violently, hitting her in the face.

"I can't do this," she sobbed, gasping for air, her words completely lost in the noise of the storm. *"I can't be alone."* She curled up into a tight ball and wrapped her arms around her legs. Her voice dropped to a whisper. *"You knew that, Peter, didn't you? Didn't you?"*

She closed her eyes and lay there, silent, as the furious night continued to rage around her.

37

Nora felt a stinging pain in her finger. When she looked down, she was surprised to see that she'd bitten her thumbnail to the quick.

"I sure hope you don't have to scratch anywhere for the next few weeks," Eloise said, laughing sympathetically.

Nora regarded her in surprise. Eloise and Kip were seated side by side on the 1930s' porch swing that Nora's sister, Wendy, had bought at a flea market years before and refurbished to a high sheen, with handmade pillows covered in fabric patches she'd acquired for next to nothing from Shabby Chic and sewn together to a perfect plumpness. The women had cups of coffee in their laps, while Wendy and Nora, seated on comfortable padded outdoor chairs on either side of them, were drinking lemonade out of oversize ceramic mugs. Nora had gone to watch her sister at a kiln a few times when she'd begun to learn pottery. She'd even tried to fashion a soup bowl, which she'd painted in colors she suspected a six-year-old would also have chosen. Wendy, meanwhile, had been the teacher's favorite student, achieving an even glaze with her first ashtray that would have done a professional proud.

Nora examined her fingers, the bleeding mess of ragged nails and picked-over cuticles. What used to look like adult hands now resembled those of an anxiety-ridden child. More disturbing than that was the fact that she'd had no idea she was doing it. She looked around her sister's screened-in porch. There were the three people she felt closest to in the world. So, she asked herself, what are you doing acting like a mental patient?

"Listen, guys," Eloise said, putting the cup in her hand on the table next to her. "I have some news. In fact, I have two pieces of news."

The other women looked at her.

"Guess who doesn't work for her father anymore?" She smiled broadly.

It was Kip who answered. "Do we assume you're talking about you?"

"Yup."

Nora nodded her head. "And this is a good thing, right?"

"Actually, it's a great thing." Eloise became more serious. "It seems wrong to attribute anything good to Peter's death, but in a way, that's what gave me the courage to do what I'm doing." She reached for Kip's hand, holding it for a few seconds. Then she smiled once more. "I'm sorry, but I've never been so excited."

"First things first," Nora said, waving with impatience. "What is it you're doing? And, while we're at it, since when have you wanted to do something else?"

Eloise looked at her in amazement. "I can't have done that good an acting job! I've been dissatisfied for months, no, make that years. And I could never put my finger on exactly what was bothering me. Well, it turned out not to be such a big mystery. Except, of course, to yours truly. I'm sure you guys always knew how frustrating it was for me to still be Daddy's little girl."

"Actually," Nora said, "no, I didn't really know that at all."

"Hmm," Eloise said. "Maybe I'm more like him than I realized. The old one-foot-in-front-of-the-other Bentleys ride again. I may have acted as if everything was hunky-dory, but it wasn't. All my life, I've wanted something of my own, and now I'm finally doing it."

"Doing what?" Nora practically shouted the question this time.

"I'm starting up a boomer magazine, complete with Web site. It's geared to sophisticated women between thirty-two and fifty-five, and it's going to have health and fashion and finance and every other subject anyone that age could possibly be interested in." She smiled at Wendy. "I'm sorry. This must be boring you to death."

Wendy laughed. "How very kind of you to think I might be bored with something that pertains to a woman in her late thirties."

"So, who's supporting this venture? I presume it's not Bentley Communications," Nora said.

"Nope," Eloise said.

"Thus spake Gary Cooper," Nora said.

"Oh, Kip," Eloise said as if in apology. "How horrible it is for me to be taking such pleasure in something and even mentioning Peter's name in the same breath."

Kip sipped at her coffee. "If Peter's death has led to anything even vaguely good, I can only be happy about that." She sighed. "God knows I'm not happy about anything else these days."

Eloise's eyes sought contact with Nora, though neither of them was sure of what to do for their friend. Nora realized that Kip had caught their shared glance when she fixed a smile on her face and looked expectantly back toward Eloise.

"So, where are you getting your funding?" Kip asked.

"Well," Eloise answered, "part of it is coming from the settlement John and I have come to. We've agreed to liquidate some of the things we've been fighting over."

Nora wondered about the implications of what Eloise was saying, and her anxiety showed on her face.

"Don't worry," Eloise said, smiling at her friend's chagrin, "I found myself fighting and fighting, and then one day I realized that I didn't want to see anything that had belonged to the two of us ever again. Including," she said with a glance at Kip, "the house in Rhinebeck. When I'm up here from now on, you will probably find yourself with a houseguest."

"That's fine by me," Kip answered with enthusiasm.

"Anyway," Eloise went on, "as to the major share of the magazine's funding, there's a British consortium that has several American branches. They own one of the book publishers and several of the shelter magazines." She began to describe the inner workings of the Patria Corporation at length.

Nora was thrilled at Eloise's news. She wasn't especially knowledgeable about the publishing business anymore, but she could imagine how big a deal this was for Eloise. Kip was also listening intently, although Nora couldn't stop noticing how quiet she'd become. If only she could really help Kip, Nora thought, knowing how little help one day's companionship—or, for that matter, a year's companionship—was likely to be. She knew that Eloise shared her frustration. Both of them longed to get Kip and her family through this horrible time, and both of them were powerless to do so.

"So, what's the second piece of news?" Nora asked, suddenly remembering how Eloise had begun.

Eloise's jaw clenched slightly. "Well, I hope you guys are going to be okay with this. But all the horrible drama of the past year—Peter's death, the robbery—even starting up the magazine . . . well, it's made me act on something I've been thinking about doing for a long time." She looked from Nora to Kip. "I don't want to ever feel as powerless again as all three of us did in that store."

Nora heard the abrupt intake of breath from Kip, while she herself felt almost stunned. The three of them so rarely raised the subject directly. They spoke of being afraid, of the decisions they'd come to. Sometimes they even joked about triple-locking their doors or hearing nonexistent noises in the night. On a handful of occasions, one of them would mention a dream about Todd Lyle, a passing, hateful thought of the boy who'd taught them fear. But they never went back into the emotions he'd made them experience, the terror-filled minutes when they were certain they would be killed and there was nothing—*nothing*—they could do about it.

Nora managed a slight nod, indicating that Eloise

should continue with what she was saying, and after another glance at Kip, she did.

"I've come to see that I have to do something to keep
from feeling so powerless. And what I've decided to do
may not seem like much, as if I'm just throwing money
at a problem. But it's the one thing I can think of to do,
and any measure of good that comes from it makes it
worthwhile." She took a deep breath. "Todd Lyle was
emotionally disturbed. What he did was horrible, but if
someone had noticed how damaged he was, if there had
been someplace for him to go, for his parents to go,
maybe he wouldn't have carried through with it." She
licked her lips, which had gone dry. "So I'm setting up
a foundation. It's for the kind of kid who gets lost in the
shuffle, the way Todd Lyle did. And it's for the mothers
and fathers who don't know which way to turn."

"You're doing this with your own money?" Nora asked.

Eloise nodded, adding, "And with the help of at least
seven other companies, including, by the way, the Bentley Corporation. We're planning our first fund-raiser
for March."

"I'll be there with you," Nora said. "How about if I
plan the music?"

Eloise smiled. Then she gazed at Kip, the one who'd
been physically harmed, the one who'd lost so much. It
was hard to know how she would react.

Kip looked thoughtful. "You know what? I bet I can
get Peter's publisher to contribute. I think they'll be glad
to." She smiled at Eloise. "I think the idea's terrific. Just
let me know what I can do to help."

Nora watched Eloise's shoulders sag in relief.

The sounds of the children screaming in the backyard
took Nora's attention outside to the lawn, which was
being used as a makeshift softball field. Her niece Sarah
was at home plate, holding a lightweight metal baseball
bat, clearly so surprised to see the ball sailing out toward
second base that she forgot to start running.

"Go, stupidhead," Tamara yelled from the grass behind her sister.

The sentiment was echoed more politely by Wendy's husband and by Kip's children, all of whom were imploring the child to run. Nora watched as, finally, Sarah took in what they were saying and began to speed toward first. Will scooped up the ball at short center and threw it to Casey Clark, the twelve-year-old boy from down the street, who was guarding the denim seat cushion that served as the base. But Nora realized that Will had waited a few seconds before sending the ball off and then had thrown more softly than he needed to. She grinned as her niece's foot touched the base just a hair before Casey caught the ball. In the dimming early evening light, she could see the look of joy spread across Sarah's face.

Well, Nora thought, she was glad it was a banner day for someone she loved. It certainly was not shaping up as a banner day for her. When she'd picked up her messages on Wednesday during a break in a meeting she was having with Will and two camera people, she'd had no intention of inviting Will once again into her life. But, if that hadn't been her intention, calling Wendy back from Will's office had been quite a mistake. Her sister had wanted a telephone number, and Nora had mentioned where she was only by way of explaining why she couldn't check her Rolodex. Wendy had insisted that Nora put Will on the phone. Nora's heart had sunk as she listened to Will's end of the conversation. "Saturday afternoon? Kip and the kids? Sounds great."

It had been nice of Wendy to invite Kip and her family. Since Peter's death, Nora had been spending much more time up in Rhinebeck, and Wendy and Kip had become friendly. It would be great for the kids to get to know each other, Wendy had said, to have a day when something besides tragedy was on the agenda. And, of course, Nora had agreed. But she had no idea why Wendy had chosen to include Will Stanley, a man she barely knew, in the party she'd planned. Nor could Nora imagine why Will would say yes to such a thing. It clearly wasn't because he wanted to see more of Nora. She had offered him a ride up to Rhinebeck and he had turned her down flat with some excuse about enjoying the train trip along the Hudson.

In fact, for the past few weeks, Will had been oddly neutral with her. Not hostile. Certainly not attentive, as he had—well, she admitted to herself, *almost* had been just before Peter's death. Now, when they were spending a lot of time together, working on the plans for the documentary, she had obviously become merely a colleague, one with whom Will had a professional, courteous relationship.

And that was just fine, she thought. Which made it even more peculiar for her sister to have included him in today's festivities. He was wonderful to one of your best friends, Wendy had insisted, hearing the hostility in Nora's voice when she had taken the phone back from Will. You should be glad to see him included. And Nora could hardly argue. Will might make her uneasy, but even she had to acknowledge how important he had been to Kip. Besides, Wendy had added, there were plenty of other people invited.

Despite the fact that Wendy had not known Peter, his death had had a profound effect on her. After all, Nora realized, Peter had been about the same age as Andy, just as Wendy was the same age as Kip. They lived within five miles of each other, each had two children, each had a marriage that was stable and happy. The tragedy had been a reminder of how tenuous the good times really were. How people owed it to themselves to appreciate every day they had. Wendy wanted this party to celebrate life, she'd said, and life had a lot more to it than your sister and your two closest friends. And, indeed, as Nora looked out toward the lawn, she saw a number of unfamiliar faces in addition to Kip's family and Wendy's family.

Nora watched the ballgame continue as Sarah's team took their third out and returned to the field. Sarah and Tamara had been placed in the outfield, where Nora knew the ball was unlikely to be hit. Andy was pitching, while Ted Kantor, a chiropractor who lived right across from her sister, was a tiger at shortstop. Nora smiled as Ted ran down a fast fly ball that should have made it to centerfield. She'd met Ted and his wife, Eleanor, several times, and he'd always fascinated Nora. Eleanor was quiet and dignified, while Ted was the kind of guy who plowed in to everything. Even today, he'd come to the party bearing the oddest gift Nora could imagine. It was a brightly painted wooden stick, decorated with red and yellow birds, about an inch in circumference and a foot in length. It was, he explained enthusiastically, a talking stick. When not a single person at the party recognized the term, Ted explained that it had been used in his men's group. "We go around in a circle and the man who holds the stick must go to his inner child and tell the whole truth. And while someone is holding the stick, no one else is allowed to talk."

He couldn't have been more serious about it, though Nora was not the only person at the party who smiled at his explanation. Nora had always found his excess zeal both amusing and, at times, irritating. Yet, she had to admit that to a woman like herself, someone who preferred to stay on the periphery, Ted was an object lesson in getting involved. He was a guy who poured himself into sports, into his family, into his patients, and, evidently, into spirituality. She had to admit that as silly as she might sometimes find it, his passion was not such a bad quality.

Nora continued to watch the game as one of Wendy's neighbors hit a hard single to third. A girl who must have been about eleven or twelve scooped up the ball and threw it toward first. But instead of going in a straight line, the ball wavered in the air, threatening to fall several feet short of the base. The first baseman shot forward grabbing the ball in midair and arriving back at the base in time to put out the runner.

"He's pretty great, isn't he?" Wendy said.

Nora turned to the other women and realized that all of them had been watching the game.

"The kid can certainly catch a ball," Nora answered, looking at Casey Clark with admiration.

Wendy turned to her. "I wasn't talking about Casey. I meant your friend Will. Surely, you had to see what he just did for Sarah."

"No, I'm deaf, dumb, and blind." She smiled at her sister. "Why don't you just call me stupidhead?"

Wendy frowned. "You know, *stupidhead* might just be appropriate."

"Hey," Nora laughed, "what did I do to deserve that?"

"I think it's a question of what you're not doing, not what you are doing." Wendy looked to Eloise and Kip, as if asking for their support, but the two women kept quiet.

"Meaning?" Nora asked.

Wendy raised her arms in the air. "I give up!" She waited a beat and then went on. "Meaning, Will Stanley is an incredible man, who I firmly believe is in love with you."

Nora reddened. "That's idiotic."

"Idiotic?" Wendy responded. "You think he came up here for the Hawaiian Punch?"

"I think he came up here because you invited him."

Eloise and Kip had begun to stare at Nora, making her crawl with self-consciousness. But still they stayed quiet. To her distress, Nora could see that Wendy had no intention of doing the same.

Her sister stood up and reached for the empty pitcher that had contained lemonade. She walked toward the entrance to the house and turned.

"Would you even recognize it if someone were in love with you?" Wendy asked. "No," she answered her own question. "Let me put that another way. Would you know it if *you* were in love with someone?" Without waiting for an answer, she strode off toward the kitchen.

Nora felt herself rising to the bait. She knew she should keep quiet, but she felt compelled to defend herself. "I was there and you weren't," she raged. "We had our night and it amounted to zero."

Wendy was too far into the house to hear her, but Kip leaned forward.

"What night was that?" she asked.

Nora suddenly realized what she had said. She had never mentioned the night in Mississippi to anyone. Not to her sister and certainly not to Eloise and Kip.

"Oh, it was nothing," Nora said. She noticed that Kip seemed engaged in the conversation for the first time that afternoon. She only wished it had been any other subject that had engaged her.

Kip looked at Eloise. "Do you think the word *nothing* covers it?" she asked.

Eloise widened her eyes. "Gosh and golly gee, Kip, I guess it must. 'Cause you know our friend Nora would never hold anything back from us."

"Oh, shut up," Nora muttered, sitting back in her chair and closing her eyes.

Eloise smiled at Kip, then looked around. Her eyes alighted on the wooden truth stick. "Let's let the stick decide if Nora is telling the whole truth," she said, taking it in her hand. "We'll all take a turn." She held it up in front of her face. "Let's see," she said, "I wish I could have three scoops of pistachio ice cream right now." She turned to Kip. "Now, that's the entire truth."

Then she handed the stick to Nora. "Okay, so what's your entire truth?"

Nora grabbed the stick from her and laid it to one side of the chair, but Kip reached across and placed it back in her hands.

"Uh-uh, Nora," Kip said, her voice soft and insistent. "I'm sorry, but the three of us made certain promises to each other, and this happens to be nonnegotiable. Did something happen with Will?"

Nora put the stick down once again, but this time she kept it in her lap, her fingers grasping it as if for emotional support. She did not want to be having this conversation, yet she realized she was feeling too guilty to go on lying to them. She was going to tell them the truth, even if it killed her.

"Okay," she admitted, looking down at her lap. "There was one night when Will and I got together. It was a few months ago, when we were in Mississippi. It didn't mean anything then, and it doesn't mean anything now."

There was a silence, then Kip reached for the truth stick and held it up in the air. "If it hadn't meant any thing, you *would* have told us. And that really *is* the entire truth."

She handed the stick back to Nora, who, in turn, threw it to the floor.

Eloise shook her head. "You know it's fine to laugh about the inner child nonsense. But for the little scared kid in you to still be the one making your most important decisions when you're almost forty years old is not funny at all. And to throw away a chance at some real happiness—well, that's downright tragic."

Nora refused to meet her eyes. "You're both being crazy."

"We're not and you know it," Kip retorted. "You have this fantasy about relationships. We've talked about it before. Your father bullies your mother and somehow you think that every relationship is like that. Somehow, magically, if you admit you're in love with Will, you'll turn into your mother and throw away every bit of your creativity and power."

"Could you be a little more pretentious, Mrs. Freud?" Nora smirked.

"Could you be a little more dishonest and cowardly?" Kip answered, unamused. "I had the kind of love you could walk away with tonight. It was the most incredible gift I could ever have had, and I would do anything, anything, to have it again for even an hour."

Nora felt a terrible shame. She ached to run from the porch, to leap into her car and drive back to the city at ninety miles an hour. But something inside her made her look out to the yard. She saw Will, her eyes finding him near home plate, standing next to Kip's son, J. P. As she gazed at them, Will raised his right arm, offering the boy a high five. She had no idea what it was about. Maybe the child had just scored a run, or maybe he'd told a funny joke. But she realized how characteristic the kindness of the gesture was. Will was nice. And smart. And funny and talented and interesting and adult. He was unlike any of the men she'd dated. And as painful as it was to admit to herself, she knew just why that was so.

Because she'd never before allowed anyone near her whom she could love this much. If there were any possibility of someone getting to her like this, she had always run. Run so fast, she didn't even have time to think about what it was she was running from.

And she also knew why she'd never owned up to this before tonight. Because she was exactly as stupid and as cowardly as Kip and Eloise were telling her she was.

Nora lifted her face, taking in both her friends. "And, let's say you were right. What if I were in love with him?"

Eloise answered. "You'd have to put yourself on the line and tell him so. And then you'd have to go on every day fighting the part of yourself that would long for him to leave so you could stay alone and safe."

Nora sat quietly for the rest of the evening. She didn't say anything more to Kip and Eloise. Nor did she explain anything to her sister. She remained in her chair, trying to cope with the terrible ball of fear in the pit of her stomach. Not that she was successful. When she approached Will at ten, asking him if he wanted to drive home with her, the fear was alive and well. Yet, when he demurred, saying he could catch a train at eleven, she didn't let the fear stop her.

"No, Will," she said, fighting her rising panic with all her might. "I want you to come with me. We have things to talk about."

He looked at her in surprise. Then he shrugged his shoulders. "Okay," was all he said.

They made their good-byes, each thanking Wendy and Andy for a wonderful day. When Wendy offered them both leftover cake, Nora said no, but Will surprised her by accepting. Nora waited, impatient and edgy, while Will went with her sister to the kitchen. He returned a few minutes later with an aluminum-foil-wrapped package in his hand. They walked to the car, Nora leading the way, neither one saying a word.

When she took her place behind the wheel, the silence was hard to break. What was she supposed to say to him, for Christ's sake, she thought. I love you and my friends think that you love me. Is that true? Do you think about me? Do you even give a damn about me? As the phrases floated through her mind, the fear inside her expanded. She couldn't do this. She shouldn't. If it were meant to be, it wouldn't be so damned hard. And, for sure, she wouldn't be feeling this awful.

She looked over at Will, who sat calmly in the passenger seat, gazing out the window. He said nothing about the fact that she still hadn't started up the engine. As the two of them sat there in stony silence, he picked up the foil packet Wendy had given him and began to pick at the cake inside. Nora felt infuriated as she watched him take a smear of the chocolate icing on his finger and lick it off. He was so nonchalant, so blasé, sitting there staring into the night. After all, she thought, they were in absolute country darkness. What the hell was he looking at? Whatever it was, he certainly wasn't looking at her. No, she decided, he didn't give a damn about her. Kip, Eloise, Wendy—they couldn't have been more wrong. To say anything to him, she told herself, would be to make a total fool of herself.

Angry now, she turned the key, forcing the engine to life faster than it was meant to go. The loud start covered up a different sound, one that she didn't hear at first. Only when the car had quieted to a steady hum did she realize that Will was laughing.

"What's so damned funny?" she asked.

Will stuck his finger in the icing once more and turned to her. "You."

"What do you mean, me?"

Will stopped laughing long enough to pop his finger into his mouth once more, this time murmuring "Mmmm" as he tasted the rich chocolate.

Whatever else he might have wanted to say, he seemed to prefer keeping it to himself. Once again, there was not a sound in the car. Yet Nora couldn't bring herself to put the machine into gear and start the long trip home. She was in turmoil, just as she had been in his apartment the night that horrible Claudia woman had been there, frozen with fear, and, at the same time, aching to connect with him, to crawl into the warmth of his body, to feel his arms around her, to feel him wanting her as she longed for him.

"Okay, Nora. Out with it."

The sound of Will's voice in the silent car startled her.

"What makes you think there's anything to come out with?" she answered, knowing how foolish she sounded. She was, after all, keeping him in the car, not driving, not going anywhere while the night got later and later, and New York City remained exactly as far away as it had always been. But, there was nothing she was capable of coming out with because she was too frightened to say anything at all.

"Jesus," Will muttered as he opened the car door and started to step out.

Nora's indecision turned to alarm. "No," she cried out, circling his upper arm with her hand to stop him.

She was relieved when he pulled the door half-shut and remained in the car. Yet, again, she sat there, paralyzed, having no idea what to do when, out of nowhere, she felt his index finger opening her mouth. She was shocked at the taste of chocolate on her tongue, even more shocked to feel the fire in her body as she sucked on his finger. He left it there until she had licked off all the icing. Then, instead of pulling his finger away, he moved it to her lips, tracing them slowly, making her insides feel as if they'd been lit up with an electrical charge.

"Say it, Nora. Tell me what you want."

Nora had never heard a demand issued with such tenderness. It left her breathless with that familiar combination of excitement and fear. But, for the first time, along with the fear was a longing so powerful, she couldn't keep it to herself anymore. She reached up and circled his finger with her hand. "I want this. I want you." She looked into his eyes. "And I'm scared. I'm so terribly scared."

Will turned in the passenger seat to face her. He dropped the packet of cake onto the floor and reached across for Nora. In one powerful, fluid motion, he lifted her out of her seat and onto his lap, facing him. Her legs encased his thighs, while he lifted her arms around his neck. Nora melted into him until every part of her body touched his. With a flush of pleasure, she realized that it was the very first time she had ever *not* felt alone.

Will held her face between his hands, his mouth only inches from hers. "Like you're the only one who's scared," he whispered.

He kissed her finally, so deeply, so completely, she felt as if they had become one being.

Nora's body cried out to join with his. She reveled in the strength of his back, her elbow coming to rest against the car door. As her hands stroked his shoulder blades, her elbow pressed downward, freeing the latch and sending the pair tumbling out of the car. Will held on to Nora, keeping her from hitting the ground. As they landed on the grassy hill beneath, they both began to laugh.

"See," he said, as he turned them over so he was lying on top of her, "that's the good part of loving someone. You get to be terrified together."

Nora smiled as his mouth met hers once again. Maybe she'd always be afraid, but, God, how she wanted him. Wanted him more than she'd ever wanted anything. She tugged at his shirt, pushing it up as her hands dug into his flesh. She could tell that Will felt the same urgency. He was impatient as he pushed her sweater over her head and unclasped her bra. His mouth devoured her breasts, her nerve endings coming alive at the insistence of his tongue.

She gasped as his hands moved down to her blue jeans. He wasted no time unzipping them, raising up her lower body to enable him to pull them off. Within seconds her underpants were flung to the ground several feet off.

Excited beyond measure, Nora tore at his belt. She wanted him inside her, on top of her, enveloping her for the rest of time. And, within moments, he was. She cried out as he entered her, her hands digging into his upper arms as she pulled him to her. Their movements were frenzied now. There was nothing of the taunting silence that had come before. She found herself saying his name over and over again, holding on to him for dear life, joining him in an outpouring of joy so profound, she felt as if she'd just been born.

38

Kip finished lacing up her skates. She rose from the bench, putting on her gloves as she went toward the ice. At the entrance point, she paused. The bright whiteness was so familiar, so soothing. Just staring at it made her happy.

"A balm to the soul," she intoned.

"What'd you say?" J. P. came up behind her, adjusting his woolen cap. He had spotted a friend from school, and stayed to sit with him while she and Lisa put on their skates.

"Nothing." She smiled at him.

He looked at her outfit, shaking his head. "How you can wear that tiny little skirt and leotard thing, I'll never know. You're insane, Mom. It's, like, zero degrees in here."

"How you can move around in all those layers, *I'll* never know," she said with a grin. "You get warmed up as you move. That down jacket is going to slow your jumps and spins."

"Very funny." He made a face at her as he stepped out onto the ice.

She watched him take a few tentative glides. His motions grew a little smoother as he relaxed a bit. He wasn't used to this. Standing there, she thought about how strange it was that she had no idea who had ever taught him how to skate, or when. That was back when she was still pretending skating didn't exist, that it had been banished from the face of the earth the day she quit the sport. She sighed at her own folly.

Lisa emerged from the ladies' room, where she had stopped off to brush her hair. Kip watched her sixteen-year-old coming closer, surprised by how completely grown up Lisa looked, much closer to a woman now than a girl. Would that have been the case if she hadn't been through the past few months? Probably. It was one of those facts of their growing up, that one day you looked at your children and they were no longer your children, but adults; your job was nearly done.

But they weren't at that point just yet. And, despite her outward appearance, Lisa was going to need plenty of mothering for a while to come. She had been wrung out by her father's death. The teenager she was had been destroyed, suddenly, as if in an explosion. It had taken some time, but she was recovering. She would never be the same, of course. The luxury of her self-absorption was no longer an option. She—like J. P. and Kip—had to concentrate on living with Peter's absence. That absence was big, solid. It was something to be contended with every day. The three of them found that their concern for one another had become the most important part of their lives. Kip wished that both her children would get to the point where they could once again get caught up in typical kid stuff. But for now, they—and she, too—were different. They were raw, still hurting. They needed to rally together. And, thank God, she thought, they had.

Lisa was wearing black pants and a long, off-white cable-knit sweater. She was putting on a pair of red ear-muffs as she walked. Kip noted how graceful her movements were.

Lisa came closer. "Ready, Mom?"

"You ever consider taking up skating as a sport?" Kip asked. "I'll bet you'd be good at it."

Lisa arched her eyebrows. "Surely you jest."

"Not competitively, just for fun."

"That's your thing, Mom, not mine." Lisa stepped out onto the ice.

Kip followed her. "I didn't actually expect you to agree. But I gave it a shot."

"Nice try."

They skated together in silence. Lisa was comfortable on the ice.

She was the first to speak. "Actually," she said in a hesitant tone, "there is a sports matter I wanted to talk to you about."

Kip had been enjoying the feeling of gliding, not thinking about anything, just sailing along. She turned her attention to her daughter. "Shoot."

"I've given it a lot of thought." Lisa drew a deep breath. "I want to swim in the Olympics."

Kip turned sharply. "You *what*?"

Lisa nodded. "The Olympics. I think I can do it."

"Well, well, well." Kip faced forward again. For so long, until this very instant, she realized, she had always assumed her daughter would lose interest in swimming, and quit. This was quite the surprise.

"What do you say?" Lisa understood that she was asking Kip herself to make an even bigger commitment than in the past. Without her mother's support, Lisa would have a difficult time of it.

Kip stopped short on the ice. "You realize what you'd be getting into?" she asked. "You'd have to keep up your schoolwork, but you'd also have to swim and train and a score of other things a million hours a week."

"I know," Lisa said. "And I know you'd have to deal with all that, too. But I really want this, Mom. Really."

Kip was quiet, realizing the extent to which she had misread her daughter. She had never given her the slightest credit for the work and dedication it took to win all those swim meets last year. Kip always assumed it was a passing fancy, and that she hadn't really worked hard for it. Of all people, Kip thought, I should have known better.

She reached for her daughter's hand. "If you're willing to do what it takes, then you should do it." She bit her lip. "It's a hard road, baby. But I can't tell you how much I admire you."

Lisa's entire face brightened at the words. "You do?"

"Oh, yes, of course. It's brave and wonderful and exciting beyond anything." She put her arms around Lisa and drew her into a hug. "I'm proud of you."

J. P. had made it around the rink for the third time, reaching the two of them just in time to see them hug. "Oh, come on, you guys. What the heck are you doing? It's embarrassing."

"Bug off," Lisa said good-naturedly as she broke away from her mother. "Come on, let me show you a few pointers here." She held out her hand to him. He regarded it with horror, clearly mortified at the idea of being seen holding hands with his sister. "Oh, don't be such a baby," she prodded him. "Nobody cares."

"*This* is what's going to make me look like a baby," he informed Kip. "This, right here." He nonetheless took Lisa's hand, and she rewarded him with a yank forward that nearly pulled him over. He recovered, and the two of them took off together.

Kip watched them, thinking that this was the best day J. P. had had yet. He was coming back to himself, but it was a slow process. He was quiet a lot of the time, and more prone to get angry than he used to be. Yet, there were sparks of his old sweetness and good humor, like this moment with Lisa, and Kip had noticed they were occurring more frequently in the past few weeks.

She began to skate backward in a circle, her arms extended. If any of them had been in serious danger of not recovering from Peter's death, it had been she, she knew that. After that night in the movie theater, she had spent most of the next several weeks in bed, in a kind of daze. All she could think was that she couldn't. She couldn't, she couldn't, she couldn't. Couldn't live without Peter. Couldn't be a grown-up. Couldn't be a mother. She couldn't *anything*.

The children were petrified. They didn't understand what was going on, but they were scared out of their wits that they were going to lose their mother, too. Kip was aware of their fear, but she was somehow beyond caring, as if she wasn't even part of the world anymore. She was beyond everything. Amazingly, it was her sister, Nicole, who figured out what was going on in the house and stepped in to look after her niece and nephew. She was there every morning to get them off to school and came by every evening to cook them dinner and make sure their homework got done. Kip had no idea how she ran her own household during that time. All she knew was that her sister had made up for every nasty crack, and then some. Kip couldn't imagine how she could ever repay her.

Nicole never pushed Kip to get up. On the morning Kip finally ventured out of her bed and went downstairs, Nicole was still there, cleaning up after the children's breakfast. When she saw Kip wearing the same nightgown she'd been wearing for a week, her hair unwashed and uncombed, she only smiled and made them both some tea. They sat at the table with their drinks, neither of them saying a word. As Nicole stood up to clear away the cups, she paused and then put a hand over Kip's and let it rest there. Kip didn't say anything. But she nodded her head. It was enough.

Slowly, Kip resumed her life. It would have been nice, she thought, if she had done it because she felt she would be fine, that it was no problem for her to stand on her own two feet. But it didn't happen that way at all. She came to understand that she would be afraid for a very long time. She wasn't going to change overnight, just because Peter was gone. But she saw that she could be afraid and still go on. And she wasn't alone, of course. She had her sister and brother, she had her parents and Peter's parents, and she had friends. All of these people would help her with the children and the burdens of the day-to-day stuff if she needed it; all she had to do was ask. And she had the miracle of her friendship with Nora and Eloise. There wasn't anything they wouldn't do for her, she knew that.

Kip saw the children skating toward her. She glided over to meet them halfway.

"We want hot chocolate," J. P. informed her. "You want to come?"

"Sounds good."

The three of them walked to the concession stand and took their steaming cups of cocoa over to a bench. They sipped contentedly.

"Mom," J. P. said suddenly, "can I ask you something?"

"Sure."

"Could you do Thanksgiving again next year?"

Kip looked at him in surprise. J. P. hadn't seemed to care when she told him that Aunt Nicole would be making the holiday dinner. Kip had been grateful to her sister for offering to do it. This would be the first big holiday without Peter, and there was no way she could face it at her house. But she hadn't considered how the children would feel.

"Gee, honey," she said, "would it make you feel better because having it at our house is a tradition? Because it reminds you of Dad?"

He looked abashed. "No. It's just that Aunt Nicole always makes such weird food. All that no-fat, special tofu stuff is so gross."

Kip stared at him; then she burst out laughing.

They finished their drinks and went back onto the ice for another half hour. At that point, both children said they had had enough and were ready to go home. As they all sat down to change into their shoes, Kip raised her eyes to take a good, last look at the ice.

It would be a long time before she came here again, she knew that now. She was lucky to have had the chance to go back to the one thing she regretted most in life and do something about it. Without Nora and Eloise, she never would have. She would have kept it buried deep in her heart, untouched because it was too scary to face. But she had reclaimed her love of skating, her interrupted passion. If Peter hadn't died, she would have continued to skate for as long as she could. Certainly, she would have made it to the Adult Nationals. That wasn't possible anymore, though. She couldn't pursue the classes and practice, and all the rest, and give her children what they were going to need from her in the next few years. Peter had left her plenty of money, so she didn't have to worry about that. But she needed to find something to occupy her free time and her mind, something of her own, and eventually she would go back to work. It just couldn't be something with the demands of this sport.

Skating would always be her special love. She was so incredibly fortunate to have had it, and then found it a second time in spite of her own foolishness. But real life was more important. That was what was going on now. What made her so happy was that she had discovered she didn't mind. The simple act of taking that first step, going back onto the ice that first day, turned out to be the moment her regret dissolved. She was free of it, free to go on to whatever was going to come next.

"Mother," Lisa said, interrupting Kip's reverie. She and her brother were standing there looking at her, their skates already tied together and slung over their shoulders. "We're ready to go, and you haven't even gotten one skate off yet." She rolled her eyes. "Come *on,* already."

You hear that, Peter? Kip asked her husband silently as she loosened her laces and yanked off the skates. They're going to be okay. I really think they are.

She jumped to her feet and smiled. "I'm ready."

39

Eloise uncapped a thermos of steaming coffee, filling the three mugs she had set out on the bench beside her. She handed one mug to Kip and one to Nora, both seated to her left.

"Thanks," Nora said, as all three women sipped their drinks. "I would have paid you a thousand dollars for this coffee, but, luckily, you didn't ask." She pulled an errant strand of hair away from her face. "God, all this makeup—I feel as if I'm wearing a mask. What happens to me if I smudge my lipstick?"

"Too frightening to imagine." Kip wrapped her hands around the mug to warm them. "Who would have thought we needed to wear parkas for a little boat ride in April? At least we don't have to pose in bikinis."

Eloise raised an eyebrow. "Bikinis, sure. Over my dead thin-but-not-*that*-thin body."

Nora pulled the collar of her jacket around her more tightly. "Where are the tables with croissants and caviar? Where are the male models? If I get my behind on a ferry at six-thirty in the morning, I want perks!"

Sonny, the photographer's assistant, came into view. "Okay, we're set up for you."

Eloise was the first one on her feet. "Ready to shoot?"

The women hurried along behind him as Sonny spoke over his shoulder. "No, but we need to do a few things before we get the background view right."

As they came around to the ferry's starboard side, Ian,

the hair and makeup artist, appeared beside them. "A touch-up, everybody," he said, waving a brush with powder across each woman's forehead and nose. He reached into the carpenter's apron he wore tied around his waist, extracting a handful of lipsticks. "Your mouth is ruined," he said, pointing at Nora. "Let's go over here."

"See? Why can't I ever get away with anything?" she asked the others as she followed him to an area that was protected from the wind.

Kip watched him fuss with the eyeshadow he had put on Nora earlier. Then he brushed her hair, lifting it in sections and spraying underneath to accentuate its wild curliness. Kip turned away to see what was going on near the boat's railing, where the three of them were to pose. Eloise was standing there with Chris Larkin, the photographer. He was tall, his prematurely graying hair a sharp contrast to his young-looking face. Chris was pointing toward the Statue of Liberty as he talked to Eloise, who listened intently, one hand on the railing. Kip was startled to see him turn to Eloise and reach for her hand. He held it only momentarily, but the look that passed between the two of them was unmistakable. They continued talking, their heads close together.

"Well, I'll be damned," Kip muttered.

Ian came up behind her, hairbrush in hand. "The wind will wreck it, but that's okay," he informed her as he wielded the brush to turn under the ends. After re-applying her blush, he went to concentrate on Eloise, whose hairstyle was the most conservative of the three. Kip understood that the photographer wanted to exaggerate the hair and clothes as a way of highlighting the differences in their personalities.

She buttoned her jacket against the dampness and wind. Initially, she had been reluctant to be part of this article. Eloise had come up with the idea, and Kip had been surprised that her usually private friend was willing to reveal so much of her life in print. Discussing your biggest regret and what you did about it was one thing. But Eloise insisted the story had to contain all their failures and struggling, and what each woman's efforts said about her. Kip wasn't sure she wanted to invite that kind of scrutiny. But as soon as Nora pointed out that it was a way to help Eloise's new magazine, Kip agreed that it was the least she could do for her friend.

Eloise let another editor handle the story, knowing she couldn't be objective. A writer interviewed the three of them separately and together. It had been eye opening, that was for sure, Kip thought, to go over the past year with the benefit of hindsight.

Apparently, the writer had done a terrific job, because Eloise reported that the entire staff at her magazine was intrigued with the story. Although they weren't supposed to, virtually everyone in editorial and advertising passed the story around while it was still in the editing process. They were all talking about it, Eloise said. About how they cried over Peter's death, and how bad they felt when Kip walked away from her dream a second time. Eloise's admission that it wasn't losing weight that changed her life, but breaking free of her family, brought her dozens of admiring comments from the staff. And Nora's wedding to Will started all kinds of heated debates about the nature of marriage.

Eloise was delighted with the reactions. She hadn't planned on making it a cover story, but her features editor insisted. So here the three of them were, about to pose on the Staten Island Ferry as it passed by the Statue of Liberty. Symbol of change, a new life, that sort of thing, Eloise had explained.

"Let's try it," Chris Larkin called out.

Nora and Kip joined them at the railing. He positioned Kip in the middle, Nora to her left, Eloise on her right. As the stylist had instructed them in advance, they all wore black, with black jackets, but no gloves.

The wind whipped their hair in all directions. Chris yelled out instructions over the noise of the ferry's engine, telling them to hold hands, to huddle closer together, to smile, to put their arms around each other. At every change, he snapped Polaroids.

"Kip, get down a bit," he shouted, "that's right, bend your knees. Eloise and Nora, lean in behind her."

He switched their positions, this time putting Eloise in the middle. The ferry passed the Statue of Liberty.

"Don't worry," he said, "we'll do the actual shots on the ride back. I want to sit with the Polaroids first. So far, they're good. The wind is making everybody healthy-looking."

"Sadist," Eloise said.

He laughed, but went on. Satisfied at last, he told them to take a break. "Sonny and I will call you when we're heading back." He smiled at them. Kip saw his eyes linger on Eloise.

"Let's find a furnace and stick our heads in it to warm up," Nora said, leading the way inside. They sank down onto a bench, all three rubbing their hands to warm them.

Kip turned to Eloise. "*Not* that I would dream of interfering in your business, and *not* that you have to tell me . . . but what's the story with you and our photographer?"

Eloise wasn't fast enough to conceal that the question struck a nerve. "What on earth do you mean?"

Her weak attempt to recover only served to make Nora lean forward to get a better look at her face. "I seem to have missed something."

"I'm not that fast to pick up on such things," Kip said, "but anybody could see you two have—shall we say—*met* before."

Eloise reddened.

Nora folded her arms. "We're waiting. And, let me remind you, we're trapped on a boat, so we've got nothing else to do but wait."

Kip held up a hand. "Hang on, Nora, now I feel bad. Maybe she doesn't want to talk about it."

"No, it's okay. It's time," Eloise said. "I didn't want to say anything in case it fell apart. We're—this sounds so idiotic—dating. About two months now."

Nora's eyes widened. "Well, well, *well.* I can't believe you didn't tell us. You know, normally, I don't approve of dating people whom you meet at work, but . . ."

Kip laughed. "Yes, we know how Nora frowns on that sort of thing."

"I met him at a shoot," Eloise said. "It just sort of happened when I wasn't looking. We were talking, we continued talking after the shoot was over. It seemed natural to go for some dinner. By the time I got home at two in the morning, I realized I could easily have spent another fifty hours talking to him."

"Those cute crinkly eyes didn't have anything to do with it, did they?" Nora asked. "Or those long, sensitive fingers. Or that—"

"Okay, okay, so I was attracted to him," Eloise broke in. "Sue me."

"Do people know about this?" Kip asked.

Eloise shook her head. "Officially, no. He works for the magazine, so it would lead to gossip. Mind you, I'm not the one who hired him to begin with, or even for this shoot today."

"Judging from the way he looked at you and touched you before, it's not going to be a secret for long," Kip said. "It was written all over his face."

Eloise's face lit up with pleasure. "Was it, really?" Her expression turned serious again. "But you can guess what people will say about it, the boss dating the photographer. Not to mention that he's younger than I am."

"It can't be by much," Nora put in.

"He's thirty-six," Eloise said. "It's not that many years, but I feel a little weird about it."

"El, I'm going to say the predictable, but apparently, it's got to be said." Kip rested a hand on Eloise's arm. "If you want to be with him, you don't need to give a damn what anybody says or thinks."

Eloise nodded. "I should be smart enough to learn from you not to take love lightly if you're lucky enough to find it."

"We're talking *love?*" Nora slid forward on the bench, turning her entire body in Eloise's direction.

"It's too soon to say that, I suppose." Eloise hesitated. "But it doesn't seem out of the question." She grinned. "Oh, hell. Yes, we are."

"This is fantastic." Nora reached across Kip to squeeze

Eloise's hand. "I'm thrilled for you. And God knows, you deserve it."

Kip laughed. "I'd say that qualifies as a best moment, even if it's not exactly this week's. And even if today's not Monday."

Eloise nodded, beaming. "Yes, it does, doesn't it?"

"If only they could all be moments like this one," Nora said.

"Unfortunately, I do have a worst moment, if you want to hear it," Eloise said. "The focus group we did on Tuesday. Some of the comments about the magazine were not at all what I was hoping to hear. I was so flipped out, I went straight home and ate about forty Oreos and a pint of chocolate ice cream." She sighed. "It made me see that I'm always going to use food to cope with things. Yes, I finally lost the weight, but I'll be fighting to stay this way forever."

"At least you understand yourself now," Nora said. "That's a big deal. You'll know what's going on, and you'll be able to do something about it."

Eloise nodded. "I suppose. What about you, Nora? You want to do your moments, even though it's Friday?"

"Now that you mention it, I happen to have a best moment right at my fingertips," Nora answered. "I got hired to do the music for Kevin Cunningham's new movie. To be in charge, completely."

Kip applauded. "The top music dog, as it were?"

Nora laughed. "Exactly."

"That's sensational," Eloise added. "I've seen all Cunningham's movies. He's an incredible director."

"I'll be spending some time in L.A. when they shoot, but I can do most of it from here until we get to postproduction. Forty-million-dollar budget. A real movie."

"You don't have to share any of that forty million dollars with anyone else working on the movie, do you?" Kip grinned. "It's all strictly for you and your music."

"If only," Nora replied. "Anyway, that's my best. My worst moment was a doozy." She searched for the right words. "Will was away for a week doing research for his new film. We had really settled in at last in our new place, everything was rolling right along. Then I had this week alone, and I forgot what it was like to be married. I was my old, alone self. When he came home, I was thinking 'Who on earth are you? Why are you in my apartment?' I had to restrain myself from screaming at him to get out, to stop moving things around and touching things. I was in a panic."

"If I may be permitted an understatement, that's not so good," Eloise remarked.

"Total regression," Nora agreed. "But you know what? After a couple of hours, it was okay again. He went back to being Will, instead of some terrifying intrusion in my life. I survived it. And we're still married."

Eloise laughed. "We'll all dance at your fiftieth wedding anniversary, you'll see."

Nora looked horrified. "Please, let's not make appointments for the blue hair rinse just yet." She turned to Kip. "You go."

She nodded. "Worst moment first. On Wednesday, I was in the kitchen, and I noticed that some papers had fallen behind a drawer into the cabinet below. They must have been there a long time, behind this big pot. Anyway, in the pile was a picture of Peter and me, taken when the kids were really little. It was at a party for one of his books. He was in this great suit, and I was wearing a black dress that he really liked on me. We were sitting at a table, but we had our arms around each other, and we were looking at each other, not realizing our picture was being taken." She stopped and sighed. "It was one of those times—when you're supremely happy, and the whole world is perfect. He was looking at me with all this love on his face. I can feel it exactly, how much I adored him."

"Oh, Kip." Nora took her hand.

"I went up to my bedroom and I cried," Kip went on. "I couldn't stop. Rivers, oceans. I just couldn't stop. That was my worst moment of the week."

The three of them were quiet.

Kip drew himself up. "But I have a best moment as well. And you're not going to believe this one." She reached into her jacket pocket to extract an envelope. "I was going to tell you this today anyway." She pulled a typed letter out of the envelope and extended it out in front of her so Nora and Eloise could both see it.

"It's from Vassar?" Eloise leaned over, noting the letterhead.

"Wow, did Lisa get accepted for the fall?" Nora asked. "That's terrific."

"No," Kip said. "Lisa's only in eleventh grade this year."

"Then what?" Nora reached out to bring the paper closer so she could read it.

"It's me," Kip said. "*I* got accepted."

"What?" Eloise leaned forward to get a better look at the letter. "You never said anything about applying to college."

"I *didn't* apply," Kip said. "That's what so unbelievable. Lisa applied *for* me."

"Lisa? What are you talking about?" Nora said. "You can't apply for somebody else."

"It turns out that you can," Kip said. "After I got this letter the other day, she explained the whole story to me. She got hold of my high school transcripts, and my old SAT scores. Even though I didn't go to college, I took the SATs along with everybody else, assuming I would want to go at some point. She dug them up. Then she got recommendations from old teachers and from my skating coach. She went to our local elementary and high school principals, and asked them to write letters about all the stuff I've done for the schools. On her own at night, she put together a résumé with all my skating awards and the basic story of what I had done with my time since high school."

"I don't believe this," Eloise said.

"The topper was that she tricked me into writing an essay for the application form. She told me they were doing some assignment in her class about how different generations had different aspirations, or some such thing. She had me dictate this whole story into a tape recorder about what ice skating meant to me and why I was willing to work so hard at it as a teenager, and so on. She typed it directly onto the form and sent it in."

"I love that," Nora said. "So underhanded, but in the service of such good."

"Why did Lisa do it?" Eloise asked.

Kip smiled. "She knew I wasn't sure what step to take next. This way, she said, I could try lots of things and find out what I want to do. Also, it would get me out and back into the world. It's a short drive from the house, so it's easy to manage." She laughed. "Can you picture me with homework?"

"Eloise and I can visit you at our alma mater," Nora said. "Imagine. Frat parties with kegs, pulling all-nighters before exams. And, oh, that institution food."

A man's voice called out to them. "We're ready. Come on back."

They looked over to see Sonny gesturing to them from outside.

"So, the dreadful Lisa has turned out to be something else entirely," Eloise said as they got up. "Something special."

"Yes." Kip said. "A lot of things this year turned out differently than I might have expected. Some of them far, far worse, of course. But several of them turned out to be something special. Very special."

The three of them paused to smile at one another before heading out once more onto the boat's windy deck.

ONYX

CYNTHIA VICTOR

"Cynthia Victor tells a riveting story!"
—Julie Garwood

"Excitement and emotion on every page."
—Sandra Brown

CONSEQUENCES   0-451-40901-9
Page and Liza. Strangers raised a continent
apart....Rivals for love, money, and success...Sisters
bound by a betrayal no woman could ever forgive.
Or forget.

Also Available:
THE SISTERS   0-451-40866-7

To order call: 1-800-788-6262

The smash *New York Times* bestseller

A thoroughly modern love story for
all ages.

JULIE AND ROMEO

BY JEANNE RAY

A family feud blossoms into love for Julie Rosemar
and Romeo Cacciamani in this deliciously witty
story—a romance for all generations.

"A comic gem of a love story...completely
entertaining." —*Denver Post*

0-451-40997-3

THE CURTAIN RISES ON THE FABULOUS NEW
CARSON SPRINGS TRILOGY
FROM BESTSELLING AUTHOR

EILEEN GOUDGE

STRANGER IN PARADISE

Caressed by the golden California sun, a valley nestled
in a ring of hills flecked with orange groves, Carson
Springs has for four hundred years remained a near-
mystical sight where the local convent still houses nuns
whose prayers mingle with the hum of their famous
honeybees. Yet, beneath the tranquil surface of this
idyllic village disputes flare, feuds simmer, and
secrets are guarded.

In *Stranger in Paradise*, the opening novel, a woman's
love for a much younger man ignites a blaze of disap-
proval. Readers will be drawn irresistibly into the life
of this beautiful, lush, and unique valley, where family
histories have dangerously deep and tangled roots.

ISBN: 0-451-20577-4

To order call: 1-800-788-6262

Goudge/Stranger S380